WHAT DOESN'T KILL HER

ALSO BY CARLA NORTON

The Edge of Normal
Perfect Victim
Disturbed Ground

WHAT DOESN'T
KILL HER

CARLA NORTON

Minotaur Books
New York

WHAT DOESN'T KILL HER. Copyright © 2015 by Carla Norton. All rights reserved. Printed in the United States of America. For information, address St. Martin's Press, 175 Fifth Avenue, New York, N.Y. 10010.

www.minotaurbooks.com

Designed by Anna Gorovoy

Library of Congress Cataloging-in-Publication Data

Norton, Carla.
    What doesn't kill her : a novel / Carla Norton.—First edition.
        p. cm.
    ISBN 978-1-250-03280-5 (hardcover)
    ISBN 978-1-250-03281-2 (e-book)
    1. Women college students—Fiction.   2. Kidnapping victims—Fiction.   3. Escaped prisoners—Fiction.   I. Title.
    PS3614.O78253W48 2015
    813'.6—dc23

                                                                                    2015013519

Minotaur books may be purchased for educational, business, or promotional use. For information on bulk purchases, please contact the Macmillan Corporate and Premium Sales Department at 1-800-221-7945, extension 5442, or write to specialmarkets@macmillan.com.

First Edition: June 2015

10   9   8   7   6   5   4   3   2   1

To survivors of kidnapping and captivity everywhere.
Your real-life courage inspires this fiction.

ELEVEN YEARS AGO

The last time she would ever go swimming, all of Seattle was baking beneath a sky of blameless blue. For two whole days, temperatures had soared while she begged her family for a quick trip to the lake. An hour? Thirty minutes?

But no one else cared about swimming. They seemed oblivious to the oppressive heat. Her parents were busy working, and her older sister had commandeered the coolest room in the house as her private rehearsal studio. Rachel was now glued to the piano bench, practicing that same concerto over and over, while Reggie was stranded with nothing to do. Her best friend had gone on a family vacation, and a long, lonely, humdrum summer loomed ahead.

So, if she wanted to go to the lake, she would have to take matters into her own hands. Any kid with a bike would have done the same thing.

She'd ridden down to the local scrap of beach a dozen times last summer. She knew the way. And she made the quite responsible calculation that she had plenty of time to ride downhill, plunge into the lake, swim for twenty-five minutes, ride back uphill, get cleaned up, and be ready for her sister's recital before her parents got home.

All doable. No one even needed to know. Maybe during dinner she would tell them. Or maybe not. Now that she was almost a teenager she felt entitled to some secret independence.

Reggie put on her new peach-colored swimsuit and covered it with a favorite T-shirt that fell to her knees. There was no need to bring a towel because, cleverly, she would wear her wet swimsuit home, and that would keep her cool for the long, hot return trip uphill.

She shut the back door on her sister's endlessly repeating concerto—which she'd liked the first ten or twenty times but had grown to hate—and wheeled her bike to the curb.

There was a thrill in setting out alone and unsupervised. She stood up on the pedals and the speed lifted her hair off the back of her neck. The air seemed to cool with each smooth turn downhill, and she coasted all of the last block, feeling strong and happy and alive.

She found the secret path between the hedges and dumped her bike in a patch beside a discarded beer bottle and an empty cigarette pack speared with broken toothpicks. Then she headed down toward the lake . . . left . . . right . . . The path wound through the overgrown shrubs to a small stretch of beach known only to locals.

She emerged from the foliage onto a slope as big as her front yard. Two boys with a dog glanced her way and then ignored her, as if she were intruding on their private shore. She watched the dog swim out to fetch a ball. Then, with the boys turned away, she self-consciously stripped off her T-shirt and dropped it on the grass.

She quickly made her way down to the water's edge, as far from the boys as she could get, where she kicked off her sneakers and plunged into the water. She gasped to the surface, checked the indifference of the kids with the dog, and started stroking through the cold water.

At a good distance from shore, she flipped over and floated on her back, catching her breath. When she turned back to the beach, the boys with the dog had gone. She looked up and down the shoreline.

Big houses had private docks with boats of all sizes, and the blue water slapped against hulls as she swam past. There was a woman in a hat cutting flowers. There was a man starting a fire in a grill. Reggie spied on their private worlds, feeling mischievous and invisible as she moved through the deliciously cool water.

Sounds carried across the lake. She heard motoring boats in the distance and children's laughter somewhere out of sight.

With a start, she realized that she had strayed far out into the lake. What time was it?

Kicking strongly, she swam in closer and then started following the shore-line back to the beach. It seemed to take a long while before she could swim close enough to touch bottom and wade ashore. Dripping wet, she slipped back into her sneakers and hurried up to her T-shirt. She shook it once, thinking there might be bugs, and then slipped it on over her head. She had no pockets and had neglected to bring a watch but knew she must hurry.

The T-shirt clung to her wet swimsuit as she ran up the path to where she had stashed her bicycle. She kicked a beer bottle aside, righted the bike, and climbed astride.

It was like trying to pedal through tar. She grunted with effort and managed only a few feet before noticing the flat.

She got off the bike and moaned at the deflated tire, now certain she'd be late. How could this happen? Despair pulsed in her throat.

The glassy whisper of crickets slid back and forth on the air as she muscled her bike out from the shrubbery, off the dirt path, and onto the asphalt. A neighbor getting into his van turned to watch her.

"Got a flat tire?" he called.

"Yeah." She trudged toward him, pushing the bike along. "Unfortunately."

"You live nearby? You need a ride?"

She stopped and looked at him: a chubby guy with an unkempt beard, younger than her father, but older than a teenager. She could never guess the ages of adults.

"You need some help?" the man asked again. "I can't fix your bike, but I can give you a lift. It's no trouble."

"Uh, no thanks. I better not."

He looked nice enough, and in all her twelve years she'd never met anyone dangerous or crazy, but she'd been warned many times about strangers. She trudged on, pushing the bike around the corner and up the hill. It weighed a ton.

All the coolness of the lake drained out of her. She felt hot and sweaty and exhausted as she pictured her parents and her sister dressed and waiting beside the car. Anxious, pacing . . .

The certainty that she would be late coiled in her stomach. She reviewed her defenses—*I am nearly thirteen, after all*—but instantly heard the rebuke: "Old enough to know better."

She heard a car approach and slow alongside her. She glanced over and saw that it was the guy in the van. He rolled down his window and put out an elbow.

"I'm just heading out. You sure I can't give you a lift?"

Reggie felt embarrassed to have to explain it to him. "I'd get in trouble," she said, as though she were a child of nine rather than a mature individual with an age in double digits.

"Even for a flat tire?"

She shrugged and kept pushing the bike up the hill.

"Okay. I get it. But you live uphill from here, I gather. So here's an idea. We can put your bike in my van, and you can go on ahead and run home, and I'll deliver the bike to your door. No harm, no foul, right?"

She stopped to consider this. "What time is it?" she asked.

"Uh, a little before five."

She felt encouraged. She might still get home in time. She could take a two-minute shower, get dressed, and be ready on time if she hurried. No one even needed to know.

"It'd be a lot easier for you to walk home without having to push that heavy bike, wouldn't it?"

She smiled at him, grateful for this solution. "Yeah, I guess that would be okay."

He pulled over to the curb and stopped while she wheeled her bike over behind the van. When he got out and came around to the back, she saw that his right hand was bandaged in gauze. He opened the back doors with his left hand.

"If you could just help me lift it," he said, smiling with uneven yellow teeth.

"Sure."

She gripped the bicycle with both hands, ready to hoist it up and into the van. As he got close and moved around behind her, she noticed his smell.

He helped boost the bike off the ground while she maneuvered the front tire into the van. It wasn't that difficult, but as she was shifting her grip, he hit her with a jolt like a snakebite that spun the sky red.

TODAY

ONE

Most of the men incarcerated in the forensic unit of Washington State's largest psychiatric hospital play basketball or cards during rec time. The more delusional converse with imaginary friends. A few spend time exploring their private parts.

As Daryl Wayne Flint steps into the rec yard, he hears an older guard say to a rookie, "See that longhaired guy with the wild beard? The one that looks like Charles Manson? Watch what he does."

Flint ignores the comment and struts across the damp grass toward the asphalt basketball court. Exactly at center court, he stops, opens his arms wide, and starts a slow spin.

The familiar scenes flash past: the parking lot, the cafeteria windows, the blank wall, the iron-girded windows of the warden's corner office, the lawn extending to the fence, the woods beyond, and—what's this?—a wink of light from between the trees.

He wishes he could stop and study but must continue his rotations.

A huge patient named Galt dribbles the basketball toward him. "Hurry up, man."

Flint sticks to his routine. Again: the cafeteria windows, the bare wall, the warden's office, the hospital grounds . . . and then, yes, he sees it distinctly: A car is coming down the road, sunlight splashing off its windshield.

"Move your ass, man!" Galt circles Flint, bouncing the ball hard and grunting obscenities. A group of men toeing the asphalt call for the game to begin.

Galt dribbles in a tight pattern, crowding so close that Flint's fingertips brush his T-shirt. The other men yap and holler. But Flint continues spinning and does not hurry.

He glimpses the car again. White, it comes winding out of the trees. Then, with his third rotation complete, he drops his arms.

The ball smacks the asphalt and the basketball game starts behind him as Flint strolls off the court. He steps onto the grass, where he always turns left. Always counterclockwise.

Now he sees the car approach the gate, but then it moves beyond his peripheral vision. He cannot stop and gawk, but continues walking around the court, looking straight ahead. When at last he makes a turn and has a clear view of the white car, his pulse quickens. He need barely move his eyes to watch it turn into the parking lot.

He calculates: an unfamiliar car, arriving at this particular hour, on this particular day . . . It can only be the new barber.

This might be the perfect day for a haircut.

Keeping the smile off his face, he watches the car cruise past. The driver is a white male wearing some type of hat.

A beret? The guy must think he's some kind of artist.

Flint aches to turn his head and study the driver as the car continues in search of a place to park, but now his feet have arrived at the next corner. He must turn south. He keeps a steady pace as he walks past the cafeteria, past the long blank wall, past the warden's ironclad windows. All the while, he's straining to hear any sound from the new arrival. The car door slamming shut? A cell phone conversation as the driver crosses the parking lot?

But he hears only the trash talk of the basketball game, the ball slapping asphalt, thwacking the backboard, rattling around the rim.

He swallows his disappointment.

At the next corner, he turns east, heading toward the guard tower that over-looks the nine-foot fence and the deep woods beyond. He has no interest today in the colors of the leaves or the gathering clouds. Instead, he's weighing risk versus opportunity.

And he's wondering just how much he can trust his mother.

Has she done everything needed? It's hard to know.

Visiting hours aren't so lax in the medium-security wing that inmates can speak freely, no matter what their status. No matter how addled they might be. No matter what meds might be flooding their brains. People are always listening. So, of necessity, most of his conversations with his mother have been in code.

During their most recent visit, his mother had said, "I've been thinking about your dear, departed father."

He'd nearly choked.

"Thinking about our wedding day," she said, widening her eyes at him. "You remember the date, don't you?"

He shifted uncomfortably, wondering where this was headed.

"Don't you remember? It was April."

"Uh, no—"

"Shush. April fifth, 1968. Repeat it back to me."

Perplexed, he recited, "April fifth, 1968."

"That's exactly right. The fourth month, the fifth day. The fourth month, the fifth day."

That's when he realized she was speaking in code.

"It's hot in here," she said abruptly. "I wish they'd open a window or something. Let in some air."

He nodded to let her know he was following.

"Oh, it was such a lovely day. In the early fall, like this." His mother gestured toward the girded window.

He scowled. Hadn't she just said it was April?

But she went on describing "the perfect little church—the ideal location for an April wedding. And it was so close to our first house. We got a few things out of storage," she said with emphasis, "and moved right in."

Her meaning dawned. "So, the church and the house weren't that far distant."

"You could say that." She looked to the north. "Less than three miles apart."

His lips curled into a smile.

"Anyway, we were just starting out, your father and I. But we had enough cash for essentials. Food and water, a little gas for our motorbike." She lifted a penciled-on eyebrow, waiting for a response.

He sat forward. "Not much, but enough to get started."

"Oh, yes. *Enough.*" She gave a sideways glance at the guard.

Flint stroked his long beard. "Tell me again, how were you dressed?"

Noticing the guard, he added loudly, "I mean, for your wedding day, Momma. You know I love this story."

"I wore white, of course," she replied, with a wave of her hand. "But your father, he wore black."

"All black?"

"Completely," she said, squinting at him. "From his cap to his toes." She seemed to wait for the guard to turn away before adding, "You know, he was about your size when he died."

Flint replays this conversation as he reaches the corner and turns again toward the parking lot. He scans for the white car, quickly locates where it is parked, and studies it as he marches forward. A Honda. Compact and non-descript. Washington plates.

The sun disappears behind the clouds, and a cold wind whips Flint's hair across his face as he continues his walk. No one pays any attention. He's the repetitive inmate with post-concussive syndrome who never causes problems.

"Mentally disordered, with frontal lobe dysfunction, obsessive tendencies . . . antisocial behavioral problems that render him unsuitable for incarceration in the state penitentiary," his psychiatrist had said.

Sure, let them think that.

Let them think that.

Let them think that.

Because every crazy thing he does is useful. And each day brings him closer to Plan B, closer to recapturing his favorite girl.

The daily rec yard routine? Three spins at center court allow him to take in the entire 360-degree scene within minutes of exiting the building. Three turns around the basketball court? It's a leisurely way to observe all the inmates and the staff. And three tours of the fence line? Well, one needs a daily search for weakness along the perimeter. All very innocuous, all due to his mental impairments. And none of the doctors—not even the brilliant Dr. Terrance Moody—has found a way to cure him.

During rec time he gathers information about the comings and goings of visitors and staff. He knows, for instance, that the regular barber's car is the color of Dijon mustard, not the bland mayonnaise-white of this new vehicle. Wanda-the-Warden drives a BMW, which she parks in the slot marked "Chief of Psychiatry," just beside the head cook's Cadillac. The cook's car is as black as his hair. The warden's car is the same red as the scarf she wears like a slash across her throat.

His exercise regimen has melted away the pounds he packed on after dropping out of college. He's never been so fit. And sometimes he finds useful objects. Just yesterday, he spied a plastic bag wrestling with the fence. He snatched it up and tucked it inside his underwear. Last night, he pulled it out to inspect it and found it beautiful. He secretly carries it with him now.

Flint turns west, heading directly toward the cafeteria. Sunny days can cause a glare on the glass, but most days are cloudy, like today. The individuals inside are lit up like actors on a stage.

People stream past with their trays of food, and he wonders about those who occupy the other, less secure sections of the institution. What are their afflictions? What are their routines? What happens in those realms that clink and moan just beyond the forensic unit's locked doors?

He imagines focusing a camera lens on the men in the cafeteria and spots a new face: A pudgy man in a beret. He smiles. The new barber is getting coffee.

Three times, Daryl Wayne Flint strokes his wooly beard, recalling that the last time he let a barber touch him was the day before his trial.

TWO

San Francisco, California

Six cyclists come pumping up the hill, turn, and then glide in single file onto the wide expanse of the Golden Gate Bridge. It stretches before them with picture-postcard splendor, its famous tangerine towers rising into a sapphire sky, and the cyclists whoop and shout as they wheel onto the wide promenade that runs the length of the span.

One by one they maneuver past clusters of tourists, coast over to the railing, and dismount to marvel at the view. Yachts and sailboats, tankers and tugboats cut across the jade-green bay, while to the right, San Francisco's distinctive skyline crowns the scene.

The cyclist in the lead removes her helmet and the brisk autumn breeze ruffles her flame-colored hair. She gazes around, then peers over the railing, where the dark water is pushing seaward so fast and so far below that it brings a flash of vertigo.

Just then, a sturdy blonde with an animated smile angles up beside her, grips her arm, and says, "Oh my lord, Reeve, thank you for making this happen. This is the most gorgeous trip yet."

"It is amazing, isn't it?" Reeve grins, pleased that her first attempt at organizing the group's monthly bike ride is going so well. They cluster around as she points out the Berkeley hills, Angel Island, and then Alcatraz, which glows like a pearl, belying its dark past.

"How crazy is it that I've been in California for over three years," the blonde says, waving at the view, "and this is the first time I've actually stood on the Golden Gate Bridge."

Reeve gives her friend a nudge. "Lana, you're not in Kansas anymore."

Lana's boyfriend joins them. Toned as a whippet, David is the most serious cyclist of the bunch. "Just look at this," he says. "It's spectacular!"

"We need pictures," someone shouts, and the group jostles together, holding up their phones, snapping selfies. Then a passerby offers to serve as photographer and the six of them grin while striking poses. After a few moments, the group unknots and continues walking their bicycles along the span, gawking.

Reeve notices that a baby in a stroller has lost his shoe. She hurriedly scoops it up and hands it to the distracted mother, who says something in a foreign language while beaming gratitude. Reeve smiles in answer and continues weaving past joggers, couples, and families.

As she walks her bike along, enjoying the sunshine and breathing in the fresh, crisp air, she fully appreciates that a day like this brings the kind of healing that even years of psychotherapy can't.

At the far end of the bridge, the cyclists mount their bikes and follow Reeve through the last knots of foot traffic. She leads them away from the bridge, the tour buses, and the busy highway, onto a two-lane road that winds downhill. The glittering views of the bay diminish, turn after turn, as they sweep through green hillsides and quickly descend into Sausalito, a scenic bayside community with expensive homes climbing the hills to their left, the waterfront stretching to their right, and plenty of upscale shops, restaurants, and galleries in between.

As the road begins to flatten, Reeve stands on her bike pedals, exhilarated by how mysterious and strange and wonderful life is. How marvelous that she has fit in with this tribe. How completely her life has changed.

It had all started last spring. Just as Reeve was re-enrolling in college, her apartment building was sold, and the new management announced a nosebleed increase in rent prices. The next day, she met Lana on the beach during a coastal cleanup event. They started talking while picking up trash, and it turned out that Lana's house was in need of one more roommate. Serendipity, pure and simple. Reeve was soon unpacking boxes in a noisy household not far from the UC Berkeley campus.

Shortly thereafter, she was invited to join this cycling club, and now she owns her first bike since that ill-fated summer when she was just an average twelve-year-old kid. She doesn't need her psychiatrist to tell her that this marks another milestone in her recovery.

Now, at twenty-three, Reeve feels that her life as an adult has finally bloomed and ripened. Each day seems to drop into her palm like sweet, plump fruit.

The group wheels through town to the ferry terminal, where they lock up their bikes and buy tickets for the ferry ride back across the bay. Then they stroll around the picturesque waterfront, their cycling shoes clacking loudly while they eat snacks and drink smoothies.

Right on time, the ferry appears in the distance. It grows steadily larger, pulling a white wake as the cyclists retrieve their bicycles and prepare for boarding.

Megan, the tallest woman of the group, maneuvers up beside Reeve and asks about their route home. "The Ferry Building is near the BART station, right?"

"That's right, we'll take the train back to Berkeley," Reeve replies, watching as the ferry slows, reverses engines, and nudges into place. "Sorry this is kind of a short bike for you hard-core riders."

"Don't be sorry. There's no way I'd be able to keep up," Lana says. "Good lord, David is doing sixty miles tomorrow, can you imagine?"

"The ferry will be going right by Alcatraz, won't it?" Megan asks.

Reeve nods but says nothing. She watches deckhands scramble out to secure the ferry to the dock with rope as thick as her arm.

"Alcatraz must be cool," Megan continues. "There are guided tours of the old prison, right? I'd love to see the old cells, hear all the stories."

"Reeve, you're the San Franciscan," David says. "What do you think of Alcatraz? Is it worth doing a tour?"

"For you, maybe." She gives a tight smile. "But I have zero interest in prisons."

Lana—who is Reeve's sole confidante and the only one aware of her old name and her tragic, headline-grabbing past—quickly changes the subject. "This trip was a great idea," she says, looping her arm through Reeve's. "And I love the Ferry Building. Let's run in and get some sourdough bread before heading home."

Reeve feels a rush of gratitude for Lana, for her new life in Berkeley, and for every single minute that adds distance between ever-loving now and those wretched years spent locked in her kidnapper's basement.

THREE

Olshaker Psychiatric Hospital

Daryl Wayne Flint wanders down the corridor to the lavatory, checking out the line of inmates waiting for a chance to sit in the barber's chair. It has diminished to two guys now, but they look like they don't even need haircuts. Like this is some sort of entertainment, a diversion.

Okay, after all these years, he can certainly understand that.

A short time later, Flint returns to stand behind the one guy remaining in line, a guy with a cap of blond curls. Then the door opens and a huge guy with a shaved head shuffles out.

"How was it?" the blond guy asks.

"Quick," the bald guy replies.

They both lock eyes on Flint for half a second, smirk, and turn away.

The blond guy disappears inside, the bald one ambles away, and Flint leans against the wall, unhappy about this moment of scrutiny. He would have preferred to remain unobserved at this particular juncture, but his thick mane and wild whiskers make him conspicuous.

He waits. He fidgets. He starts to pace. When a guard walks by and looks toward him, Flint pretends he's simply walking past the door, as though returning from the lavatory. This would draw less notice, he reasons, so he begins pacing the entire length of the corridor, purposefully heading in one direction and then the other. Out of habit, he does this three times.

Still, no one opens the door.

Flint considers another set of three but, disconcerted by the prospect of an interrupted sequence, stops to wait beside the door. He taps his toes in sets of three. At last the door creaks open and the blond comes out with his curls shortened to a row of waves.

"You're up," the blond says, jerking a thumb at the door.

Flint slips inside, where the barber, still wearing his beret, is tipping a dustpan full of hair into the trash.

"Are you my last—" The barber glances back, sees Flint, and straightens. His eyebrows shoot up as he breathes out, "Oh."

Flint's hands go up to his long locks. "Guess I'm a little overdue."

The barber places the dustpan on the floor with an audible sigh. "Okay, well, have a seat and let's take a look."

Sitting in an orange plastic chair, Flint looks around. He's never been in this room, this makeshift barber shop, which seems to be nothing more than a small office with an attached bath. The chair faces a mirror mounted on the wall. The day's used towels are heaped in a corner. The barber's tools are arranged on a small table beside a stack of fresh towels the color of undercooked pancakes.

The barber tents his last customer in a drape and begins circling—tugging at his hair and humming thoughtfully—while Flint studies the barber in the mirror: midthirties, with short brown hair and a neatly groomed goatee. A bit too young, a bit on the pudgy side, but the right height and roughly Flint's size.

"So," the barber says, "what did you have in mind?"

"I'm not sure." Flint meets the man's eye in the mirror. "Short, I guess."

"How short?"

"Short." Flint cocks his head and grins. "Like yours."

Later, when the floor is covered with hair, Flint gazes at his reflection with something close to awe. "Damn, don't I look handsome?"

"You sure look a lot better, but . . ." The barber puts a hand on his hip. "With that nasty beard? Seriously?"

Flint lifts a hand from beneath the drape and strokes his beard once, then gathers it in a fist. "I've had this for a long time, you know."

The barber rolls his eyes. "Clearly."

"You think it's time to get rid of it?"

"Past time, dude. Way past time."

"Okay, uh, what did you say your name is?"

"Ricky."

"Okay, Ricky, let's just say, for the sake of argument, that I decided to let you trim it a little. What would you suggest?"

The barber scoffs. "Trim it? Are you kidding? Chop off six inches, just for starters."

"Oh, man. . . ." Flint groans, pretending reluctance, enjoying this little game. "I guess . . . yeah, it needs to go. But are you going to use those scissors?"

The barber makes a face. "How about I use a chainsaw?"

Flint considers the scissors and then rejects the idea. Too much blood. He sighs dramatically. "Just be careful, okay?"

"Good." The barber beams at him. "You won't regret it. How short do you want it?"

"I don't know, what do you think?"

"The shorter the better." The barber stands behind Flint, grasping the beard with both hands, feeling its thickness. "I mean, this is out of control."

"Okay, okay, okay," Flint says, grinning into the mirror. "How about a goatee? Like yours."

The barber hums a note and sets to work. "When I'm done, your own mother won't recognize you." He smiles at Flint's reflection. "And I mean that in a good way."

"Understood. And my little cricket will be impressed, too," Flint says, rubbing his palm across his groin beneath the drape.

"Is that your girlfriend?"

"My dearest one." Flint considers explaining, but why bother? People who remembered his trial always said stupid shit about pedophiles. So instead he closes his eyes, pictures the designs on her back, and inhales deeply, as though savoring her aroma.

"Well, your girlfriend is definitely going to be impressed," says the barber. "Why on earth didn't you get this beard taken care of before? You didn't like my predecessor?"

"Never met him."

"But he had this gig for awhile, right? Came every month, didn't he?"

"Timing is important with these things," Flint says, studying the pile of dirty towels heaped in a corner.

The barber frowns at this non sequitur but says nothing, as though suddenly recalling that this is, after all, a mental institution. He falls silent, hands busy while whiskers drift to the floor.

Flint watches the electric shears buzzing away the whiskers from his neck, his cheeks, beside his ears. The planes of his face emerge, familiar yet strange, like the long-forgotten neighborhoods of his youth. As the heavy beard goes, his lips seem naked and pink as areolas.

"Today's your first day, right? So, how do you like this new job?" Flint asks.

"It's not a bad gig. Kind of a long drive, but it pays pretty well. No complaints so far." Facing him, the barber takes a wet towel and wipes Flint's forehead, cheeks, neck, then cups Flint's chin, tilting his face back and forth, inspecting his work. Then the barber steps away and asks, "What do you think?"

Flint grins. His trimmed whiskers appear to bracket his mouth in clever parentheses. "Better than ever."

"Absolutely," the barber says with satisfaction.

Flint notes the barber's jacket hanging on the knob of the bathroom door. Car keys in the right pocket, he figures. Beneath the drape, he slides his hand down his stomach and pinches the plastic bag hidden in his underwear. He extracts it and clutches it in his fist just as the barber unties the strings of the drape, lifts it off.

"Man, I'm hungry," the barber says, shaking the trimmings to the floor. "I'm glad you're my last customer."

Flint rises to his feet and moves in close. He nods toward the floor. "I'm afraid you have quite a lot of sweeping up to do."

The barber looks down, and in the split second before he can take in a breath to speak whatever comment he has in mind, Flint punches him hard and square in the stomach.

The barber doubles over with a cry as Flint slips the plastic bag over the man's head, then wrenches back in confusion, but Flint is already behind him, locking an arm tight around his neck, shoving him off his feet. The man struggles, making horrible sounds as he fights for air. The plastic clings to his face as he bucks and thrashes, knocking things to the floor. He wrenches right to left, but Flint crushes him beneath his weight, and as the barber weakens, Flint presses harder, feeling the man shudder and finally go still.

He waits, counting to one hundred to make sure the barber is dead before releasing his iron grip and rising to his feet. Breathing hard, he surveys his work. Not an ounce of blood spilled.

He begins stripping off the man's clothes. The shirt comes off easily, but when he removes the barber's trousers, he winces at the freshly soiled underwear. He lifts the khakis, sniffs, and shrugs.

The barber's clothes fit a bit too loosely, so Flint folds two towels across his belly, then cinches the belt. The leather shoes pinch his toes, but Flint manages to get them on. Then, with no time to waste, he drags the body across the floor into the bathroom and hides it beneath the dirty towels.

He snags the jacket from where it hangs on the doorknob. Lastly, he puts on the beret. A nice touch. "Hey now! Don't we look jaunty?" he says to himself in the mirror, mimicking the dead man's high-pitched tone.

Noticing that his neck looks white as gooseflesh, he buttons the shirt all the way up and pulls in his chin. Better. Next, he pulls the man's wallet from his back pocket, flips it open, and studies the ID. Richard Baker. Baker the barber. He smirks.

Quickly, he gathers up the barber's gear and stashes it in the large case—a two-tiered piece of luggage resembling a tackle box on wheels—takes a deep breath and shakes the tension out of his shoulders. As he rolls the case into the hallway, a gray-haired guard whom everyone calls Snake is coming toward him. Flint knows him too well. He puffs air into his cheeks to make himself look plumper.

"It's after five, kid. I'm supposed to take you through the gate," Snake says. "You ready to get out of here?"

Flint shuts the door behind him. "Am I ever," he replies in a mild falsetto. "What a day!"

The guard stops a few feet away, eyeing him. "Yeah, you're looking kinda beat, kid."

Flint adjusts the beret, partly blocking his face, and tightens his grip on the rolling case.

"Let's go," the guard says, turning on his heel and starting down the corridor.

Flint puffs out his cheeks and follows in the tight leather shoes, careful not to wince at every step.

FOUR

Flint pauses at each intersection, craning his neck to look up and down the street, hoping for something that makes sense. He might have only seconds before the barber's body is found. Then what? An alarm? Dogs? An APB will go out on this white Honda, for sure, but he can't afford to stash it. Not yet.

"About three miles away," he grumbles. "April fifth, 1968. What the hell is that supposed to mean?"

He peers into the rain-smeared dusk, hoping for numbered streets. Instead, he's in an area named after women: Dana Lane . . . Cassidy Lane . . . Barbara Lane . . . *April!* He brakes hard in the middle of the intersection, wrenches the wheel to the left, and speeds down the block, searching madly.

He sees nothing but ramshackle houses and defunct businesses before reaching a dead end. He makes a sharp U-turn, races back to the intersection where he started, then speeds in the opposite direction, nearly zooming past the storage facility at the corner of Church and April streets.

Church Street Storage. That's gotta be it!

He slams on the brakes, slaps the car into reverse, cranks the wheel to the left, and wheels up to the gate. Above a keypad is a posted sign: *Please enter your security code.*

He studies the instructions, then looks around cautiously. Seeing no one, he turns back to the keypad, considers the numbers in April 5, 1968, and decides that a standard code would be a sequence of four. He tries entering one, nine, six, eight. Nothing happens.

An alarm sounds in the distance—a strange, deep-throated drone.

He spits out a curse and punches in zero, four, zero, five. Again, nothing. He groans in frustration, trying to recall what his mother had said.

He hears her laugh. "The fourth month, the fifth day. The fourth month, the fifth day."

He punches in four, five, four, five.

The gate slowly rolls open as the siren scream of a police car starts nearby, then turns away, heading in the direction of the hospital.

Flint drives through the gate and realizes there are dozens of storage units here, and he hasn't got a clue which way to turn. The gate slides shut behind him, and he has a sudden uneasiness at being locked inside, but shakes this off and drives forward.

The facility is laid out with one long building on the left and perpendicular buildings jutting out to the right. Which one? He cruises along slowly and tries to sift through all his mother's nonsense for some clue. She'd been prattling about that wedding for months, becoming increasingly elaborate in her details. What else had she said?

He notices that the buildings are numbered in sequence: One, two, three . . . yes *three*! And now he recalls that she'd said, "I insisted on an afternoon wedding. Not morning, not evening, it had to be 3:15. The perfect time, don't you think?"

He'd thought she was humoring him, but he turns and follows along building three, studying the numbered doors, starting at ten, eleven . . . He stops in front of unit fifteen and gets out of the car.

Another siren sounds in the distance while he steps close enough to notice two initials scratched in the paint: "D.W." This has to be it.

A black combination lock hangs from the door. Thinking April 4, 1968, he tries various combinations before spinning the dial right to nineteen, left around twice to six, and right to eight. The lock pops open in his palm.

He barks a laugh, but then hears an engine rumbling toward him. He glances over his shoulder at a pickup truck, waits until it passes, then lifts the rolling door and hustles inside.

Smack in the middle is parked a motorbike with a helmet resting atop the seat. His fingers stroke the bike's shiny fender. At his feet, a backpack sits atop a cardboard box. He moves these tight against the wall, then eases the motorbike off its kickstand and rolls it out of the storage unit, parking it beside the building.

There's now enough room for the Honda. He noses it forward until the front bumper kisses the wall. The car door opens just wide enough for him to slide out.

Finding clothes inside the backpack, he quickly strips off the barber's clothes and tosses them into a corner. He pulls on a black T-shirt, a black sweater, and black jeans, which are a tad too big.

Next, he opens the box and lifts out a black leather jacket and a pair of boots, which fit perfectly. Inside one jacket pocket is a Swiss Army knife; the other holds a wallet containing cash, which he doesn't stop to count. Quickly, he plucks cash and credit cards from the barber's wallet and adds these to the new one. He's cramming the wallet into a pocket when—what's this?—he feels something there and pulls out an envelope.

It smells faintly of perfume. Not his mother's, surely, so it must be that blonde's. He smiles at a memory of the short skirts she used to wear to the courthouse.

The envelope holds a map and a key. Excellent.

He turns his attention back to the box. Packaged food and water. And, at the bottom, an assortment of license plates from three states, all with current registrations. This is Walter Wertz's doing, no doubt.

A chorus of sirens commences just as he shoulders the backpack. The sirens grow louder as he slams down the rolling door and secures the lock.

He finds a pair of gloves tucked inside the helmet. He slips these on, mounts the bike, turns the key, and kicks it to life.

It coughs and dies.

He tries again, and the bike sputters and then roars.

A patrol car races past with its light bar flashing as Flint exits the storage facility. He turns the opposite direction, heading toward the freeway, closely watching his speed.

FIVE

Berkeley, California

The aging house has only one bathroom, which the four roommates manage on weekdays, thanks to their varying class schedules. But on weekends, a hot shower is less likely than a cold water dance, which is exactly what Reeve is doing now. She sucks air through her teeth and rinses off quickly.

Twenty minutes later, she's dressed and wearing her good shoes, which sound loud as she comes down the stairs, causing David and Lana to look up from where they're snuggled on the couch.

"Well, look at you," Lana coos. "Makeup and everything. Who's the hot date?"

"No hot date. My sister is having a dinner party is all."

Reeve feels a telltale heat creeping up her neck and into her cheeks. She has met Brad only twice—first at her sister's wedding, and then about a year ago—so there's no reason to expect any spark between the two of them tonight. Still, she can't help thinking about how he flirted with her and made her laugh.

Megan and Maria, the self-professed foodies of the student household, enter from the kitchen. The two couldn't be more different—Megan is tall, freckled, and athletic, Maria is short, tawny, and plump—but they mirror one another as they check Reeve's attire, raising their eyebrows in silent comment.

Megan pops the last bite of something into her mouth and dusts off her fingers, saying, "I can give you a lift if you need a ride. We're just heading out."

Reeve glances down at her shoes. "If you could drop me at the BART station, that would be great."

Arriving at her sister's neighborhood ahead of schedule, Reeve strolls past the neat, candy-colored houses, figuring she'll have plenty of time to chat with her sister and calm herself before Brad arrives. There's no reason to be stressing out, she thinks, unconsciously fingering the scar on the back of her neck. It's true that she has problems with intimacy, but she is not unattractive. And what's the worst that can happen? If she makes a fool of herself, the fact that Brad lives in Dallas makes it a nonissue, doesn't it?

She climbs the front steps and presses the doorbell.

In a moment, Rachel flings open the door, wearing jeans and looking frantic. Her hair is mussed and she's clutching a teddy bear.

"I'm so glad you're here," she says, grasping Reeve's arm and pulling her inside. "Greg is taking the baby to his mother's, and just look at me. And look at this mess!" She waves an arm at an obstacle course of scattered toys.

Reeve takes the teddy bear from her sister, saying, "Go get dressed. I'll clean up."

She carries armloads of toys into the baby's room, stuffing as many as she can into the toy box and cramming the rest into some semblance of order. Next, she straightens the living room, plumps the pillows on the couch, and has just finished setting the dining room table when the first guests arrive.

Reeve offers them wine, casting anxious glances at her sister's closed door. But before their glasses are filled, Rachel floats into the room in gossamer blue, looking pretty and poised as a movie star.

Enticing aromas waft from the kitchen as Rachel takes over the role of hostess. Meanwhile, Reeve carries a glass of sparkling water over to the baby grand piano in the corner. She studies the framed photographs arranged on its glossy surface. Wedding photos, family portraits, baby pictures . . .

Here's one she remembers: a photo of Rachel holding a bouquet of long-stemmed roses after a high school play. There's one she does not: Rachel in a graduation cap, bracketed by their parents on a sunny day, when their mother was well and her honey-colored hair was still as thick and beautiful as Rachel's.

Her mother's image evokes a sigh of longing. Next month, she recalls, would have been her fifty-first birthday.

Reeve turns her back on the photos and perches on the piano bench to watch the room. Music and laughter fill the air. Now Greg has joined Rachel in greeting guests. And there is Brad, a little plumper than she remembered, but still good-looking, with a youthful face and puppy-dog eyes.

He grins and comes toward her.

She stands, smiling, as he takes her hand. His palm is warm and dry.

He steps aside and introduces her to an elegant young woman with black bangs and an Audrey Hepburn smile, saying, ". . . and this is my wife."

Reeve doesn't even hear the woman's name. She just keeps smiling and nodding while the two talk. She feels ridiculous. Why on earth had she nursed such a stupid, one-sided crush? She excuses herself and heads toward the appetizers, where she loads a plate with food that she can hardly taste through her chagrin.

A minute later, Rachel startles her by clasping her arm and saying, "Come and sit down. There's someone I want you to meet."

The young man's face seems bland and pleasant and forgettable. Reeve makes an effort to smile as she's seated next to him.

Soon, the guests are toasting the chef. The arugula salad is delicious. The entrée is extraordinary. Everyone agrees that Rachel ought to write a cookbook. But while her sister beams, Reeve discreetly pushes her mushrooms aside and scrapes the dill sauce off her perfectly cooked salmon.

When she notices the young man beside her doing the same, they share a look.

He leans over and whispers in her ear, "Here we are in the fussy-eaters' section."

She grants him a dimpled smile as her cell phone rings. "Sorry," she mumbles, fishing it out of her purse to shut it off.

She checks the display—Otis Poe—and tenses.

"Is something wrong?" he asks.

Reeve mutes her phone, saying, "No, nothing, sorry," but thinking, *Why would Otis Poe be calling me?*

Probably nothing.

Poe is a reporter she met last year. He'd seemed intimidating at first—with his domed head and football-player physique—but he eventually gained her trust. The last time they'd spoken—was it in February?—he was writing a book about a series of abductions in Jefferson County. In order to shield a young survivor named Tilly from public scrutiny, Reeve and Poe had cut a deal: She agreed to provide exclusive information about her role in what had transpired in exchange for Poe's promise never to disclose their new names or locations.

Maybe Otis Poe's book is being published. Or maybe he wants to clarify one final detail.

Still, for the rest of the meal, Reeve itches to snatch up her phone and call him back. She scarcely responds to small talk and seizes the first opportunity to leave her sister's table.

"Let me help you clear the dishes," she says, slipping her phone into her pocket and scooting back her chair.

While her sister prepares dessert, Reeve steps onto the back deck, shuts the door, and checks her phone. She finds two messages: One from Otis Poe, simply asking her to call back; the other from the King County district attorney's office.

She frowns at the phone and decides to call Poe first.

"Hey, Reeve," he answers. "Have you heard the news about Daryl Wayne Flint?"

Something knots in her chest. This is what she's feared all along. "They found the remains of another victim, didn't they?"

"Uh—"

"I told them they would. I told them I wasn't his first. I told them they'd find more girls if they just kept looking."

"Reeve—"

"Who was she? Where'd they find her?"

"Would you please stop talking for two seconds and just listen?"

"Okay." She forces herself to be still. "I'm listening."

"Flint has escaped. He broke out of the psychiatric hospital just a couple of hours ago."

She grips the phone. "No, that's not possible."

"I know it sounds crazy, but he killed someone."

It's as though Poe is speaking a foreign language. Struggling to understand, she parrots back, "He killed someone."

"A barber. He took his clothes. The security camera shows him walking out the door wearing the guy's beret."

"He's in disguise?" Her voice sounds thin.

"Yeah, and he sure looks different. He lost that wild hair of his. And the bushy beard is gone, too. He's got a goatee now."

"But . . . how . . ." The ground seems to shift underfoot and she leans heavily against the house.

"Anyway, I'm sorry to be calling with such awful news. I just thought you should know."

A thousand noxious thoughts crowd into her head. She listens mutely, feeling ill while Poe recounts what he has learned so far. Each detail makes her feel worse.

When he falls silent, she moans, "How could this happen? How could they let him get away?"

"I know. You'd think forensic lockup would be secure, right? But I'm sure they'll catch him pretty soon. I mean, it's not like you have to worry about him coming after you."

She stares out at the night and says nothing.

"I'll let you know as soon as I hear anything new, but there's no trace of him yet, according to these latest reports." He pauses a moment and his tone changes. "Do you want to know what I think? I think someone on the outside is helping him."

"Like an accomplice?"

"Exactly."

She tries to picture this. Who would want to help a psychopath like Flint?

"His mother," she says, jolting upright.

"Really? You think so?"

"It's got to be her. She's as bad as he is." An image of Flint's mother hardens in her mind. "She even petitioned the judge to lower his security status last year."

"Is that right? Well now, this is getting interesting."

Hearing the appetite in his voice, she says, "Oh crap, you're going to write about this, aren't you? I hate seeing my name in the paper."

"Reeve, give me some credit. A promise is a promise. I won't mention your new name or anything about what you're doing. But Edgy Reggie is already part of the story. Your kidnapping, your rescue, the trial. Sorry, but that's unavoidable."

Reeve is shaking with emotion. She says good-bye to Poe and takes several deep breaths, trying to process this news. With effort, she regains her composure and returns the call from the district attorney's office.

A man with a reedy voice tries to gently break it to her that Flint has escaped. She listens intently, hoping for something encouraging, but hears little more than what Poe has just told her.

She hangs up, grappling with this seismic shift, and realizes that she must get home, quickly, before she falls apart.

She steels herself and swings open the door to find herself face-to-face with her sister.

Rachel gasps at the sight of her. "Reeve, what's the matter?"

"Don't worry, I'm—"

"What is it?" Rachel grips her shoulders and peers into her eyes. "Look at me. Are you okay? God, you're so pale. Tell me what's wrong."

There's no denying her sister when she gets like this. The story pours out.

The moment Reeve stops talking, her sister steers her over to a deck chair, saying, "Sit down here and wait. I'll be right back."

Rachel turns on her heel. The door slams shut. And then Reeve overhears her sister announce to the dinner guests—in a pitch-perfect stage voice—that she is so very, very sorry, but her sister is ill, and unfortunately she must say goodnight and drive Reeve home.

An instant later, Rachel reappears with her keys, her purse, and a small bag. She hustles Reeve across the deck, down the steps, and around to the garage.

All the while, Reeve is protesting. "Please don't make a fuss. Really, I'm okay. I can take the train home."

Her sister gapes at her. "Don't be ridiculous," she says fiercely. "You *cannot* take the train. You're in shock. Don't argue with me. Get in."

Reeve wordlessly climbs into her sister's car.

"Buckle up."

Once Reeve does so, Rachel sets the bag on her lap, saying, "We've got brandy, Ambien, and some aspirin. I'm taking you home and putting you to bed."

Rachel starts the engine and backs out to the street, adding, "We need to tell Dad."

"God no, this will only upset him."

"Honestly, Reeve," Rachel says, her voice going up a notch. "Do you want him to get the news from TV? Do you? Seriously?"

Reeve pictures the infamous footage of her teenage self swatting at news cameras and groans. Even if Flint is apprehended tonight, she's sure to be all over the news. The celebrity victim, once again. She rubs her face, dreading the coming onslaught.

Rachel seems to read her mind. "Wouldn't it be better to take you to Dad's, rather than home to all those roommates? No explanations. No prying questions. Dad and Amanda won't mind, and you can sleep in their guest room, at least for tonight."

This makes perfect sense, of course. Her father and stepmother would offer the perfect refuge.

"What do you think?" Rachel continues. "Wouldn't that be better?"

Reeve is about to answer when her phone rings. She fishes it out of her purse, checks the display, and says, "It's Dad."

SIX

Dr. Terrance Moody regularly rewards himself for his achievements with a particularly fine meal. He thinks of this practice as a kind of enlightened behaviorism, and he places his order from the excellent menu at Daniel's Broiler with the idea that he is justified in writing the meal off his taxes, even though he's dining alone, because anything that contributes to his productivity is a business expense, isn't it?

The wine steward eases the cork out of a bottle of Silver Oak cabernet and offers it on a white linen napkin for Dr. Moody's approval. A sniff, a nod, a taste of the ruby liquid, and Dr. Moody's world is near perfection. He gazes out the window at the lights sparkling on Lake Union, savoring the wine's satin texture, the subtle flavors of sandalwood, cherry, and cassis in this wonderfully complex vintage. He is so relaxed, so lost in the moment, so enjoying the wine and the skill of the pianist in the adjacent room, that he almost doesn't hear his cell phone ringing.

He regards the call display with some surprise. Dr. Wanda Blume. It has been several weeks since he last spoke with the chief of psychiatry at Washington's largest mental hospital.

Their relationship got off to a rocky start. Shortly after Dr. Blume assumed her new position, one of Dr. Moody's patients was alleged to have broken a condition of his lowered security status by placing a call to his former victim, that LeClaire girl. No real proof of this arose, however, so ultimately it was decided that Daryl Wayne Flint could remain in the forensic unit's medium-security wing on probationary status. Still, Dr. Blume has been waspish since.

The whole point of hospitalization, in Dr. Moody's view, is treatment, not punishment, even in the forensic unit, which houses a handful of his most interesting cases. He and Dr. Blume have strong philosophical disagreements, and he considers ignoring her call . . . but, as an attending physician at Dr. Blume's hospital, he has an obligation to keep the peace, even if she interrupts a fine meal.

Dr. Moody sighs, lifts his wineglass, takes a sip, then picks up his phone and answers. "Dr. Blume, how diligent of you to be working on a Saturday night." He means this—as he's certain she'll understand—as a mild rebuke, since her call can surely wait until Monday. Still, he keeps an even tone, adding, "How are things at Olshaker?"

"Not good, Dr. Moody," she begins curtly. "Your patient, Daryl Wayne Flint, has escaped."

"Really?" Dr. Moody lets the skepticism leak into his voice. "But no one ever escapes from Olshaker, Dr. Blume. Perhaps you're mistaken."

"He's killed someone, Moody."

Dr. Moody pulls the phone away from his ear as if burnt. He glares at it for a beat, partly missing Dr. Blume's accusatory rant, ". . . despite your assurances that he was not a threat, and despite that you argued so persuasively about lowering his security status last December so that the judge—"

While she talks, Dr. Moody fills his mouth with cabernet and swallows, tasting nothing. When she pauses for air, he asks sharply, "How could you possibly have allowed someone like Daryl Wayne Flint to escape?"

"Aren't you listening? He took the man's clothes and walked right past our security cameras as if—"

"That's an excuse? That he wore a disguise?"

"You said he wasn't dangerous, which was clearly—"

"He's been controlled on medication for years. I don't understand how a patient who is not fully functioning, and who is certainly not hard to identify, could be allowed to simply walk away. His beard alone—"

"He shaved, goddammit!" Dr. Blume shouts. "Or, to be more precise, he killed the barber who did it for him."

Noticing that other diners are casting disapproving glances in his direction, Dr. Moody forces himself to pause and lower his voice. "Have you alerted the sheriff?"

"Of course we've alerted the sheriff. And the FBI. They've launched a search and they're setting up roadblocks right this minute."

"Wanda, calm down. I'm sure you have search dogs that—"

"Search dogs? Don't be ridiculous. He took the man's car, Moody. They've put out an APB, but so far it's turned up nothing. The man has vanished."

"I see."

"Either Flint has gone to ground or he's already slipped through."

Dr. Moody takes another gulp of wine before saying, with ice in his voice, "You've unfortunately got a very serious security breach on your hands."

"Yes, *we* certainly do," she snaps. "For Christ's sake, Moody, you assured me he was fit for his lowered security status. You said he tested low in dangerousness and risk assessment, but clearly—"

"Predicting the behavior of the mentally ill is an inexact science, Dr. Blume, as you very well know. And Flint's history, coupled with the brain trauma he suffered, makes him a unique case."

"Spare me your justifications. You've misdiagnosed this man. Badly. I'm looking at your report right now, which states that Flint's fixation on that LeClaire girl renders him unlikely to commit violence in an institutional setting. That's a false reading if I ever saw one."

Dr. Moody clears his throat, unused to having his judgment challenged. It's time to steer this conversation in a more constructive direction. "An APB has gone out, correct? And his mother's residence is staked out?"

"Absolutely."

"Good. If law enforcement does their job and watches Tacoma like they should, Flint ought to be back in custody before tomorrow morning." Dr. Moody remains outwardly calm, but he's starting to sweat. He listens grimly while Dr. Blume summons him to her office for a Monday morning meeting.

She won't take no for an answer.

He loosens his tie and reluctantly agrees, grumbling about the inconvenience of having to contact his assistant over the weekend in order to rearrange his scheduled Monday appointments.

"Well, too bad for your *inconvenience,* Moody, because even if Flint is caught within the hour, this episode is going to blow up into a disaster. And if I get burned, you can damn well expect to share the heat."

He's about to respond when he realizes that she has hung up on him. He stares at the phone. How dare that unqualified, bureaucratic bitch speak to him this way!

He sends his Caesar salad away uneaten and tears off a crust of bread, which he washes down with a gulp of wine.

Unfortunately, Dr. Blume is correct about the coming criticisms. A board review, a scathing report . . . How could she possibly have let Flint slip away? It's inexcusable!

He pours himself another glass of wine and struggles to put her call into perspective.

Flint's escape is sure to make headlines. But it's also certain to be Wanda Blume's headache. She's the one who will have to face the cameras. He resolves to stay in the background and provide only limited information. He must choose his words beforehand and carefully consider what, if any, public role he'll play.

Dr. Moody gained his national reputation because Flint's defense attorneys had wisely retained him as an expert witness. He was the best possible forensic psychiatrist available for such a high-profile case, particularly since Dr. Ezra Lerner had been retained by the prosecution.

Flint's case had been complicated by the head trauma he suffered in the car crash the night he was apprehended. Now Dr. Moody ponders how the damage to Flint's frontal lobe might explain this unexpected violence.

Of course, everyone understands that an advocate for a mental patient in a criminal case bears no responsibility for the failures of the institution subsequently tasked with confining said criminal. Forensic patients can be unpredictable. That's obvious.

By the time the waiter sets before him a perfectly cooked medium-rare Porterhouse steak with green peppercorn sauce and steaming baked potato, he is feeling somewhat better.

More than an hour later, after drinking nearly an entire bottle of wine, Dr. Terrance Moody leaves the restaurant and climbs into his classy new Audi R8.

When his wife moved out, the bitch took the Mercedes, leaving him with the Toyota. But the instant their divorce was finalized, he bought the gorgeous Audi coupe he coveted. It was well worth the cost . . . although it did pain him to have to have it repainted. He felt sure he knew the identity of the culprit who had keyed his car doors, but he couldn't prove it.

In any case, the paint is again perfect. The Audi R8 is a spectacular automobile. And Dr. Moody has taken several beautiful women home in it, though tonight he's alone as he wheels along the rain-swept roads. The familiar drive is so automatic that, despite the wine, he obsesses the entire way home about the trouble he's about to face.

He will have to call his new assistant, Mrs. Simms, early tomorrow morning and instruct her to reschedule all his Monday appointments. He groans aloud, but any dent in his schedule is nothing compared to how he fears he might be portrayed in the coming news cycles: The clueless forensic psychiatrist who didn't understand the risk presented by his star patient. The expensive expert witness who billed the state of Washington an ungodly sum for his testimony. The coddler of a hardened criminal. And the author of several formerly respected books that will now be tossed into the trash.

He stiffens at the thought.

Dr. Moody has worked hard to gain the respect of his peers at each stage of his career, but it wasn't until Flint's sensational trial—now nearly seven years past and many cases distant—that he'd attained a national reputation. He had been instrumental in getting Flint a relatively light sentence (far less than the decades in a maximum-security prison that the prosecutor wanted).

Afterward, he'd been invited to speak at many prestigious events. And of course he'd received acclaim for his book, which correlated Flint's compulsions and mental peculiarities with a handful of other mentally disordered sex offenders. It was Dr. Moody's signature field. He'd practically launched his own subcategory in DSM-5, the diagnostic bible used by every mental health professional.

But now his prize patient, who had behaved so passively for so many years, had gone and done something that no one could have predicted. He'd killed someone—that bastard!—and his escape from mental lockup was going to create a media frenzy.

Dr. Moody groans again as he turns toward his large, empty, waterfront home in fashionable West Seattle. He had been looking forward to a relaxing evening. Instead, he'll have to work on preparing a statement. With luck, Daryl Wayne Flint will be caught—or found dead—and news teams will take the story in an entirely new direction. Because blood is always more interesting than psychology, as any reporter will tell you.

He turns into his driveway, hits the remote-control button. The moment he parks his Audi beside the dusty SUV, he feels less stressed. He gathers his things. While exiting his car, he fumbles and drops his keys.

Perhaps he's drunker than he thought.

As he bends over to scoop them up, his stomach bubbles. He abruptly straightens, regretting the big meal and particularly the mixture of cabernet and cheesecake. He enters the house vowing to add an extra mile to his run tomorrow morning.

He moves inside, turning on lights. A faint odor greets him in the kitchen, and he casts a scornful glance toward the trashcan, wondering what the cleaning woman neglected to carry outside. His stomach bubbles again, and he decides that whatever it is, it can wait until morning.

But the odor nags at him as he lights up the rest of the house and steps into the dining room, where he empties his pockets onto the table and removes his jacket and tie, which he drapes over the back of a chair. That smell is familiar, but . . .

Dr. Moody lets out an uncharacteristic belch. It sounds loud and startling in the empty house, but he immediately feels better. Lightly pressing his fist to his chest, he's relieved to think that's all it was, just a bit of gas.

He surveys his spacious home, looking for some welcoming spot to settle. Television on a Saturday night is often disappointing, but it's too early for bed. His eye strays toward the liquor cabinet. What the hell—if today's news about Flint doesn't warrant a nightcap, nothing does.

He selects a glass of Waterford crystal and uncaps a bottle of Glenlivet. Two fingers, neat. He inhales the aroma, takes a first sip, and smacks his lips with satisfaction. That's more like it.

He's not going to let the bizarre escape of Daryl Wayne Flint cast a pall over what has otherwise been a stellar week, which included signing a new, moneyed client, and an invitation to give the keynote address at an important conference. Instead of worrying about a blip of bad publicity or a wrongheaded assault on his professional reputation—worries which might darken his mood for no legitimate reason—Dr. Moody decides to spend an hour or so looking over his investments. He takes another sip of scotch, thinking that, since the stock market has been up nicely the past few days, maybe it's time to take a little profit and book another trip to the Cayman Islands.

He heads down the hallway toward his den, and there's that smell again, stronger. What could it be? He'll have to have a few pointed words with his cleaning woman.

Seeing that a light has been left on, he frowns and turns in the doorway.

"Hello, Terrance." Daryl Wayne Flint's face is nearly unrecognizable without the wild beard, but then he smiles, showing his distinctive yellow teeth.

Dr. Moody nearly spills his drink.

"Long time no see," Flint says, leaning far back in the leather office chair and swinging his boots up onto the massive desk.

Dr. Moody works to keep the shock off his face as he takes in the scene: the files and papers strewn across his desk, the bottle of beer, the plate of crackers and sharply aromatic cheese.

"Sorry to drop in unannounced like this." Flint rolls his tongue across his teeth. "Bet you thought I'd be heading toward my mother's place, didn't you?"

Moody swallows. This is precisely what he'd told Dr. Blume.

"It cuts both ways, doesn't it," Flint says, smiling. "All those hours we spent together, I studied you as much as you did me."

Dr. Moody hesitates as questions flash through his mind—*What are you doing here? How did you get in?*—but he discards these as weak and pointless. Instead, he forces a smile onto his lips and lies: "I'm relieved that you've come to see me, actually, because you clearly understand that I can help you."

"Yep, you sure can." Flint gestures toward the papers before him. "You've got lots of useful information here. It's interesting to read all this stuff about myself."

Dr. Moody's hands twitch with irritation. His desk notes are sacrosanct. He never shares his work product with anyone unless forced to do so under subpoena.

"I see that Reggie changed her name. Reeve. It's an odd choice, I think." He places one fingertip on an evidentiary photograph that shows the scars on her back. "It's nice to see my old artwork, too. But it's disappointing that you never told me she'd moved away to San Francisco. Very disappointing." He narrows his eyes at Moody and nudges the photo aside.

Moody licks his lips. "Confidentiality. You know how it is."

"So does that mean you also kept quiet about my father? And about Wertz?"

"I did, yes, of course."

"You're sure about that? No new book in the works?"

"Nothing to say, right?" Moody swallows. "Your case is old news, right? And both Wertz and your father are dead."

Flint hesitates a moment before nodding. Then his expression darkens. "But you didn't say very nice things about my mother. Did you?"

Moody inhales sharply, pursing his lips, and then replies with careful diction, "You realize that virtually everything noted about your mother was merely a reflection of your own comments and feelings. Don't you remember? In nearly every session you—"

"Hey, I'm just messin' with you, Terrance," Flint interrupts, grinning. He brings his feet back to the floor, taps his toe three times. "Why don't you sit down? You look kinda tired," he says, waving toward the sofa as if he were the homeowner and the psychiatrist his guest.

Dr. Moody sidles over to the sofa and sits, but immediately regrets doing so. The sofa is low while Flint sits up higher, in what Moody himself designed as the "power position." He licks his lips and searches for a way to regain control of the situation, but it now occurs to him that he didn't even think to ask Dr. Blume how his formerly docile patient has today managed to commit murder.

Moody's mouth has gone dry. He takes a quick slug of liquor for courage.

SEVEN

San Francisco, California

Reeve gasps awake. She sits up in the dark, heart thudding, and the nightmare vanishes, as though too terrible for her mind to haul to the shore of consciousness. But then reality dawns: Daryl Wayne Flint has escaped.

Her nightmares are real.

She tosses off the covers and snatches up her phone to scan the headlines. The news hasn't changed—Flint is still at large—but now the stories have metastasized and there are many more photos. Photos of Daryl Wayne Flint, both from when he was arrested, looking heavy and untamed, and from when he escaped yesterday, looking neat and trim and wearing a beret. Photos of "Edgy Reggie" LeClaire, with fierce eyes and tight lips.

"Dammit!" she says aloud. Tossing the phone aside, she plunges her hands into her hair and curses Flint, curses their shared and twisted history. Why couldn't that animal stay locked up where he belongs? It has taken years of hard work to shove his memory aside, but it's like a living, breathing thing, and now it has snarled awake and found its feet.

She checks the clock—6:13—much too early to disturb her dad and Amanda, especially after they'd stayed up late last night, trying to reassure her while answering calls and e-mails from concerned relatives who'd heard the news.

She jumps to her feet and begins to pace, telling herself to cool down. What have years of psychotherapy taught her?

Breathe in and breathe out.

She inhales, exhales . . . and wonders what time it is in Brazil.

Two weeks ago, when Dr. Ezra Lerner had called to let her know that he was heading to Rio, she'd had to stop herself from teasing her psychiatrist about being overprotective.

He'd explained that he was going to Brazil to help a family deal with a hostage situation. "I don't know how long I'll be, but if you need to reach me," he said, "leave a message with my office and I promise to get back to you."

She had smiled into the phone, bemused that Dr. Lerner, an expert on captivity syndromes, was still so worried about her. She'd felt confident that her years of fuming and weeping on his couch were over.

Of course, she never expected her kidnapper to walk the earth again, rising up like some undead creature in a bad horror flick.

She tells herself to get a grip. Dr. Lerner is out of reach, and she needs to buck up and cope with Flint's escape on her own.

Do something. Go for a run.

It's the best she can come up with. But then she looks around and realizes she hasn't brought a bag. No way she's going running in those shoes from last night.

After a few minutes of rummaging through the closet, she comes up with some old gym clothes and a pair of Nikes that she left behind when she moved out.

She grabs the spare key, and minutes later she's running along the Embarcadero, past the early risers and tourists streaming through the Ferry Building. Her muscles warm and loosen as she heads uphill.

By the time she reaches the park, sweat has saturated her clothes. She slows to a walk and shakes out her muscles, then unzips her hoodie and pushes the sleeves up to her elbows, revealing pale forearms dotted with small, circular scars.

The park smells fresh, and as the noise of the city falls away, she hears the parrots overhead and cranes her neck to watch. The birds' distinctive green bodies and cherry-colored cheeks make them easy to spot. The wild parrots—made famous by a documentary film years ago—swoop and squawk and perch in pairs. She always takes pleasure in watching them flit from tree to tree, relishing the idea that so many South American parrots have escaped their cages to form this unlikely flock.

Once she has cooled, Reeve heads back downhill. As she passes a woman who is unloading boxes from the trunk of a car, the woman turns aside and calls, "Honey, I need your help with this."

Reeve glances into the garage just as a man lifts his head from his task to call back, "Okay, one second."

How nice it must be to call a spouse so easily for help. She tries to imagine having someone like that in her life, but intimacy eludes her. And at this particular moment, the only person she really wants to talk to is far away in Brazil.

And just like that, a realization looms.

She stops and shuts her eyes, coaxing it closer, and the idea snaps into certainty: Daryl Wayne Flint will seek out Dr. Moody.

She opens her eyes and stands up straight. "Dr. Ick," she says aloud.

She's often skeptical of intuition, but this insight unfolds with perfect logic: If she wants to talk with her psychiatrist, then Flint must also want to talk to his. Of course. Because, just as Dr. Lerner is the one person who has worked to understand Reeve, Dr. Moody is the one person who has worked to understand Flint. Who else has spent so many hours listening to that madman? Flint's twisted psyche has been Dr. Moody's bread and butter for years. He even wrote a book about his infamous client.

She absently touches the scar on the back of her neck, thinking that she and Flint are each bonded to their psychiatrists. They've likely been treated with some of the same drugs.

With a sudden chill she sees that they are, and ever will be, linked by their shared past. They are two sides of the same crime—captor and captive—and that's a tie that can never be broken. They define each other. She can still feel him breathing on her skin.

EIGHT

Because Reeve's father works as a software consultant, his name and number are easily found on the Internet. After the second call from a news scout seeking an interview with his daughter, he mutes the phone and shuts it inside his home office. Then he steps to a front window and checks the street below.

Thankfully, no one seems to have located this address. Not yet.

He and Amanda have conspired to keep Reeve out of sight until Flint is caught. Her grades are good and she can afford to miss a few classes. Luckily, cooking is one of Amanda's talents, and the house is well stocked with the kinds of foods that college students crave but can't afford.

Amanda is just setting out the makings of an elaborate breakfast when they hear Reeve come in from her morning run.

Amanda meets his eyes and whispers, "It's not going to be so easy keeping her indoors."

Reeve smells coffee brewing, but instead of heading toward the kitchen, creeps back to the guest room, where she kicks off her Nikes and snatches up her cell phone.

She calls Otis Poe. When he answers, she blurts out, "Otis, I just realized something important."

"Um, Reeve? Is that you?" His voice sounds sleepy.

She bites a lip, picturing Poe's new bride pulling the covers over her head with a groan. "I'm sorry, did I wake you up?"

"Um, no, we're awake. What were you saying?"

"I just realized where Flint is."

"You did? Where?" Poe sounds instantly awake. "His mother's, right? Because—"

"No, he won't go to his mother's. He'll go to Dr. Ick's."

"Who's Dr. Ick?"

"Sorry. Dr. Ick is just a nickname. I mean he'll go to Dr. Moody's, his psychiatrist."

"Dr. Moody? Wasn't he an expert witness at Flint's trial?"

"Right. And I figure that's the first place Flint will go."

"Interesting. So, did you call the cops?"

"No, I don't want to get even more involved than I already am. Would you do it?"

"I could, but it's your theory. And you're the one with the cred."

She grimaces. "I'd ask Dr. Lerner to call, but he's in Brazil, working with those hostages who were just rescued."

"Really? I didn't see anything about that in the news."

"No, you wouldn't. The family paid a huge ransom. It's very hush-hush."

Poe starts to speak, but Reeve quickly says, "Oh, crap, here I am blabbing to a reporter. Forget I said anything, okay?"

"Okay." He chuckles. "Unless, of course, it turns out there's a link to Jefferson County."

Each shuffles through their thoughts for a moment, then Poe says, "Do you want the sheriff's number? He gave a statement yesterday. I've got his name right here."

She suddenly has an idea. "No, never mind. I think I know someone," she says, and hangs up.

It takes no effort to conjure the name of the FBI agent who was so kind to her during Flint's trial. "Special Agent Milo Bender," she says aloud.

It's been years since she's thought much about Bender. He was the case agent who stayed with her almost from the moment she was lifted from the trunk of her captor's wrecked car.

She remembers the crash, the spinning car, the abrupt stillness. She remembers being lifted onto a gurney, lights flashing all around. She remembers lying in a hospital bed, where Milo Bender's lined face appeared even before her own parents'.

"What's your name, young lady?" he'd asked, bending over her.

She swallowed hard and told him.

"Glad to finally meet you, Reggie. We've been looking for you. But you're safe now, okay?" he said, patting her hand. "Your parents are on their way. You're going to be fixed up good as new, and then you can go home."

And when she looked into his pacific blue eyes, she knew it was true.

Later, Agent Bender had been the one to escort her family into the courthouse. He'd taken them via the back entrance to a private elevator used by the judges. She balked at entering that tight, windowless box, but being with Agent Bender and her family made it tolerable.

Once the trial was over, her family moved to San Francisco, leaving the ugliness of what happened in Seattle behind. And so the FBI agent, who had been so kind to her family, so patient with her, and so stony with the media, also faded into the past.

She remembers that Agent Bender had programmed his number into her first cell phone. Seven years and several phones later, his number is still there. So, after mentally rehearsing what to say, she keys it up and calls.

An electronic voice promptly announces that the number has been disconnected.

She swears under her breath, wondering if something has happened to him, wondering if she should have stayed in touch. What's the etiquette for crime victims and federal agents? Here's another type of problem that normal people don't have.

A quick search yields the number for the FBI's Seattle office. Figuring she can reach Agent Bender through them, she punches in the number.

A recording says, "If this is an emergency please hang up and call 911."

She paces while the voice continues listing numbered options. But she does not want to report a crime, she does not know her party's extension, and so she disconnects, mocking, "If you'd like to report a wild-ass guess, please hang up and get a life."

NINE

West Seattle, Washington

For the first time in many years, Daryl Wayne Flint sleeps late, awaking in a comfortable, king-sized bed. A momentary disorientation dissolves as he stretches, enjoying the luxurious sheets. Then he sits up and looks around, taking in the elegance of Dr. Terrance Moody's master bedroom in the soft morning light.

He hums three notes of approval in quick succession and climbs out of bed. He goes first to the window and peeks through the drapes to admire the view: a stretch of blue water dashed with white boats. He watches the clouds smudge across a green island in the misty distance.

"Well, yes, Terrance, your home will do just fine, thank you very much," he says aloud.

The master bathroom is larger than Flint's entire room at the hospital. Every surface gleams. Flint urinates, puts on a plush terrycloth robe, and heads downstairs to the kitchen, where he manages to figure out the coffee machine.

While the coffee is brewing, he rummages through the pantry, examines the contents of the fridge, and helps himself to a large glass of orange juice. Next, he makes a simple ham-and-egg sandwich on a toasted poppy seed bagel. It is by far the best meal he's had in seven years, so he fixes himself a second bagel sandwich, this one with cream cheese and lox, which he eats while roaming around the house, leaving a trail of seeds and crumbs.

He turns on the television in the living room and finds a news station, but there's nothing interesting at the moment, so he leaves it blaring while he heads back upstairs.

The robe falls to the floor. The oversized shower draws a flicker of interest, but after sniffing the fancy soaps, Flint decides he prefers his own scent. He enters Moody's walk-in closet. The choices make him smile. Ignoring the wool suits and crisp shirts, he selects a pair of jeans. He is not as tall and long-limbed as Moody, but the fit isn't bad, so he grabs several more items and piles them onto the bed.

What else?

Back in the closet, Flint eyes Dr. Moody's collection of hats. He tries on a few, laughing at his reflection, and adds two to the pile. Halloween is coming, after all.

Next, he runs his fingers along a selection of leather belts and lifts out three, each of which he snaps in the air. One does not snap to his satisfaction, so he replaces it and finds another.

He leaves the closet and approaches a large chest of drawers, where he finds underwear and socks, plus a Rolex watch, a diamond ring, and a wallet containing six crisp hundred-dollar bills. He tosses these onto the bed as well, then stands there with his hands on his hips, realizing that there's no way he can fit all this into the backpack he brought with him.

He finds a black rolling suitcase in a closet, sets it on a chair, opens it, and discovers a neat toiletry bag that contains an assortment of stuff, including vials of pills. He reads the labels with a smile. Viagra! He doesn't anticipate any problems in that department, but, hey, it might be fun.

Flint returns to the bathroom and searches the medicine cabinet, which yields a few more medications worth bringing. After adding them to the suitcase, he checks out Moody's shoes. Most are too big, too fancy, but the sneakers will be okay. And these soft, woolly slippers? Why not?

He tosses everything into the suitcase, zips it closed, and carries it downstairs to the den.

Files, notebooks, and papers are still strewn across the desktop where he left them. He hurries over to gaze at the evidentiary photographs of the girl's back. His fingertips hover over the small, careful whorls and intricate lines. The long slashes, beautiful as impressionistic art. He hungers over them for several long moments before gently slipping the photographs into a protective sleeve.

Next, he turns his attention to the files. She has moved to California, which will require—what?—a twelve-hour drive? It will take some planning, of course, but later, once Plan B is rolling . . .

He sucks his teeth.

He'll want to spend more time reading through all this before destroying what he doesn't want, so he shuffles pages back into their files, amazed at how much Dr. Moody has accumulated over the years, and chastened by how much he blabbed. Why had he ever talked about his father's burial? And how could he have been so stupid as to mention Walter Wertz?

"Risky behavior, Daryl. Risky, risky, risky," he says, mimicking Wertz's voice.

Truth was, he'd been showing off for his shrink, watching the color spread up Moody's neck. The old goat was turned on by it all, scribbling away in his notebook while his forehead glistened with that telltale sheen.

Flint locates a briefcase and fills it with Moody's papers and notebooks.

What else? He looks around. The door to the safe is still wide open.

He smirks, recalling how Moody's cranky behavior last night had turned quite reasonable once he'd revealed the gun. With a moment's encouragement, Moody had shown him the safe, which was hidden behind a false front in the closet, just like in the movies.

After spinning the combination and opening the door, Dr. Moody had said, "You can just take the money and go. There's nearly ten thousand dollars here. How's that?"

"Are you sure? That's a lot of money, Terrance," Flint said, looking over Moody's shoulder while stroking the man's ear with the gun barrel's tip.

"You can count it," Moody said, his voice going up a notch. "I was planning on . . . never mind. Take it. It's yours."

"That's generous of you. How about we leave it right there for the moment, and I'll count it later."

"And you can take my car," Moody continued, speaking rapidly. "You could be over the border into Canada before dawn. The car has GPS, and I know a way you can get across without even a passport, no border guards, nothing but open road. You can simply disappear and no one will even know you were here."

"That's a fine idea," Flint said, playing along. "And I sure appreciate your generosity." He stepped back and lowered the handgun, grinning. "In fact, I think that kind of plan deserves a toast, don't you?"

"Uh, sure. What's your drink of choice? Vodka? Gin? I have a full bar, and I'd be happy to serve whatever you'd like."

"Well, I'm not really in the mood for hard liquor."

"Beer then? I've got some good pilsner."

Flint began to stroke his beard, forgetting it had been cut off, so he rubbed his chin. "Don't you have a wine cellar?"

Dr. Moody's expression dimmed. He swallowed and said softly, "Yes, I do."

"Let's go down there and get a nice bottle," Flint said, gesturing toward the door with the gun. "You pick it out."

Dr. Moody then led him downstairs, through the basement, to a door at the back. It was a cold room with a musty smell.

Flint stood back and whistled. "That's a nice selection of wine, Terrance. How many bottles have you got there?"

"Nearly four hundred, I believe." Dr. Moody faced the racks, lifted a hand, and asked, "What would you prefer? Red or white?"

Flint shot him in reply.

Then he stood there for a long moment, letting his ears recover, studying the way the light reflected on the rows and rows of bottles. The pattern was pleasing to the eye.

Flint had tilted his head from side to side, interested in how the gleam on the bottles changed as he did so. Then he stepped back, watching Moody's blood spill across the floor, appreciating how its ruby color contrasted with the stark whiteness of the shirt stretched across the man's back.

Now Flint smiles at the recollection and turns his attention back to the safe.

Using both hands, he lifts out the bundles of cash and gold coins and places them on the desk. Then he lowers himself into the soft leather chair while savoring one final memory: In a nice trick of light, Dr. Terrance Moody's pooling blood had looked dark as wine.

TEN

It's obvious to Reeve that her father and Amanda are trying their best to distract her. But while lingering over the kitchen table and then watching a charming film on their big-screen TV, Reeve itches to grab her phone and check the news. She fidgets on the sofa, doing her best to be genial while inwardly obsessing over Flint's escape. Because a man like that won't just fade away. He's a kidnapper. He's a sadist. She can't just sit here pretending that he'll slink off and vanish. She has to do *something*.

She excuses herself and slips back into the guest room, where she scrolls through the headlines for the hundredth time. It's just a repeat of the same news.

Frustrated that Flint hasn't been caught, and angry at herself for failing to call earlier, she finds the number of the sheriff that Otis Poe mentioned. The phone rings and again a recording advises her to call 911 in an emergency, but this time she endures the full spiel until an actual human being answers.

When she explains that she's calling about Daryl Wayne Flint, the man who escaped from mental lockup, a woman's voice responds, "State your name, please."

"I'd rather not."

A pause. "Are you calling to report a sighting?"

"No, not a sighting. I just think I know where he's headed."

"You think you do. Okay, what makes you think that?"

"I'd rather not say."

Another pause. "Do you have something specific for me or not?"

"Well, the thing is, I believe I have some insight into this case."

"Uh-huh. And why is that?"

"I'd rather not say."

The woman's tone sours. "Listen, we deal in facts here, and we've had our share of psychic readings for today."

"It's nothing like that."

"Well, if you have any solid information, I'd love to hear it."

"The thing is, you need to make sure that you watch Dr. Moody's house."

"Whose house?"

"Dr. Terrance Moody's. He's the psychiatrist who testified at Flint's trial."

"Okay, and why do you think that?"

"Well, it's just a hunch, really."

"A hunch?"

"That's what I said."

"That's it?"

Realizing this is going nowhere, Reeve steels herself and tries to explain in simple terms who she is.

"Seriously? You're that girl? The one he kidnapped? The one he kept locked up in his basement?"

"Correct. Regina LeClaire, and I think—"

"Edgy Reggie, right? Isn't that what they called you?"

She stiffens. "I changed my name."

"Well, that's good, because it wasn't a very complimentary—"

"The point is," Reeve interrupts, "you haven't found him yet, have you?"

"Not yet, no."

"And there are already people staking out his mother's place, am I right?"

"Why do you think that?" the woman asks with a suspicious tinge.

"Because that would seem logical. But he won't go to his mother's."

"And why not?"

"Because he's insane, not stupid," Reeve snaps. Hearing herself, she tries a softer tone, adding, "He'll anticipate a trap. But I'll bet no one is watching Dr. Moody's place. Am I right?"

Another pause. "And where exactly is that?"

"Somewhere in Seattle, I'd imagine. Don't you have records?"

"Seattle's not our jurisdiction, but everyone's on the lookout for that stolen Honda, so it's highly unlikely he could drive all the way to Seattle without being seen. It makes more sense that he's hiding out locally. That's what I think, anyway."

"But he won't do what you expect. He won't. He has a plan of some kind." Reeve strangles the phone, realizing that the more urgently she speaks, the crazier she sounds.

As if thinking the same thing, the woman's tone turns placating. "Thank you for calling with this information. I've got it down, and I'll be sure to relay your suggestion to the investigator in charge."

Reeve grinds her teeth. "Can I speak to that person directly?"

"Don't worry, I'll make sure to relay your information. Is there anything else?"

Reeve hangs up, sinks down on the floor, and plunges her hands into her hair.

Later, wearing her good shoes and dressed in her clothes from last night, she returns to the living room saying, "Dad? Amanda? We need to talk."

Her father and his wife exchange a look and her father clicks off the television.

"I know you're trying to help, and I really appreciate it. I do," she says, settling on the couch. "But I can't just hide out here like some kind of fugitive. I need to get home. I've got classes tomorrow."

"Are you sure? Because it's quiet here and your roommates—"

"They're my friends, Dad. It's okay. I just talked to them. They understand."

She couldn't ask for better roommates, and that's become clearer now than ever. But she has deeper reasons for wanting to get home.

"I can't let my past ruin another minute of my life. I've worked too hard to get back on track. So now I need to focus on my studies and forget all about Flint. Because whatever he's doing up in Washington, it has nothing to do with me."

She nods briskly, looking from one to the other, willing these words to be true.

ELEVEN

The next morning, Daryl Wayne Flint rises early, eats a large breakfast, and then begins searching through Dr. Moody's garage. He ignores the expensive bike, the kayak, the snow skis. When he finds an ice chest, he carries it inside, sets it on the kitchen floor, and packs it full. When he lifts it he realizes he should have loaded it in place, but manages to muscle it back out the garage door, where he pauses. The shiny new Audi is tempting, but it's a showpiece—far too noticeable—so he loads the ice chest into the Toyota.

A black and nondescript SUV. Perfect.

He finds a screwdriver and squats down to remove the license plate, replacing it with one that had been included with the supplies in the storage unit. Finished, he considers the screwdriver for a moment, then finds a duffle bag and selects several more tools to bring along, plus zip ties and a roll of duct tape. He then goes back into the kitchen. A selection of sharp knives and three large plastic garbage bags get added to his stash.

Satisfied, he rummages through the freezer, and opens a tub of ice cream. He admires the design of chocolate swirled through vanilla.

Just as he spoons in, a phone begins ringing.

Has it started?

He carries the ice cream into the living room, where he picks up the remote and flips through channels, searching for news until there he is: a picture taken before the trial, when he was younger and heavier, with his unruly hair and full beard.

He sits on the sofa to watch. Here's a brief clip from his trial, with just a glimpse of his little cricket. He jerks forward, eager to see more of her, but now the newscaster reappears, describing his "daring escape that was captured by security cameras Saturday afternoon."

Flint leans in, studying the grainy black-and-white video that shows him exiting the mental hospital. The frame freezes and zooms in. It's a poor-quality image and he barely recognizes his own features, so pale between the dark beret and dark goatee.

Dark, white, dark. Like an ice cream sandwich, he thinks.

When the news shifts to the next report, Flint clicks off the television and hurries upstairs to the master bathroom, where he stares into the mirror, rubbing his palm over his distinctive goatee.

TWELVE

Seattle, Washington

Efficiency and punctuality define forty-two-year-old Mrs. Simms, and for this she's being well compensated. As Dr. Moody's new assistant, her salary is nearly twice what she formerly earned teaching history to ungrateful adolescents. This job is proving to be a joy in comparison.

Mrs. Simms arrives at the office each weekday morning well before Dr. Moody, and she makes sure the relevant papers are organized and the coffee is hot by the time he reaches his desk at 9:00 A.M. This Monday is no different than usual except for two things: First of all, the phone begins ringing the moment she steps in the door. Reporters, reporters, and more reporters.

Mrs. Simms handles these adroitly, saying nothing quotable and belying none of the anxiety she feels about the escape of Dr. Moody's most notorious patient. The instant she first heard the news, she'd anticipated this unpleasantness. Now she can hardly wait to see how Dr. Moody will deal with these vultures.

Much more troubling is the second thing: She has received no word from Dr. Moody himself. On the few occasions when Dr. Moody was running late, he has always called to let her know why he was detained and when to expect him. Always.

She checks her cell phone as well as the appointment calendar, but finds nothing to explain this lapse.

Mrs. Simms doesn't usually touch the coffee until Dr. Moody has finished his first cup. But when the doctor hasn't arrived by 9:30, she fixes herself a mug with sugar and sits at her desk, sipping the excellent Kona coffee while debating what to do.

Should she call his former assistant and ask the correct protocol? No, better to call Dr. Moody, though she hates to bother him. There could be some kind of emergency. He could be in deep consultation with an important client or a suicidal patient. Or perhaps he just forgot, with all this bother about Daryl Wayne Flint.

More likely, he's having another dispute with that ex-wife of his. That's certainly possible. After all, the woman seems terribly obstreperous. Mrs. Simms even suspects that Dr. Moody's ex is the culprit responsible for that nasty gouge in the doctor's beautiful new car. She can't understand why Dr. Moody won't confront the woman. In her experience, bad behavior needs to be nipped in the bud. Otherwise, it blooms into something worse.

At 9:40, having heard nothing from her employer, Mrs. Simms decides she must act. She mentally prepares a carefully worded apology and calls the doctor's cell phone.

No answer.

When the phone switches over to voice mail, she leaves a brief and polite message reminding him of his ten o'clock appointment. Then she gets up, smooths her skirt, and carries her coffee mug to the small kitchen, where she washes it out and sets it in the drainer to dry. She debates whether to pour out the coffee and make a fresh pot, but decides to wait until after the doctor's first appointment. She hates to waste expensive Kona coffee.

Mrs. Simms handles two more phone calls from reporters, then considers whether to call Dr. Moody again. Perhaps there's something wrong with his cell phone. Or perhaps he's ill.

She checks the time. What's the best way to handle this?

With a growing sense of foreboding, she sends a text message. When she gets no response, she phones Dr. Moody's home.

The phone rings three times before Dr. Moody's recorded prompt to leave a message. "I'm very sorry for the intrusion, doctor," she says, "but it's now nearly ten, and you have a patient scheduled, and I'm concerned that I've heard no word about why you are, uh, detained."

She hangs up and frowns at the phone as if it has committed some offense, then turns her attention to her computer.

A moment later, Dr. Moody's first appointment, a sloppily dressed young man wearing expensive shoes, enters the door, states his name, apologizes for being early, and makes himself comfortable on the couch.

At 9:58, she explains that Dr. Moody hasn't yet arrived and offers the young man coffee, which he declines, asking for green tea instead.

In the kitchen, while preparing the young man's tea, she pours herself another mug of coffee and has a taste. It has gone bitter. She pours it down the sink and rinses out the pot, then serves the tea and retakes her seat.

The phone has stopped ringing and the atmosphere in the office grows tense as Dr. Moody's absence lengthens. Mrs. Simms offers the young man a copy of the *Wall Street Journal*, which he declines, pulling out his smart phone.

Mrs. Simms tries to concentrate on bookkeeping, but now her worries have gained an appetite. Her mind reaches from one scenario to the next, trying to find some explanation for Dr. Moody's uncharacteristic behavior. Has she neglected something?

She wonders what the psychiatrist's previous assistant might have done in her situation. She double-checks the calendar, wondering if she could have overlooked a court date.

The young man coughs, setting aside his empty cup of tea, and Mrs. Simms offers another apology for Dr. Moody's tardiness. She again checks the time, and at that moment—10:11—the phone rings.

Mrs. Simms blurts, "That must be him," and quickly answers.

But the voice that replies is not her employer. "This is Dr. Wanda Blume at Olshaker Hospital. I must speak with Dr. Moody immediately."

Mrs. Simms recognizes the name of the hospital's chief of psychiatry. "I'm so sorry, Dr. Blume, but Dr. Moody unfortunately is not in the office."

"No? Well, he's supposed to be *here* for this morning's meeting. But since he hasn't appeared, I thought—"

"What meeting?"

"He didn't tell you?"

"No. Tell me what?"

"He didn't call you yesterday?"

"On Sunday? No. Is something wrong?"

The young man on the couch sets his phone aside and gives Mrs. Simms a curious look.

"This is strange. I talked with him Saturday evening," Dr. Blume's voice rises as she continues, "and he said he would instruct you to cancel today's appointments."

"But he didn't call, and I've been trying to reach him all morning."

"When did you last speak with him?"

"Friday afternoon, when we closed up the office. What's wrong?"

Dr. Blume says nothing.

"Does this have to do with that man who escaped?"

"Oh my god."

"What is it?"

Dr. Blume chokes slightly. "I'm afraid someone needs to check on Dr. Moody."

THIRTEEN

Cascade Mountains, Washington

While white Hondas are still being scrutinized on every highway across the state, Dr. Moody's dark SUV is speeding east with Daryl Wayne Flint at the wheel. A steady rain turns the interstate into a slick ribbon, but he's soon through the pass.

He exits the highway, and the road narrows as it skirts Cle Elum Lake. He winds deeper into the mountains until he spots Granite Reach Mini-Mart, looking every bit as dingy as he recalls. This is his last chance for a pit stop, so he parks and hustles inside where he selects a few provisions, including fishing line, beer, cigarettes, and a weatherproof camouflage hat.

As the pimply faced teen is ringing him up, Flint studies a display of faded photographs of happy fishermen. "What's biting these days?"

"Hell if I know," the kid responds. "My dad says I couldn't catch a cold in a kindergarten."

"You mean catch a cold in a storm."

The kid rolls his eyes. "Whatever."

Flint notices a map on the counter—Granite Reach Wilderness Area—but resists picking it up. Not good to look like an outsider. Besides, he figures he can remember the way.

But three turns later, he's wondering if maybe his memory got dented in that car crash years ago. Or if all those meds they fed him damaged his brain. Because these rain-drenched surroundings sure look different than he remembers. Nothing familiar. Nothing but forest, with thick green moss hugging rocks and trees.

The windshield wipers beat back and forth. Maybe he missed the turn. Another mile, he thinks, and then he'll have to turn around, get reoriented, take another run.

Something up ahead on the left catches his attention. He brakes, slows, and sure enough, there's the one-track bridge crossing Shadow Bark Creek. Old and weathered, just like he remembers.

Farther along, the road narrows and cuts into a rocky hillside. A bullet-riddled sign warns of falling rocks.

Twilight arrives early as the sun dips below the crags to the west. A rare set of headlights appears up ahead, cutting through the rain. Flint eases over to the shoulder to make room, but doesn't look at the other driver as the pickup rolls past. His eyes are focused on the sign up ahead.

Granite Reach Wilderness Area.

Flint makes the sharp turn into the forest, and the rutted road begins to feel familiar. When he recognizes the old fallen tree, he slows for a good look.

The tree doesn't seem near as big now, but it's surely the fallen fir that blocked the road that first day his father brought him to Granite Reach. His father had jolted to a stop, cursing. But then a strong young man named Walter Wertz had shown up. Pretty soon there was a noisy competition, his father wielding a chainsaw on one side of the road, Wertz working on the other, sawdust flying.

Daryl had stood back to watch the two slicing fat rounds out of the fallen tree, impressed with their skill, envying their strength. Soon they'd removed enough of the big fir to make the road passable.

The tree doesn't look as impressive now, settling in decay, but the way it brackets the road is unmistakable. He recalls patting the pattern of freshly exposed rings, then helping to roll the fat rounds off the side of the road, where they were later split into firewood.

He smiles at the memory of that first meeting with Wertz, and knows he's getting close.

Soon he spies the moss-covered boulder and the turn.

The driveway is little more than a path, overgrown and muddy. Flint cranks the wheel hard, dodging trees and splashing through puddles.

There's the old shed up ahead. It looks the same as always, years past decrepit. He slows and stops, angling the SUV's headlights to illuminate the padlocked door. The rain has eased to a drizzle, but he puts on his new weatherproof hat and climbs out, leaving the engine running.

The keys are easy to find if you know where to look, hanging on a nail beneath the eave. He lifts them off and pockets all but the smallest.

It fits into the padlock which clicks open, and he chuffs a laugh.

The inside of the shed is dusty, but he finds exactly what he remembers: two shovels, a pickax, a hatchet, handsaws, duct tape, a knife, and a snakebite kit.

He hurries back to his vehicle, checking the ground for signs of recent tire tracks. You can never be too careful. Finding none, he climbs back into the SUV and leaves the shed behind.

As he eases along the winding, bumpy drive, he glances sideways at the overgrown footpath that leads past the graves to Shadow Bark Lake.

The road has become so rugged it's scarcely navigable. Saplings brush the doors and windows as the SUV winds through the trees. Uphill . . . downhill . . . uphill again.

At last, the SUV's headlights glare on the cabin's front windows. He parks, angling for the best illumination, and leaves the lights on as he climbs out. A layer of wet pine needles cushions his tread until he steps onto the front porch, where he fits the key into the lock and the door creaks open.

Except for the splash of headlights, the inside lies in deep shadow. Flint gropes along a table, finds a box of matches, and lights a kerosene lantern. He holds it high. The place is cold and dusty, but everything is pretty much as he remembers: woodstove, sofa, table, chairs.

His eyes go to the floor. He sets down the lantern, peels back the rug, and locates the seam in the floorboards. It takes a knife and some effort, but the floorboards come free. He sets them aside.

Inside, he finds the stun gun, a set of handcuffs, and two types of high-powered binoculars. Here's the rifle with plenty of ammunition, and a full selection of fine knives, still sharp. He pauses to admire the blades, glinting in the light. A knife is not as good as a scalpel, but these aren't bad.

"Ultimately, none of this stuff is going to do me any good," Walter Wertz had said to him one day long ago. "I might as well enjoy it while I can, right? Because once the dialysis starts, it's all downhill. They won't put me at the top of any donors list. And when my kidneys start to fail, I'm a dead man."

"Come on, you're not that old," Flint had said. "Don't be fatalistic."

"Realistic. We both know it's the truth. I saw what happened to my father. It's genetic, Daryl. The same thing's gonna happen to me."

Flint's antennae had gone up. He smelled opportunity. His older partner had money, property, resources. Why let it all go to waste? So, over the next few weeks, Flint had coaxed him along. "You're the end of the line, eh? That's a shame, isn't it? If only there was a way of passing along the family legacy, you know? I mean, you worked hard for all this. *We* worked hard for all this."

Flint planted the seeds so subtly that Wertz thought it was his idea. "What would you think of taking over once I'm gone, Daryl? You'd be, like, my heir. That would be fitting, wouldn't it?"

Flint had feigned surprise. "That's hard to imagine. But if anybody could make a crazy idea like that work, it'd be you."

It hadn't taken much effort to draw Wertz along, one detail after another, until the idea began to take form.

"It's the ultimate bug-out plan," Wertz announced one day, handing him a large metal box. "When my kidneys give out, you can just step into my shoes. No paperwork, no trail. What do you think? We'll call it Plan B."

This was classic Wertz. He always had a plan. Plan A was business as usual; Plan B was the bug-out plan; and Plan C was always ready in case they had to drop everything and run north across the border to Canada. Three plans ready, just in case.

Of course, Flint's arrest hadn't been in anybody's plans.

He'd loaded his little cricket into the trunk of his car, trying to move her on a rainy night, and hadn't even seen the car that hit him. The next thing he knew, he was behind bars.

His bad luck.

Now Flint lifts the metal box from its hiding place and opens the latch. Inside, he finds cash, credit cards, and keys to Wertz's house in Olympia. Here are the horn-rimmed eyeglasses. He grins at the bifocals, squinting through the clear glass at the top, the minor magnification through the lens at the bottom.

Next, he lifts out a messy wig and places it atop his head. He'll need a mirror to do it right. He sets the wig aside.

At the bottom of the box, he finds several pairs of panties—which he lifts out to sniff one by one—and a driver's license with a photograph of a bushy-haired guy with heavy eyebrows and horn-rimmed eyeglasses.

Walter Wertz has left it all to him.

He sets aside what he'll need and closes the trap door. He'll make himself comfortable for the night and rest up for tomorrow. Then he'll order his tasks, take inventory. Once the cabin is ready, he'll head into Olympia and get Plan B underway.

He sets the lantern on the table and heads back outside to unload his gear. He's methodical. Back and forth, back and forth, his boots loud on the wood floor.

When he's finished, he stands in the middle of the room and taps a toe three times, enjoying the sound so much that he does a quick jig, chanting, "Off the grid, off the grid, off the grid."

FOURTEEN

University of California
Berkeley, California

The moment the professor stops speaking, Reeve snaps her laptop shut and checks her phone for news about Flint. The first thing she sees is a text message from Otis Poe:

> Breaking news! You were right about DWF paying a visit to Dr. M. But not in a good way.

All the information the professor has imparted over the past sixty minutes empties from her head as she follows Poe's link to an article, "Fugitive's Psychiatrist Found Dead." The news seems so unreal she has to read it twice. Flint is running rampant, and now he has killed Dr. Moody.

"Good lord," she groans. Startled by her own voice, she looks around and realizes that the lecture hall is empty.

She crams her computer into her backpack, jumps to her feet, and hustles along the row, up the aisle, and out the exit into the chilly air. She takes a deep breath, trying to clear her head. Too antsy to stroll, she jogs along the path through the trees, hurrying toward her next class.

The last thing she expects is to be ambushed.

A scarecrow of a man shouldering a heavy camera steps in front of her while a tall woman with heavy makeup sticks a microphone into her face.

"Reggie LeClaire!" the reporter barks. "Tell us, how did you feel when you heard the news that your kidnapper had escaped?"

"Leave me alone," Reeve says, flinching away.

"He was your captor for four years. During that time, did you believe he was capable of murder?"

"Please go away," she says, jamming her hands into her pockets and ducking aside.

The cameraman follows Reeve's movements with a lens like a hungry mouth. Her first impulse is to swat it, but she's gone that route before. And wouldn't the media just love to capture her making the same mistake twice?

"What were your first thoughts when you heard about Flint's escape?" the reporter persists.

"No comment."

"Are you aware that Flint's psychiatrist was found murdered earlier today?"

A group of students has turned to stare. Reeve recognizes a guy from chemistry lab, and suspects that he's the one who pointed her out to the news team.

She does a quick pivot, half hoping to clip the news people with her bulging backpack, but they gamely dodge around in front of her.

The microphone again waves in her face. "Reggie, what would you like to say to the families of Flint's victims?"

She glances around at the spectators and flips her hoodie up over her hair.

"Were you shocked when you heard the news of Flint's escape?"

She's taking a deep breath, preparing to shout something she'll regret when a thin man steps between her and the news team. He butts the cameraman aside, saying, "Leave her alone."

"Hey! What are you doing?" the cameraman protests.

Reeve is relieved to see Lana's boyfriend, David.

"She says she doesn't want to talk to you, man," he says, blocking the camera's view.

"You don't understand," the tall reporter says, standing with him toe-to-toe. "We're working on a news story."

"Well, you'd better work on it somewhere else before I break your damn camera."

"Yeah, leave her alone," calls another voice, and Reeve turns to see Lana running up.

The reporter's nostrils flare but she takes a step back.

"If you don't beat it, I'm calling security," David says.

"Yeah, we're calling security." Lana squares her shoulders. "So you better leave before they get here."

The reporter glares at Reeve, narrows her eyes at her friends, then turns away, telling the cameraman, "That's it for now. Let's pack it in."

Reeve stands with her friends, assuring them that she's fine, but feeling far from it. Because now it has begun. She watches the news team receding down the path with their cell phones high and glowing, and then closes her eyes with that image still burning on her retina. And it's like watching a lit fuse.

FIFTEEN

Reeve is in the kitchen slicing an apple when her cell phone rings. She wipes damp fingers on her jeans, checks the phone, and frowns at the Seattle area code.

The caller identifies himself as Agent Pete Blankenship with the FBI. "Miss LeClaire? I understand that you placed a call to the Turvey County Sheriff's Department yesterday morning, is that correct?"

"I did."

"And you were calling to warn them that Daryl Wayne Flint might target his psychiatrist, is that right?"

She frowns. "Well, no, not that he would 'target' him. That's not a term I would use."

"So what was it, exactly, that led you to make the call?"

There's no way she's going to explain her reasoning to this stranger. What's she supposed to say? *I figured that Flint would want to talk to his psychiatrist because I wanted to talk to mine?* No way.

Instead, she answers blandly: "It just seemed logical."

"Logical in what way?"

"Flint was in mental lockup. How many people ever showed up to visit him?"

Blankenship says nothing.

"I mean, his psychiatrist would see him regularly, right?"

"Did you ever visit him?"

"Of course not."

"How did you know Dr. Moody?"

"I saw him during Flint's trial. And I've read his books, of course."

"So you're saying you came to this conclusion without any direct information?"

"It wasn't a conclusion. It was a hunch."

"And how did you arrive at this hunch?"

She can't help but scoff. "Have you read any of Dr. Moody's work?"

"Excuse me?"

"Dr. Moody's books, his journal articles. Have you read them?"

"Why?"

"Because he wrote about Flint, obviously."

A dry cough. "Listen, the point is, you were right about the danger Flint posed to Dr. Moody. So where do you predict that he will head next?"

"I've no idea."

"Do you have any information about his mother?"

"If you're thinking that Flint will head to his mother's, well, that's not very smart, if you ask me."

"Why not?"

"Because Flint knows what you'll expect. That's his advantage. He'll do what you do *not* expect."

"So, what's your assumption, since you apparently know him so well. You have my full attention."

She stands very still, wrestling with her thoughts, clutching the phone to her ear with one hand and rubbing the scar on the back of her neck with the other.

"Miss LeClaire, we're interested," he prods. "Given your personal knowledge of Flint's nature, what is your expectation? What's your best guess?"

"Well, I'm not a profiler," she says sarcastically.

"Exactly. Which is why we're so interested in your point of view."

She says nothing.

"Tell me, when was the last time you had contact with Daryl Wayne Flint?"

"What? Not since the trial. I'm a student at UC Berkeley."

"He called you last year, didn't he? What did you talk about?"

"Are you kidding?"

"Did Flint express any resentment toward Dr. Moody?"

"What?"

"Did he tell you he was planning an escape?"

"Of course not."

"Has Daryl Wayne Flint communicated with you or shared his plans with you in any way?"

"That's a ridiculous question."

"What about his mother? Has she been in touch with you?"

Something snaps shut inside her. "I'm sorry, but I've told you all I know."

"But we have more questions, and we'd like to interview you further. Would tomorrow be convenient?"

She blows out air and has a sudden vision of a tall, Nordic-looking man with a sweep of blond hair and crinkle lines around blue eyes. "Could I speak with Agent Bender?"

"Who?"

"Special Agent Milo Bender. Is he there?"

"Bender?" A pause, a muffled exchange, and then the voice comes back on, saying, "Uh, no, Agent Bender is no longer with the bureau."

"Well for god's sake, he's the one I need to talk to."

SIXTEEN

Seattle, Washington

Milo Bender used to dream about retirement. He'd imagined that he and his wife would travel. First, they'd visit Sweden and Norway, where he would breathe the air and walk the landscapes of his maternal ancestors. Next, they would tour the British Isles, the sunny Mediterranean, and the Swiss Alps. After that, the Caribbean, Asia, and the distant Southern Hemisphere beckoned.

That had been his plan, but now he's careful not to remark on any of this to his wife. The most exotic trip they might hope to manage is a sailing excursion down the coast with their son. But even that has to wait, since Yvonne is still working full-time as a nurse.

Bender hadn't planned on being out of the game so soon. One minute he was solving cases, the next he was flat on his back, having his sternum sliced open. The zipperlike scar running down his chest rebukes him each morning while he shaves. It has now faded from vivid pink to a waxy color. The only thing still hurting is his pride.

But who wouldn't be bitter? His early retirement had coincided with the tanking economy. So Bender's travel these days is limited to the route from home to the hardware store to one of four aging rental properties that have done nothing but demand major repairs and drain his savings. Of necessity, he keeps tools and a change of clothes in the back of his minivan. This morning, he's buying what's needed to fix a leaky toilet.

As he pockets his receipt, he notes with detached irony that ABBA is playing on the store's soundtrack, as if mocking his dreams of touring Scandinavia.

When his cell phone rings, his first thought is that it's one of his renters calling to gripe. He fishes the phone from his pocket, ready for bad news, then stares through his bifocals at the familiar number displayed: FBI Field Office.

He clears his throat and answers crisply, "Milo Bender here."

"Bender, this is Stuart Cox. Remember me?"

Bender pauses. He'd heard that Cox was fully capable as Seattle's special agent in charge, but he never much liked the man. Data driven and impersonal, that was Bender's impression. But maybe it was a generational thing. Cox and all those younger agents were always clicking keys and scanning screens and talking in acronyms.

"Stuart, it's been awhile," Bender says coolly. "Congratulations on your promotion."

"How's retirement? How's Yvonne? How's your health?"

"Yvonne's great, and I'm not dead yet. What's up?"

"Listen, if you have time, I'd like to talk."

"Sure, okay. Shoot."

"The thing is, I missed breakfast and I'm starving. Can you meet me in, say, half an hour?"

Bender pictures the rental's leaking toilet and the damage the water is doing to the floor beneath. He has torn up floors before. It's costly, unpleasant labor, and he knows it's important to catch a leak early. He swallows, knowing the answer but asking anyway, "What's this about?"

"I need to pick your brains about the Daryl Wayne Flint case. He's still at large, as I'm sure you're aware."

In all his years with the bureau, Milo Bender never saw another criminal like Flint. Hearing the man's name still makes his blood pressure spike. "Name the place," he says. "I'll be there."

Exactly twenty-five minutes later, Milo Bender is sitting across from Stuart Cox at a café on Pioneer Square. Eyeing the bureau's new boss from behind his menu, Bender is surprised by the change he sees in Cox. The ruddy man who was bulging out of his suit now looks gaunt, and his face has assumed a terrierlike sharpness.

After they order, Cox says, "It's on me today. Official business." Moving the silverware aside, he pushes a thick file across the table.

Bender recognizes the case file as his own. He doesn't touch it, but remembers every item of evidence, each awful photo. A flutter in his chest reminds him to check his watch. Wordlessly, he pulls a vial of pills from his pocket, shakes a dose into his palm, and pops the tablet into his mouth.

Cox watches him swallow, then leans forward and says, "Before we get started, what's your take on what happened with Flint's conviction? I mean, not guilty by reason of insanity didn't fly, right?"

Bender sighs. "Because he was guilty—insane, sure, but still legally culpable. His actions showed he knew exactly what he was doing."

"Obviously. Hiding a girl in your basement for years is not exactly a rash act."

Bender's face tightens.

"So," Cox continues, "Flint was rational, organized, and cognizant of his actions. The guy's guilty as hell under the law. So how'd he end up in mental lockup?"

"After he was convicted, things went sideways. He apparently had some kind of brain injury in the—"

"The car crash, yeah. Pretty dramatic finding the girl that way, right?" Cox shakes his head. "Just a lucky fluke that she was in the trunk when his car got slammed."

"A fluke. Right. So anyway, Flint had a closed-head injury, some kind of postconcussive syndrome. And after he was sentenced, the DOJ decided that Olshaker was the only suitable institution for someone with his mental problems."

"What bullshit."

Bender opens his empty palms. "They decided he needed treatment. So they turned around and sent him to the hospital's forensic ward."

Cox sits back and looks past Bender's shoulder. "Where's our food? Damn, I'm hungry." When his eyes come back to Bender's he asks, "So, what was your take on Dr. Moody?"

"What do you mean?"

"Well, did he screw up? Was he an asshole?"

"He was a fully competent asshole. He never screwed up." Bender frowns at the file on the table. "You're trying to figure out why Flint killed him."

"Exactly. Why take that risk? Why target Moody?"

"Robbery? Revenge?"

"Yeah, maybe, but revenge for what?"

Bender shakes his head. "I've been off the case for years. You've got the file and the transcripts. I'm sure you've got plenty of new agents with fresh opinions. Come on, Stuart. You didn't call me here just to speculate about Flint's motivations."

"I've got some questions about the victim. That girl he kidnapped. You two were close, right?"

"That was years ago. She was just a kid."

"Sixteen, I know. But you interviewed her. And you've got good psychological insight, that's your reputation. Not like me, I'm a numbers guy. Data, I can analyze. People?" A shrug. "My wife says I'm hopeless. Anyway, this was your case. You were there during Flint's trial, so the girl got to trust you, right?"

"Well, she never tried to smack me, if that's what you mean," Bender says, referring to the time she swatted at the cameramen dogging her through the courthouse.

"Right. I remember that. The press started calling her Edgy Reggie, right?"

"She hated that name."

"Yeah, well, she's had it legally changed since then." Cox is about to say more when their food arrives, and they fall silent while the plates are arranged before them.

Once the waiter has gone, Bender asks, "So, what's her new name?"

Cox pours a dollop of catsup onto his plate. "Oh, it's *Reeve*. Reeve LeClaire."

"She calls herself Reeve?" Bender smiles.

"Yeah. Weird, huh?"

"No, I like it." Bender cuts into his omelet, takes a bite, and reaches for the salt.

Cox watches him for a moment. "Here's the thing about Miss LeClaire: She called the sheriff's office on Sunday, with a tip that Flint would go after Dr. Moody. Now, how on earth would she know that?"

"Sunday?" Bender puts down his fork.

"Right."

"When was Moody killed?"

"Best guess, around midnight Saturday, a few hours after Flint escaped. Looks like Flint lounged around, slept in Moody's bed. He must have enjoyed a nice little rest. His prints are all over the place."

"But Dr. Moody's body wasn't found until when? Yesterday?"

"Right, around midday. He's divorced, lives alone. Nobody missed him until he didn't show up for work."

Bender exhales loudly.

"Here's what we're thinking," Cox says, putting his elbows on the table. "That girl knows something. Could be Flint still holds some kind of influence over her."

Bender scowls. "After all these years? No, I seriously doubt that."

"But she was, what? Twelve when he took her? Who knows what years in a basement with that scumbag might do to a kid? Who knows about the long-term effects?"

"You're talking Stockholm syndrome."

"Of course."

"Listen, you're wrong if you imagine she would cooperate with—"

"Maybe not that she'd cooperate outright. Not overtly, but maybe they're still connected somehow. Otherwise, how would she know what Flint's up to?"

"Why don't you ask her?"

"We did. She wasn't exactly forthcoming." Cox polishes off the rest of his meal while giving Bender the gist of what happened.

Hearing about the case agent's botched attempt to interview Reeve, Bender looks at the ceiling, shaking his head. "Your man pissed her off. But anyway, it sounds to me like she told him what she knows."

"Maybe, maybe not. That's where you come in."

"Me? But I haven't seen her since her mother's funeral." He suffers a recollection of the girl's stricken expression, her listless bearing, and recalls talking with Dr. Ezra Lerner about her fragile psychological state.

"You went to her mother's funeral? Sounds to me like you were close to the whole family."

"In some ways, perhaps. But it's been years. I'm afraid I can't offer much insight anymore."

"Well, isn't it time you got back in touch?"

"What, you want me to call her?" Bender scoffs. "What am I supposed to say? 'Hey kid, remember me? Wanna talk about old times?' Besides, your case agent already talked to her."

"Listen, even I can understand that she might have trust issues. But you befriended her. You were always good at this stuff. And besides, she asked about you."

"She did?"

"Yeah."

"What did she say?"

Cox waves this away. "The question is, can she help us? Does she have some kind of insight into our fugitive? Where is he hiding, and what the hell is he going to do next?"

"He took the barber's car, right? But now he has Moody's?"

"A black Toyota Highlander, correct." Cox pulls a face. "But that's another thing. We never found the barber's Honda. You'd expect that he'd have left it near Dr. Moody's, but that's not the case. Or maybe it's at the bottom of a lake. We're working on that. But since the LeClaire girl figured out one part of the puzzle, maybe she can offer something more."

"And maybe not."

"But she's a lead, isn't she? And we don't have much better out of the hundreds we're following. You know how it is."

"Sure." Bender knows how frustrated Cox must be, slogging through false sightings, sifting out poor information, weighing the value of lame guesswork. "What about Flint's relatives?"

"His father's been dead for decades. There's only his mother, still in Tacoma. And we're watching her, believe me."

Bender knows without asking that her phone has been tapped and she's under twenty-four-hour surveillance. He takes off his glasses, rubs his eyes, then puts the glasses back on before asking, "You've got no other leads?"

"Nothing hot. But listen, this LeClaire girl helped with that case in northern California last year, in Jefferson. Remember that?"

Bender nods.

"So what I'm thinking is, maybe you can talk to her, maybe find some kind of leverage to use that—"

"Leverage?" Bender's expression sours. "If that's your approach, you really do need my help."

Cox pushes his plate away and leans back. "Exactly. Don't make me beg."

"Look, I'm retired. I'm rusty. And I'm not an agent anymore."

"All I'm asking is that you contact her and report back."

"In what capacity?"

"Nothing formal, okay? I'm just asking for a little help between old friends. How's that?"

"But hasn't her case been reassigned?"

"No, actually, her case is closed. You closed it. But now that Flint has escaped, we've got a whole new ballgame. And this comes on top of everything else going on. You know, counterterrorism, cybercrimes, human trafficking—"

"Sure, I know. Limited resources, skyrocketing caseload. Some things never change."

"Exactly. We're swamped, so if you can help . . ." Cox opens his palms. "Listen, it's not like I'm asking you to carry a badge."

"Or a weapon, either, because I promised my wife—"

"Of course not. I'm just asking for a favor. Whaddya say?" Cox leans toward him across the table. "Come on, come back to the office. It won't take long to get you up to speed."

Bender closes his eyes, thinking. He wonders how the bureau will proceed if he declines, but instantly knows the answer: Another pushy agent will try to coerce information. And he can picture how Reggie—*Reeve*, he corrects himself—will respond to being badgered by some amped-up stranger.

Bender opens his eyes and relents. "Okay, I'll give her a call. But I can't promise you anything. And if she doesn't want to talk to me, I'm out."

SEVENTEEN

Reeve jams her fists into her pockets and marches toward her next class. She has donned sunglasses and a hoodie, determined to stick to her schedule and evade any news teams that might be prowling the campus.

When her cell phone rings, she narrows her eyes at the Seattle area code and answers briskly, ready to scold the intruder who has managed to locate her number. But she recognizes the voice and pulls up short.

"Agent Bender?"

"Well, it's not 'Agent' anymore. Call me Milo."

"You're not an agent anymore?"

"I'm retired."

How old is old enough to be retired? An image comes to mind, but Milo Bender seems fit and tall and ageless. The tension leaves her shoulders as she remembers the man who could always be persuaded to bring her chocolate ice cream during Flint's trial. Even after Agent Bender's testimony, when he didn't need to be there and surely had other things to do, he would show up at the courthouse to check on how she was doing. Her family seemed to orbit around him. She pictures him talking with her mother, their heads tipped together, and suffers a pang of longing.

Releasing the image, she forces herself to confront the subject lurking in the background. "You're calling about Flint, aren't you?"

"I'd hoped that soulless devil would stay locked up forever."

"You and me both." She sighs. "Anyway, I'm glad Agent Blankenship asked you to call me."

"I spoke with his boss, actually. I gather that Blankenship's not the most tactful guy in the world."

"Yeah, he was kind of a jerk. He practically accused me of being Flint's accomplice."

Bender grunts his disapproval. "They're desperate to find a solid lead. Desperation makes people stupid. And now Flint's trail has gone cold."

"How could they let him escape?"

"That's what I'm wondering. And what triggered this? And why now? I mean, he causes no trouble for years and then suddenly murders two people. What's that about? No one has any idea. And Reeve, you won't like this, but you're the only one who seems to have any real insight into the man, now that Dr. Moody is dead."

She flinches. "The thing about Dr. Moody . . . I didn't know that Flint would kill him. I never expected that."

"Of course not. No one could have. Besides, you called the sheriff's department, you tried to warn them."

"I tried to call you first."

"You really did?"

"But your line was disconnected."

"I'm sorry. Perhaps I should have called you when I retired. I considered it, but thought a call from me might be upsetting."

Hearing Bender's voice, remembering his intelligent blue eyes behind wire-rim glasses and his gentle manner, she says, "You're the last person I'd find upsetting."

"Well, if you don't mind, may I ask a few questions?"

She steels herself. "If I can help."

"How did you know that Daryl Wayne Flint would go to Dr. Moody's?"

"It was just a guess, but it seemed obvious that Flint would seek out that connection. Besides, he'd see an opportunity with Moody."

"In what way?"

"His arrogance, for one thing."

"Flint's?"

"No, I mean Moody's."

"What makes you say that?"

"Well, haven't you read his books?"

A pause. "Um, no, I'm afraid I've fallen behind in my reading. I've had some health issues."

She tenses. "What kind of health issues?"

"Just a little surgery."

"What kind of surgery?"

"Heart surgery. No big deal. They fixed me right up."

"Heart surgery? Are you okay?" she asks, her voice rising an octave.

"That was years ago. I'm fine now, but I lost track of Dr. Moody. So please continue. Tell me how you figured that Flint would go after him."

She exhales loudly. "Not that he would go *after* him, no, not that. But think about it: Dr. Moody was his confidante."

"Hmm, yes, as well as a link to the outside world. So you realized that Flint might have become . . . somewhat dependent on that connection. Is that what you mean?"

"But I have no idea why Flint killed him. Maybe he resented Dr. Moody. Maybe he disliked the notion that his psychiatrist had the audacity to pretend he understood him."

Bender hums a note. "So you think Flint wanted to prove to Dr. Moody that he was the one in control?"

"But it's not rocket science. The profilers should have figured this out."

"You'd think so. But Flint's case was considered closed."

"Was. Past tense."

"Correct. So now they're at a loss. The initial theory was that Flint's mother might be hiding him, since she's the only person who visited him at the hospital."

"She was weird." Reeve frowns, picturing the woman. So charming on the witness stand, so menacing in private. An unpleasant encounter in the women's restroom flashes through her mind and she adds, "Weird in a witchy kind of way."

"I remember. You and your sister made up a term for her, uh . . . what was it?"

"Obsessive-repulsive disorder."

He laughs. "That was it."

"I was wondering, how many times did his mother visit him? Do you know?"

"Good question. Let's see . . ."

It seems as if he's flipping through pages, and it occurs to her that Bender has a copy of Flint's records. She recalls the heavy briefcase crammed with files that he always carried with him.

"Here it is," he says. "Hmm, this is interesting. Flint's mother used to visit about four times a year, but she visited fifteen times in the last year, twelve times in the last five months."

"Really? So what changed?"

"I'm wondering the same thing. I'm sure the bureau is looking into it."

She rubs her forehead. She's getting a headache. "So, why are you working on this? I thought you said you were retired."

"I am. But the FBI stays on you like a tattoo, I'm afraid. And I'm the one who's most familiar with Flint's case."

"Unfortunately for you, right?"

He utters some agreement as she spies a news crew lurking beside Sather Gate. They don't spot her as she veers away. "Sorry I can't be more help, but, uh, I'm afraid I'm going to be late for class. I really need to go."

"One more thing. Where do you think Flint might head next?"

Dark recollections wash through her, but the past has faded. "I've no idea," she says at last. "He has a plan, I'm sure. But he won't go to his mother's."

"So where?"

"Maybe someplace off the grid, like a hideaway in the mountains, like a fishing cabin."

"Fishing cabin? What makes you say that?"

She closes her eyes, trying to conjure a memory, but the connection has slipped away. "I don't know, it just popped out."

Their conversation bothers her for the rest of the day. It dogs her around campus. It nags her on the way home. It worries her as she orders a take-out dinner from a Thai restaurant. And just after she enters her door, as she's lifting the fragrant meal out of its paper sack, the realization sinks its claws into her chest.

Her breath stops. She goes utterly still, weighing the cost of struggle, but sees no option but surrender.

Reeve's father, who often consults for Microsoft, has flown to Seattle on Alaska Airlines so many times that he's on a first-name basis with nearly every flight crew flying out of SFO. He claims an excessive number of frequent-flier miles, and repeatedly offers to fly his daughters to Hawaii or Florida. (Reeve always declines, preferring chilly San Francisco, where she can comfortably wear long sleeves.) Nevertheless, she knows her father won't be happy with her request.

She tries to keep her voice steady as she sits at his table and relays her conversation with their old friend, Agent Bender. "The thing is, Dad, I know Flint better than anyone. I knew he would head to Dr. Moody's. Nobody else expected that."

He makes a noncommittal sound.

"And now there are news cameras stalking me all over campus. And it might sound crazy, but I can't sleep or study or think of anything except that he's out on the streets again." She takes a breath. "So, the thing is, I think I need to go to Seattle."

"You can't be serious."

"I hate to ask, but I can't just sit around here and hide from reporters. And this story isn't going away until he's caught."

"You want to go up there *now*? I don't think that's a good idea. What does Dr. Lerner say about this?"

"He's out of the country, so I haven't actually spoken to him," she answers carefully. "But the FBI thinks that maybe I can help."

"But it's not safe for you up there, is it? Besides, it's unnecessary. They've got a full-scale manhunt underway."

"Which Flint has completely evaded. He's smarter than they think he is."

"But you said you never wanted to go back there."

"I know, but now that he's out, things have changed. I'm having nightmares again. I just feel like I need to do whatever I can until he's caught. You can understand that, right?"

"But . . ." He shakes his head. "No, actually, I can't."

"Dad, I can't concentrate on my classes, anyway. Besides, it'll only be a couple of days. I won't lose much time."

"I just don't think this is a good idea."

"You said yourself that they're going to catch him. And I'll be with Milo Bender. What could be safer than that?"

His face creases with concern. "Reeve, call me overprotective, but I hate it that you're even considering this. What point is there in you going up there? What good can possibly—"

"But Dad, that's exactly it! If anything good can come out of those years I spent locked in that basement, if I can squeeze anything positive out of all that misery, then I've got to try. I've got to do something. Besides, I can't move on with my life with this hanging over my head. And I'm the only one who really knows what he's capable of." She's pleading, she's talking too fast but can't stop. "Maybe I know more than I think I do, maybe I can jolt something loose that I've blocked out, maybe I can help catch him."

She grips her hands in her lap, waiting for him to respond.

He says nothing for a long moment, then his eyes meet hers. "How about if I go with you?"

"No Dad, I need to do this alone. I'm not as fragile as you think I am." After a beat, she adds, "But if you can't get me a ticket I'll—"

"Reeve, if you insist, then of course I can get you a ticket." He shakes his head sadly, cupping her hands in his. "But I'm worried about you. So don't take this the wrong way—I know you're not a fragile little girl anymore—but you and I both know that your desire to go back to Seattle has more to do with your own issues than with actually helping to catch that madman."

EIGHTEEN

Sea-Tac Airport, Washington

Milo Bender arrives at the airport a bit early and finds a good spot in the parking structure. He checks his watch, then spends a few minutes reviewing the file.

An old photograph catches his attention. Regina Victoria LeClaire. Her thin face, her solemn expression. At the age of sixteen, she wore the haunted look of a refugee.

He remembers how brave she was at Daryl Wayne Flint's trial, sitting on the stand and recounting what she'd endured. Every detail still pains him. He hates to think of what she suffered during those years in her kidnapper's basement. And he hates himself for not having stopped it.

There must have been something that could have led him to Flint's lair—the guy didn't suddenly appear out of thin air; he must have made mistakes somewhere along the line—but what? Other victims always seemed probable. A predator like Flint would typically evolve over time. He would have practiced his appetites on others before Reeve, but either the girls disappeared or they suffered in silence. Sex crimes are notoriously underreported. But Milo Bender still believes there was something they'd missed.

He heaves out a sigh and puts the file away, then checks his watch. Still early.

Reeve's call had taken him by surprise. "You want to come up here? Are you sure?" he'd asked.

His first suspicion was that Stuart Cox had been unhappy with his report and had then resorted to other means of prying information out of her.

"Honestly," he asked, "is this your idea, or did someone from the bureau call you?"

But Reeve had insisted it was her idea. And then she'd surprised him further, saying, "I want to check out the mental hospital."

That struck him as odd. "Olshaker? Really? Why?"

"Maybe if I look around, I can get a sense of what Flint was thinking. Maybe I'll remember something important. Maybe I'll have some kind of insight."

He'd smiled and said, "Maybe you will," without adding, "but I doubt it."

It was gutsy of her to want to help, but he didn't understand it. She'd suffered so much here. Why return to the scene of such dark events? He could scarcely imagine the emotional toll. Still, if Reeve had some deep reasons for coming, even if she just wanted to confront her personal demons, the poor kid would need an ally. So, he'd called Cox, who quickly warmed to the idea of having Flint's former captive close at hand.

Bender insisted on handling the logistics on his own, without involving the case agent. No pressure, no expectations, no formal interviews. And no bloody protocols.

Then he'd called the hospital and arranged their visit, telling Dr. Blume that he was consulting with the FBI and that they were hoping that perhaps Reeve LeClaire—whose name Dr. Blume instantly recognized—could shed some light on Flint's psyche.

She was skeptical at first, but he'd persuaded her, saying, "The investigation has stalled, so why not try unconventional methods?"

He checks the time, locks up his vehicle, and heads into Sea-Tac airport, wondering if he'll have trouble recognizing Reeve as a young woman of twenty-three. He hopes she's not covered with tattoos and studded with piercings, like so many young people these days.

He'd last seen Reeve when he'd flown down to San Francisco for her mother's funeral. Her teeth had been fixed, her hair had filled in, and she was meticulously groomed. But she was still as thin as ever. And what he noticed most was her shell-shocked demeanor.

The death of a parent can do that to you. What was the term Dr. Lerner had used? *Secondary wounding?*

He checks the board for arrivals and finds that her Alaska flight from SFO has arrived ahead of schedule, so he's already late. He hurries toward their rendezvous point and spots her immediately.

Her hair is longer, colored an attractive shade of red, and she is turned away from him, yet she's unmistakable. Look for the girl in any crowd who moves most gracefully, and that's her.

"Reeve!" he calls, and when she turns around, he's struck by what a lovely young woman she has become. Her mother would have been so proud.

She comes toward him with a backpack slung over one shoulder, pulling a rolling suitcase behind her. "Thanks for meeting me, Agent Bender."

"Milo," he corrects her. "I'm retired, remember?"

"Milo?" She dimples one cheek and rolls her eyes. "I'll never get used to that."

"Just Bender then, how's that?"

"Okay." She cocks her head and gives him an appraising look. "You look just the same."

But he knows she's just being polite. "And you look all grown up," he says, because it would seem frivolous to say she looks pretty.

"Let me help you with that." He stoops to take the rolling bag and is glad that she lets him without protest.

Bender steals sideways glances at her while they head toward the parking structure, talking. She wears the same worried expression he remembers. Always so pensive.

So he's not surprised when, after only a few minutes, she drops the small talk and asks, "How long will it take us to get to the hospital?"

NINETEEN

The sturdy woman who heads up this mental institution is nothing like Reeve's psychiatrist. There is no scent of citrus, no delicate orchid blooming from a cobalt pot as Reeve and Milo Bender enter the office of Dr. Wanda Blume. She wears a somber suit and sits behind a heavy walnut desk stacked with files, giving the impression that she's anchored in administration rather than psychiatry. Her salt-and-pepper hair is pulled back in a no-nonsense bun, and the dark circles around her eyes bespeak a run of sleepless nights.

Milo Bender thanks her for meeting them. "I'm sure these past few days have been stressful. I hope it's not too much of an imposition."

Without getting up, Dr. Blume gives them a tight smile and waves them toward two leather chairs. "I took a look at your file notes after you called, Agent Bender. Given the work you've put into Flint's case, I can surely spare a little time."

"I'm not an agent anymore. You can call me Milo," he says.

Reeve scans the walls of books, recognizing several, and then spots an excellent model of the human brain. Resisting an urge to pick it up, she takes a seat.

"Are you just moving in?" Bender asks, nodding toward several framed paintings leaning against the wall beside a bookcase, apparently waiting to be hung.

Dr. Blume flashes a look of surprise. "I've been here since January, but I'm afraid it's taking me awhile to get settled."

All the walls are bare save one, which is crowded with framed diplomas and certificates. Reeve studies the scrollwork. "You moved here from Nevada, is that right? Are you getting used to the rain?"

Again, the flash of surprise. "Let's just say that the greenery here is a nice change." Dr. Blume spreads her hands on the desk. "Now, Miss LeClaire, I of course understand that you have a personal interest in seeing Daryl Wayne Flint apprehended, but it seems unusual that a former victim would make the effort to become involved in an ongoing investigation."

Reeve holds her breath, sensing that something unpleasant is coming.

"And as you are surely aware, there's very little I can tell you." Dr. Blume lifts her palms off the desk and holds them up, empty. "There are confidentiality issues and protocols involved."

"We're not here to violate anyone's privacy."

"This is an unofficial visit," Bender says. "We'd merely like to look around."

"Well, you know that everyone here has already been questioned extensively. All our security tapes have been examined. Individuals at every level, employees and patients alike, have been interviewed and exonerated."

"Of course. That's understood," Bender says.

"How long did you work on Flint's case, Mr. Bender? Four years?"

"Let's see . . . From the time of the kidnapping, right through his trial and sentencing. More than five."

"He knows Flint cold," Reeve interjects.

Dr. Blume sighs. "Well then, perhaps you might have been better than Dr. Moody at predicting Flint's propensity for violence."

"*I* certainly would have," Reeve mutters. She shifts in her seat and notices a tower of books stacked neatly on the floor beside Dr. Blume's desk, with Dr. Moody's most recent on top. Glancing back at Dr. Blume, she catches the woman studying her with interest.

"Reeve is the one who seems to have the most insight into Flint," Bender is saying.

"Because of your years as his captive?" Dr. Blume shakes her head sadly. "That's a very unfortunate way to gain insight."

Reeve nods and abruptly stands, wanting to sidestep this particular discussion. She finds herself drawn to the plastic model of the human brain. Placing her fingertips lightly on the clear plastic skull, she asks Dr. Blume, "May I?"

"Certainly, if you wish."

Reeve lifts the model by its skeletal jaw and carries it to Dr. Blume's desk, setting it down gently.

The doctor's curious expression deepens. "Are you studying anatomy?"

"I've always had an interest in brain function." Reeve removes the clear skull and lightly taps the frontal lobes above the eye sockets. "This area, the orbitofrontal cortex, controls decision making, social behavior, and aggression."

Dr. Blume steeples her fingers with just the hint of a smile.

"Flint's brain would likely show impairment here. And"—Reeve lifts out a part of the brain and points to a section colored in blue—"psychopaths have reduced activity here, in the anterior cingulate cortex, the center of empathy."

Dr. Blume nods. "The ACC does show reduced activity in psychopaths. But researchers don't know why."

Reeve points to two areas located deep within the brain, the amygdala and hippocampus. "These are the centers of mood and memory, which can be affected by stress hormones."

"Especially during childhood," Dr. Blume says. "And Flint's brain likely had some impairment in this area, since his father was by all accounts a brutal man."

Reeve can't muster any sympathy. No doubt her own brain suffered a flood of stress hormones, thanks to Flint. Each time she struggles to keep her feelings in check, each time a memory eludes her, she blames him. But she doesn't mention any of this. Instead, she says as lightly as possible, "The man is also a sadist, of course."

"A sadist, an opportunist, and a narcissist," Dr. Blume agrees. "But he doesn't easily fit into classification, perhaps because of his closed-head injuries."

"Ah, from the car crash," Bender says. "As I recall, Dr. Moody testified that brain trauma caused some kind of obsessive disorder. Isn't that right?"

"He exhibited some ritualistic behaviors, yes."

"What kind of ritualistic behaviors?" Reeve asks, staring at Dr. Blume.

"Repetitions. An obsession with sets of three, apparently. I never spoke with the man directly." After a beat, Dr. Blume adds, "I did meet his mother, however."

Reeve notices that the doctor compresses her lips, as if sealing further comment.

Bender asks, "Did Flint have any violent episodes prior to his escape?"

"None. But Dr. Moody and I had our disagreements regarding Flint's long-term treatment. His prognosis was based on somewhat questionable results, in my opinion."

"Meaning what?" Reeve asks. "His psychological evaluations were inconclusive?"

Dr. Blume cocks an eyebrow at her. "Somewhat. Dr. Moody administered all the standard tests, but Flint tested in the midrange."

Reeve rests her fingertips on the plastic brain. "Didn't I read about a new type of evaluation, a new technique that can diagnose psychopathic subcategories?"

Dr. Blume smiles at her. "You have done quite a lot of reading on this subject, haven't you?"

"Excuse me," Bender says, "but could you two fill me in on what you're talking about?"

"Certainly," Dr. Blume responds. "There are new tests which measure the brain's response to various stimuli, such as olfactory stimulations."

"Odors?" Bender adjusts his eyeglasses.

"Yes. The smell of fear, for instance."

"Is there such a thing? I thought that was a myth," he says.

"It's a physiological fact." Dr. Blume again steeples her fingers. "You see, there are three types of human sweat. The one associated with fear is distinct. When afraid, human skin actually sheds cells along with fluid, unlike what is produced during exercise or sexual activity. And fear produces a smell to which psychopaths respond. Measurably."

"Respond in what way?" Reeve asks. "I mean, in real life."

"Brain imaging shows that their pleasure centers are stimulated by fear."

Reeve shudders at the thought that her own scent must be stored somewhere deep within Flint's brain.

Bender clears his throat. "I'm guessing this is somewhat controversial."

"New ideas are always controversial. But classification hardly matters at this juncture, does it?"

"Right," Bender says. "We're just trying to figure out where to find him."

"And as I told your colleagues, that's anyone's guess. Because without his medications, Flint's behavior will likely become more erratic, more unpredictable, more impulsive."

The talk turns to risk assessment, and Reeve half listens while lifting the plastic model with both hands and returning it to its place on the shelf. Before setting it down, she peers into the eye sockets and whispers, "Where are you, you monster?"

TWENTY

Daryl Wayne Flint grabs his jacket and heads outdoors to survey the grounds. The air is brisk, and he can smell winter coming. He hikes down to the shore, scarcely glancing in the direction of the graves, and scans Shadow Bark Lake. The dark water stretches out like smoked glass. He studies the sky and listens to the birds. Finding no clue of another living soul, he trudges back toward the cabin to complete his inventory.

There's a charcoal grill with two bags of charcoal, and a gas grill with three spare propane tanks. There's a small cistern that efficiently collects rainwater, plus fresh water from a creek that flows through the property. A canoe and fishing tackle, all neat and ready.

Perhaps best of all is that Wertz has constructed a narrow garage since Flint was here last. It's tucked into the pines, well camouflaged. Inside are two vehicles: a snowmobile, and a Ford Bronco with excellent tires, registered to Walter Wertz. Nice.

Flint wishes he had a van, but this big Ford is just what he'll need when he heads down to Wertz's house in Olympia. Just in case he ever needs it, he'll keep Dr. Moody's SUV packed up and ready to go. He parks it in a well-hidden spot between the trees and sets to work. When it is thoroughly concealed beneath a canopy of pine boughs, he steps back to assess his handiwork, saying, "Good, good, good."

Next, he considers the woodpile. He needs to split firewood, a task he has always hated, but he grabs an ax.

A few minutes later, he's raising the ax high and bringing it down hard. The wood splits with a loud *crack!*

He tosses the freshly split wood onto the pile and sets up another log, his muscles warming in the brisk mountain air. He repeats this process over and over, the sound of splitting wood ringing through the forest. This is the routine Wertz had dictated early on. Get everything ready first, decide on a target later. And for now, Flint is sticking to what works. Once the firewood is stacked high and the cabin is in good shape, he'll put on his disguise and head into Olympia, where his new life as Walter Wertz awaits.

Wertz had never visited him in lockup. Not once. Flint knew it would be out of the question. Then, one afternoon about five months ago, he received a postcard with a picture of a fish. The message read: *How you Be?*

Flint knew immediately who it was from and what it meant.

So, the next time his mother appeared in the visiting room, Flint lowered his voice and told her, "I need you to call Walter. Tell him we're on for Plan B."

Funny how things turn out.

He grasps the next log, positions it, raises the ax high, and brings it down with a satisfying *crack!*

TWENTY-ONE

Olshaker Psychiatric Hospital

A loud noise grabs Reeve's attention and she peers out the blinds. A group of men are playing basketball. The ball sails through the air and again smacks the backboard with a loud *thwack!*

Dr. Blume is saying, "So, Mr. Bender, might I suppose that you and Miss LeClaire are here at least partly because you're interested in the reward?"

"Reward?" Reeve shoots Bender a puzzled look.

He shakes his head. "I forgot to mention it. Fifty thousand dollars."

"I'm sure they'll be more than happy to write you that check if your contribution leads to Flint's apprehension. God knows, they seem to have no idea where he is."

"I'm not here for any reward," Reeve grumbles.

"We're ineligible, in any case," Bender says. "Or at least I am, I imagine, given my connection with the bureau. But a reward can bring some good leads."

"Or plenty of bad ones," Dr. Blume exhales, rubbing her temples. "I was about to say, you have no idea. But with your experience, I'm afraid you do."

Conversation has just turned to Dr. Moody's funeral when noise again erupts outside. Reeve cranes her neck to watch the hooting men on the basketball court.

"Did Flint play basketball?" she wonders aloud.

The other two look at her blankly.

"Basketball?" Dr. Blume says after a beat. "I would imagine so. Why?"

"Well, the thing is—" Reeve glances out the window "—I'm sure you're busy, Dr. Blume, but would you mind if we just look around?"

A tight smile. "I'm afraid you can't just wander through the forensic wards. However . . ." Dr. Blume taps her chin, then raises an index finger, signaling an idea. "We have a wonderful public relations person," she says, picking up her phone. "Why don't I have Vincent show you the facility?"

Five minutes later they're in the airy office of a slight man in a blue shirt and tie who hands each of them a colored brochure printed in calming hues. Reeve studies the pretty pictures, the inspirational quotes. "Don't you have anything about the forensic wards?"

The corners of Vincent's mouth tighten. "That literature is being redesigned. People are usually more interested in the gardens, the food, visiting hours, that kind of thing."

"But we're here about one particular patient: Daryl Wayne Flint."

Vincent leans across the desk and drops his voice. "We're not supposed to talk about that."

"You don't know who we are, do you?" Reeve says, tensing at the prospect of having to explain her history.

He gives her a puzzled look, but before he can reply, Milo Bender says smoothly, "Allow me to explain. My colleague and I are consulting with the FBI on this case."

Reeve hides a smile while Bender mentions several agents by name and drops a few choice phrases.

Vincent goes wide-eyed. "Oh, of course. They came in and questioned everybody, just like in the movies. I talked to them."

"Right, so we're following up on a few matters today, and Dr. Blume said you'd be the best person to show us around."

Vincent's face brightens. "Absolutely no problem." He stands, clasping his thin hands together. "What would you like to see first?"

While Bender strolls ahead with Vincent, Reeve trails behind and watches how Bender walks in stride, echoing body language. Intentionally putting Vincent at ease, no doubt.

A red sign above a security door announces: *Forensic Unit, Medium Security.*

Vincent pulls out a plastic key card, opens the door, and sticks his head inside. A man dressed in scrubs who seems to be guarding the door questions Vincent a moment. He looks them up and down, then stands aside and swings the door wide, gesturing to the left.

They file in and proceed down an austere corridor while Vincent explains, "It's rec time for another few minutes, so all the rooms are empty. Don't worry, it's completely safe." He stops and opens a door, saying, "This was Daryl Wayne Flint's room. It's been cleaned out, of course."

Reeve stops in the doorway of the bright, white room. The cot has been stripped bare. A metal toilet and a metal sink jut from the wall. It's a relatively humane confinement, she notes bitterly, but her feet stay glued to the floor, refusing to step one inch into her captor's cage. The lights are hot. She can almost sense his presence, almost see the imprint of his back on the mattress.

Milo Bender is standing beside her, watching her closely when he says, "Vincent, could we please see the visiting area next?"

The visitors' room has all the charm of a cardboard box, with a color scheme ranging from brown to beige. Two rows of brown tables with brown benches, all affixed to the floor. Beige walls, beige flooring.

Vincent introduces them to a tall man with an etched face who wears his long, black hair pulled back in a ponytail. He looks classically Native American to Reeve, but his name is Snyderman.

"The regular patients, you know, they can walk around the grounds," Snyderman says, gesturing with long fingers. "They have a nicer place with couches and a TV and stuff. But this is what we've got for forensic lockup."

"It's better than I expected," Milo Bender says. "No cubicles with barriers."

"Oh, we have those, too, but that's maximum security."

Vincent pipes up, "This is where Mr. Flint met his visitors. Snyderman talked with the FBI because he was most often the guard on duty."

"Yeah, but I guess I don't know much," Snyderman says. "All the guys we get in here are on the weird side, so it's not like he stood out, you know? Besides, his mother was his only visitor. There was nothing suspicious or anything."

"Do the prisoners and their visitors sometimes share a table with others?"

"Nah, that wouldn't be allowed. But sometimes they greet one another, you know, call back and forth. That's okay."

"And did Flint interact with others? Friends, perhaps?"

"Only Sven. He and Flint were buddies, I guess. I'm sure he's been questioned already."

Reeve hangs back, listening while Bender asks questions in his gentle, persistent manner.

"Yeah, Sven's girlfriend is kinda flirty. But there was nothing suspicious, like I said."

"What about Flint's mother?"

Synderman rolls his eyes. "You ask me, she's a sentimental old bat."

"Really? In what way?"

"Well, she was always talking about her dead husband."

"Flint's dad?"

"Yeah."

"That's odd. What did she say about him?"

"I don't know. Um, like reminiscing about their wedding day, stuff like that."

"Can you be more specific? Did you overhear the particulars of their conversations?"

"Well, she would say, like, we had such a nice wedding, in such a nice church, and la-de-da. And she'd say, you remember our wedding anniversary, don't you? And she'd make him recite it back to her."

"The date?"

"Yeah."

"Do you remember what it was?"

He shakes his head, saying, "Nah, I can't remember particulars like that. I told those FBI guys already. Sorry."

When Synderman can remember nothing more, Vincent checks his watch and leads them down a wide corridor to the cafeteria.

Reeve touches Bender's elbow and asks softly, "Flint's mother was married twice, wasn't she?"

"That's right. She's been married to a Tacoma pharmacist named Pratt for years."

"When was her first marriage?"

Bender shakes his head. "The date's in the file, I believe."

She closes her eyes, trying to recall anything that Flint might have said about his parents, but comes up empty.

A few moments later, the greasy, layered smells of the hospital cafeteria spark an unbidden memory. She blinks rapidly, trying to quell a painful recollection of waiting with her father in the hospital cafeteria while her mother endured those final rounds of chemo.

Bender glances at her and whispers, "Are you okay?"

She nods and follows Vincent, who is striding ahead, waving toward the refrigerated salads and brightly lit steam trays. "The kitchen staff takes pride in preparing healthy, nutritious meals," he is saying, seeming most comfortable with this part of his tour.

Bender asks about how the forensic unit is treated differently from the rest of the population, and while Vincent explains, Reeve murmurs, "Excuse me," and crosses the room to the gleaming wall of windows. She stands with hands clasped, studying the basketball court, which is now vacant. It seems foreboding, black and wet beneath a low ceiling of clouds.

Rejoining Bender and Vincent, she asks, "Did Flint play basketball?"

"Uh, he could have. All our patients are given daily rec time."

"May I go out and take a look?"

"Now?" He wheels toward the windows and frowns. "In the rain?"

"That's the idea."

Vincent shifts from foot to foot. "Well, I don't have a key." He glances out the windows with a grimace. "Let me find the orderly."

The orderly, a heavy man who introduces himself as Gary, gently cups Reeve's elbow and asks, "You're sure, miss?"

"Yes, show me exactly what he did."

"Okay." He lifts the hood of his weatherproof jacket up over his shaggy hair and says, "Follow me."

The two descend the steps and proceed toward the basketball court. There's no wind, but drizzle has turned to a pattering rain. Their boots splash out to center court, where Gary stops.

"Right here. He'd stand right here and spin in circles."

She edges the man aside and starts to turn, but the man stops her, saying, "No, miss, the other way. Counterclockwise. Three times. That was his thing. And he would put his arms straight out," he says, demonstrating, "like this."

She stands in the same way, arms extended, and looks across the court, through the chain-link fence toward the parking lot. She turns slowly to the left. The view wheels past: the bright windows of the cafeteria; a stretch of blank wall; and then the ironclad windows of a corner office, which she recognizes as Dr. Blume's. Next, her eyes follow the tall chain-link fence, beyond which the greenery thickens to forest.

"Miss? You need to see the rest now?" Gary shifts uncomfortably. "Or is this enough?"

"The rest? What else did he do?"

She listens intently while Gary explains, then says she'd like to try it, if he has a few minutes.

He shoots a glance at the dry steps beneath the overhang.

"Why don't you wait beside the building, out of the rain?" she suggests.

"Well, sure, I guess so."

The moment he turns to go, she hurries to the edge of the asphalt and begins circumnavigating the basketball court. As the scene glides past, she notes the people inside, framed by the windows and lit up with bright fluorescent lights.

Next, she walks across the grass toward the fence line. Rain drips in her face and dampens her jeans, and she's grateful for Milo Bender's oversized weatherproof jacket. As she studies the parking lot, a heavy man in a parka appears. She hears the chirp of the keyless entry and watches as he ambles toward a black sedan, opens the door, and climbs inside. The car exits the parking lot, and when it disappears through the trees, she heads back to join Gary on the steps.

"The rain doesn't bother you, does it?" he says. "You're just like him."

"Excuse me?"

"I mean, it didn't matter what the weather was, he'd still come out here and do his thing. And everyone just kinda left him alone. Some kinds of crazy you just don't mess with."

"What do you mean?"

"Let's just say he wasn't the kind of guy you'd introduce your sister to." He laughs. "Maybe an ex-girlfriend."

"Can you think of anything else?"

He holds open the door for her. "Oh, he had some quirks. He'd tap his foot three times, or repeat something three times. He called all the orderlies guards, and he called Dr. Blume 'Wanda the Warden.' Stuff like that."

They shed their dripping jackets and head down the corridor, back toward the visitors' lounge.

"Hey, can I ask you something, miss?" he says, giving her a sideways look.

"Sure."

"You here for the reward? Is that right?"

"No, I have, uh, personal reasons."

"Yeah? Well, if I was you, I'd go for that reward. Fifty grand, that'd pay some bills. I'd sure go after it if I could, but employees, you know, we're not eligible. I guess they figure we'd be helping guys escape just so we could rat 'em out and collect some cash, right?"

"I guess." She stops and gives him a look. "Does that happen a lot?"

"What? Escapes? Nah, never. I've been here sixteen years and this is the first one I've ever heard of. People don't escape a place like this. Most of the patients are voluntary. Nonviolent. And this is a pretty good treatment facility, really. Even the forensic wards."

Reeve and Bender exit the building the same way they came in. They're hastening through the rain when she says, "Give me one second," and stops beside a red BMW. A sign on the curb states *Chief of Psychiatry*.

She stands in the rain, surveying the road and the parking lot. She peers through the chain-link fence toward the basketball court, then dashes across the parking lot and climbs in beside Bender.

He looks at her quizzically. "I see wheels turning. Come on."

"I keep thinking about motive and opportunity." She gives him a sideways glance. "That's what you guys always look for, right?"

"Sure, partly. Go on."

"It just seems obvious that he was playing them."

"How so?"

"That routine of his out in the recreation yard? He could watch whoever was coming and going. I bet he saw the barber arrive. He knew which car was his and where he parked."

"The investigators thought so, too. That's in the file."

"Oh." A beat of disappointment. "Well, so much for my brilliant powers of deduction."

"Shows you're on the right track. What else?"

She crosses her arms. "Nothing."

"What? I'll bet you're thinking we ought to talk to Flint's mother."

"God, no. That woman gives me the creeps."

He smiles and starts the car. "Well, that's a relief."

While the hospital recedes behind them, Reeve scowls out the window as if studying a Rorschach. Flint drove this same road, dressed in the barber's clothes, driving the dead man's Honda. . . . But there's not a glimmer of intuition in her head. Why did she even bother to come up here?

"What I'm wondering," Bender says, "is what triggered all this? Flint was nonviolent and appropriately managed, and then he went haywire."

"Maybe we should put together a timeline."

"Good idea. What has changed?"

Reeve fishes a pen and notepad from her purse. "The only real change since he's been at Olshaker was last winter. Dr. Lerner had to come up here for a hearing and the judge ruled that Flint could be moved from maximum to medium security."

"And shortly after that, Dr. Blume became the new chief of psychiatry."

"But she said she never even spoke to him." She huffs out a sigh. "I keep coming back to his mother and Dr. Moody. I wonder if they had some sort of connection."

"That's possible. Another question: What did Flint do with the barber's car?"

"It hasn't been found?"

"Nope. Best guess, he stashed it someplace near Moody's house, but it hasn't turned up yet. One theory is that he stashed the car with a friend, perhaps a former inmate, maybe an orderly. But the bureau has interviewed the staff, plus anyone significant in the patient population. Nothing popped."

"Frustrating." The windshield wipers beat back and forth as she stares out at an area of mixed residential and industrial use. A vacant lot, an auto body shop, houses in need of paint. The nondescript outskirts of small-town America.

The tip of her tongue reaches for her upper lip while she pictures Flint speeding away in the Honda. "Flint got away before anyone even knew he was missing. And then he headed to Dr. Moody's. So maybe we should do the same."

"What?" Bender turns to look at her. "You want to go to Dr. Moody's? Now? Are you serious?"

"Why not? That's what Flint did. How long does it take to get there?"

"I hate to be a spoilsport, but it's getting late and my old bones are tired. How about tomorrow?"

She slumps in her seat. "Okay, but promise you'll pick me up at my hotel first thing in the morning."

"Hotel? No way. You're staying with us."

"Really? Oh, I don't want to impose."

"We insist. Yvonne's looking forward to seeing you."

She lets out a yelp. "Wait! Stop! Stop the car," she says, slapping the dashboard.

He slams on the brakes.

"Go back, go back!" she says, twisting in her seat to stare out the back windshield.

"Why?"

"Just turn around!"

"What is it?" Bender says, cranking the wheel and doing a quick U-turn.

"Look there, that sign," she says, pointing.

"What sign?"

"That street sign. Church Street. The guard said Flint's mother talked about her wedding in a church. He called her a sentimental old bat. Does that sound like her?"

"No, but what—"

"Just turn here, okay?"

Bender turns onto the street. "What are we looking for?"

"I'm not sure," she says, scanning from side to side. "But why would Flint's mother get all sentimental about her wedding to Flint's dad? I mean, she's remarried, so what's up with that?"

Bender drives along slowly while he studies one side and she studies the other. "I don't see anything. Besides, Mrs. Pratt has already been investigated, and I'm sure the bureau has—"

"Look there!" She jabs a finger toward a building and Bender hits the brakes.

"Church Street Storage?"

"Yes, and see the street signs? We're at the corner of Church and April. Couldn't that be code for a wedding date?" She leans far forward, trying to see inside the facility. "I'll bet they've got units big enough for a car."

He turns into the driveway, saying, "Well now, let's take a look."

TWENTY-TWO

Church Street Storage

For the first time since his retirement, Milo Bender could really use a badge.

The scruffy man in charge of the storage facility refuses to show his records to a civilian. He's within his rights, of course, so Bender has no choice but to excuse himself and call Stuart Cox, who practically bellows, "You're *what*? Investigating a lead with that LeClaire girl? Are you kidding me?"

"Calm down and listen. No guarantees, but I think we've got something."

He keeps talking until Cox sees the larger picture.

"All right, Bender, I'll send an agent. Wait right there while we get a warrant."

When Bender climbs back into his vehicle, Reeve is biting a knuckle. "This makes sense, doesn't it? I'm not crazy, right?"

"It makes sense to me. And I'll tell you what, it must make sense to the bureau, too, or they wouldn't be scrambling to get a warrant."

"But what if there's nothing here?"

"Welcome to Investigation 101: Waiting to be wrong." He drums his fingers on the dashboard, then says, "Excuse me, but I need to call Yvonne," and he reaches across to get his cell phone out of the glove box.

Her eyes go wide. "That's your cell phone? Can you even text on that thing?"

Bender gives her a look. "You sound just like my son."

"Then your son is right, because you clearly need a new phone."

"I don't need to text, and I don't need another fancy gadget."

"You can't text? Seriously?"

"Sure, I *can,* but they make the keypad so damn small, and with these fat fingers?" He wiggles his extra-large digits for emphasis. "Besides, I don't need to text. I'm retired."

He phones his wife to tell her they'll be late for dinner. And he cringes when he has to admit that he forgot to bring his evening dose of pills with him. Yvonne scolds him, like she always does, before promising to have a nice dinner ready for them when they arrive.

While they wait, Reeve pulls out her smart phone, which seems to keep her busy while Bender thinks about the things he has no intention of sharing, things that he can't get out of his head.

While she was out on the basketball court, tromping around in the rain, Bender had made a point of interviewing another patient, a rat-faced guy named Sven, who had apparently been Flint's closest buddy behind bars. Sven was a fellow sex offender, and Sven and Flint had spent time together in art therapy.

Most of Flint's drawings had been seized as evidence, but Sven showed Bender two drawings that Flint had given him. Bender recognized the patterns in those drawings and immediately resolved that Reeve would not see them. She doesn't need to know about Flint's artwork. It's bad enough that she's wearing so much of it on her skin.

He pulls at an ear, worrying that Flint's artwork reveals a man who is perfecting his designs, a man planning for his next victim.

He glances at Reeve and feels a familiar tug of regret. If he'd found a way to nab Flint, he could have saved her from years of abuse. He was the case agent, the lead investigator, and his failures still pain him far more than any medical condition.

Flint's name had popped up on a list of potential suspects because of a complaint that was filed against him when he was a student at the University of Washington. Bender had questioned Flint briefly and found nothing. The guy didn't smell right, but Bender had to follow procedures. So he'd gone through the guy's trash. He'd parked outside Flint's house and watched his comings and goings. But Bender had found nothing suspicious, and he'd never been able to rally enough to persuade any judge to issue a warrant. All the while, young Reggie LeClaire had been chained in that monster's basement.

Yvonne tells him he shouldn't blame himself, but he can't help it.

The other thing he's not going to discuss with Reeve is that Flint's going to be hard to catch. It's the methodical criminals who will, given enough time, reveal themselves. But the longer Flint is off his meds, the more peculiar his behavior might become. Their best chance to catch him is long gone, and who knows what his plan will be tomorrow?

It seems a long wait before Bender spots a black SUV coming around the corner. "I'll bet this is our man," he tells Reeve.

She stops checking e-mail and puts away her phone as the SUV pulls up. Everyone gets out of their vehicles. They ignore the rain and stand bareheaded as they exchange introductions.

The agent looks fit and serious, as Bender expected, with an unsmiling mouth, a pointy nose, and a prominent shining slope of forehead.

"Pete Blankenship," the agent says, extending a hand.

Bender shakes his hand, recalling that this is the very same agent who botched Reeve's first phone interview.

Upon introduction, Blankenship frowns at Reeve. "What are you doing here? I thought you were a student at Berkeley."

"You haven't caught Flint yet, have you? I thought you might need some help."

There's a brief, clipped exchange between the two, but Bender smooths it over and shepherds them into the manager's office. It's a small room with a stale odor. A TV mounted on the wall blares a reality show.

Agent Blankenship takes charge, showing the manager his badge and the warrant. The manager, a scruffy man with heavy jowls, makes a show of rolling his eyes before complying. While he's pulling up the records on an old desktop computer, Reeve steps over and switches off the TV.

The man looks up sharply, and she raises her eyebrows, as if daring him to say anything.

He looks back at the computer and says to Blankenship, "Yeah, so what time frame are you looking for?"

Blankenship peers over the manager's shoulder at the screen. "The past couple years."

Reeve compresses her lips to a thin line, and Bender knows what she's thinking, but figures it's best to let the agent proceed at his own pace.

While Blankenship and the manager scroll through names, Reeve stands off to one side, massaging her left hand and studying a chart on the wall. Bender steps up beside her, and she points toward the row of twelve-by-fifteen foot units. "Those are the biggest ones," she says. "Building three."

It takes a few minutes for Blankenship to check the list for matches to any of Flint's known associates. No surprise, he comes up empty.

"How about we target the units large enough for a car?" Bender says. "And may I suggest focusing on those rented within, say, the past year?"

The scruffy manager scrolls and grumbles and comes up with four units. One is promptly ruled out because it's vacant. "These other three are locked," he states, as if that finishes the conversation.

Blankenship scowls. "We've got a warrant. Have you got a bolt cutter?"

"Man, I hate to do that."

"I've got one," Bender volunteers.

Shooting him a sour look, the manager says, "Hold on, I'll do it. Shit."

They find the white Honda inside the second unit they check. Blankenship leans in, inspects the license plate, then wheels around, barking, "No one goes inside!" as if a crowd were about to stampede the door.

Bender and Reeve exchange a look while Blankenship gets on his phone to summon an evidence response team.

Back inside the stale-smelling office, the manager's horse-faced wife has joined him, and the couple seems energized. Bender has seen this before. People drag their heels until something is found. Then they perk up, knowing they're going to have something juicy to tell their friends.

"Okay now, let's just find out who rented that unit," the manager says. "Let me check for you. . . . Oh, yeah, here it is. That one's on the annual plan. Pre-paid. Cash. Five months ago."

"What's the name?" Blankenship says, turning the computer screen so he can see better.

"Ted Springs, it says."

Reeve says something under her breath while Agent Blankenship mutters a curse.

"Do you remember anything about this man?" Blankenship asks.

The manager scratches his chin. "No, but maybe if I saw a picture."

"Are you sure it wasn't a woman?" Blankenship pulls out a photo of Flint's mother and shows it to the manager. "Do you recognize this woman?"

The jowly manager and his wife peer at the picture, shaking their heads.

"What if she'd been dressed up as a man? Try to picture that. Did the man who rented the unit look anything like her?"

"You kidding? I can damn sure tell the difference between a man and a woman."

"Look again. Maybe in disguise, with different hair?"

The manager shakes his head in disgust. "Nah, if someone came in here trying to pull something like that, I'd remember for sure."

Bender notices that the man's wife has slipped outside, where she cups a cell phone to her ear, its glow on her cheek. He sees the woman talking excitedly and gives Blankenship a nudge, but the case agent remains preoccupied with questions about the man who rented the storage unit.

The significance of the woman's phone call doesn't fully register until later, when a big van rolls up and a news team spills out. Bender grabs Reeve's elbow to pull her aside, but not before they're both caught in the camera's glare.

TWENTY-THREE

Bear's Den Sports Bar

Sorry, buddy. No smoking inside," the bartender says.

Flint's first impulse is to argue, but he stops himself, wary of causing a scene. Instead, he drops the match into his empty glass and orders another beer, discreetly scratching beneath his wig.

No one pays him any notice. He blends in with the other flannel-clad men, who are mostly focused on beer and burgers and the televisions flickering over-head. None of the women in the bar warrant his attention, so he takes a cold French fry and drags it through a glob of catsup on his plate, creating a swirl. Nice. He doodles another swirl, then another, embellishing the design into something arty, which he admires while sucking the foam off his fresh glass of beer.

He's feeling much better now that he has locked up the cabin and come partway out of the mountains. It's been seven years since he last enjoyed the ordinary pleasures of civilization, and this seedy sports bar is just the ticket. He feels much more relaxed.

He glances around. The bar is decorated with silly skeletons. "Halloween, Hallo-week, Hallo-Wertz." Flint smirks into his beer.

He can almost hear Wertz reminding him to get a costume. "Because Halloween is the one day of the year, more than any other time, Daryl, that provides cover and opportunity. The hunter's necessities."

He touches the horn-rimmed glasses, thinking that he's already in cos-tume, thank you very much. Once he gets set up in Wertz's house in Olympia, Plan B can become fully operational. Daryl Wayne Flint will cease to exist—as long as he keeps his fingerprints to himself—and he can slip into the man's big shoes.

He sips his beer, wondering if, after all this time, Wertz will have left the same systems in place. He smirks. It doesn't really matter because now that he's on his own, he'll be the one in charge. He can pick and choose his targets. Sure, he'll look closely at the ones Wertz has mapped out, but now he can improvise. And who says he has to wait until Halloween? If he wants, he could be cruising the streets as early as tomorrow.

"Will that do it for you, buddy?"

Flint nods at the bartender and asks for his check. He sets aside the last of his beer and glances at the television screens. One shows robust men in suits talking on ESPN. Another shows a frenetic music video, but without the sound. A third screen features the local news.

And there, suddenly, is his little cricket. His eyes widen in astonishment.

The old footage shows her just as he remembers, small and feisty as she swats at the camera. He gawks at the screen, remembering how pretty she looked for him during his trial. He itches to ask the bartender to turn up the volume, but doesn't dare draw attention to himself.

Now the image is slashed with red type declaring *Breaking News,* and he recognizes a picture of Church Street Storage.

They've found it already.

He spits a curse, trying to read the newscaster's lips, but the face abruptly disappears, replaced by a video that fills the screen. The camera zooms out from a man wearing an FBI vest and pans and . . .

What? Can he trust his eyes? Off to the side, scowling at the camera before disappearing from the frame, that was *her.* She's not in San Francisco, she's here!

TWENTY-FOUR

Seattle, Washington

Hot water beats down on her head and steamy air fills her lungs. She closes her eyes and lingers in the shower, soothed by this reprieve. But a stream of water is a slim tether to comfort, and mere soap and water cannot clear her head of the day's jumble, or wash off the sensation of having spent hours rolling in Flint's muck.

She steps from the shower and as she towels off, glimpses her back in the mirror.

She tends to shy away from mirrors, particularly those that offer a view of her back, but now pauses. The scars have faded some. The ones from the whip still crisscross her spine, long strips resembling feathers. She lifts her hair and squints at the small design at the nape of her neck, the intricate one Flint created with thin, sharp blades.

Dropping her hair, she wants only to crawl into bed and sink into forgetfulness. Instead, she dresses in clean clothes and blow-dries her hair. She's not hungry, but Milo Bender's wife has a hot meal waiting, and common courtesy requires an appearance at the dinner table.

She walks down the hall toward the kitchen, dreading an onslaught of questions. The day's events have left her feeling bruised, but she promises herself that, if she can just make it through the next hour with some semblance of good manners, she will get to bed early and then go for a nice, long run in the morning. At least she can hang onto some sliver of her routine in the midst of all this chaos.

Just outside the kitchen, she overhears Milo Bender telling his wife about their discoveries at the mental hospital and the storage unit. It now occurs to her that the former agent has the gift of seeming open while withholding information. She has no idea, for instance, what he was doing inside the hospital wards while she was outside, tromping around the basketball court in the rain.

"I hope I didn't keep dinner waiting," she says, as a means of announcing herself, and they both smile as she enters the kitchen.

"Just in time. Come and sit down," says Yvonne Bender, a husky, no-nonsense woman whose short stature makes her seem the reverse image of her long-limbed husband. "I'll bet you're exhausted after everything you've gone through today."

Reeve takes a seat, murmuring something polite while wondering how she might satisfy any questions about this difficult and complicated day. But before Yvonne can ask a single question, her husband says, "Let's set all of today's business aside and simply enjoy this wonderful meal."

Reeve smiles at him and spoons gratefully into a cup of minestrone.

She has just rediscovered her appetite when a side door opens, and a taller, younger version of Milo Bender enters. Without a glance their way, he sets a canvas bag on the floor and hangs his denim jacket on a peg, saying, "Well, it took longer than I thought, but—" then he turns and sees Reeve. "Oh, sorry, I didn't know you had company."

Yvonne is already at his elbow. "Come in, JD. Let me get you a plate."

"No, Mom, don't let me interrupt."

"I'd like to introduce you to Reeve," Yvonne says. "Reeve, this is our son, JD."

He cocks an eyebrow at her. "Have we met before?"

"I don't think so," she says, feeling heat rise up her neck.

They had not been introduced, but she remembers him clearly from the day he came to the trial to watch his father testify. JD had sat with the other spectators just behind the railing, but he'd been hard to miss. And Reeve's sister, who was about his age, had gushed about his Nordic good looks for days afterward.

"I'd shake your hand, but . . ." He holds up smudged palms.

"What on earth have you been doing?" his father asks.

"Didn't Mom tell you? I fixed that bathroom floor for you. New tile, new baseboard, the works."

"You didn't have to do that."

JD grins. "Yeah, well, now you owe me big time." He glances at the canvas bag, adding, "But I had to borrow your power drill. Mine crapped out."

Yvonne takes control, directing her son to set the tools inside the garage and insisting that he join them for dinner. "Go take a shower. I'll find some clean clothes of your dad's that will fit, and I'll keep a plate warm for you."

As soon as he's out of the room, Yvonne settles into her seat and puts a hand on Reeve's shoulder. "You'd think he had nothing else to do but help out. The truth is, our son just won't sit still."

"He keeps hijacking my repair projects. I think he's afraid I'll drop dead by lifting a hammer." Bender taps his chest. "But my old heart's better than ever. More likely I'll get struck by lightning."

"Or fall off a ladder." Yvonne waves a fork at him. "You better let JD do that from now on. No more roof repairs."

Reeve sits quietly, observing their easy exchange, glad to be outside the center of attention.

A few minutes later, JD enters with damp hair, wearing a clean University of Washington T-shirt. While Yvonne serves him shrimp and pasta with grilled asparagus, Reeve learns that JD lives aboard a sailboat, which strikes her as mildly eccentric.

"One day he'll sail us down the coast, won't you, JD?"

"I'm counting on it, Dad. I could use a crew."

"We'll go down to Mexico," his father continues. "Maybe even to Panama, through the canal, and then cruise the Caribbean."

Yvonne rolls her eyes. "Color me seasick."

"So, Reeve, are my folks taking in boarders now without telling me?" JD asks. "Because if they're renting out my old room, I'll need to throw out the last of my junk." He looks chagrined. "Not much room for storage on a boat."

"Reeve and Milo are investigating a case together," Yvonne says, widening her eyes.

"Don't tell me it's Daryl Wayne Flint?" JD looks from Reeve to his father and back, the realization dawning on his face. "Wait, aren't you . . .?"

Stiffening, she explains that she has changed her name.

Milo Bender briefly recounts what they've been doing over the past several hours. Then Yvonne places a warm hand on Reeve's forearm, asking, "How are you holding up, dear, with all this ugly business? Are you having trouble sleeping? I sure would be."

Everyone is looking at her. Her face flushes. She hates being the object of pity.

As she's trying to come up with a response, JD leans over and stage-whispers, "Mom's a nurse who believes that a good night's sleep is the cure for all ills."

"Sleeping is very important, it certainly is," his mother huffs. "And so is good nutrition."

"Which reminds me, could you please pass the pasta?"

As JD remarks on each ingredient, Reeve discerns that he's intentionally drawing attention away from her. They share a smile. And she watches his hands while he eats. Strong, scrubbed hands with nice, clean nails.

"So, you're going to UC Berkeley," JD says, "What's your major?"

"I haven't decided yet."

"Undeclared? Hey, that was my major, too." He grins. "But I eventually got a doctorate in marine biology. Which I highly recommend, by the way, if you're hoping for years of lucrative employment working in a gym and fixing up old boats."

His mother says, "But I thought the University of—"

"Nope, they hired someone else."

Reeve watches his parents exchange a look.

"What about that grant?" his mother asks.

"Which one? I've applied for so many." JD laughs and his blue eyes return to Reeve's. "So, what do you do for fun?"

"Fun?"

"You know, that thing you do when you're not going to class or helping my dad chase down criminals. Hobbies? Pets? Sports? Games of chance?"

Reeve has learned that mentioning a pet tarantula—even one going through the fascinating and natural process of molting—is a guaranteed conversation stopper. She gives a shrug. "Just the usual college student stuff. Movies, concerts. My Japanese class is interesting, and a few of us are learning to make sushi. But the best thing, really, is my cycling group. We take rides through gorgeous places like Napa, Monterey, Yosemite. . . . And I love to run."

"JD was a track star," his mother interjects.

"Hardly. I have a few second-place trophies."

"You kept letting Jimmy win."

"Jimmy was fast." JD tips his head toward Reeve, adding, "The truth is, I was never competitive enough. Or at least, that's what my coach kept telling me."

The conversation ambles along while Yvonne serves a delicious dessert of baked pears with caramel sauce. Everything seems normal on the surface, but Reeve observes that each time Yvonne starts asking about Flint, the father or the son somehow manage to change the subject. It seems to be an underlying family dynamic. Perhaps years of having an FBI agent in the house has created paths of communication that diffuse charged discussions, leaving secret information unshared.

Meanwhile, phones softly ping and chirp in the background, but no one moves to answer them. Milo Bender seems distracted, and Reeve wonders what messages wait for him at the end of the meal.

As she carries her plate to the sink, JD sidles up beside her. "I was wondering, would you like to come to my gym? I could get you a guest pass."

"No, thanks. Gyms have too many mirrors. I'd rather just run."

"Do you want some company? I've got mornings off. I could show you some nice trails."

She looks at him, surprised, and hears herself asking, "What time?"

TWENTY-FIVE

Olympia, Washington

It's nearly midnight by the time Daryl Wayne Flint drives down out of the mountains. He cruises through Olympia's quiet streets until, in the midst of an ordinary neighborhood, he turns toward the unremarkable home owned by Walter Wertz. The driveway is long and the trees are overgrown. The automatic garage-door opener works, and he parks the Ford Bronco inside. So easy. So familiar. But as he gathers up his supplies, he remembers the last time he was here at this house.

Wertz had been furious.

The fight had started because Flint had finally confessed that he was the one who'd kidnapped a schoolgirl named Reggie six months earlier. He'd done it all on his own. And he'd gotten away with it. The girl was secure in his basement, his own private project.

No harm, no foul, right?

But Wertz didn't see it that way. Maybe he hated the fact that Daryl had gone off and done something on his own initiative, because he balled his fists, yelling, "Why the hell would you want to keep one?"

They had carried their argument through the house, and now it replays in Flint's head as he unlocks the door, flips on the lights, and sets his bags on the kitchen table.

"We've got the perfect arrangement," Wertz had yelled, stomping through the kitchen. "Why would you want to risk screwing that up?"

"What's it to you?" Flint spat back. "It doesn't make an ounce of difference to our business. I can keep her and still do everything else here."

"Are you out of your goddamn mind? Don't you see how dangerous this is?"

"I shouldn't have even told you. You didn't even need to know."

Now Flint shakes his head, muttering, "Drama, drama, drama."

He looks around and finds the place much the same, except for some dust and a few spiderwebs. Wertz hasn't been gone all that long. The house still carries the faint odor of cigar smoke.

Somewhere, there should be a letter for him, but the countertops and table are bare. He heads into the den, where glassy eyes stare back from the heads mounted on the walls: an elk, a six-point buck, a wild boar, a bull moose, a wolf, and a grizzly bear. This room always gave him the creeps, but Wertz thought it was grand. He was always boasting about his family's hunting adventures.

"That's the difference between you and me," Flint had said, waving at the heads mounted on the wall. "You like your trophies dead. I want mine breathing."

Wertz had wheeled around, eyes wild. "This is no joke, Daryl. This is way out of bounds. Don't you see that?"

Flint had tried to reason with him. "Try to understand, man, I'm not like you. The photos, the hunts, they're not enough for me. I want to keep one for a while."

"How long?"

"I don't know. A while."

For Christ's sake, he'd taken precautions. The girl was locked up quiet and secure in his basement. She had nothing to do with any of the work they did together. What was his problem?

But Wertz wouldn't listen. He hated the fact that his junior partner had taken the lead, that he'd applied his wits and ingenuity to do something solo for once. . . . Plus, that he'd waited six months to tell him about it.

Wertz had yelled at him, nose-to-nose, "Never again, Daryl. This is the last time you step one foot inside my house. From now on, we meet at the bar or the cabin. Because I'm not having you lead the cops straight to my door!"

"You're overreacting. I told you, there's no evidence and no witnesses. It's as clean as anything we've ever done together."

"You really don't get it, do you? You're goddamn nuts to try this. And if any blowback comes at me, I'll kill you."

Flint scans the den, muttering, "But you're the one who's dead now, eh buddy?"

Or at least, that's his best guess.

Flint glances around, wondering what he'll find waiting for him. He approaches the side wall, which is lined with bookshelves, and locates the button on the underside of the bottom right shelf. One push, and the middle sections slide apart.

Flint enters the secret room, roughly six-by-twelve, with full shelves and cupboards. A laptop computer and a thick folder wait for him on a work surface. He carries the folder to a worn leather chair and eases down into the seat. Inside, he finds a handwritten note.

> *D: If you're reading this, welcome back. Don't know what's taking so long, but glad you made it out.*
>
> *Most everything is pretty much the same as before. I carried on with business for awhile, but it wasn't the same kinda fun. Anyway, that damn disease is doing its ugly. No hope for me, unless I stop smoking & drinking. Ha!*
>
> *So Plan B is all set and welcome to it. My daddy left it to me, and it's a helluva lot better passing it on to you than giving it to the goddamn government!!!*
>
> *Plan C is ready if need arises. Remember that place up by Anacortes? All set. Give yourself enough time for the boat to come around. Palms greased, cash ready.*
>
> *One change, I'm heading north for my own private version of Plan C. I'll feed myself to the wolves if I have to. Ha!*
> *WW*
>
> *P.S. I always told you that keeping one was a mistake, didn't I?*

Flint grunts, crumples the note, and gives it a toss.

Inside the folder, he finds all the expected paperwork, the sort of information that any homeowner accumulates—the water and electricity bills, the property taxes, the deed—as well as a list of instructions. A post office box, where mail is being held. Bank accounts, where the money flows in and all the bills are on autopay. Flint smiles. Wertz was always a supremely organized man. He has made it all so easy to slide into his life.

Flint shuffles the papers back into the folder, then fingers a large envelope marked "Plan C." He knows what's inside, but it would be bad luck to open it. Besides, Plan B is going to work out fine. Plan C won't be needed.

He sets the envelope aside and stands, taking stock. One shelf is lined with camera gear. Other shelves are lined with yearbooks. Some are fat, some thin, several have cracked spines. They are a testament to Wertz's many years of work as a photographer.

Flint raises a hand to pull one off the shelf, but then stops. Not yet. He has other things to attend to first.

A third shelf is lined with wigs, placed atop neat, round, Styrofoam heads. Flint tilts his head from side to side, assessing the shades of mousy brown and dull gunmetal. Wertz never had a sense of color.

Flint had teased his friend about the wigs, but Wertz chastised him, "Don't laugh, Daryl. Someday this could all be yours."

"Dull, dull, dull," Flint says aloud, fingering the lank hair. Tomorrow, he'll purchase some new wigs, add some color.

He returns to the kitchen, puts the groceries away, then begins refamiliarizing himself with the house. The pleasures of the cabin and the great outdoors had grown thin, and this house makes a nice change. With central heat, comfortable furniture, and plenty of room, it has everything he'll need for day-to-day life as quiet, responsible Walter Wertz. He won't return to the cabin until he has a girl.

After getting settled, he pours himself a shot of Jägermeister on ice and returns to the secret room, where he opens the laptop computer. It's been years since he's used one, but he gets it booted up and clearly remembers the password: PlanABC.

It takes a few minutes to figure out the icons and get online, but then it's a simple matter to type in a search. His name brings up an impressive number of articles. He mutters curses while scanning the news. Eventually, he finds what he's looking for: the news clip of the discovery at Church Street Storage.

He replays the video three times. Each time he glimpses Reggie, his mood lightens.

She has left her California address and is back in Washington. So close. But how can that be? There's got to be some special meaning in her reappearance.

He closes the laptop and gets to his feet, trying to clear his head. With a flash of inspiration, he snatches up one of Dr. Moody's files and spills its contents across the countertop.

Here are the photographs. Even with that ugly lighting, her skin looks sublime.

He fetches a magnifying eye loupe from a drawer and bends over the photos, studying each detail, fingertips hovering as though they might actually touch the perfect edges of the designs he created on her skin. It's electrifying to see them again.

His need for release has become urgent. He unzips and comes almost immediately.

But afterward, as he's cleaning up, he can almost hear Wertz's voice in his ear, chiding him: *Don't screw up, Daryl. Stick with the plan. Stick with the plan. Stick with the plan.*

Wertz is right, of course. He must carry on. That was the deal. Besides, all of the arrangements Wertz set in place are working perfectly, despite that unscheduled detour to Dr. Moody's house.

Flint smirks. Wertz would have objected to any deviation from his plan. But look at how well that all went, thanks to his clever mother and that hot blonde.

TWENTY-SIX

Seattle, Washington

He's dead, Cybil keeps reminding herself. But the idea seems so unreal that it dissolves each hour like sugar in a cup of hot tea. Perhaps tomorrow's funeral will help solidify the fact in her mind.

"May I help you find something?" asks the shopgirl at her elbow.

"Yes, I need a black dress."

Nothing in her closet will do. Not dull business black, not casual black, not shimmery black. His funeral calls for something altogether different, but she's been shopping intently and she's running out of time. The selections have been meager.

She'd been tempted by a nice little dress at Nordstrom's, but there was no way around the fact that it was really too short. Increasingly discouraged, she finally had to stop and take a break. And now, after a lunch of Caesar salad with a glass of chardonnay, she has stumbled upon this boutique.

It seems promising. The shopgirl guesses her size correctly and leads her deeper into the store, where she plucks a dress off the rack. She holds it up. "How about this one?"

"No, nothing with bows. Too fussy."

The shopgirl returns the dress to its spot and turns her attention elsewhere. After a moment of rifling through the rack, she lifts another. "Something like this?"

"No, no. Something classy."

"Yes, I see." The shopgirl purses her lips, and an instant later holds up another. "What do you think of this one?"

The woman tilts her head. "Worth a try, I guess."

A few minutes later, she's in the dressing room with four black dresses of different cuts and textures. The first one bunches at the waist. The second has a neckline befitting a nun. She tosses them aside.

Next, she slips doubtfully into a black sheath. A few months ago, this would have been much too tight, but she's not as voluptuous as she once was. It fits.

Exiting the fitting room, she comes out into a well-lit area and stands before the three-way mirrors, checking the back, the profile.

"Oh yes, this is very nice," coos the salesgirl. "Blondes look very elegant in black. And you have the perfect figure for it. Absolutely stunning."

She turns left and right, admiring the way the dress hugs her curves. Panty line would be a problem, but maybe if she wore a thong . . . And the back drops so low that, if she were to wear it for cocktails . . . Well, she'd definitely have to go braless.

But of course she'll have to wear a jacket tomorrow, anyway.

"Beautiful! This is the classic black dress for so many occasions," the salesgirl continues. "Not many people can wear something like this, but on *you*? Perfect. This little dress was made for you."

"Yes, it does fit well," she muses aloud, studying her reflection.

But still, the back . . . Isn't it too daring?

He's dead, she reminds herself.

She turns quickly and heads back to the dressing room, saying, "I'll take it."

TWENTY-SEVEN

When rookie Agent Nikki Keswick hears that Milo Bender is in the building, she jumps at the chance to meet him. She finds him at the center table in the Violent Crimes Center, hunched over files. He's thinner and grayer than in his photos, but there's no mistaking his ice-blue eyes and lined features.

She stops inside the door. "Excuse me, aren't you Agent Bender?"

He quickly gets to his feet, taller than she expected. "Well, I *was*," he says. "Past tense. Now I'm retired."

"I'm Nikki Keswick, still a rookie, so I guess we cover both ends of the spectrum," she says, shaking his hand. "I studied some of your work at the academy. Child forensic interviews are a special interest of mine."

"That's good to hear. Kids need all the help they can get."

"Your interviews with Reggie LeClaire were really inspiring. And now I'm helping with the Daryl Wayne Flint investigation, so—small world—I guess that means we're colleagues." She flashes a grin. "I heard you're consulting with us."

"So is Miss LeClaire. And she calls herself Reeve now, by the way."

"Reeve? Nice name."

"It helps her gain distance, I think."

"How's she doing?"

"Physically, she seems fine. But she's wound a little tight."

"Understandable."

"I can introduce you, if you'd like. She's in the ladies' room."

As if on cue, a slim young woman enters the room. She's much healthier than she was at sixteen, and her hair is now a gorgeous shade of red, but Keswick immediately recognizes those intense eyes, the heart-shaped face.

After introductions, Reeve says, "You're young to be an agent, aren't you?"

Keswick shrugs. "It's the Hawaiian genes. My mother says the women in our family look like teenagers until our hair turns gray. Anyway, it'll be good for undercover work." She smiles. "By the way, great work with that storage unit yesterday. Agent Blankenship told us all about it."

"So, have you figured out how Flint got from the storage unit to Dr. Moody's?"

Keswick raises her eyebrows at how quickly Reeve dispenses with chit-chat. "Not yet."

Reeve keeps glancing over at the crime board. "Is that all about Flint's escape?"

"It is."

They walk over to the display of maps, diagrams, and crime-scene photos. Reeve stands with her hands clenched, scanning the board, then narrows her eyes at a blown-up image of Flint, taken from the security footage of his escape. "What's your theory about his motivation for killing Dr. Moody?" she asks. "That's unusual for a pedophile, right?"

"That's the question. Is Flint a pedophile, or an opportunistic offender? I think I need to defer to Agent Bender on that one." Keswick turns around and asks him, "You worked his case. What do you think?"

Bender opens his palms and gives a shrug. "We used to argue about that, back in my day. Pedophiles usually target a particular type of victim, and there are typically several botched kidnapping attempts before one is successful, so it makes sense there would be other victims. But we found no evidence of that."

"No pattern?"

"No pattern." He sighs. "And if I may ask, what's your role in this investigation, Agent Keswick?"

"Researching known associates, classmates, family. Turns out, our fugitive has a lot of relatives."

"But he was an only child," Reeve says.

"Right, but his late father had two brothers with two kids apiece, and his mother has seven brothers and sisters, who had a total of twenty-three children, all still living."

"That's a lot of aunts and uncles and cousins."

"Right, so we're starting in Washington and heading east, checking out who might be harboring a fugitive. Plus, cross-referencing known offenders. They're all over the map, so it's pretty slow going."

Bender adjusts his glasses. "What about Flint's mother?"

"She's got to be involved somehow, right? But we've got nothing more than speculation."

"Nothing popped in her records?"

"No, sir, nothing so far. Her phone records, her bank accounts, her credit cards are unremarkable. There's nothing linking her to Flint's escape or to the storage unit. And she refused to take a polygraph, of course."

"Any other leads from Church Street Storage?"

"Motorcycle tire treads, which we're following up. And a few strands of hair, which might prove helpful. Long, blond hair and also short, brown, synthetic hair."

Bender's eyebrows shoot up. "That's interesting."

Keswick gives a shrug. "Hard to say. They could have been left by previous renters."

"The manager there wasn't much help, was he? Any leads on the man who rented the unit?"

She shakes her head. "The manager couldn't give us anything. He doesn't photocopy driver's licenses, and his only security camera is just for show. The thing's been broken for years."

At that moment, Case Agent Blankenship bursts into the room. "Sorry to keep you waiting, Bender. What did you want to see me about?"

Keswick stands aside, listening as Bender explains that he and Reeve would like to go to Dr. Moody's residence to take a look around.

The muscles in Blankenship's jaw bulge. "That's not necessary."

"But no one's living there, correct? So there's no occupant to be disturbed."

"That would be correct, however—"

"And the crime scene has been processed and released, hasn't it?"

"Yes, it has."

"Well, Reeve asked to have a look around. And she's been right twice now, Blankenship. So what's the harm if she wants to see Moody's house?"

Keswick can feel the heat rising in the room. But she observes that, while Milo Bender may not be an active agent, he still possesses his powers of persuasion. When Blankenship starts objecting, Bender smoothly persists, saying, "We'll be in and out in less than an hour. We won't touch a thing. And the key will be back on your desk the instant we get back into town."

Blankenship's expression sours, and Bender says, "You know what? I shouldn't be bothering you with this, should I? My apologies. I'll just have a word with Cox. It's really his decision, isn't it?"

Blankenship wipes a hand across his shiny forehead. This is his first turn at running such a big investigation, and he seems pissed off that a retired agent might circumvent his authority.

With a quick glance at Reeve, he says, "I'll be the one to talk to Cox," then bolts from the room.

Bender seems calm and unruffled, clearly a man who has seen it all.

He smiles at her. "What are you planning for Dr. Moody's funeral, Agent Keswick? It's tomorrow, is that right?"

"Yes, sir. There'll be surveillance, of course, in case Flint or his accomplice decides to enjoy the show. I've got my black suit ready." She grins at him. "I get to be an undercover guest."

"Excuse me, but what are these drawings?" Reeve asks, standing in front of the crime board, arms crossed, staring at Flint's confiscated artwork.

"Those?" Keswick has been so focused on Bender that she almost forgot about Reeve. "Those are from Flint's art therapy sessions." She walks over to join her. "A sadist who thinks he's an artist. Creepy, right? Some of them look like lace or filigree, don't they? And that small one is so stylized and intricate," she says, pointing with her chin, "it looks like an insect."

"It's a cricket," Reeve says softly.

Bender hurries over. "I'm sorry I didn't tell you, Reeve."

"You knew about this?"

"I didn't see the point in upsetting you."

Keswick looks from one to the other. "What's so ominous about these drawings?"

The room goes quiet as Bender removes them from the crime board and places them flat on the table. "You're not going to like this," he says to Reeve. He opens his briefcase and lifts out some photographs, which he places on the table with the drawings.

Reeve visibly recoils, muttering something inaudible.

Keswick swallows, recognizing evidentiary photos of what can only be

Reeve's scarred back. She had never guessed that the scarring was this extensive. She watches in silence as Reeve moves closer to the table and begins placing photos beside specific drawings, pairing up patterns that bear a chilling resemblance.

"Do you see what this means?" Reeve demands, straightening.

Keswick's voice fails her. She clears her throat and says, "Flint apparently remains fixated on scarification, and he's refining his designs."

She looks again at the paired images and inhales sharply. A close-up image of a particularly intricate scar nearly matches the drawing of the cricket.

TWENTY-EIGHT

Betty's Wigs & Beauty Prosthetics

Betty's Wigs & Beauty Prosthetics is on a side street just a few blocks from the hospital. All the oncology patients shop here. The shopkeeper, Betty Niveen, prides herself on supplying the most lifelike breast prosthetics, the best-fitting undergarments, the most colorful scarves, and the best selection of both synthetic and human-hair wigs.

Most of her customers are women, but now a gentleman strolls in with the kind of serenity enjoyed only by healthy individuals. Betty immediately recognizes that he's wearing a wig—synthetic hair, somewhat neglected but good quality—but of course would never be so gauche as to mention it.

"Are you looking for something special?"

"I need something for my wife." His demeanor grows sober. "She's losing her beautiful hair."

She sweeps a grand gesture toward the shelves in the back. "You'll see that we have an excellent selection. Every type and color of head covering. Hats, scarves, and wigs to suit every budget. What do you think she'd like?"

The man lightly touches a red polka-dot turban, seeming to consider it, then shakes his head. There's something familiar about him. . . . Betty has a good memory and she prides herself on recognizing every wig she has ever sold, but this one, no. It's not one of hers. Perhaps he's been in here before with some other hairpiece.

She's trying to picture this when he says, "My wife has been so depressed. I just want to cheer her up."

"Perhaps she'd like a wig. What's her coloring?"

"She's a brunette."

Betty resists saying, "Like you." The wig doesn't suit him, in her opinion. She'd love to suggest something else, but instead she steps over to the rows of bland-faced mannequins topped with hair of every style and color. "These synthetic wigs are our most affordable. And these"—she says, gesturing— "are our human-hair wigs, our finest quality."

He smiles, eyeing the selection.

Betty always starts with the most expensive. "They're breathable, comfortable, and very natural looking," she says, showing him a brunette shoulder-length cut. "These human-hair wigs are excellent quality. Might this style suit your wife?"

He strokes his chin. "It might. But I think she'd like an assortment. You know, there's so little she can enjoy at this stage of her treatment. And it would amuse her, I think, to have blond hair one day, maybe black the next, you know?"

"Of course."

The man glances indifferently past the most expensive hairpieces of long, flowing locks, and his eyes stop at a short, sassy, blond wig.

"That one's very popular," she says. "Synthetic hair, but it's a fine wig." She lifts it off the mannequin to show him the inside. "See? It's quite well made."

He smiles, accepting the blond wig, turning it around, cocking his head from side to side. The way he holds it when he glances in the mirror reveals that the wig is not for his wife, but for him.

The sick wife is a fiction, but this does not shock her. Drag queens are some of her best customers. Still, this man . . . He lacks the charm and sparkle of a drag queen. She wonders for a moment about his personal habits.

He interrupts her thoughts, asking, "What about that one?" He points behind her.

She turns toward a black synthetic wig with a tousled look. "Oh, yes, very stylish. This hairdo looks good on anyone."

She turns back around and is startled to find that he has crept up so close.

"Oh yes, I'm sure she'd like it," he says, and there's a strange scent on his breath. Something alcoholic and herbal, almost like cough medicine.

He lifts the wig from her hands. "I'll take it. Plus, I need one more. I need three."

Another customer enters the store, a woman that Betty recognizes with a wave, and the man suddenly seems in a rush. Without any encouraging remarks from Betty, he selects a mannish, helmet-shaped auburn wig and then hurries over to the cash register.

"One, two, three," he says. "Very good. What do I owe you?"

To the shopkeeper's pleasure, he pays for all three wigs in cash. But it bothers her that he seems so familiar, and the image of his face seems to linger like a bad smell.

TWENTY-NINE

West Seattle, Washington

Reeve tries to forget about Flint's drawings and focus on what lies ahead at Dr. Moody's house. The FBI has already done a thorough search, so they can't expect to discover any significant evidence. But she wants to retrace Flint's steps, and she's grateful that Bender has managed to arrange it.

While Bender drives, she sits alert in the passenger seat, an open map in her lap and another one on her phone. She looks at one, then the other, then out the window, studying road signs and landmarks. "I guess it might be different if I'd been old enough to drive when I lived here, but this area's confusing. Mount Rainier is about the only thing I recognize."

It's a clear October day and the mountain dominates the southern skyline. She'd forgotten how majestic it is, rising cold blue and snowy white. They cross a bridge and exit into West Seattle, heading toward the water. In a few minutes they're driving south along the waterfront, past a park of dense conifers. The Evergreen State, true to its name.

As traffic slows near the ferry terminal, she wonders aloud what compelled Flint to drive here. "I don't get it. He stashed the barber's car at the storage unit, and then came here on a motorcycle? That seems risky. Why not just disappear?"

"Good question."

"And Flint apparently acted alone in killing Dr. Moody, is that right?"

"The bureau found no evidence of another person."

"So if he came here solo, who set up the storage unit?"

"A friend, maybe someone Flint met at the hospital. Or someone who had a grudge against Dr. Moody." Bender nods toward the ferry terminal. "One thought is that he's hiding out on Vashon Island, but I doubt that. Unless, of course, he's got a connection with someone there."

She frowns. "It's hard enough trying to figure out what Flint is up to, much less some mysterious accomplice."

"It could be accomplices, plural. Meanwhile, that reward money is bringing in a slew of half-baked leads, which means a lot of extra work. I don't envy Agent Blankenship."

Bender maneuvers through the congestion and follows the waterfront to Moody's neighborhood, where the homes become progressively more upscale, with expensive cars in the driveways.

"So how did Flint find Moody's house?" Reeve asks, searching for the address.

"Well, perhaps Moody talked about it. He was the type to boast about his property, don't you think?" Bender turns into the driveway and parks.

"Yeah, I guess he could have shown Flint pictures on his phone during their chummy sessions together," she says, getting out of the car. "But I don't think he would have drawn him a map."

A curved walkway leads to wide stone steps and tall double doors. Bender sets down his briefcase and is fitting the key into the lock when Reeve stops him with a touch on his sleeve. "Wait. How did Flint get inside? If he could find a way in, I could too."

"What makes you say that?"

She gives him a look. "Entrance and egress is something I've given a lot of thought."

"Right, sorry. Well, hold on and I'll check." He stoops to open his briefcase, pulls out a file, and in a moment puts his finger on a paragraph. "It says there was no sign of forced entry."

"So Dr. Moody let him in?" She frowns.

"That's interesting," he says, putting the papers away and turning back to the door. It swings open, and Reeve follows him into a large, cool foyer with marble floors and a high chandelier.

She glances around, then turns to study the door, hands on hips. "Moody lets him in? After hearing that Flint killed someone? I can't picture it."

"Maybe he found a spare key."

She raises her eyebrows in reply.

The house is impressive, with hardwood floors and high ceilings, expensively framed art and fine furnishings. Wood gleams and a faint smell of polish hangs in the chilly air. All of the surfaces are immaculate.

"Somebody didn't waste any time cleaning up," Bender observes. "There's no residue of fingerprint powder."

"So, what did the FBI find here?"

Bender has studied the file, and as he leads her through the now-spotless house, he details what was found: the empty beer bottles and dirty dishes, the rumpled sheets, the missing clothes. "Flint felt no compulsion to clean up or hide the fact that he'd been here. And he didn't worry about leaving prints."

"Your guys would call that evidence of a disorganized offender, wouldn't they?"

He gives a shrug. "Or someone who just doesn't care, someone very confident that leaving behind a lot of evidence is of no great importance."

When they enter the den, she notices that Bender's eyes go immediately to the desk. "What is it about the desk?"

Bender explains that Flint left food crumbs and enough trace from his shoes to make it clear that he'd put his feet up on the desk. "Very territorial behavior."

She narrows her eyes at him. "What else? There's something more, right? What is it that you're not telling me?"

He sighs. "There are some missing files. It appears that Flint took everything that Dr. Moody had about him and . . ." Casting a rueful look her way, he adds, "I'm afraid some of those files would have contained information about you."

She stiffens. "What kind of information?"

"It's hard to say. Dr. Moody would have kept notes from his sessions with Flint, of course. And he likely kept files related to the trial."

Questions spin through her mind as she sinks onto a low sofa facing the desk. She can picture Flint enjoying a snack while pawing through files with his greasy fingers.

Bender is staring at her. "Are you okay?"

"What time did Dr. Moody get home?"

"He left the restaurant around ten, so he would've gotten home by ten-thirty or so."

"I think Flint was already here," she says, looking at the desk, "waiting for him."

"That could fit."

"Did Flint take anything else from the office?"

"The safe was open and anything of value was taken. Apparently, Dr. Moody had recently purchased several thousand dollars in gold coins, which may have been what Flint was after. Money is a pretty good motivator. Could be Dr. Moody was a victim of his own affluence."

Something nags at her. She gets to her feet and scans the room. "Where was Moody killed?"

He hesitates, and she asks again, "Where?"

"In the basement. You might not want to go down there."

She takes a breath. "I've had lots of therapy. I can handle basements."

"Are you sure?"

She nods.

"Okay, your call. But let's finish up here first."

They head next to the garage, where Bender stops short, whistling a long note. "Now this is what I call a car. Look at these lines." He circles the Audi R8, clearly resisting the temptation to touch it. "I'd say Dr. Moody was having one heckuva midlife crisis."

She frowns at the car. "Too bad Flint didn't take this one instead of Moody's SUV."

"Sure, the SUV is much less conspicuous."

"What else did he take?"

Bender quickly runs through the list, pausing after he mentions fishing tackle.

"You're wondering if I remember anything more about a fishing cabin." She rubs her eyes, trying to summon up an image, but any notion slips away like noodles off a spoon. "Sorry."

They leave the chilly garage and head back into the house. The moment they reach the kitchen, the front door bangs open, followed by the rapid clicking of a woman's heels.

A trim woman in black bursts in, shouting, "Who the hell are you? And what the hell are you doing in my house?"

"Mrs. Moody?" Bender says. "We're so sorry to intrude. We were told the house was vacant. We're consulting with the FBI." He rushes through introductions and shows Mrs. Moody the key with the case number attached. "Again, I apologize. We didn't expect you."

"Well, you better not touch anything," Mrs. Moody warns. "If anything's missing, I . . . I . . ." She looks around and says angrily, "The house is *mine* now, you know. You really have to leave."

"Yes, of course." Bender takes a step toward the door, but she blocks the way, standing with feet apart, and doesn't move.

"Can you believe he divorced me?" she demands. "But now *I'm* the one who has to deal with his mess. With the funeral, with his family, with all this bullshit. That lying bastard. I'm glad he's dead." She hiccups a laugh and starts to weep.

Reeve watches, chewing a lip while Bender offers the woman a tissue.

"Thank you," she says, dabbing her eyes. "I'm sorry. I'm usually not like this."

"Of course," he says in a sympathetic tone. "This is a difficult time for you."

"At least he left me the house. At least he didn't change his will." She stares blankly out the window a moment, then her red eyes find Bender's. "Did you see that ridiculous car? I don't want to even think about all the whores he had in that thing. I'll sell it like *that*," she says with a snap of her fingers.

Reeve fidgets, shooting Bender a look.

"I don't mean to be rude," Mrs. Moody says, straightening, "but you two really need to go."

"We were just about to head out. Again, we're very sorry to intrude."

Still blocking the doorway, she says, "Shit, I forgot why I came." She looks around as if lost, then blurts, "Oh, I remember! I need some kind of memorabilia, photographs or something for the funeral, but I don't—" Her face crumples and tears slide down her cheeks.

Again, Bender tries to soothe her, handing her another tissue.

"I saw some trophies in the den," Reeve suggests. "Maybe you'd like to take those?"

Mrs. Moody flashes a fierce smile. "Excellent idea." Stepping quickly past them, she opens a cupboard and snatches out a shopping bag. "A couple of trophies, a few photos, and I'll be out of this place. This damn house, I'll sell it, too. I can't live here."

She leads them into the foyer, saying, "All I need to do is keep it together for his family. All I need to do is make it through the funeral. All I need to do is make it through one day after another."

But she doesn't open the door. Instead, she stands there with the empty shopping bag, staring at something they can't see, whispering, "This is what happens, this is what happens."

Bender opens the door and they exit quietly, without any acknowledgment from Mrs. Moody.

"Well now, wasn't *that* interesting?" Bender says, climbing into the driver's seat.

"God, she seems unstable, doesn't she? I can't tell if she's happy or sad that Moody's dead." She puts on her seat belt. "So, when did they get divorced?"

"Why? You've got that pensive look."

"I'm guessing not long ago. Because the Audi is brand new, right? And look . . ." She gestures toward the Mercedes parked in the driveway. "His ex-wife took the luxury sedan."

"I see. She left him with the utilitarian SUV, so then he goes out and buys the car of his dreams. Sounds reasonable."

A beat of silence.

"I wonder what Dr. Moody drove to the hospital."

Bender cocks an eyebrow. "Your point being. . ."

"Flint made a habit of watching the parking lot. Suppose he always sees Dr. Moody driving a Mercedes, then he's suddenly driving an ordinary SUV, and after that, he shows up driving that flashy Audi."

"So maybe Flint made a point of asking about the new car."

"Or Moody bragged about it."

"In any case, Flint figured out—"

"—that Moody was living alone," they say in unison.

They share a conspiratorial look and then fall silent as Bender wheels away from the house.

Reeve unconsciously massages the numb side of her left hand, a permanent reminder of her captivity. "But why did he kill Dr. Moody? Why not just tie him up, hit the road, and disappear?"

"That's what we're all wondering. But think about risks versus rewards. What are the consequences of getting caught, from his point of view? He'd probably enjoy another trial, where he'd be in the limelight for a while. And then he'd be returned to forensic lockup."

This stops her. "You're serious? He'd just go back to Olshaker?"

"He's mentally ill."

"Well, crap, then what difference would a couple of life sentences make?"

Bender coughs a sound of disapproval. "Flint has had a lot of time to think about that."

"Yeah, spending years of being locked up, craving freedom."

He gives her a sad look. "As you know too well."

She tries to imagine what her kidnapper is up to, where he's hiding, how he's reinventing himself. "We still don't have a clue where Flint could be."

"He can't just go back and start over, but ordinarily, a fugitive will try to reclaim his old life, his old routines."

"But—" She bites off the sentence, unwilling to say aloud that *she* was his old life.

The car slowly winds out of the neighborhood, and she stares glumly out the window at houses bedecked with Halloween decorations. One lawn is pocked with tombstones, skeletal hands reaching from mock graves. And the sudden sensation of Flint breathing on her neck makes her shiver.

THIRTY

Just as Daryl Wayne Flint is turning into Wertz's driveway, a neighbor comes out onto his porch with an aging spaniel, does a double take, and gives a wave.

Flint doesn't curse. He doesn't smile. He just nods his bushy wig and raises a palm off the steering wheel in a gesture midway between casual and contemptuous.

The last thing he wants is to encourage nosy neighbors.

Once inside, he stashes the groceries and supplies and his newly purchased pirate costume, then heads down the hallway toward the den. He pauses midway, noticing the framed map of the Pacific Northwest. He remembers how Wertz liked to point out his ancestors' timberland, especially the high-profit areas, while griping about all the acreage bequeathed to national parks.

"Gripe, gripe, gripe," Flint says, heading into the den, where he ignores the glass eyes of the dead animals mounted on the walls.

The door to the secret room rolls open. Inside, he adds his newly purchased wigs to the shelf, and then stands back to admire them. Wertz would not approve, but the colors are certainly a big improvement over that old selection.

Now it's time to focus on Plan B.

Flint sits down with the computer, starting with their bank accounts. Wertz had been a master at setting up untraceable websites and offshore accounts. Wertz was the businessman, Flint was the artist. It worked well. Wertz managed all the technical stuff, but he had thoroughly schooled Flint about using only anonymized e-mail accounts. So now, no matter where his imagination takes him, Flint is certain the Tor program running in the background is cloaking the laptop's IP address.

He logs out of the bank account and peruses one of their websites, all of which are running on servers somewhere overseas, perhaps Norway, where strict privacy laws protect it from the reach of US authorities. He scrolls through the pictures and smiles. Specialty porn always draws a moneyed clientele.

Recalling the instant of capturing each image, Flint admires the play of light and shadow on young skin. Then he leans back in his chair and glances up at the shelves of yearbooks.

The school photography had been a stroke of genius.

As a legitimate business, Walter Wertz Photography had given them access to literally thousands of children every year. Wertz spent his days behind the camera, smiling at all the pimply faced coeds. Later, the two of them would study the photos—catalogues of young faces—culling the ugly ones, selecting those with the most potential.

After that, Flint went to work, scouting out their homes, identifying the ones worthy of serious attention. No dogs. Distant neighbors. Careless habits. He was stealthy by nature, good at surreptitious work, and spent long hours prone on hillsides, coiled in trees, crouched on balconies, aiming high-powered lenses through windows and capturing unguarded moments. The bedtimes. The evening baths. He especially loved the summers, when damp swimmers were always peeling off wet swimsuits.

He scrolls through the websites featuring beautiful young flesh that never ages. But the unmarked skin seems strangely bland and uninteresting. Imagine how much better it would be after many long months of careful work, after it scabs and heals and blooms.

He stops at a familiar torso. Her name is lost to him now, but he remembers her curves. She had been Wertz's favorite that season. He now recalls that, after they'd smuggled her away to the cabin, Wertz had laid full claim and sent him away with scarcely a chance to photograph her.

Wertz always preferred the chesty ones, but Flint followed his friend's lead because there were often sisters more to his taste. Like Reggie.

He savors a memory, then stands, faces the shelves of yearbooks, and runs his fingers along the colorful spines until he locates the middle school yearbook he seeks. He plucks it off the shelf, opens it, and the pages fall open to precisely the page he wishes. He retrieves the magnifying eye loupe and bends so close to the smiling photograph that he can count the freckles sprinkled across young Reggie LeClaire's cheeks.

He taps his toe three times, then boots up the laptop. He finds the news clip of the discovery of the storage unit, and stops the frame when he spots her, enlarging the image until her face begins to pixelate. The sight of her warms him.

He replays the video, wondering how she ended up here when, according to Dr. Moody's files, she's supposedly living in San Francisco. He sits back in the chair, tapping his chin.

If she's here in Seattle, where would she be? Staying with an old friend, perhaps?

An idea occurs to him that's so tantalizing, he doesn't know why he didn't think of it before.

He vividly recalls Reggie as a girl of twelve, coming home from school, roaming her neighborhood, visiting with the girl two doors down, the one with the charming gap between her front teeth. What was her name?

Jenna.

It's a risk, but a few minutes later, he's loading up his gear, humming a tune, eager to get started. He always enjoyed surveillance. The camera's spotting scope brings details in so close—the hand on the hip, the curve of the spine—you can almost smell their skin.

Just in case he gets lucky, he'll bring the metal box loaded with his tools.

THIRTY-ONE

Seattle, Washington

Sitting on an outcropping of granite, Daryl Wayne Flint squints through his binoculars, scanning Reggie LeClaire's old neighborhood. He can be a patient man when he needs to be, and he has been waiting for the sun to dip below the horizon, as it does now. There's no breeze as twilight creeps in, painting the clouds with streaks of gold.

This was not in the original plan—Wertz would certainly not approve—but he's now free to improvise. And he'd be a fool to overlook this opportunity.

It makes sense that his cricket might have returned to this neighborhood on Strawberry Lane, where she has old ties. Her family has moved to California, but perhaps she's visiting old friends, perhaps even staying in this Tudor-style house, where she and that coltish, gap-toothed girl used to play.

Jenna. How old would she be? Early twenties, like Reggie, so perhaps she's moved out. But she might still be living here. Nowadays, kids fail at natural independence, hanging onto their mother's tits as long as possible. Not like when he was a boy. Once his father was dead and buried, his mother's plans didn't include him, so at thirteen it was time to man up. He'd shot into adulthood, and after a short apprenticeship, Wertz invited him into a partnership. None of this lifelong coddling and indulgence, like today's youth.

The sun disappears below the horizon. He adjusts the camouflage hat on his head and peers through the binoculars, watching as the lights come on in the houses, just as he did years ago. But now, instead of focusing a camera lens and following Wertz's dictates, he carries a stun gun in his pocket and follows his own interests.

What's this? A car pulls up to the curb and out hops a girl. He gets to his feet for a better look.

She's young, perhaps only fourteen, with short bangs and honey-colored hair. He focuses on her perfect skin as she waves goodbye to her friends in the car, then he watches her lithe form mount the steps.

Might this be Jenna's little sister, all grown up?

She unlocks the door, and a moment after she enters, the lights come on.

He smiles, pleased that no one is waiting for her at home, and gets to his feet. He creeps down the slope, inhaling the woodsy aromas, and pauses at the road. When all is quiet, he slips across unseen to crouch in the shadows, then follows the hedge along the side of the house.

A light shines from a bathroom window. He hears a toilet flush and rises up on his toes, but the frosted glass obscures what's inside. He moves to the back of the house, where he finds a wide, flagstone patio. He checks the neighbor's windows, careful to stay out of their line of sight, and creeps along the perimeter.

Sounds of movement. A cupboard closes, a dish clinks. He locates a kitchen window and gets a glimpse of the girl—lovely up close. He can almost feel her skin beneath his fingertips.

He moves across the flagstones, tiptoeing through the potted plants, and approaches the sliding glass door. From here, he can view the entire living room, a staircase, and all the way through to the front door. Light glows from the kitchen, but the rest of the house falls darker by the minute. He approaches the patio door, eyeing the locking mechanism. Sliders can be iffy. Some lock securely, others are easy to—

The front door suddenly swings open. He freezes as two adults enter with shopping bags. He holds his breath and watches their eyes, but they turn immediately toward the kitchen with a call of greeting, and neither parent glances his direction.

He eases away from the door to retrace his steps through the potted plants and along the hedge. He pauses before crossing Strawberry Lane, then hurries back up the slope.

A few minutes later, he's behind the wheel of his vehicle, feeling both frustrated and exhilarated at having come so close.

THIRTY-TWO

In her dream, Reeve is late for a trip. She barely has time to throw a few clothes into a suitcase and run. The suitcase is heavy and she misses her plane, so she has to take a train.

The train is dark and crowded and grim.

She disembarks in a strange country where the looming trees are huge, gnarled, black things, completely bare of leaves. They have learned to talk, and they mutter nasty things at her as she rushes past.

She makes it into town but discovers that a long funeral procession is blocking the street. She must wait in the crowd for it to pass. She stops, trying to be respectful, craning her neck to see. She is expecting a hearse to appear, but realizes there are no cars. Instead, throngs of people come marching toward her with their arms raised above their heads.

She strains to see what's happening.

Thin, naked bodies are being passed overhead.

She turns to run away but stumbles, falls, and is horrified to realize that she has tripped over a skinny girl sitting on the ground. Reeve blurts an apology, and as she starts to rise, sees that the girl's legs are scarred and broken like twigs.

The girl glares into her face and spits out, "No one will help us!"

Reeve jolts awake with a shudder, the girl's words ringing. She pulls the covers over her head, but the nightmare grips her like a chill. The bed turns cold. Sleep is hopeless.

She gets up, pulls on a robe and goes to the window, where she stares out, grappling with the dark insinuations rising from her psyche. She once studied her dreams with the avidity of Freud's disciple. Over the years, she became more skeptical, but this is one she cannot ignore.

What would Dr. Lerner say? Survivor's guilt?

Before leaving for Brazil, he'd said to call him any time. Reeve chews on this a moment, then pulls her cell phone from the charger, keys up his number, and listens to the recorded message. Her psychiatrist's voice is usually a balm, but she grips the phone, working her jaw, searching for words.

Beep.

"Hi, it's me. As you know, Daryl Wayne Flint is at large and . . . I'm having a hard time with this, is all." Her words sound so weak that she flushes with shame and says hurriedly, "That's all. Never mind. Sorry to bother you."

She hangs up, feeling unsettled, and stands at the window, watching daylight begin to dawn. Then she pads down the hall to the bathroom to splash water on her face.

On her way back to bed she hears a sneeze. A line of soft light shows beneath a door. She creeps up to it and listens to drawers opening and closing, the rustle of paper, a man's voice mumbling.

She raps lightly and whispers, "Are you up?"

Milo Bender opens the door. He, too, is wearing a robe, and his hair is uncharacteristically tousled. "I'm sorry, did I wake you?"

"I'm just restless."

He gestures her inside, saying, "Who can sleep with all that's going on?"

"Is this your office?"

"Partly. This over here is Yvonne's," he says, pointing at the computer. "And all that is mine." He waves at a wall of metal filing cabinets. "I'm old school."

Several drawers are open, and the desk is covered with papers.

"You're awfully busy for so early in the morning, aren't you?"

"Bah. The old man's curse is that you can never sleep. And the old agent's curse is that when you can't move forward, you must look behind."

"What does that mean?"

"It's just an old saying for times when you're stuck. Like now, with no leads."

"It sucks, doesn't it?"

He gives a twitch of his shoulders. "Not a phrase I would use, but yes, it does."

They sigh in unison.

"Have a seat," he says, shifting a stack of files off a chair.

She perches on the chair, kneading the numb edge of her left hand. "I thought he would've been caught by now."

"You and me both." He shakes his head. "Seems like we're several steps behind him. And who knows where he's hiding?"

"So you're digging through old files, looking for clues?"

He gestures at the papers splayed across his desk. "Just an old dog doing the same old tricks, I'm afraid."

"Doesn't look like much fun." She glances at the files wondering what the retired agent might have kept. "So what's next? Dr. Moody's funeral?"

Before he can answer, the sound of her ringing cell phone carries down the hall. She bolts out of her chair, leaving "Excuse me!" hanging in the air as she dashes back to her room to snatch up her phone.

The number is foreign, but Dr. Lerner's voice is familiar. "Good morning, Reeve. How are you?"

"Hi. Are you still in Brazil?"

"Yes, but we're wrapping up. I'll be home in a couple of days."

"You sound so close. What's the time difference there? Three hours?"

"Five, so this is a good time to talk." The background noise diminishes, as if Dr. Lerner has moved to a quieter area. "It's terrible news about Flint. I'm sure all of this is very upsetting for you. How are you sleeping?"

"Crappy."

"Understandable. I wish I were there to help you through this."

Reeve slumps on the bed and brings him up to date.

"Wait. Did you say you're in Seattle? Why did you—"

"I felt like I could help. Because I predicted some of what Flint would do." She shares more details and explains what has transpired over the past few days, with Dr. Lerner stopping her at several points to ask questions. She can hear the concern in his voice when he says, "You've fully immersed yourself in this case, haven't you?"

"I had to. But we don't have a clue where he's hiding, so I'm looking back at my initial reaction—which is usually the most reliable, right? Why did I just blurt out that Flint would go to a fishing cabin someplace in the woods? Where did that come from? Why can't I remember?"

"Is that a memory you're trying to retrieve, or simply a guess?"

"I don't know. How can I judge?"

"Flint's escape has surely rekindled a great deal in your subconscious, and I understand that you want to help, but this isn't your fight. Besides," he continues, "we talked about your memory issues. You know it's not unusual to block out details of traumatic events. It's good how much you have recovered, given the deprivations you suffered during those important years of development, but—"

"But I can't really access it, not in a useful way. Can't you give me some techniques to help me remember?"

A pause. She can almost see Dr. Lerner's penetrating look. "You mean like hypnosis?"

"No, I mean something I can do on my own. Something fast. Right away. Certain sounds and smells can trigger flashbacks or intrusive memories, right? So I could do that intentionally, couldn't I?"

"Reeve, that might be dangerous. I'd recommend that you only undertake this with close supervision, in a clinical setting. Even then, treatments of traumatic amnesia are controversial."

"But Flint is going after new victims *now*," she says hotly. "He's out there stalking again, I'm sure of it." She chokes slightly. "So maybe it's crazy, but it feels like it's my fault."

"Why do you feel that it's your fault?"

"Because I failed to stop him, don't you see that? If only I'd, if only—"

"Reeve, you're not being rational. You survived, that's the most crucial thing. You survived and you've made tremendous progress considering that—"

"That I was kidnapped by a sadist?" She's on her feet and pacing. "That he made my skin his canvas? I know. That's my point."

"Reeve, take a breath. You're only hurting yourself by trying to reengage like this. You've made so much progress. Don't let Flint's escape drag you back into the torments of the past."

She stifles a groan.

On Dr. Lerner's end, there's the sound of a knock on a door and some muted exchange before he says, "I'm so sorry, Reeve, I really need to go. But I'll be heading home soon, and once I get back, we'll talk, okay? I can help you get more perspective on Flint's escape. An emotionally charged situation like this would be difficult for anyone to process, and you don't have to do it alone. So listen, when I get back to San Francisco, we'll resume our sessions for as long as you feel it's helpful. How's that?"

After they say goodbye, she replays this conversation several times, pacing.

He's right. She knows he's right. But she keeps hearing that girl's voice from her dream: *No one will help us.*

If Dr. Lerner were here with her in Seattle, rather than thousands of miles away, she could explain all this to him. Then he would understand that she has no choice.

She sets her jaw and heads back down the hallway to Milo Bender's office, where the light is still leaking from beneath the door. Rapping softly, she lets herself in.

Bender is at his desk. When he looks up, she says without preamble, "There are some things you don't know about me."

"Well, yes, I'm sure that's true."

"Things about my memory."

He adjusts his glasses, watching her.

"You know how I said that Flint would go to a fishing cabin in the mountains?"

"Have you remembered more details?"

She hears the hope in his voice and gives a rueful shake of her head. "No, that's the problem. I have a gut feeling that it must be in there somewhere, but, um, I have an impairment, you might say. There are some things from my past—long periods, actually—that I've just blacked out."

"That's not really an impairment, is it? A lot of people who've suffered traumatic events as children don't remember them. It's a defense mechanism. It's self-protective."

She relaxes a notch, relieved that he understands. "The thing is, memories can be triggered all of a sudden by certain circumstances."

"Like flashbacks, right?"

"Right. So listen, I have an idea. It's going to seem weird, but I need your help."

THIRTY-THREE

Sunset Breeze Mortuary

Agent Pete Blankenship squints through the camera's viewfinder and adjusts the high-powered telephoto lens, beginning to regret that he gave Nikki Keswick the plum assignment of mingling with the crowd. She's down there, getting a close-up look at all the possible suspects, smelling the flowers and expensive cologne, while he's stuck in the brush on this windy hillside.

He zips his jacket up tight, refocuses, and snaps a photo of Mrs. Moody.

It's much too early to rule out anyone, particularly since they've found no actual evidence that Flint's mother, Mrs. Pratt, acted as his accomplice. So Blankenship is working a new theory. He suspects that Dr. Moody may have unwittingly aided Flint's escape. Moody had enemies—many of them female—so perhaps Flint's buddy teamed up with one of Moody's disenchanted girlfriends.

Shifting position, Blankenship focuses on each woman as she approaches the door, then catches her again as she exits. Each time, he silently curses the way sunglasses and hats cast shadows across their features, making them hard to identify.

Seems like there are an awful lot of hot babes at this funeral. Old Dr. Moody had it goin' on. By every report, he had a slew of girlfriends over the past few years, which was a big factor in his divorce. Here's another nice figure in black, slim and blond. That's about all he can make out, but he snaps her picture.

They'd found two strands of long blond hair and six of synthetic brown ones in the storage unit. Impossible to say when they were left behind, or by whom, but possible leads, nonetheless.

Of course, with that fat, friggin' reward, they had no shortage of leads. They were getting calls about sightings from all over, from Fargo to Phoenix. It just made his job harder.

Whenever there's a lull in the action, Blankenship scans adjacent hillsides, hoping Daryl Wayne Flint might pop up. There's always a chance that a killer will appear for the thrill of watching his victim's funeral. He checks for a man lurking in the parking lot, in the hedges, behind trees. . . . Nothing.

Swinging his lens back to the funeral, he focuses on one of many men with brown hair. Natural or a wig? He can't tell, so Nikki damn well better be paying attention.

The good news was that the motorbike treads they found in the storage unit have led them to Flint's getaway vehicle: a Ducati motorcycle found abandoned near the ferry terminal, easy walking distance to Moody's house. The bike had been reported stolen a year ago in Yakima, so one theory is that Flint's accomplice resides in eastern Washington.

Agent Blankenship notices that Mrs. Moody is holding hands with a frail-looking old woman who must be her ex-mother-in-law. That's gotta be awkward, he thinks, though he's never been married.

He again scans the crowd and the surroundings for any suspicious-looking men, but again sees nothing. He takes photos of those men who appear to be Flint's approximate height, since that's the toughest characteristic to conceal, but he is not optimistic that Flint or his accomplice will appear. Or that the storage unit manager would even recognize the man who rented the unit, even if handed a nice sharp photo. The guy didn't seem all that bright. And eyewitness accounts have the reliability of a coin toss.

Who is that Nikki's talking to now? Yet another fair-haired woman in black, with a nice figure. That makes eight he's counted so far. A natural blonde? Who knows? He snaps another series of shots, cursing the sunglasses, wishing the damn sun would give him a break. Of all the days for a cloudless sky over Seattle.

At least Milo Bender and Reeve LeClaire haven't shown up. With luck, they'll butt out of this investigation altogether. What was Cox thinking, inviting those two to meddle in his case? That LeClaire girl imagines she has a proprietary interest because of some weird connection with Flint. A former victim, okay, she has some insight. But all he needs is a reckless civilian messing with evidence. Besides, he's done his research. Last year, she wormed her way into a California case and almost got herself killed.

Some shit like that could end his career.

He'll make one last scan of the crowd, finish up here, and get back to the office so he can grind out some real evidence, make a good impression on Cox. He brings the lens back to Nikki Keswick. She cleans up well. With her tight figure and glossy black hair, his young colleague is the best-looking woman at this funeral.

Why the hell not, he thinks, and snaps her picture.

An hour after the funeral, Cybil hangs her beautiful new dress in the closet and puts on jeans and a sweater. She fixes herself a cup of tea, then flips through the stack of bills on her kitchen table, wondering how much money Daryl Wayne Flint managed to lift from Terry's safe. Thousands? Tens of thousands? She can only speculate.

It surprises her that the newspapers have made no specific mention of what was stolen. But she knew Terry's habits. Three times, she'd fitted bundles of hundred dollar bills into her suitcase and helped him carry cash to his account in the Cayman Islands.

She closes her eyes, remembering the impossibly gorgeous blue-green of the Caribbean. The silly, pineapple-flavored drinks they'd sipped at sunset. The extravagant breakfasts they'd eaten in bed. When she opens her eyes again, she sees only the coming winter crowding thick against her windows.

If only he'd truly loved her.

All those years, Terry had kept promising he would get a divorce so they could be together. Just give me another six months, another year, he'd begged. But she'd been a fool to hang on all that time. He'd filed for divorce and then cast her aside like an old pair of shoes, claiming it would be easier on both of them if they didn't have to work together. He'd even had the gall to ask her to train his new assistant, that matronly Simms woman.

What an act he'd put on, pretending to be so distraught and spouting all that nonsense about celibacy. Did he really think she'd buy that? She'd followed him, naturally. And when she saw him driving that hot new car with one girlfriend after another, she'd scratched the lying bastard's shiny new paint.

The pleasure in that act of vandalism proved fleeting. She next posted some nasty things online, but that was small potatoes. Burning down his house crossed her mind.

She was trying to figure out some clever way of getting away with serious sabotage when Daryl Wayne Flint's mother called. The two of them had been friendly during Flint's trial. And as soon as Cybil heard Mrs. Pratt's voice, she calculated how she might use the woman to hurt Terry.

As it turned out, Flint's mother was on exactly the same page. She wanted to help her son escape. She even had a storage unit all set up, so it didn't take long for the two of them to cook up a plan. A map and a key was all it took. Mrs. Pratt gave her directions to the storage unit, where Cybil stashed a perfumed envelope.

No fingerprints, she was careful of that.

Perhaps it's a shame that Terry's pet patient is now loosed upon the world, but at least the lying bastard got what he deserved. She chuffs a laugh, but it sounds empty in her apartment. The helium-light thrill of his funeral is already dissipating. Too bad. She'd expected the heady sweetness of revenge to be much longer lasting.

She pushes the stack of bills aside, wishing she'd made more lucrative plans. Mrs. Pratt's generous contribution is long gone, and the unemployment checks aren't covering her costs. She walks her fingers across the table to last week's newspaper, which remains open to the same page, the same story: "Reward Offered for Dangerous Fugitive."

Fifty thousand dollars.

That's a fat sum, though god knows Terry's parents can afford it. She sighs. Tempting as it sounds, it's hardly worth the risk. . . . Is it?

She sips her tea and, pinching the edge of the paper, rereads the article, wondering if there's a way she can get more out of this yet.

THIRTY-FOUR

Seattle, Washington

Milo Bender accelerates onto the freeway and asks, "Are you sure about this?"

Reeve gives him a sharp look. "The arrangements are made, aren't they?"

"Yes, but . . ."

"When you can't move forward, look behind, right?"

He gives her a sideways glance. "Okay, you've got me there."

"Tell me about the new owners."

"They're a gay couple, seemed very nice on the phone. Educated, respectful. They know what happened. They've only been in the house about a year."

"I was kind of hoping it would be vacant."

"It was vacant for a while, but it's a big place in a nice area. High demand, you know." He gives a shrug. "The house has changed hands a few times since Flint lived there, apparently."

She doesn't say another word during the drive. She grips her hands in her lap. As they get closer, she begins massaging the numbness that runs from her wrist to the little finger of her left hand.

They exit the freeway and turn onto Twenty-third Avenue. She cringes when they pass the spot where the drunk driver smashed into her captor's car, remembering the crash, the sounds of crunched metal and broken glass as she was flung about in the trunk. Then the night went still, with only the ticking of the hot car. She had filled her lungs and checked for blood, making sure she wasn't dead, but stayed quiet, listening for her captor's voice, expecting him to take charge, waiting for the engine to start up and the car to drive off. Instead, she heard a growing wave of strange voices, followed by sirens. And though it has been more than seven years, she recalls cowering in the trunk, afraid to shout for help.

She takes a deep breath, lets it out slowly as Bender turns onto the road that winds through the arboretum, past the Japanese garden. Soon they're cruising past houses with cartoonish black cats in the windows and ghosts haunting the trees.

"When is Halloween?" she asks.

"The day after tomorrow."

"Crap. That's not good."

"Why?"

"With Flint out there? I hate to think about all those kids walking the streets after dark."

Bender makes a *tsking* sound.

As he parks the car, she sits rigidly, staring out the window at the house. She has never seen it from the front other than in photographs and is surprised that the new owners have managed to make it appear attractive. It's painted a sunny yellow. The massive hedges are gone, the gloomy trees have been cut back.

Bender puts a hand on hers. "You don't have to do this, you know. No one expects this of you."

"But I've got to," she says without moving.

"No rush. Take your time."

She rallies her courage, removes her jacket, and puts it on the backseat. "I won't be needing this."

A long walkway leads to a porch decorated with several pumpkins and bright pots of mums. The doorbell chimes and an Asian man opens the door to greet them. She studies him while introductions are made. He's a pleasant-looking man, dressed in black jeans and a black sweater, just as she is. His name is Yoshi, so he's clearly Japanese. She takes this as a good sign, given her study of the language and love of the culture.

He shows them inside to where he introduces his partner, Yev, a sharp-featured man sitting at a table covered in blueprints. Yev removes his reading glasses, stands, shakes hands, and is making genial remarks when his cell phone rings. He excuses himself, carrying his phone toward the back porch.

Reeve pictures rushing after him, fleeing the house out the back.

Be still, she tells herself.

A delicious aroma fills the air as Yoshi leads them into a bright kitchen with shiny appliances. "Could I offer you something? Coffee or tea? A slice of homemade pumpkin pie?"

When they decline, Yoshi's smile falters. He stands in awkward silence. Then, in a voice low as a whisper, he says to Reeve, "Mr. Bender explained to us that you'd like to look around. We are so, so sorry for what happened to you. Of course we saw it on the news. And we know the history of this house, which is why we've done so much remodeling. Anyway, we're happy to help in any way we can."

Reeve's field of vision narrows on the door across the room. "I'm just here to see the basement."

"Oh!" He looks from Reeve to Bender, who gives him a nod.

Yoshi hurriedly opens the door. "We almost never go down here."

As they descend, the temperature drops. A step groans. Her throat constricts.

The three stand in a pool of cold air at the foot of the stairs. She turns away from them, studying the rows of neat crates that line the wall. "It feels smaller than before, with those shelves."

"We put those in for storage."

She looks at their expectant faces and says, "I'm going to need some privacy."

"Of course. We'll give you a minute," Bender says.

"Uh, better make it thirty."

"Oh." Yoshi looks stricken. "Are you sure?"

Her mouth is dry. Her palms are wet. "I'm sure." Turning her back, she closes her eyes and listens to their shoes ascend the stairs. As they reach the top, she calls, "Could you please shut off the light?"

"Oh! Really?"

The light goes out and the door closes. She braces herself, waiting for the *clink* of the keys and the sound of the lock. When it doesn't come, she re-creates it in her mind. And when she starts breathing again, she realizes she's been holding her breath. She sniffs the air. The basement no longer carries her scent. Or his.

Not a basement, she corrects herself. *Torture chamber.*

She turns in a slow circle, waving her hands in the air, seeing nothing. It feels so different. Wrong, somehow. . . . Too comfortable. She peels her sweater off over her head. Her skin chills, but it's still not right, so she sits on the hard concrete floor and removes her boots, her socks, then stands again, feeling the shock of cold on the bare soles of her feet. She paces back and forth, her toes losing heat.

She hears the scrape of a chair overhead, then footsteps that are different from her kidnapper's tread. She recalls the *thunk, thunk, thunk, thunk* of his pacing, the heavy way he walked on his heels. Each time his steps approached the basement door, she would freeze with dread, wondering whether he was bringing food or some new torment.

As the familiar darkness closes in, the pounding of her heart grows loud, and images flash behind her eyes—the tray of tools, the hooks in the ceiling— and she starts to hyperventilate. If she resisted, he would press the cruel prongs of the stun gun into her thigh and set her skin on fire.

His voice rasps in her ear: "Don't you dare move. Not one chirp."

She nearly swoons and reaches out to steady herself, locating the stairs without thinking. The second her fingertips touch the wood, her breath stops and her eyes go wide in the darkness.

Quickly, she steps around to the back of the stairs, where she gets down on her hands and knees. She feels along the underside of the third step from the bottom, and her fingertips touch the tiny gouges—still there—which she made years ago.

After her capture, she'd wanted to keep track of time, but when she first asked for pens and paper, Flint had refused. Eventually, he allowed her one pen, but he required her to always return the pen to its place at the top of the stairs, so that she would never have an opportunity to stab him.

Using the pen, she secretly started keeping this calendar. The first marks were sporadic and uneven. Over time, they became ordered into neat blocks of seven. She'd recalled her mother's voice, reciting, "Thirty days hath September, April, May, and November. All the rest have thirty-one, save February, which has twenty-eight."

Time shaped into weeks, months, and seasons as the basement warmed and cooled. On rare occasions, she latched onto clues to actual dates. He might bring down leftover turkey and stuffing on Thanksgiving, or ham and cold mashed potatoes on Christmas. She faintly heard firecrackers popping on the Fourth of July.

But Flint never found her calendar. The underside of the stairs was her private territory.

Now her fingertips trace the little marks in the wood. The careful "X" on each day identified. "X-C" for Christmas. "X-TH" for Thanksgiving. "X-H" for Halloween, with long dashes indicating each day that Flint left her alone.

He was always gone for a few days around Halloween, leaving her with protein bars and a sack of fruit, returning with a bag of cheap candy. It was hard to gauge time without a clock, but she'd come to figure two bottles of water per day, and always felt a small rush of victory when Thanksgiving or Christmas arrived on the days expected.

Where did Flint go every year at Halloween? And what did he call it?

The pads of her fingers trace the markings made during those long, dreadful days, and she says the words out loud: "Halloween, Hallo-week . . ."

Her skin crawls.

She scoots out from beneath the stair, puts on her sweater, and climbs the staircase in the dark. Opening the door, she calls, "Agent Bender? Could you come down here, please? There's something you need to see."

Two minutes later, Bender is flat on his back, playing a flashlight beam across the underside of the stair.

"What is that?" Yoshi asks, bending for a closer look.

"A calendar."

Yoshi gasps and looks at Reeve with alarm.

"I'm sorry to tell you this," Bender says to him, shimmying out from beneath the stairs, "but we're going to need some tools. I've got to confiscate this board."

THIRTY-FIVE

Milo Bender places the board on the car's backseat, reminds Reeve to buckle up, and speeds directly to the FBI Field Office, where he raps on Stuart Cox's door, tips his head inside, and says, "You're going to want to see this."

Bender has wondered for years what more he could have done as an agent, how he might have connected Flint to any number of missing girls, and now he feels as though he's holding the answer in his hands. This simple plank of wood holds something significant. He's certain. It's as unmistakable as the smell of death.

It doesn't take long for Cox to assemble a group of agents, including Pete Blankenship, Nikki Keswick, and a few other faces that Bender recognizes. They take their seats in the conference room, casting questioning glances at the board and at Reeve.

"Quiet down," Cox says, holding up his hands. He introduces Reeve, then holds up the board and sets it on the table in front of her, asking her to explain.

She speaks clearly as she describes where the board was located in the basement and how she kept track of her days of captivity. Meanwhile, someone arranges for the photos she has taken with her camera phone to appear on a large screen behind her. The scratches in the wood appear like hieroglyphs, and a buzz of interest rises while the board gets passed around the table.

"Reeve, tell them about the horizontal lines," Bender says, pointing to the small, secret marks. "They seem especially significant."

Reeve explains that the horizontal dashes designate prolonged periods of isolation. "He left behind food and water, but for two or three or four days at a stretch, Flint would simply disappear."

Blankenship picks up the board and frowns. "Why wasn't this brought to our attention before?"

"It was my case," Bender says, rubbing his forehead and remembering how damaged and frail Reeve had seemed when they'd pulled her from the trunk of Flint's car. Had he let her safe return overshadow everything else? "It's my fault," he says, "because I should have—"

"Milo, you didn't prosecute the case or run the crime scene," Cox says.

"Hey, I remember working that scene," a man says with a note of defensiveness. "We searched that basement and recovered all kinds of weird stuff. Implements of torture, evidence of deprivation. We lifted fibers, prints, and DNA. It was a slam-dunk. No one ever said we needed to dismantle the friggin' stairs."

"I must have talked about it," Reeve says, "but I'm not sure. There was so much going on during the trial, it's kind of a blur."

"Not the best prosecutor, either," someone mutters.

"All right, people. We all know it takes a big team to handle a major crime scene," Cox says, holding up his palms. "Let's not waste time assigning blame. The point is, we've got something new here. Let's examine what we've got."

Reeve clears her throat. "If you want, I can reconstruct all the dates."

THIRTY-SIX

Missing Persons, FBI Field Office

The walls are lined with photographs. Reeve looks around, aghast. "All of these people are missing?"

Faces stare back at her from all sides. Cherubic toddlers. Wholesome, scrubbed schoolkids. Teens with bright, hopeful smiles. A few elderly people. There are individuals of all ages, some clearly loved and happy, others unkempt and discarded, with sad eyes and chipped teeth. "All of these people were kidnapped?"

"All missing," Keswick corrects. "Some were kidnapped, no doubt. But the senior citizens are often Alzheimer's patients who've wandered away, and they usually show up within a few days. Still"—she sighs—"some of these individuals have been missing for more than a decade, some longer than that."

Reeve tries to speak but the words lodge in her throat.

Keswick waves broadly. "We've got parental kidnappings on this wall— custody issues, you know. And over here are the violent abductions."

Reeve approaches that wall and leans in close, kneading her hands together, wondering how many of these people might still be alive. She searches their eyes, as though hoping to find some secret message. Each person seems so precious, caught in midbreath long ago. Laughing, smiling, unconcerned, wistful. There are snapshots of birthdays, and celebrations, and special events. Emotional, candid shots. Stiff portraits. A few are professional photographs, the subjects posing like models. But most are simply school pictures, taken for yearbooks and then shared like precious currency.

Some of the photos are paired with age-enhanced versions, a youngster as she appeared when she went missing alongside what she might look like today. Reeve's stomach knots. Her own photograph must have been posted here, too.

She is one of the weirdly lucky ones, recovered after years, who make the news and give the other families hope. A cruel injection of hope, she thinks bitterly.

"Come sit over here," Bender says, "and let's try to pair up some of these missing girls with those days when Flint went AWOL."

With a last look at the photographs, she folds into a seat beside him. Open files lie on the table, along with the wood plank from the basement stairs.

Keswick opens her laptop and types. "Okay, I've got the calendar keyed up here. Let's try to identify the actual dates when you were left alone in that basement."

"Okay." Reeve steels herself, adjusts the board in front of her, closes her eyes, and carefully places her fingertips on it. She suffers a sense of vertigo as she's swept back into the basement, but she shakes it off and begins reading the small gouges like braille.

She counts from day one, getting oriented. After a long moment, she opens her eyes and taps a spot. "Here's the first Halloween after I was kidnapped. He was gone for three days."

"Before or after Halloween?"

"Halloween was the day in the middle. I figured out Thanksgiving that year and then counted backward to be sure. I remember he was gone every year at Halloween. And Flint used to say something—it was three words: Halloween, Hallo-week, and . . ." She frowns. "And something else."

Bender adjusts his bifocals, looks at the board, then at Reeve. "Let's just continue, okay? Because there are other dashes, too. Can you identify other specific periods?"

She closes her eyes again and runs her fingers across the rows. Counting the days, weeks, months. "Here," she says at last. "Memorial Day weekend. He was gone three days again."

She opens her eyes to see Bender and Keswick exchanging a look. "What?"

Keswick frowns, her fingers flying over the keyboard. "Let's just keep working. We'll pair up the missing at the end, okay?"

"Okay."

Counting days with her fingertips, she goes through week after week, and it's as if each thin mark in the wood is a step backward, as if she is descending into that awful darkness. She's again a child chained in a basement, hungry. Some days she was suspended and whipped. Others, she was drugged and woke to the bite of a blade.

She had promised herself early on that he would not make her cry. It had taken only weeks of practice before she'd mastered that skill. It was the one thing she could control.

Reeve fingers the marks she made during those terrible days, checking and double checking dates until she has identified ten periods when Flint left her alone in the basement for more than twenty-four hours, usually for just two or three days. Twice for four days, once for five.

"I ran out of water that time," she recalls. "I was really thirsty when he got back."

When her fingers reach the end of the calendar, she blinks and looks around.

The room is bright and clean. She is safe and healthy. She sits back and takes a deep breath.

"Okay, good," Keswick says. "Now, do you remember anything he said that might have indicated where he'd gone?"

She casts a look at Bender, remembering what she'd blurted about a fishing cabin, but shakes her head. "I wish I had some idea where he went, but he never explained anything to me. He never answered questions. Sometimes he'd come back angry. Sometimes he'd seem almost giddy. But he never mentioned any other girls, or not specifically, anyway."

After a beat of silence, Bender says, "I'm sure that wasn't easy for you," and pours her a glass of water, which she clasps with both hands.

An idea flickers behind her eyes. "There's one other thing, though. I always knew there must have been other girls because he sometimes told me I was his favorite."

Keswick mutters something unintelligible, shoves back her chair, and gets up to leave the room. She returns a moment later with Agent Blankenship, and the two of them begin conferring over lists of missing persons on the computer screen.

Reeve watches, feeling ill, as Keswick begins retrieving photos of missing girls from the wall, which she places in sequence on the table.

The picture of one pretty teen with a heart-shaped face and a cascade of honey-colored hair makes Reeve gasp.

"What's the matter?" Bender asks sharply.

She says nothing, bending over the picture.

"Do you know her?" Blankenship asks.

Reeve swallows hard.

"What?" Keswick asks, looking from the photo to Reeve and back again. "Do you think she looks like you?"

Blankenship bends over the picture, saying, "Yeah, she kind of does."

"No, it's not that. She doesn't look like me. She looks like my sister." She points a shaking finger at another girl's photo. "And so does she."

THIRTY-SEVEN

Rachel answers on the first ring, and after hearing repeated assurances that her sister is fine, Reeve's galloping heart begins to slow.

"Of course I'm fine. Why wouldn't I be? You're the one we're worried about," Rachel says. "We saw you in that news clip when they found Flint's getaway vehicle. You're getting way too close to this, Reeve. Dad wants to know when you're coming home."

Reeve offers vague reassurances, asks about the baby, and soon says good-bye.

When she hangs up, she grips Agent Blankenship's arm. "Promise me you'll send an agent to watch my sister's house."

"Right, we've got it handled." He pries her hand free and turns to Keswick. "Nik, why don't you and Reeve take a break?"

Reeve hates being dismissed like this, but swallows her protests and follows Keswick out of the room. They take the elevator to the cafeteria, where Reeve chooses a seat near the back corner. Out of habit, she keeps an eye on the exits.

While Keswick gets some lunch, Reeve sits alone, mulling the connection between her kidnapper and the missing girls. She can't get their faces out of her mind. Could Flint have had a role in their kidnappings? Could any of them still be alive?

"Okay, I've brought your hot chocolate," Keswick says, setting down a fully loaded tray of food. "Help yourself to anything. I've brought more than I can eat."

Reeve barely glances at the food. "How many of those missing girls match up to days when Flint left me alone in the basement?"

"That's what we're trying to find out. Don't worry. Blankenship might lack social skills, but he's a smart guy and a solid agent. And with what you've given us, we'll be able to scour old cases for possible correlations."

Reeve hunches in her seat, saying nothing.

After eating a few bites, Keswick says, "Tell me about your sister. What's she like?"

"You're trying to calm me down, aren't you?"

"Tell me about her."

She sighs. "Okay, fair enough. Rachel is one of those beautiful, gifted, talented people who can do anything. Unlike me. She cooks, she sings, she plays piano, and she's mad about dance, especially ballet. When we were kids, she always said she wanted to be an actress. She was in a lot of school plays, and she was really, really good, but . . . I guess my kidnapping messed her up. Plus the trial." A pause before Reeve adds softly, "And then our mother died."

"Oh." Keswick puts down her sandwich. "I'm so sorry."

Breathe in, breathe out.

"Anyway, Rachel is married and has a son and seems exceptionally happy. But she's less bubbly than she used to be. And when it comes to me, she over-compensates."

"How do you mean?"

"She's always trying to . . . ." Reeve pushes her cup away. "I think she blamed herself when I was taken. As if she should have kept a closer eye on her kid sister. Of course, Flint is the one to blame. Flint and no one else. But it's like she's always trying to make it up to me, trying to fill my life with good cheer. Or that's my two-cent analysis, anyway."

"The blame thing?" Keswick shakes her head. "I see that over and over. The criminal is the one to blame, but people are always either assuming blame, or assigning blame to someone else. It makes no sense, but it happens a lot."

Reeve frowns, recalling the faces of missing teens and young women. "If Flint went after older girls, does this mean he isn't a pedophile?"

"Maybe he's a situational offender. Maybe it's not the age of the victim so much as the opportunity to grab someone who's vulnerable."

Reeve chews on this for a minute. "So what's your theory about Flint's accomplice?"

"We're looking at family, past associates, the whole gamut. Plus anyone who might have had a grudge against Dr. Moody. His ex-wife, former girlfriends. Could be more than one person involved."

"But what would motivate anyone to help Flint escape?"

"Like I said, we're working on it, looking at disgruntled business associates, former patients. . . ." After a beat, she asks, "Did Flint ever bring anyone else down into the basement?"

"Never. He seemed like a complete loner." Reeve groans, rubbing her forehead. "I feel like there's something we're missing."

Keswick studies her for a moment before asking, "With all you've been through, can I assume that you have a gun?"

Reeve gapes at her. "What? Me? God, no."

"Well, maybe you should get one."

"I don't think so." Reeve looks away, trying to frame her response. "I'm no good with guns."

"Think about it. You could get some training, then you could sign up for a permit to carry. Really, you should be armed. As a precaution."

"But what if you don't see the guy coming? What if he grabs you and you're down before you know it? Flint used a stun gun." Her stomach clenches as she recalls the searing jolt that came out of nowhere. "There was no time to react. Besides, I'm not a big person. I can't rely on something that can be taken away."

Keswick raises an eyebrow. "How about self-defense? Aikido or judo or karate? Have you tried that?"

A twitch of the shoulders. "I took a one-day class once."

"You know that eighty-one percent of foiled abductions are due to fighting back, right?"

Reeve gives her a flat look. "I'm aware of the statistics."

"I hear that Bender's son teaches self-defense. I guess he's pretty good."

Reeve heaves a sigh, thinking about the missing girls of the past, the potential victims of the future. Halloween is just around the corner, and Flint is still on the loose, circling and stalking. She itches with frustration that there's no way she can't stop it.

Just then, she sees Special Agent in Charge Stuart Cox entering the cafeteria accompanied by a tall, lanky woman with stylish glasses. The two talk briefly, then scan the room until their eyes find Reeve.

The woman seems to ask a question. Cox nods. All the while, they keep their eyes fixed on Reeve, as if taking her measure.

"Who is that talking with Stuart Cox?"

Keswick glances over. "Oh, that's the bureau's public information officer."

Cox and the woman continue conspiring together. Then Cox nods and is out the door, but the woman heads toward their table with purposeful strides.

"She's coming over here."

Keswick sets down her fork and looks up. "Well, shit. I'll bet she's going to ask you to make a statement."

Reeve blanches. "To the press?"

"I'm afraid so."

"Why? I'm not an agent."

"But you're a sympathetic figure. They probably think you'd provide a fresh angle."

"A fresh angle? Meaning what, exactly?"

"A fugitive at large gets to be a one-note story. Maybe they think you could warn the public in some new way." Keswick starts to rise, adding, "Don't worry, I know you hate facing cameras. I'll tell her that—"

Reeve grabs her sleeve. "No, I'll do it," she says, getting to her feet. "Let's set it up."

THIRTY-EIGHT

Triangle Park Shopping Center

While the FBI is preparing for tomorrow's event, Daryl Wayne Flint is watching young girls come and go. He pulls the cellophane off a packet of cigarettes, places one between his lips, produces flame with a flick of his lighter, and inhales deeply.

Isn't it marvelous how easy it is to slip back into old habits?

Flint has given up on Strawberry Lane and has returned to a place he remembers from his old prowls. Triangle Park was once a sleepy patch of grass with just a few benches and swings, but as Seattle grew, the park was sliced up and paved and developed into a low-budget shopping center. The developers spared only a few trees. And Flint is leaning against one now, thinking that the nice thing about a triangle is that it's so easy to view the whole area from one point, especially when the shopping center has no big chain to draw business, half the shops are vacant, and the parking lot is nearly empty.

The three girls he's been following emerge from a shop that sells girly things—cheap jewelry and cheery T-shirts—each carrying the same bag, as if they've made identical purchases.

A trio of pretty girls. Leggy and smiling. They huddle together on the sidewalk, talking, and their giggles carry like music on the air.

A minivan pulls in and a horn blares. The girls look up. Two hug their friend good-bye, hurry over to the waiting minivan, and wave as they get in. While the vehicle drives away, the third girl, intent on her cell phone, starts walking in his direction.

It's Hallo-week. Even Wertz would agree that it's not too early to get started.

Flint takes three quick puffs, then crushes his cigarette underfoot and walks toward his vehicle. He pulls his baseball cap low over his wig of short, black curls and pretends he has no interest in the girl as he opens the driver's side door. A gag, a knife, and the zip ties are ready. A set of handcuffs is already secured to the metal bar beneath the passenger seat. The stun gun waits in his pocket.

He climbs into the Bronco, wishing he had a van, wishing he had Wertz there to drive so he could spring out from the back. That always worked well.

He fits the key in the ignition, sparks the engine, and the girl doesn't even look up.

He shifts into drive, calculates her trajectory, and looks around. No headlights. No pedestrians. No witnesses. Just a few dim shops in a dying shopping center.

Gently, he eases down on the accelerator and rolls forward until he pulls up beside her. He stops, opening the door while saying, "Excuse me, miss, you dropped something."

She looks up. The twilight shines on her face. Lovely, clear skin, so like his cricket at that age.

She sings out, "Oh, thank you!" And as she steps back, making a half turn to look at the ground behind her, he jumps out and zaps her with the stun gun.

Her body slumps and he catches her as her cell phone skitters across the asphalt. Drops of urine sprinkle her bright new purchase as his strong arms loop around her waist. He hauls her off her feet and they surge as one toward the vehicle.

As he lifts the girl's limp body, shoving her toward the yawning door, someone shouts, "Hey!"

A figure comes barreling up behind him, shrieking, and hits him hard on the back of his head. He wheels around to face his attacker and finds a short, stout woman standing barefoot, brandishing a shoe in each fist.

He laughs, releasing the girl with one hand and smacking the woman so hard that she falls sideways.

He turns back to his task, lifting the girl, but the woman is on her feet, shouting, beating at him with the heels of her shoes. He grunts in pain, shoving her aside while awkwardly struggling with the girl's weight. He muscles the girl onto the seat, but now the screaming woman has grabbed onto the girl's ankle and is pulling hard.

He wheels, backhanding the woman, who staggers but doesn't let go. She pulls with both hands and the limp girl slides off the seat, landing hard on the asphalt.

He stoops to grab the girl under her armpits, struggling to lift her dead weight, but now more shouting commences.

Shit!

Without turning to look, he drops the girl and scrambles into his Bronco. He slams the door, pops it into gear, and the Bronco lurches forward.

Now another woman rushes out, waving her arms like crazy, trying to block him. He clips her hard as he accelerates out of the lot, then speeds away, keeping one eye on the rearview mirror as he races toward the freeway.

THIRTY-NINE

Flint zooms down the freeway in a state of disbelief. Everything had been going fine. How could things get out of hand so fast?

This is bad, this is bad, this is bad.

He left witnesses. They can ID his vehicle.

He swerves to the off-ramp and exits the freeway, watching his speed.

Minutes later, he's wheeling into a shopping center near the University of Washington campus that he remembers from his years as a student. He drives into the parking structure and keeps cranking the wheel, climbing to higher and higher levels. At the top, he cruises slowly through the dark structure, keeping his eyes on the rearview mirror, until he finds a good spot. He parks between an old sedan and the back wall, but leaves the engine running. He retrieves the gun from beneath the seat and holds it ready.

His breathing gradually slows. When he's sure no one is following, he turns off the motor and listens.

No one around. Marginal lighting. Perfect.

He sets the gun on the seat where it will be handy and leaves the door cracked open while he goes around to the back. First things first.

In a couple of minutes, a fresh license plate is in place. One down.

He walks around to the front of Wertz's Bronco and barks a curse. The front headlight is smashed.

Footsteps.

He squats between his front bumper and the concrete wall, listening.

A woman's heels click past. He's tempted for half a second, but this is not the time to push his luck, which has already turned sour.

A car door opens and closes. An engine turns over. A car rolls past, heading toward the exit. As it wheels away he stands, feeling stiff and sweaty. Now what?

He doesn't dare drive down the freeway with one headlight broken. He'd be asking to be stopped.

Steal a car? No, another red flag.

Be logical, he tells himself.

He scoots around to the front of his vehicle, wondering if he can make repairs. After a quick inspection, he decides he can switch the bulb from left to right, at least that. He's worked on this vehicle before, when he was in college. And in that instant, he recalls visiting an auto supply store located near here. This is why he was drawn to this parking structure. Of course. They can't drug the smarts out of you completely.

He climbs back into the driver's seat, wedges the pistol back into its hiding place, and grabs his wallet. He removes the baseball cap, replaces the wig, and fits on his horn-rimmed glasses. Just like that, he becomes Walter Wertz.

He locks up the vehicle and descends the stairs, looking utterly bland and nonthreatening.

First, he must fix the headlight. After that, he'll go get something to eat. Best to kill some time and not drive until it's well past dark. He strides toward the auto supply store, which he finds situated exactly where he remembers.

FORTY

Milo Bender tries to keep the conversation light through dinner, steering it away from Reeve's ordeal in the basement, the cases of missing girls, and the news of an attempted kidnapping at Triangle Park, a place not far from where Reeve grew up. But he can't help noticing that Reeve barely speaks.

After the dishes are done, Yvonne says, "Let's watch a movie, a comedy or something, help take your mind off things."

But Reeve doesn't sit with them to watch the movie, saying she has to prepare her remarks for tomorrow's press conference.

Just as well, he thinks. The eleven o'clock news comes as a crescendo to the day's events. Every station airs the sensational reports of the attempted kidnapping of a fourteen-year-old girl at Triangle Park. The attack culminated with the girl's mother, thirty-nine-year-old Molly Sullivan, being hit by the suspect's vehicle, which is described as a large SUV, probably brown or maroon.

The man's description doesn't match Flint's, but each time the kidnapping attempt is recounted, the newscast segues to his escape. Flint's image fills the screen while viewers are reminded of the reward offered for information leading to his arrest. And every newscast seizes the opportunity to include a picture of sixteen-year-old "Edgy Reggie," along with the news that she's expected to make a her first public statement tomorrow morning.

Shortly before midnight, Reeve sticks her head in the door to bid them good night. The minute she leaves, Yvonne pulls her husband's sleeve, saying, "Now, would you please fill me in on what really happened today?"

Then she listens, clasping and unclasping her hands, murmuring, "My god. Going back to that basement must've been awful for her."

Milo Bender removes his glasses, rubs his eyes. "She said it would jog her memory. It sure did."

"And now she wants to make a statement to the media? That's not going to be easy for her."

He agrees, but doesn't share more details. Yvonne would not approve of Reeve's plan to use herself as "bait"—her word—to lure Flint.

Would he come circling? Would the surveillance team be able to spot him? What if it's an accomplice who shows up? He doesn't mention these concerns. Nor does he tell Yvonne that he felt compelled to call Reeve's father, who has made it clear that he wants his daughter back on a plane and home again as soon as possible.

"It would be hard on anyone," Yvonne is saying. "She seems stoic, but the poor girl surely has post-traumatic stress. Did you hear her scream last night?"

"Nightmares. Yeah, she woke me up, too." He strokes his chin, worrying that Reeve's mental state seems more fragile now than when she first arrived. "She's so preoccupied, like she's brooding about something."

His wife gives him a sympathetic look. "I know you're concerned about her. But she's going to JD's gym tomorrow, right? That can't be bad."

He raises his eyebrows.

"He likes her," she says with an impish smile. "And do you know why?"

"He was always fascinated with her. Plus the usual reasons, I suppose. She's pretty. She's smart."

"No, there are plenty of those girls at the gym. What JD likes about her is what makes her different. She lacks vanity, she's genuine, and she doesn't giggle or pretend."

He hugs his wife's shoulders and feels momentarily better. But then he remembers the faces of the missing girls and something twists in his gut.

"About Halloween," Yvonne is saying, "I'll be working late, so I'm not even going to bother getting candy, unless you plan to hand it out."

Bender recalls Reeve's words—*Halloween, Hallo-week*—and tells her no.

Yvonne pats his hand. "You look exhausted, sweetheart. Let's go to bed."

Milo Bender's unease grows late into the night as he lies under the covers, awake, listening to his wife's breathing deepen and slow. Worries churn inside him.

Unable to get comfortable, unable to clear his mind, he rises quietly, grabs his robe and slippers, and tiptoes to his office. He closes the door softly behind him and goes to the wall of filing cabinets, where he starts rifling through drawers.

He carries a stack of his old notebooks to the desk and begins flipping through, refreshing his memory, hoping something will jump out at him. There must be some bit of overlooked evidence. He searches page after page, but if there's any clue in his notes, it eludes him.

There's a rap on the door and Reeve tips her head inside.

He closes his notebook. "Having trouble sleeping?"

"How's the girl's mother, Mrs. Sullivan? Have you heard?"

"Out of ICU and recovering pretty well, last I heard."

She comes in quiet as a cat and folds into the chair across from him. "I hate it that Flint tried to grab that girl. I hate it that he hasn't been caught."

"They're not sure it's Flint. The descriptions vary."

"It's him. He used a distraction and a stun gun, right?" She chews a nail, then adds, "You know they're saying she looks like me, that girl he tried to kidnap."

He gives a wince and a nod.

After a beat of silence, she asks, "You talked with my father, didn't you?"

"He's worried about you. Especially since that attack at Triangle Park."

"You didn't tell him any details about tomorrow's press conference, did you?"

"Only that there would be one."

"Or about the missing girls looking like my sister?"

"That seemed . . . unkind. No need to burden him with that."

Bender sighs. Talking with Reeve's father had been difficult because the man had legitimate questions, but there was plenty Bender couldn't share. Ethical questions that once appeared clear-cut now seemed muddy.

"I've been thinking about those girls," Reeve says, massaging one side of her left hand.

He notices the pale scars that ring her wrists. Handcuffs.

"We both know, statistically speaking, that they're probably dead." She says this as if holding something bitter on her tongue. "So I can't figure out why my kidnapping would be any different. Why was I kept locked up? Why aren't I dead and buried?"

No wonder she seems so preoccupied.

"That's hard to figure, isn't it? Perhaps Flint kept you alone at his house as a . . ." He shakes his head, unwilling to say more.

"Nikki Keswick says I should get a gun."

He chokes slightly. "What do you think?"

"I think people with guns but no training are idiots. Ergo, that would make me an idiot."

"Training is important." He nods slowly. "Very important. And you're certainly no idiot."

"You have a gun, right?"

He doesn't blink. "Yvonne made me hang up my holster when I retired. She hates guns. Anyway, self-defense seems more your style."

"You think so? Well, yeah, maybe it is hypocritical for me to go on television advising girls to fight back without learning self-defense myself. I'm setting myself up as an example. . . ." She takes a breath, adding, "Which is ironic." She gets to her feet. "At the very least, a session with JD will help me burn off some nervous energy."

"Besides, you might like it. And JD's a good teacher."

"He said you started taking him to lessons when he was just a kid."

"Once he saw me doing it, he wanted to give it a try."

"He said you were a black belt."

"That was a long time ago. But a lot of agents practice martial arts." After a beat, he says, "You should try to get some sleep. Do you want an Excedrin PM? I'm sure Yvonne has something."

She makes a face. "I'll read my chemistry book. That'll put me to sleep for sure."

After she has gone, Milo Bender leans back in his chair, mulling over the case. If Flint is returning to old stomping grounds, their chances of catching him are on the rise.

He sits forward, opens a file, and pulls out the postcard that the bureau found in Flint's personal affects. It's a picture of a leaping trout, with a cryptic message: "How you _Be_?"

Bender studies the Seattle postmark. The postcard was sent five months ago, and he feels certain that this somehow triggered Flint's escape. But what does it mean? Is it a link to the fishing cabin Reeve first mentioned?

He studies the ceiling, wrestling with a decision, then leans down and runs his fingertips across the underside of his desk until he finds the key. He peels off the tape and the key drops into his palm.

He stands and carries it over to the row of metal filing cabinets that line the wall, old and battered. He unlocks the one in the middle, pulls out the drawer marked "G," and locates what he wants far in the back, wrapped in an old T-shirt.

He lifts it out and carries the heavy bundle over to the desk, placing it carefully on the surface. The office chair squeaks under his weight as he settles down to load his gun.

FORTY-ONE

Olympia, Washington

Daryl Wayne Flint had planned on sleeping late after a long night of sex and skin. Instead, a growing pile of cigarette butts attests to his frustration. Three times yesterday he targeted a girl, and three times the girl flitted away like a startled bird. Then, at Triangle Park, he'd been so close. . . . How could he have failed so completely after so many long years of anticipation?

He replays every action in his mind, following their old routine. Success or failure, with a girl or without, he and Wertz would analyze each detail. If they'd succeeded, they would smoke cigars and celebrate. If they'd failed, they would examine what went wrong and then assign blame.

Of course, Daryl was always the one to blame, according to Wertz.

He clicks on the television and scans the news channels. Sure enough, the kidnapping attempt at Triangle Park dominates the news. He gets to his feet and starts to pace.

He failed because he was impulsive.

He failed because he didn't to stick to the plan.

He must clear his head of improvisation, just as Wertz always said. Because tomorrow is Halloween, and his costume is ready. Besides, things will be easier with all the giddy trick-or-treaters streaming along the sidewalks, high on candy and careless of strangers. And he can almost hear Wertz saying, "Halloween provides cover and opportunity. Don't screw up, Daryl."

He's about to click off the news when her face suddenly fills the screen. His girl! He watches, transfixed, scarcely hearing her words. She blinks three times, unmistakably. Then she's gone, and the newscaster is saying, "Reggie LeClaire, who was Daryl Wayne Flint's captive for four years, will be making her first public statement later today in downtown Seattle—"

He grabs a pen and jots down the details, thrilled that today—just three hours from now—she will be addressing the press in Seattle. He'd feared that she'd already flown away, that he'd missed her, but she's still here. And it's surely no accident that his cricket has stayed in Washington. He begins to pace, thinking she's meant to be his again, thinking he'll drive up there right now to stake out the location.

But as he's making plans, something niggles in the back of his mind.

He shuts his eyes and tries to order his thoughts.

Yesterday's attack at Triangle Park has been all over the news, and they've posted a description of a brown or maroon SUV. The partial license plate number is no longer a problem, but he clicks his teeth, worrying about the conspicuousness of the Ford Bronco.

When a solution dawns, he opens his eyes and rushes to the secret room, where he boots up the computer.

He keys up a search and finds even more than he'd hoped for: three video clips—*one, two, three!*—which he watches in chronological sequence. There she is, wearing a UC Berkeley hoodie, with that lovely face framed with red hair. The camera zooms to close-up and he watches her pretty lips move, feeling as if she is speaking directly to him.

Next, he replays the news clip of her at Church Street Storage. He studies the video with the thrill of possibility tingling through him. But this time he notices something new. He freezes an image and sits forward.

Who is that pulling her away from the camera?

He enlarges the image and recognizes the man. Without doubt, the FBI agent who testified against him at his trial.

He sits back and taps his chin, trying to summon the man's name.

Milo Bender.

Where has he seen that name recently?

It takes only a minute to find the reports among Dr. Moody's papers. Moody had collected copies of the FBI reports during the discovery process of the trial, and each one bears the no-nonsense signature of Special Agent Milo Bender.

He lights a cigarette, replaying scenes from the trial in his mind until he recalls an interesting fact: Milo Bender's son attended one afternoon, a blond teen with even more height than his father. The boy's name won't come, if he ever knew it, but when Flint's gaze falls upon the rows of high school yearbooks, he smiles.

Walter Wertz was a bear of a man with worker-bee habits. He kept meticulous billing records from the start.

It takes only a quick search of the thousands of alphabetized orders to locate JD Bender, the only boy with that surname.

Next, Flint plucks a lime green yearbook off the shelf and scans until he finds the boy's picture. The grinning high school senior is the same teenager he recalls from the trial, and the very same JD Bender who ordered a "Special Deluxe" package of school photographs delivered to his home twelve years ago.

Flint notes the address and verifies through an online search that the house has not been sold in two decades. Bender's house seems a good place to start. Perhaps the man will lead him to her.

He stubs out his cigarette and plucks the auburn wig from atop a lifeless head. He hurries to prepare his gear. And then he calls for a taxi.

FORTY-TWO

Seattle, Washington

By the time the girl once known as Edgy Reggie arrives in the Press Room, her emotions have fluxed through anxiety, anger, dread, and every shade in between. She's been awake since before dawn and she's shaking from an overdose of adrenaline. She had no appetite for whatever food was offered, and little more sustains her now than the hope that facing the cameras might somehow spare a future victim.

Nikki Keswick has helped with makeup. Someone's hands have attempted to smooth her hair. But Reeve feels certain that she looks exactly like what she is: a distressed individual with jumbled emotions.

The news media seem pleased.

She stares at her notes, trying to remember the tips Otis Poe has suggested.

"You're the expert on Daryl Wayne Flint," Poe had said, "so just tell the girls out there what you wish someone had told you."

But what could have saved her on that hot summer day?

"I'll try to snag a last-minute ticket to Seattle," Poe said. "But if I can't make it, is there anything you'd like to share beforehand? Any quotes for me?"

She'd managed to utter a few sentences, but now has no idea what she might have said.

She digs her fingernails into her palms, watching while cameramen surge into the room with a flock of reporters. They begin setting up microphones. She can barely believe what is happening—the lights, the sense of urgency—and she hopes the pain rising from her clenched fists might somehow center her in this bizarre reality.

It does not.

The chaotic scene flows around her as she scans the crowd for Otis Poe. She instead spots Nikki Keswick standing on the periphery, dressed in faded jeans and a UW sweatshirt—undercover—and wonders how many armed agents have planted themselves amongst the spectators. How many are circling the block? And what will happen if they spot Flint in the gathering throng?

"Reeve, do you understand what's expected of you?"

She stares at the unfamiliar face, then realizes it's the FBI's public information officer, the tall, lanky woman with the stylish glasses, whose name escapes her.

Without waiting for Reeve to respond, the woman keeps talking. "I've issued a detailed press release. No one is permitted to ask questions. You won't be hassled in any way. All you have to do is speak from your heart. Do you understand?"

Suddenly, given some cue that Reeve doesn't catch, the crowd falls silent and all faces turn toward her. Someone places a chair at the table with the microphones and motions for her to come and sit down. She can't feel her legs, but shuffles the short distance and folds into the chair.

The lights press hotly on her face. She licks her lips. Her mouth is coated with paste. Someone kindly pours a glass of water and places it in her hand. She raises it to her lips, takes a drink, and her mind goes blank.

Someone whispers in her ear, "Picture a young girl and pretend you're speaking directly to her."

She squints into the lights, swallows, and tries her voice. "Hello. I'm Reggie LeClaire."

Everyone stares as she searches for words.

"Maybe you know that I was kidnapped on a summer day when I was twelve. I was just an ordinary kid with an ordinary life, and that day didn't seem unusual. I never thought anything bad would happen to me. I'd been warned, of course, that there were dangerous predators out there, but I wasn't thinking much about that."

She clutches at the water glass, takes a sip to compose herself, and continues, "I've had a lot of time to regret that day. My mistake was that I disregarded my first suspicions and accepted the help of a stranger. That's all. I gave him the benefit of the doubt. I expected that particular stranger to behave as a normal human being."

Her voice strengthens as she speaks. "But he wasn't a normal human being. He was a psychopath. And now the man who kidnapped me has escaped. You know his name. You've seen his picture. And you know what he's capable of doing."

Her hands are shaking as she continues, "But here's something very important that you might not know: The best way to get away from a kidnapper is to fight back. Eighty-one percent—that's a big statistic—eighty-one percent of foiled abductions are due to fighting back."

She looks out at the crowd of faces, but sees only the photos of missing children. "So be safe. Be on guard. And be especially wary of any stranger who insists on getting your attention. Don't be fooled by the guy who pretends he's simply asking a question or offering help. If you find yourself in a situation that feels weird, get away as fast as you can."

Her voice rises. "So trust your instincts, and don't worry about being embarrassed. It's better to be embarrassed than to be kidnapped, believe me. So don't argue with your own suspicions, just act. If someone scares you, run. Don't get close enough for him to grab you. But if he does, you've got to fight back. You've got to scream and kick and fight and run!"

A reporter suddenly shouts out, "Reggie, are you afraid that Daryl Wayne Flint will come after you?"

Reeve glares at the man, and for a heartbeat the room is completely still. She takes a breath and is about to answer when the FBI's information officer steps between them, putting up her palms and saying, "No questions. There'll be no questions. That's all for today."

When Reeve stands, it's like a curtain coming down. Everyone stirs, the noise level rises with kinetic energy. The busy young men begin removing the equipment.

She touches a hand lifting a microphone off the table and asks, "When will this go on the air?"

The young man glances around as if looking for help, then says, "Your voice will go out on radio right away. The TV stations will splice you in with other footage, you know, for the news."

The tall information officer with the stylish glasses appears at her side.

"Thank you for doing this. You did great. But I'm so sorry about that question. That was out of line."

"I was about to answer."

"I saw that." She puts a hand on Reeve's shoulder. "But we're glad you didn't, because that would've become the only sound bite we'd be hearing for days."

This is truer than the woman realizes. Reeve had pictured the armed FBI agents watching, circling, and almost said, "Let him try."

But that brash thought is quashed when Nikki Keswick meets her eye and gives a shake of her head.

FORTY-THREE

The secret is the same as hunting. You find your prey and creep in silently. Daryl Wayne Flint has a talent for it. It's all about elevation and line of sight.

The first thing is to circle the neighborhood, but Milo Bender's split-level house isn't easy to circle surreptitiously because of the way it is situated beside the park. Flint cruises around, looking for vantage points and watching for cops. He's driving a nondescript silver sedan, which he rented at Sea-Tac airport. He doesn't like it much. It's not as functional as the Ford Bronco, but it's about as close to invisible as a car can get.

He finally decides on a spot across the park, at a higher elevation. It's hard to get a good view, and he'd prefer to climb a tree or perch on a rooftop, but not while it's still daylight.

He parks the car, briefly checks his reflection in the rearview mirror, and smirks. Eyeglasses and a wig make anyone look different. He hangs the binoculars around his neck and zips up his jacket to conceal them. He pockets the stun gun and he's ready.

A shady path traverses the lip of the park. He passes a man walking a fat bulldog, then drops down a level. The path winds along an outcropping of granite. When he's sure he's alone, he scrambles atop a boulder to study the houses on the other side of the park and easily locates the distinctive roofline of Milo Bender's house.

He peers through the binoculars, angles for a better view, and can hardly believe his luck. There she is, pacing in front of the house, the phone cupped to her ear. She waves a hand, emphatic about whatever she's saying.

If he were close enough, he could grab her this instant. He scrambles off the boulder and runs back to the sedan.

It takes only a couple of minutes to circle the park, but by the time he reaches Bender's house, she's gone. Maybe she has walked down the street. He curses three times and circles the block, searching.

As he's coming around the corner, he sees that a green pickup truck is now parked directly in front of Bender's house. He drives past, glancing sideways. A blond young man sits at the wheel—Bender's son?—with his gaze focused on the front door.

Flint drives ahead, checking his rearview mirror, and parks midway down the next block, just out of sight. A second later, he hears a car door slam, and here comes the green pickup truck, with Reggie in the passenger seat, talking.

He waits for the pickup to continue down the block, and when it pauses at a stop sign, he pulls away from the curb.

The pickup truck proves easy to follow, winding lazily toward the East-lake district, where it turns into the parking lot of One World Fitness, a two-story building on the left. Flint takes the first parking spot he can find, and then hustles back up the block to a coffee shop on the opposite side of the street, which affords an unobstructed view.

He chooses a seat next to the window, where he can watch the fitness center's front door and parking lot. Even better, he can see inside, where all the young bodies are jogging and bouncing on rows of exercise equipment. He watches carefully and first spots Bender's son inside. The tall blond holds open a door, and Flint then glimpses his girl's bright red hair before the two disappear into a back room.

So close.

When the waiter brings his cappuccino, Flint considers the design swirled into the foam. It's too symmetrical, so he takes a spoon and cuts an edge here, an edge there, imagining scars on milky white skin as he licks the spoon.

FORTY-FOUR

One World Fitness Center

The gym has way too many mirrors, in Reeve's opinion, so she keeps her eyes on JD. He leads her past the rows of busy exercise machines, through an area with benches and weights, to a small room with no windows. A body-sized punching bag hangs in the corner.

He stops and faces her. "So, first question, have you ever taken any self-defense classes before?"

"Once, years ago. It was just a one-day class, but it was pretty good."

"What did you learn?"

"Hit him where it hurts. Eyes, throat, groin, knees, instep."

"Good. Take off your shoes and socks and we'll get started."

They step onto the heavy floor mats and he leads her through a series of stretches and introductory positions. Their muscles warm and loosen, and he begins demonstrating simple ways to break out of holds, doing it slowly at first, then faster, then letting her try.

"I remember some of this," she says, getting the hang of it.

"You're stronger than you look. Are you ready to try some throws?"

"Okay. But you're, like, twice my size."

"That doesn't matter. The secret is to use your attacker's momentum against him. It's all in the technique, okay?"

"Right," she says doubtfully.

"So attack me."

"Seriously?"

"Yeah, give it your best shot."

She lowers her head, balls her fists, and with a cry lunges at him with all her strength. In the next instant, her feet are swept from under her and she's flat on her back.

"You okay?"

She scrambles upright. "Show me how you did that."

"Okay, the most important thing is that you have to widen your stance and tighten your core." He demonstrates, moving his feet wide apart and bending his knees, and she does the same. "Flex your knees a bit more. Feel that? You need to keep your center of gravity low."

"Yeah. Got it."

"Okay, watch closely." He takes her through the steps in slow motion, saying, "As I try to grab you like this, you turn and grip me here, pulling my weight past you, like this. . . . See? Okay, now faster. Grab, shift, and then—"

His feet leave the mat and he's on his back.

She looks down at him, grinning. "Cool."

He stands upright, saying, "Okay, let's do it for real. Are you ready?"

"Sure."

He attacks. She grabs and pulls and shifts just as he showed her, but she lands on the floor with a grunt of pain.

"What did I do wrong?" she asks as he helps her to her feet.

"You lost your center of gravity."

"Well, crap. Show me again."

They start over, step by step, in slow motion. She understands the mechanics perfectly. They go through the movements again, working together, and he lands on his back as intended.

"Okay, I've got it now," she says.

"You sure?"

"Yep, let's try this for real."

He attacks fast, and she grabs and pulls and shifts just as before, but loses her footing and falls hard.

"Dammit!"

"That's okay," JD says, helping her up. "It's not as easy as it looks. Not everybody picks it up right off the bat."

She frowns at him. "I know what I did wrong. Let's try this again."

"You don't want to go over it slowly one more time?"

"No, no. I've got it. Come on."

He attacks, she pulls and spins, but she is again the one to land hard on the floor. She smacks the mat in frustration, and he patiently helps her to her feet, saying, "We can try something else if you want."

"No, I want to do this. Come on, show me what I'm doing wrong."

JD again shows her how to use her opponent's momentum against him.

Again, she tries to throw him onto his back, and again, she is the one who hits the mat.

"Dammit! If only I were taller."

"Or I were shorter," he says, grinning. He helps her to her feet. "It's tough to throw someone bigger than you, but you've almost got it."

They try over and over—now this approach, now that—but he towers over her, she's far outmatched, and the choreography eludes her. The room's temperature climbs and Reeve is sweaty and cross.

"Okay, try again," she snaps, taking a stance.

But JD shakes his head and moves away. "You're too tired. That's enough for one day."

"Oh, come on. I know I can do this. It's just force and motion, right? I get it."

"Do you want me to show you again?"

"No, you keep throwing yourself on purpose."

"No I don't," he says, doing a pratfall and sprawling at her feet.

"Ha ha," she says with hands on hips.

"Help me up." He puts up a hand. When she grabs hold, he pulls her off her feet and she lands on the matt beside him.

She glares at him. "What did you do that for?"

"To prove a point. I've figured out what you're doing wrong."

"I trusted you," she says pointedly. "And I let my guard down. And I lost my stance and my center of gravity."

"Good. What else?"

She makes a face.

He gets to his feet and helps her up, saying, "You're forgetting about your core. Here," he says, placing a hand firmly on her stomach. "Think about pulling your belly button toward your spine. No, don't suck it in, just keep it flat. You're tightening these muscles. See? This is the center of all action. It's not in the limbs, it comes from your core. Think of it as an affirmation. Your core is your center of strength."

Her pulse flutters. She cannot remember anyone ever touching her like this.

"Okay," he says, stepping back. "This was a good first lesson."

"Wait, I don't want to give up."

"You're not giving up. But that's enough, let's call it a day."

Reeve swipes a lock of hair from her eyes. "Well, I guess I'm not destined to become the Karate Kid."

"But you were excellent in slow motion."

"Great. So if I'm attacked in slow-mo, I'll be fine."

FORTY-FIVE

Flint smokes in the silver sedan, watching as Milo Bender's neighborhood settles into the quiet of early evening. He's certain his cricket is the only one in the house. He followed the green pickup from the gym. Bender's son dropped her off, the lights came on, and no one else has arrived.

But that damned next-door neighbor keeps fussing around his yard. First, he was raking leaves and sweeping off his sidewalk. Now the guy is rearranging a display of jack-o'-lanterns on his porch. At last, he dusts off his hands, and a moment later the kinetic light of a television fills his front window.

When nothing else moves on the street, Flint turns the key in the ignition. He moves the nondescript sedan closer to the house and parks just around the corner. He pops the trunk, leaving it closed but unlatched, and gets out of the car, the stun gun ready in his pocket.

As he approaches the house, a tall woman comes out of nowhere, walking a stubby-legged mutt. Flint lights a cigarette and crosses to the opposite side of the street, where he leans against a tree to smoke in the dark. The great thing about smoking these days is that no one does it indoors anymore, so smokers outdoors are ignored.

When no one is around, he creeps to the side of the house, listening. All his skills have come back to him. In a matter of minutes, he'll have her secure in the trunk of the car. After seven long years of refining designs in his imagination, he'll finally have the chance to see them realized in the flesh.

He edges past a camellia bush, relishing a swell of anticipation, and is letting himself into the side gate when headlights sweep the trees. He crouches low and backs into the damp shrubbery beside the trash cans.

The garage door opens and he drops his glowing cigarette to the ground, crushing it underfoot. He hears the bright chatter of talk radio as the car pulls in. The engine shuts off. A car door opens . . . the rustle of shopping bags . . . a woman's light grunt. The car door shuts, followed by the soft tread of footsteps and the closing garage door.

Mrs. Bender, I presume.

Two women in the house. He stands in the dark, calmly considering these odds.

Before he can move, headlights again sweep the trees. This time, the car parks on the street. A man gets out of the car humming.

Flint stays still as stone, listening to the jingle of keys. The front door opens and shuts.

The odds have changed, and frustration burns in his throat as he sneaks back out the side gate and moves away from the house. Unobserved, he straightens to stroll casually along the sidewalk. He returns to the silver sedan and quickly shuts the trunk. Then he slips into the driver's seat and drives away from Bender's house.

So close.

Cursing his luck, he replays events while driving toward Sea-Tac airport, but finds nothing he could have done differently. He returns the silver sedan to the car rental agency's parking lot, already thinking about his next visit to Milo Bender's residence. Perhaps his cricket will stay another week, another month. Perhaps she has become a permanent resident.

In a short while, a taxi drops Flint off at his address in Olympia. He enters the house, and when he glimpses the Halloween costume waiting on the countertop, he thinks about tomorrow and his mood lifts.

FORTY-SIX

The moment he steps from the elevator, Milo Bender detects a different vibe. The violent crimes division is charged with an electric intensity. The hunt. This is what he misses about the FBI.

When he enters the door marked "Special Agent in Charge," Stuart Cox sets down his coffee cup. "Good morning, Bender," he says, pointing toward a chair. "What can I do for you?"

"I think you need my help, actually," Bender says, taking a seat.

"With the LeClaire girl?" Cox lifts his eyebrows. "Gutsy little thing, isn't she?"

"Not with Reeve. With Dr. Moody."

"How's that?"

"The files that Flint took. I think I might be able to reconstruct them, maybe find what was worth killing for."

Cox goes still. "I'm listening."

"I recall that Dr. Moody was a bit of a Luddite, so I'd expect that what you found on his computer was disappointing, wasn't it?"

Cox pulls a face. "Unfortunately. I wouldn't call him a Luddite, exactly, but he was no technophile, either. His assistant said Moody wrote his desk notes in spiral notebooks that he kept at home. But any of those that might have had to do with Flint are gone."

"And you've already collected Dr. Moody's files from the hospital."

"They weren't especially illuminating. Prescriptions, dosages, that sort of thing. Moody clearly didn't keep extensive notes at the hospital. And if he wrote things in longhand, he didn't make a habit of scanning them to store them digitally."

"That's what I thought." Bender adjusts his glasses. "During Flint's trial, I got to study Moody's work habits. I know some of what he likes to share and what he doesn't. So if you'll let me go over whatever you've got, perhaps I can reconstruct some of what's missing."

Cox steeples his fingers on his desk, seeming outwardly calm, but his knee bounces like a piston. "That's an idea. You could reconstruct, give us a better idea of what Flint might have been after." Cox slaps his desk. "Why not? What do you need?"

"Just a desk, some coffee, and copies of whatever papers you collected from his office."

Cox pushes up from his chair. "I'll have Keswick get you set up."

Ten minutes later, Bender is at a table in an unused conference room, sifting through file boxes, extracting what he finds of interest. He's in his element. Details from Daryl Wayne Flint's trial come back to him, rising like braille from the ink on the paper. He shuffles and skims and sorts, wondering about Flint's connection with those other missing girls.

Nikki Keswick opens the door and pushes in another cart loaded with file boxes. "This is the last of Dr. Moody's stuff," she says, leaning against the door frame. "But it's mostly academic papers and clinical files. I don't envy you."

Bender gives a rueful smile. "Sometimes you just have to work your hunches."

"And you have a hunch that there's some overlooked evidence here?"

"Pieces of a puzzle. Maybe something that leads to something else." He shrugs. "When you can't move forward, you've got to turn around and look behind you, right?"

"I've heard that. And it sure can't hurt. We're kind of stuck at the moment, and Blankenship is giving everyone fits."

"You don't like him much, do you?"

"Does it show?"

"Just a tad."

She rolls her shoulders. "The thing is, he reminds me way too much of my ex-boyfriend."

"Oh? He'd probably like hearing that."

"Not if he knew my ex-boyfriend," she says with a wicked smile.

Bender is laughing when Blankenship's forehead looms behind her. "I've been looking for you, Nikki. Are you working here or what?"

"Sorry," she says, snapping to attention. "What's up?"

"A couple of things. We got a tip from a woman at a wig shop who swears that Flint came in and bought some wigs."

"Wow. Wigs similar to the synthetic hair we found?"

"Possibly. But first, I want you to check on something from the evidence team. We got an ID on those headlight fragments at Triangle Park. It's a Ford Bronco. I want you to search vehicle regs and see what pops. Do a cross-check with anyone who might have any connection with Flint, got that? Get back to me the minute you've got a lead."

"Right away." Keswick gives a wink to Bender and she's gone.

Bender gets back to unboxing Dr. Moody's files. But while sorting documents and skimming pages, something flickers in the back of his mind.

What?

He gets up and paces back and forth a few times, but the notion slips away. He tries to refocus on his work, but the distraction flickers again. It needles him. And finally, he sets the folders aside and heads down the corridor toward the men's room, intending to splash water on his face. He hesitates instead outside the Missing Persons Room, takes a breath, and opens the door.

The room is crowded with faces, yet empty of another living soul. He walks over to the wall of violent abductions, gazing up at the photographs of the many victims he recognizes, working his jaw, recalling interviews and evidence. Long, fruitless years stretch between the day of each kidnapping and this very moment. Bender stands there for a long time, choked with regret, wondering what clues he missed, craving some means of atonement.

FORTY-SEVEN

Case Agent Pete Blankenship can hardly wait to share this news with Stuart Cox. He knew the paint chips and broken headlight fragments collected at Triangle Park would crack this case. The evidence points to a brown Ford Bronco, probably a 1990s model, which fits the description of the attempted kidnapper's vehicle perfectly.

Now Blankenship's idea to canvass all the auto supply stores in the Seattle area is ringing up cherries. Not only did someone buy a new headlight for a Ford Bronco, it was the very night of the kidnap attempt, just a few miles away, and less than an hour later. *Bingo!*

This has got to be their suspect, and Blankenship is sure it's Flint. Even better, the link to the store's security-camera footage has been e-mailed to him. It's downloading right this minute.

He drums his fingers, thinking how he'll present this to Stuart Cox, thinking that all his hard work is finally paying off.

Blankenship's computer chirps, letting him know the download is complete. He cues up the security footage and grinds his teeth. The moron at the store has sent him the entire day's video recording. Twelve hours, 9:00 A.M. to 9:00 P.M.

The receipt for the headlight is time-stamped 6:44 P.M.

It takes agonizing minutes to fast-forward and locate the correct time window on the recording. Figures zip across the screen, carrying purchases to be rung up by the cashier, while other staffers rush on and off camera, fetching items from a storeroom.

At last, here's their guy. Blankenship almost gasps, the image is so clear.

Two minutes later, he's in the SAIC's office with his laptop, playing the video clip for him.

"You're right. Even with that hair, this guy looks like Flint," Cox says. "I don't suppose he used a credit card?"

Blankenship shakes his head. "I've got Nikki cross-checking Broncos with known associates. I'll let you know if we get lucky."

When he gets back to his office, Blankenship is surprised to find Milo Bender waiting for him, sitting in a hardback chair.

"I've got something I think you'll want to hear," Bender says, getting to his feet with a slight hitch.

Bad knees, Blankenship observes, hoping he won't suffer the same indignity.

"I'm pressed for time, Bender." He has no patience for hand-holding, and this old guy is becoming a distraction. Should he tell him he's getting in the way?

"The thing is," Bender says, "I believe Flint has an accomplice who links him to those older missing girls."

Blankenship frowns. "Where's the evidence? It was only Flint who kidnapped Reeve. He acted alone. Solo. Same as when he tried to grab the girl at Triangle Park yesterday."

"But think about it," Bender continues. "It's not unusual for criminals to have dual lives, an outwardly normal life at home that masks secret crimes. Plenty of serial rapists and serial killers had wives at home. Upstanding member of the community, all that, like John Wayne Gacy."

"Dual lives. Uh-huh. What's your point?"

Bender removes his glasses and polishes them on his shirt. "It's a bit out of the box, but why wouldn't Flint have a captive at home—that was normal to him, after all—but then also have another life? He'd go out on kidnapping sprees with his buddy, and then return home to his private captive. See what I'm saying?"

"Yeah, that would be out of the box. Because there's no evidence linking Flint to any other abductions. And your theory makes a big leap from just a few marks on a wood plank."

"You shouldn't overlook the significance of that calendar. And remember that an accomplice rented the storage unit. Besides, in two of the cold cases, there were witnesses who reported seeing a pair of men acting together."

Blankenship makes a nasal sound.

"Hear me out," Bender urges. "The way I see it, Flint's been locked up for seven years, and meanwhile his partner's situation will have changed, right? That's why Flint acted solo at Triangle Park. His partner might be in prison. Or there may be a power struggle between the two."

Blankenship's phone vibrates and he puts up a hand. "Hold on, I've got to check this."

It's a text message from Nikki Keswick:

> **Found Bronco registered to Olshaker patient. Tacoma.**
> **Time for a warrant?**

He needs to get going, pronto.

"Listen, Bender, I know you're trying to help, but we've got active leads. Trust me, man, we're working it." Blankenship cups the old man's elbow and shows him the door. "I think we've got this case nailed. Once we catch him, we'll consider your theory, okay? But for now, like I said, I'm pressed for time."

FORTY-EIGHT

Seattle Library

Reeve's muscles ache from yesterday's exercise, and she fidgets on the hard chair. How can anyone possibly study in this building, with its grids and sharp angles? It's supposedly an architectural marvel, but it seems designed more as an intellectual exercise than a habitable environment.

She finishes a bit of homework that she e-mails directly to her most co-operative professor, and shuts her laptop. After responding to several messages from her roommates, she starts packing up. She's supposed to meet Milo Bender for lunch, and it's still early, but her computer battery isn't the only thing that needs recharging. Caffeine beckons.

She exits onto the street and discovers that it's raining—no surprise. Seattle is called the Emerald City, but the downtown is just as gray and traffic-clogged as any metropolis, especially in bad weather. She hustles along the sidewalk, dodging pedestrians and umbrellas, hurrying from awning to awning.

She's drenched by the time she reaches the café, and the place is packed. A clown and a gypsy are waiting on customers.

Halloween, Hallo-week . . . and what else?

A woman wearing skeleton earrings orders a sandwich and a mocha latte with an extra shot of chocolate. Reeve orders the same thing. It's not her usual drink, but having tossed and turned all night, she could use an extra dose of caffeine.

The moment she places her order, her sister calls. Reeve composes herself before answering, hoping to keep the conversation light.

But Rachel has clearly teamed up with their father, because she launches immediately into a recitation of the same admonishments Reeve has already heard. "Dad wants you to come home. He's worried about your grades, and he's afraid it's not safe for you up there."

"I know, I talked to him. My flight is already booked for tomorrow, okay? But I'm fine. And I'm keeping up with my studies. I've just spent all morning ensconced in the library."

She doesn't add that she's been researching articles about kidnappings that coincide with dates when Flint left her alone in the basement. It didn't take long for her to start pairing up names and faces. But Rachel doesn't need to know any of this.

Reeve is trying to gently end the conversation when Rachel says, "One more thing. The other reason I'm calling is that I wanted to tell you again how proud I am of you. I've watched that press conference over and over, and I know it took courage for you to face those cameras. I wouldn't have been able to do it. I'd have been terrified."

"You? I thought you never suffered one minute of stage fright."

Rachel makes a *tsking* sound. "Acting in a play is a whole lot easier than real life. I could never do what you do. You're the brave one."

"*Brave?* I don't think so."

"I mean it. After what you did last year in Jefferson? I swear, sis, you're tougher than bone."

Reeve makes a small joke, deflecting the compliment, and hangs up feeling warmed by her sister's words.

She has just settled at a table in the corner when Milo Bender comes in, shedding rain from his coat. He wears a preoccupied look as he sets down his briefcase and folds into the seat across from her.

"You look tired," she says.

Bender lets out a sigh. "Pardon my saying so, but it's a bitch getting old. Nobody takes you seriously."

"What happened?"

"I was just talking to Blankenship. To him, I'm just an old warhorse with outdated ideas."

Reeve wrinkles her nose. "Blankenship is just jealous because Nikki Keswick is sweeter on you than she is on him."

He suppresses a smile.

A few minutes later, with coffee, a sandwich, and a muffin in front of him, Bender is looking better. "I shouldn't be eating all this." He takes a bite of the muffin, swallows, and adds, "Don't tell Yvonne."

"It'll be our secret."

"It's rough having a nurse for a wife. She's right, of course. My dad's heart gave out when he was just forty-eight, and she never lets me forget it." He takes another bite before asking, "So, how are you feeling? Are you sore after yesterday's session with JD?"

She huffs. "They make it look a lot easier in the movies."

He smiles. "They do, don't they?"

A sudden commotion at the door draws their attention to a trio of teens in silly costumes.

"I keep trying to remember what Flint used to say," she says, touching the scar at the back of her neck. "It was three words. Halloween, Hallo-week, Hallo . . ." She shakes her head. "And something else."

The trio of teens glances over. Reeve shifts in her seat, noticing their stares.

The smallest girl, dressed as a ninja, can't seem to take her eyes off her. The other two teens whisper in the ninja's ear. She shakes her head. Then the largest one gives her a push in Reeve's direction.

The girl approaches, hands clasped in front of her. "Excuse me, but aren't you Reggie LeClaire?"

Reeve gives a single nod.

"I thought so. We saw you on TV last night."

Reeve holds her breath.

"My sister is Jenna Dutton. She went to your school."

"I remember Jenna," Reeve says, feeling a flush of nostalgia. "We were good friends."

Best friends, in fact. She smiles at the girl, noticing the same gap between her front teeth, the same honey-colored hair as her friend from middle school.

"She said you were kidnapped while we were visiting grandma in Idaho. I was little, but we looked for you when we got home. We all looked for you. We really did." The ninja girl's eyes well with sincerity. "Anyway, I just wanted to tell you that. And hello from Jenna, too."

"How is Jenna doing?"

A shadow passes briefly over the girl's face. "She's okay. She got married, but now she's divorced, and she's moved back home. And she had a baby. He's really cute."

The girl's friends call to her that her latte is ready. She glances at them and says hurriedly, "Anyway, we're glad you're okay. And we all think you're awesome," she adds before hustling off to join her friends.

"That ought to make you feel pretty good," Bender says after she's gone.

"It does." Reeve sighs. "But what have I accomplished, really? Flint is still out there." She glances out the window. "And now it's Halloween, and I can't shake this feeling of dread."

She falls silent, gazing out at the rain and hoping it will continue all night and keep kids off the streets. Then she gives Milo Bender a quizzical look. "You've sure been working a lot in your office every morning."

He frowns. "I've been reviewing old cases, trying to make connections."

"And?"

He gives a shrug in reply.

"Hey, I've been doing a little research of my own." She tells him what she discovered at the library, matching up reported kidnappings with dates when she was left alone in Flint's basement. Two girls were taken on two different Halloweens, one on a Memorial Day weekend, and two during the summer months, just as she was. A third girl disappeared from Spokane on a Halloween two years before Reeve was abducted.

Bender knows far more about these cases than she does. He knows all the girls' names, and it clearly pains him to talk about them.

He pushes his half-eaten sandwich away, and says, "I've been giving some thought to those cases, comparing them to yours. Seems to me, your kidnapping was unique in several ways. The other girls were taken after dark, while you were kidnapped in broad daylight."

"Yeah, and three of those girls were taken from parking lots at or near their schools." Her stomach knots. "It makes me sick to think about it."

"I think he knew where you lived and followed you to the beach. He knew your bicycle. And he purposely let the air out of the tires."

She closes her eyes briefly, then asks, "Did he do anything like that with other girls?"

"Not that we know of, which is another reason your abduction seems unique."

She puts her elbows on the table and rubs her temples. "I wish I could remember something to help."

He raises an eyebrow. "Like some connection with a fishing cabin?"

She opens her empty palms in a "perhaps" gesture.

"You might be interested to hear that the bureau is investigating a new theory. Blankenship thinks that Flint's accomplice might be a fellow patient at the psychiatric hospital, someone recently released, or perhaps a friend of someone who's still locked up."

She gives him a sharp look. "You sound skeptical. What do you think?"

His eyes stay on hers and his expression softens. "I think your father is right. I think you need to put all this behind you. You need to go home, concentrate on your studies, get back to your normal life."

She looks away without responding. She doesn't want to even try to explain that she can't go home and certainly can't get on with her life while Flint is roaming free. Especially since she's convinced that he's poised to strike again.

It has stopped raining by the time they emerge onto the sidewalk. Milo Bender heads back downhill to return to the office, while Reeve heads in the opposite direction. But she has no intention of returning to the library.

FORTY-NINE

Reeve expects JD Bender to turn her down, but instead he says, "Visiting a crime scene sounds way more interesting than working on this old boat. I'll pick you up in twenty."

He arrives right on time and peppers her with questions all the way to Triangle Park. Somehow, relaying information to him helps her feel that she's getting a grip on things.

He parks his pickup truck in the half-empty parking lot in front of the shabby building, and they climb out. A brisk wind has come up. She zips up her leather jacket and points out the store where the three girls had been shopping, one of only a handful of open stores.

"Why did he choose this place?" JD asks, looking around.

Just then, a van pulls in and stops. A mother and two daughters spill out and bustle into a store.

They exchange a glance, then Reeve jams her fists into her pockets. "You know what? I recognize this place. My mom used to bring us here after ballet class." She points at a storefront on the corner with a large "For Lease" sign in the window. "That was a candy shop."

"So, what exactly happened here? Do you know any details that weren't in the news?"

A visceral memory of the stun gun's jolt shudders down her spine. She shoves the feeling aside, then tells JD everything she knows about what the evidence team found. Pointing across the parking lot, she adds, "See those trees over there? They found fresh cigarette butts that they think were his."

"Meaning he just hung out, smoking, until he saw his opportunity?"

"Apparently."

She studies the small stand of trees, then scans the shopping center from end to end. "He could watch the whole place from there."

As if by mutual agreement, they head toward the trees.

"What I can't figure out," he says, "is how he thought he would get away with it. It was sloppy. There were witnesses."

"And it seems impulsive."

They reach the stand of trees, where the scent of pine mixes with the fresh, loamy fragrance of damp earth, and turn in unison to view the shopping center and the parking lot.

"God, it really is a triangle, isn't it?" She kicks at the ground, then abruptly straightens.

"What?"

"Dr. Blume said that Flint has an obsession with threes. I wonder if he chose this place based on its name."

"Triangle Park? That's a thought. But there must be hundreds of places with some variation of three in the name. Tri-Valley High. Three Tenors Café. Third Place Books. The list is endless."

"Crap. It's like a puzzle I can't solve."

He shakes his head. "It's not your job to solve it."

"But I can't stop obsessing about those missing girls, the ones whose abductions coincide with the days he left me alone in the basement."

Worry lines his face as he scans the park. "Do they have any new leads?"

"Agent Blankenship thinks he's found a connection with a former patient, but . . ." She scowls. "I don't think your dad would agree. And I trust his judgment more than anyone's."

"Well, as my dad always says, when you're blocked and can't move forward—"

"Turn around and look behind you. I know."

They share a wry smile.

"But the thing is, I went back to the basement already. What else can I do?"

"I keep thinking about Dr. Moody," JD says. "Flint broke into his psychiatrist's house, stole various things, and then he killed him. That strikes me as very, very odd. What motivated him?"

"You think like an agent."

JD grins. "It must've rubbed off. But humor me: What do you know about Dr. Moody?"

"Arrogant, self-important. And he was kind of a celebrity. He was on *60 Minutes*."

"And he was divorced. You met his ex-wife, right?"

"Who was distraught, and apparently cleared of any suspicion."

"Dad said Moody was quite the ladies' man, so maybe one of his girlfriends played a role." JD scoffs. "Though it's hard to imagine any woman wanting to help a sex criminal like Flint. That would be perverse."

"Perverse, but it happens. Even Ted Bundy had female admirers, remember?" She starts to pace. "If Flint got help from one of Dr. Moody's ex-girlfriends, what could be her connection with—" She stops in midstride, picturing an attractive blonde who was at Flint's trial. Reeve's own hair had thinned from years of deprivation, and she recalls envying the woman's thick tresses. "Wait. I remember a blonde who worked with Moody. I think she was his assistant."

"Really? That's interesting."

Reeve has an image of the blond assistant walking in lockstep with Dr. Moody, tipping her face toward his. "They were awfully friendly."

"Friendly as in having an affair?"

"Maybe. So she would have had contact with Flint through Dr. Moody. . . ." Reeve's mind is spinning.

"But why would any sane person ever want to put Daryl Wayne Flint back on the street?"

Reeve suddenly pictures Flint's mother entering the courtroom with the young blonde, both with eyes shining, wearing smiles as if relishing a shared joke.

"Oh, crap," she says, grabbing JD's arm. "I think she and Flint's mother were friends."

FIFTY

Cybil Abbott puts her blond hair in a ponytail, slips on her jacket, grabs her keys, and heads out to her car. This is the first time in months that she has made this drive, and it will surely be the last. It's time for a purge.

They used to call the secluded cottage in Gig Harbor their love nest, which now strikes her as worse than corny. It's pathetic.

Now her car is loaded with boxes, garbage bags, and cleaning supplies. She certainly can't afford to keep the place on her own, and there's no way she's going to forfeit the cleaning deposit, so she'll work nonstop, without indulging in sloppy sentiment, until the rental is spotless. And of course she plans to strip the place of anything of value.

Turning up the radio, she sings all the way there.

It doesn't take long.

She parks in front, grabs some trash bags, and climbs the steps, pausing to enjoy the view. Then she steels herself and fits the key into the lock. The door swings open, she steps inside and feels . . . nothing.

It's an empty one-bedroom shack. That's all it is to her now.

She exhales a note of triumph, turns on the heat, and heads toward the small kitchen. Glancing around, she decides to start with the booze and the stemware, so goes back to the car to fetch boxes and bubble wrap.

After carefully packing the wine, champagne, and martini glasses, she goes through the dishes, wrapping the best pieces and tossing the rest in the trash. Pots and pans, cooking utensils, and canned goods get similar treatment.

One drawer yields an envelope filled with cash. Nice. For six years, Terry had given her cash for rent and incidentals. Well, he's still paying. *So there!*

Once all the drawers and cupboards are empty and the boxes have been loaded into her car, she sets to work scrubbing every surface. The stove, the microwave . . . Then she opens the fridge.

Shit. Why didn't she start here?

All the condiments and frozen goods get tossed. The vegetable tray, luckily, is empty, except for some crusty brown matter. The bottled waters and sodas she decides to keep. And, hey, what have we here?

Champagne!

Cybil lifts out the bottle of liquid gold. Dom Pérignon. The good stuff.

Terry had brought a box of Godiva chocolates and two bottles of champagne for Valentine's Day. They'd drunk only one. She'd forgotten all about it.

Surveying her progress in the kitchen, she decides to reward her hard work. Why not?

The cork gives way with a satisfying *pop!* A champagne flute would be nice, but they're already packed. She takes a deep swig from the bottle.

So good. It makes other champagnes, even pricey ones, taste like cheap stuff. She enjoys another few swallows, but that's enough. She still has work to do, so she'll save it for later. The champagne goes back in the fridge.

She heads toward the bedroom, where she's hit with an unexpected pang of emotion. The king-sized bed is an affront. How many hours has she wasted in this bed?

"Six years," she says aloud. "Six stupid years of swallowing his lies."

She attacks the bed, stripping off the sheets and stuffing them into a laundry bag.

The sex, unfortunately, had been fantastic. The best of her life. She'd even let herself believe they were *making love!* The lying weasel had convinced her they had something special, something much more than just a torrid affair. He'd promised they would stay together. He'd promised a ring. He'd even hinted at an extravagant wedding in Tahiti.

Divorce his wife and marry his assistant? What a cliché! She'd been an idiot to fall for such a transparent load of crap.

Feeling overheated, she stomps back to the kitchen, yanks open the refrigerator door, grabs the bottle of champagne, and lifts it to her lips. Two gulps, and she decides to carry the bottle with her back to the bedroom.

The dresser drawers get emptied into a large plastic trash bag. The few items in the closet get stripped from their hangers and added. She takes another drink, looks around, snatches up a few bottles of perfume, and tosses them in for good measure. The bag is heavy, but she wrestles it out to the car, thinking she'll sort through it later.

She returns to the bedroom and dusts every surface. Satisfied, she carries the bottle of champagne into the bathroom. The medicine cabinet is crammed so full, it's too much to bother sorting. Instead, she takes the empty trash can from beneath the sink and sweeps the contents from the shelves, sending them clattering.

A spritz of cleanser, a little elbow grease, and in minutes all the surfaces are sparkling. She rewards herself with another swig of champagne. Towels get added to the laundry bag, and then she lugs the trash can and the bag of laundry out to the car.

She's getting tipsy. So what? After she's done here, she'll drive carefully down the hill into town and use Terry's money to buy herself a nice steak dinner, followed by an espresso or two.

She stomps up the steps to the porch and glances again at the view, now softened by dusk. A bubble of nostalgia rises in her chest as she recalls a romantic picnic down by the creek, but she quickly clamps down on this emotion.

Six years she wasted in this place. No more!

The living room requires little work. She finishes dusting, vacuums the whole place, then walks through the cottage, giving it a final once-over. The vases, a framed picture, and a few throw pillows get added to the load in her car, but all the furniture belongs to the landlord.

Finished, she sprawls on the sofa to catch her breath, keeping the bottle of champagne close at hand.

She turns on the television and is flipping through channels when she glimpses a grainy image of Daryl Wayne Flint. She hears, ". . . the fugitive who escaped from medium-security lockup in the state's largest mental institution."

The still image of Flint is replaced by boldfaced numbers, and the newscaster declares, "There's been a substantial increase in what was already a hefty reward for information leading to his arrest. The number to call is on your screen. The reward has been raised from fifty thousand to seventy-five thousand dollars."

Cybil sits forward. "Well now, that's more like it."

She's raising the bottle of Dom to her lips, about to take another swig, when she's hit by a powerful notion.

Is it possible?

She gets to her feet. With a glance at the clock, she pours the rest of the champagne down the sink and grabs her keys. She'll have to skip the steak dinner. She'll grab some coffee in town and head to Tacoma. She'll have plenty of time during the drive to figure out how to get what she wants from Flint's mother.

FIFTY-ONE

Tacoma, Washington

The lead on the Ford Bronco has brought Case Agent Pete Blankenship to Tacoma, a town thirty-five miles south of Seattle. He feels certain that they're closing in on their fugitive, thanks to the headlight fragments left at Triangle Park. Because what are the odds that Flint's buddy—who just happens to be a fellow sex offender—has the same type of vehicle that was used in yesterday's kidnap attempt?

Sven Larsson and Daryl Wayne Flint were art therapy pals at the psychiatric hospital. And records show that Larsson owns a 1996 Ford Bronco. Larsson is still in medium-security lockup, but he left his vehicle with his girlfriend, a rugged blonde named Arlene Johansson, who also owns a Harley, a van, and a furniture-repair business. Records show that she visits her boyfriend with religious devotion.

It gets better. Her visiting hours coincide with Flint's mother's. And she lives not far from a wig shop where, if the owner is correct, Daryl Wayne Flint recently purchased three wigs. The connections are too thick to ignore.

But unfortunately, Arlene Johansson is proving uncooperative. After following her home from work, Blankenship stopped her outside her house. He identified himself and asked to take a look around.

"Hell, no," Johansson replied, shutting the door in his face.

The warrant has taken longer than he'd hoped, but now Blankenship is primed to make an arrest. He approaches the house armed and outfitted in protective gear. Six other armed agents are in position, ready to take down their fugitive by force.

Blankenship pounds on the door. "Arlene Johansson! FBI! Open the door."

She swings the door wide and stands with a hand on her hip. "I told you, he's not here. Jesus, don't you people listen?"

He hands her the search warrant and tells her to step aside.

"This is ridiculous. You think I'd have a murderer in my house? Christ, don't track mud in here. Wipe your feet, would you, please?"

She purses her lips and watches with a hostile attitude as the agents stream from room to room. When they find no one, she says, "See? I told you he wasn't here. Now, would you please leave?"

But they next approach a side door, and she blocks their way. "I don't want you going in there. Stay out of my garage."

"Step aside," Blankenship says, restraining himself from giving her a hard shove.

"Jesus Christ, no one is in there," she grumbles, moving aside.

Anticipating an arrest, Blankenship nods at the team leader, who gets into position and bursts through the door. Three men rush into the garage as Arlene Johansson hollers, "Don't touch anything! Don't you dare touch anything!"

The garage is crammed with furniture, including a bright pink dresser sitting atop a drop cloth with up-ended pink drawers arranged around it like sentinels. There's a strong odor of paint.

"Dammit, that's still wet," she snaps.

A large dehumidifier chugs away in the corner as the men continue their search, pulling aside plastic sheeting, uncovering bed frames, tables, and other furniture along the walls.

"Hey, I try to keep this place dust free, all right? Is that a crime?"

Blankenship faces the woman. "You have a vehicle registered to Sven Larsson here. A 1996 Ford Bronco?"

"Well, it's not in the garage, obviously. It's around back."

Three armed agents file out the back door and into the yard, where they find the vehicle up on blocks, rusty, and cannibalized for parts.

Blankenship hustles his team out of there. They shed their Kevlar and compare theories on the way back to Seattle.

His mood goes from bad to worse when he arrives back at the office and finds a bunch of nosy civilians waiting for him. Not only is Reeve LeClaire in some kind of snit, but Milo Bender and his son are now rallied behind her, tall and adamant, like a pair of damn Vikings. His first instinct is to have Nikki Keswick handle them, but she's off somewhere, probably having dinner.

With scarcely any time to collect his thoughts, he tells them to sit down and keep it brief.

Reeve shares some crackpot idea about Dr. Moody's former assistant being some kind of coconspirator.

He grunts in response. "Cybil Abbott? We questioned her the day after Moody's body was found. She's clean."

Reeve narrows her eyes at him—as if he would lie about a thing like that—and launches into some theory about how Cybil Abbott is guilty of something just because she and Flint's mother happened to have a conversation or two during her son's trial.

"Are you kidding me?" Blankenship says.

"Come on," Reeve says. "You must have found something linking her and Mrs. Pratt to the storage unit." She barely takes a breath before she's off on another wild-ass idea about a link between Flint's mother and the storage unit, simply because it was on Church Street.

Blankenship interrupts, saying, "Your supposition that Mrs. Pratt may or may not have mentioned a church wedding to her son is awfully thin proof of any involvement. Especially since it was a male that rented that place."

"But you can't completely rule out his mother," she insists. "She's as slippery as he is."

He almost makes a crude remark, but stops himself. They don't need to know about Mrs. Pratt's handful of arrests for prostitution over the years. What bearing does it have on this case? So poor Daryl Wayne had a crappy childhood. Big whoop.

"You should at least make her take a lie detector test," Reeve is saying.

Blankenship turns to Bender, looking for help. "We can't force the woman to take a polygraph, you know that."

Bender at least shows some sense. "He's right about that. There's nothing to show that Mrs. Pratt had a role in her son's escape. The forensic auditors went through all her receipts. She had no connection to the storage unit, and she never used credit cards near Olshaker except when she was there during scheduled visits."

Blankenship pinches the bridge of his nose. His head is pounding and he's got a ton of paperwork ahead of him. "If there's nothing else, I've got work to do," he says, and wastes no time shooing them out of his office.

FIFTY-TWO

Tacoma, Washington

Flint's mother knows who's calling the instant the number lights up on her phone. She nearly says, "Hello, Cybil," but catches herself, remembering that her phone is likely tapped.

"Mrs. Pratt?" says Cybil's familiar voice. "Your friend Zola asked me to call. She's in the hospital and she's asking if you can stop by."

"When?"

"Now."

Mrs. Pratt bites back a nasty comment and plays along. "I'm sorry to hear that Zola is back in the hospital so soon," she says, using their code. "It hasn't been very long."

"Yeah, but she really needs your help."

Mrs. Pratt tells her she's on her way and hangs up, irritated that Cybil has called. That blond bitch thinks she's being clever. She imagines that she is going to casually buy a vial of pills while prying loose information about Daryl's whereabouts. That hefty reward has stirred her juices, it's clear as day.

Mrs. Pratt reviews the phone call in her mind, worrying that it was a mistake to involve Cybil, which had been Daryl's dumb idea.

It all started with an idle exchange during visiting hours one day. "Who owns that gorgeous Audi in the parking lot?" she'd asked her son.

When he said it was Dr. Moody's, she remarked, "Well that's some doozy of a scratch in the side. Who'd he piss off?"

Daryl had apparently made a point of finding out during his next psychotherapy session, for an opportunity was born.

A woman scorned, and all that.

"Remember that hot blonde from the trial?" he asked. "You two were buddies, weren't you?"

"Hardly," she said, though it was true that she'd cultivated a relationship with Cybil. "We shared a few drinks, but we didn't stay in touch."

He gave her that lizard look of his, saying, "I need you to give her a call."

She hadn't guessed what he was up to, but at Daryl's insistence, she'd managed to rekindle her relationship with Cybil. She set it up innocently enough: Just a brief call to get reacquainted, a friendly chat, a lunch, and the offer of some illicit pharmaceuticals.

"Still having trouble sleeping?" she'd asked, pretending sympathy. "I can help with that."

Of course, Mrs. Pratt made sure there was no link between the two women, other than a few calls like this one, placed from one of the few remaining pay phones at Tacoma General. That was clever, if she says so herself. A woman of her age would likely have friends calling from the medical center from time to time. It had been a safe place to meet, and the arrangement had served both their needs. Cybil's various complaints got treated, and Mrs. Pratt pocketed some extra folding money. Simple.

But not long after she'd reported that to Daryl, he surprised her with another strange request. Glancing around the visiting room, he'd leaned forward and whispered, "I need you to call Walter Wertz. Tell him we're on for Plan B."

She lights a cigarette, thinking about the day she'd first laid eyes on Walter. He was a dangerous young man—all hard muscle, smelling of hormones and campfire.

It was the same summer that hot-tempered husband of hers had broken Daryl's arm. Don had decided there was need of another pair of hands up at the lake, and so he'd dragged her along, though she hated camping. "Nothing but dirt and fish guts," she said. But he left her no choice.

Walter showed up just after they'd pitched their tent. The three males had apparently made acquaintance the previous summer. But Walter calmly informed Daryl's father that they'd strayed onto his land.

"You'll have to pack up and move back down the road to the public campground," he said.

Don took issue with that. He argued that they were in a national forest, that they had every right to camp wherever they liked.

The two men were standing toe-to-toe, and it was clear they were about to fight. Then she came out of the tent and stepped between them, putting a hand on each chest.

Pretty soon, Walter was showing up whenever Don took the Chevy for a run into town. Sometimes, she'd cook dinner for him—until Don found out and beat her with his belt, that mean son of a bitch.

One night toward the end of summer, while Don was off buying liquor and cigarettes, she'd invited Walter to join her inside the tent. She was still pretty enough to attract a young buck. But if she was expecting to tame him, he certainly surprised her. He'd already worked out a whole scenario in his head.

It took all of two seconds for her to agree. It satisfied them both, didn't it? And it wasn't as if her sorry excuse for a husband had a regular job or a boss who would miss him.

The next day, Donald Flint was just a bad memory. And once all the evidence was tidied up and the authorities were convinced, she sent her boy off to live with his "Uncle Walter."

What Wertz saw in the boy she couldn't fathom. Maybe he just liked bossing him around. It was comic, the way the kid jumped to attention every time Walter showed up, ready to fetch and carry. So unlike his usual sullen self.

"My favorite helper," Walter called him.

It was a nice arrangement. After being relieved of her abusive husband and her quarrelsome son, she'd been free to do exactly as she pleased. At least, until the money ran out. Then she'd had to scramble to make ends meet, until finding Pratt, a long-faced pharmacist whose profession was his primary virtue.

Over the years, it had seemed wise not to have much contact with Walter or her son, other than the odd transfer of required school forms. Their agreement was that there would be no official record of "Uncle Walter." And once Daryl had grown to match Walter's height, those two became so secretive—like twins speaking a shared language—that she'd made sure to keep her distance. They were a menacing pair.

She hadn't seen Walter for ages until that day he showed up at her house months ago. It had never occurred to her that he even knew her address until she stepped out of the shower and smelled the smoke of his cigar.

She tied her robe tight around her and found him sitting in her living room, looking bigger, heavier, more intimidating than ever.

"Hey, Connie. Nice place you got here." He sucked on his cigar and blew smoke in her direction, smiling.

Walter lost no time in reminding her that they had a shared interest in getting Daryl away from the prying questions and greedy ears at that loathsome psychiatric hospital. "Your part is simple," he told her. "I've got everything set up. All you need to do is relay information back to Daryl."

She wasn't crazy about the risk of getting involved. But Walter wasn't a man to cross.

He showed up at odd times—always unexpected—asking about Daryl's progress. Each time, he seemed more threatening than the last.

She stepped up her visits to Olshaker, greasing the wheels of her son's escape, but had no desire to know the full scope of whatever scheme those two males had concocted. She kept her role to a minimum, remaining scarcely more than a courier of information.

Once all the wheels were set in motion, Walter suddenly went quiet. Daryl seemed to have expected this. He responded to the news with a hungry gleam. But her son remained unreadable, so she made sure to remain alert for the stink of Walter's cigar.

Of course, Walter's plan had not included anything about Dr. Moody. That was something Daryl cooked up all on his own. When her son snagged on the idea that he needed a map and key to Moody's house, she tried to warn him that it was reckless, but he wouldn't listen. Anyway, he was correct about Cybil being more than happy to oblige.

Mrs. Pratt had simply given Cybil the security codes for getting into Church Street Storage and told her to leave an envelope inside the unit. She had no intention of stepping even one foot inside that place.

Who knows what motivated her son to kill Dr. Moody—something to do with his fixation on that ridiculous LeClaire girl, no doubt—but at least Daryl isn't betraying any more secrets about his daddy.

Dead and buried and in the past.

Unfortunately, since she was Daryl's sole visitor at Olshaker, she is the one under scrutiny. And there's no way she's going to yield to pressure and take a polygraph. She's no fool. She puts out her cigarette, thinking that no matter how hard the FBI might press, they'll find nothing linking her to her son's escape, and not a scrap of paper connecting her with Walter Wertz. Nothing!

The problem now is that Cybil is sniffing around, trying to find out where Daryl is hiding, thanks to that fat reward. And Cybil may not be all that smart, but she could sure stir up trouble.

Mrs. Pratt checks the time, irked that she must rush off to meet with that meddlesome twat. As she's slipping into her leopard-print heels, an idea blooms.

Cybil has served her purpose. Now that girl is a loose end, and loose ends must be eliminated.

Mrs. Pratt opens a drawer and rummages through her private collection of pill vials, one of the perks of being a pharmacist's wife. She finds a bottle of zolpidem, a generic sleeping aid, and another of fentanyl tablets, a narcotic more potent than morphine. She slips on a pair of latex gloves, wipes her fingerprints off the bottles, and carefully exchanges the contents.

FIFTY-THREE

Seattle, Washington

Daryl Wayne Flint is getting antsy. The windows of Milo Bender's split-level home have stayed dark, and his little cricket has not appeared. Meanwhile, this is the one night of the year, as Wertz always said, that provides cover and opportunity—the hunter's necessities—and the clock is ticking.

Halloween, Hallo-week, Hallo-Wertz.

He checks his reflection in the rearview mirror, tilting his head from side to side. His beard has grown to stubble. He has darkened his eyes with black eyeliner. And with the bandanna covering his hair, and the black patch over one eye, he looks just like a pirate.

Johnny Depp, eat your heart out.

He stubs out his cigarette in the overflowing ashtray, turns the key in the ignition, and pulls away from the curb. Driving the Ford Bronco is a risk, but he's decided that, with the changed license plate and repaired headlight, it's a risk worth taking. This is a solid vehicle for the task at hand. And there must be thousands of brown or maroon SUVs like the one reported at Triangle Park.

A few minutes later, he's cruising slowly through a familiar neighborhood, scanning the sidewalks of what used to be prime hunting territory. Dusk has settled in and the streets should be streaming with trick-or-treaters, going door-to-door, filling up their bags with candy. But it's dead here tonight. Where are all the kids?

With a grunt, he decides it's time to relocate. As he's accelerating out of the neighborhood, a porch light comes on up ahead. He lifts his foot off the gas and slows to watch. The front door opens and children in costumes come spilling out. Two young boys and two older girls dressed in tights and tutus, one pink, one green.

He drives slowly past, watching the ballerinas come directly toward him, stepping with the delicacy of fawns.

Just beyond the house, he parks in the shadows where he can watch them in his rearview mirror. He cranes his neck—where did they go?—and hears car doors slamming.

An engine turns over. Headlights come on in the driveway of the children's home. A red sedan backs out. As it drives past, he glimpses the girls giggling in the backseat.

Perhaps they're headed to a neighborhood with denser homes and a reputation for better candy. He pulls away from the curb, following at a distance.

The sedan winds downhill and turns onto a busy street where Flint is caught behind a slow-moving van. He curses, afraid he's going to lose them, but sees the flash of red as the sedan turns right. He speeds up to catch them, following the car downhill and into the village, where the streets are well lit and the main street is blocked off for pedestrians only.

It's hard to find a place to park. He cruises the side streets, searching, until an SUV pulls out and he claims the spot.

He checks his reflection. A perfect pirate grins back at him. Then he opens a box and checks the items inside: the gag, the handcuffs, the blindfold, and the stun gun. He pockets the stun gun, closes the box, and heads out to have a look around.

Costumed children and adults stream along the sidewalks as he finds himself in the midst of some kind of Halloween festival. He scans past the cowboys, robots, and superheros, past the angels and fairies, searching.

Up ahead, the pink and green tutus wink at him. He jostles through the crowd, following as the pair turns left into a shop. He heads toward the same doorway.

The moment he steps inside, he hears: "Ahoy, pirate! How about some cider?"

A tall man in a fake beard and a stovepipe hat offers Flint a brimming paper cup.

Flint accepts the beverage, muttering his thanks, and turns away, scanning the store for the girls. The aisles are packed.

"Just call me Honest Abe." The man in the stovepipe hat hovers at his elbow.

"Abraham Lincoln. Got it." Flint gives him a tight smile and sidles away, sipping the cider, blending in. He spots the girls at the checkout counter, where a woman in a witch outfit is handing out candy.

"Thank you!" the girls chime in unison.

"It's not like when you and I were kids, is it?" The man in the stovepipe hat is again at his elbow.

"Uh, no, things have sure changed."

"I kinda miss the old days, with the trick-or-treaters going door-to-door."

"Uh-huh," Flint says distractedly. The girls are coming down the brightly lit aisle toward him.

"But this is great for our downtown businesses," the man continues.

The girls pass so close that their tutus brush Flint's thighs, sparking heat in his groin. He watches with longing as they disappear out the door.

The man in the hat says, "Plus, it's safer for the kids, you know?"

Flint swallows the last of his drink, crushes the cup, and heads out to resume the hunt.

As he's walking back to his car, he spots a bar and decides he needs to quench his frustration with a real drink. It's too crowded for his tastes. But while he's finishing his drink, eyeing all the young bodies in their tight costumes, he decides to check out the trick-or-treaters in Reggie's old neighborhood.

Strawberry Lane has grown quiet by the time he arrives, but lights are on at the Tudor-style house. As luck would have it, the door opens and out steps a petite girl in a curly wig and short skirt. She hurries to her Pontiac and starts up the car. He easily follows behind, guessing that this must be Reggie's cute friend, the one with honey-colored hair and the little gap between her front teeth.

FIFTY-FOUR

Three Bucks Bar

Years ago, Three Bucks Bar used to host an annual Hallow-whiskey drinking contest, but in a rare moment of sobriety, the owner realized that posed a serious risk of lawsuit. Now the Halloween celebration is more low-key, with the bartenders instructed to pour and smile for patrons right up until last call, but then to offer coffee to the heavy drinkers and stop serving alcohol at midnight.

Adding a festive atmosphere, lights are strung through the antlers of the three bucks mounted above the bar. Plastic jack-o'-lanterns glow atop the tables. And the bartenders are encouraged to dress in silly costumes.

Gunther, whose only nod to the holiday is a top hat and a tuxedo-printed T-shirt, is chagrined to realize that he has been tending bar here for six years. For six Halloweens, he's been wiping up spills, cleaning up vomit, and sweeping up broken glass.

How did he end up living on tips? He did pretty well in school. He's reasonably good-looking and has a better-than-average singing voice. He's great with cars, kids, and dogs. But women, unfortunately, are a lot more complicated. Especially the pretty ones. And here comes Jenna to remind him of this fact.

Jenna has been coming in pretty regularly since she turned twenty-one. But she's a single mother with a two-year-old son. Young. Divorced. Mother. Now, that's the *trifecta* of complicated.

Plus, she's living with her parents. That's worse. That's complicated *squared*.

Tonight she's wearing a wig of extravagant yellow curls and is poured into a tight, short costume of ruffles. Gunther can scarcely look at her without wondering how a hot little package like Jenna could be walking into this dive of a bar.

"Hey, Gunther," she says, climbing onto a bar stool. "Isn't that the same costume you wore last year?"

"Yeah, I'm dressed as a bartender. What about you, Jenna?"

"Guess," she says, grinning at him while playing with her necklace.

"Gee, I don't know. You look so young. A hot schoolgirl?"

"No." She shakes her curls.

"A living doll?"

She chirps a laugh. "Do you want a hint? Look at my necklace." She leans forward, holding out the plastic figures affixed to her cheap jewelry.

Trying not to stare at her cleavage, he says, "What? Are those bears?"

"Yeeeeahhs," she says, drawing out the word meaningfully.

"Oh, I get it. Goldilocks and the three bears, right?"

"There you go."

"Nice," he says. "You look great. So what would you like, Goldie? What would be juuuuust right?"

She rewards him with a wonderful little laugh that sounds downright musical. "I don't know. Something different. I'm bored with beer and wine."

"How about a margarita?"

"No, too sour."

"Or a daiquiri?"

"Too sweet."

They share a laugh, and Gunther is just about to suggest his own special concoction, called the "Tree Slammer," when some jerk wearing a pirate costume butts in, saying, "Have you ever tried Jägermeister?"

Jenna turns to the guy, giving him a big smile. "No, what is that?"

"It's something different, like you said."

"Really different?"

"Totally, completely different, with some special recipe with herbs and ginger and stuff like that. Trust me, you'll like it." The guy holds up two fingers and nods at Gunther, then turns back to Jenna, adding, "And if you don't like it, we'll just keep trying until we find something that's juuuust right."

And damned if Jenna doesn't reward the guy in that stupid getup with her same delightful laugh.

Jenna's mother was right: It's dumb to try to flirt with a bartender, even if he seems nice. Jenna has been trying to get Gunther's attention for over a year, but he sets her drink in front of her with hardly a smile.

If this costume isn't working, then it's just not going to happen. . . . Unless he's jealous of this pirate guy?

Liking the idea, she laughs at something stupid the pirate says. Then she takes a sip of the drink.

"It's an acquired taste, isn't it?" she says, wrinkling her nose. "It tastes kinda like medicine."

She takes another sip, thinking: Face it Jenna, you've totally screwed up your life.

"Not totally," she can almost hear her mother say. "You're still young. Once the baby is in preschool, you can finish your education, get a degree."

"So, Goldilocks, what do you do?" the pirate is asking.

"I'm a student," she lies. No way is she telling anybody tonight that she's got a two-year-old at home. She knows how that conversation goes: A baby? Really? And then before she can stop herself, she'll start showing off pictures on her phone, and then she'll begin ranting about her loser ex-husband. Better not go there.

"I'm studying to become a medical assistant," she tells the pirate. "What do you do?"

"I've just finished building a home near here. It's a showpiece, but it needs a woman's touch." He leers at her.

There's something about this guy she doesn't like.

"That's a great costume. Three bears, ha, ha, ha," he says.

She manages a weak smile, wishing Gunther would rescue her, but he's busy with other customers.

Forget it, girl. He's just not that into you.

Next year, Halloween will be a lot more fun. Next year, her baby boy will be big enough to enjoy it. She can dress him up like Spider-Man and introduce him to trick-or-treating. But she won't let him have too much candy. Ought to take that slow for as long as possible. Avoid the sugar high.

"I like your freckles. You look good enough to eat," the pirate guy says.

He's breathing on her. It's creeping her out.

"Thanks for the drink," she tells him, getting her heels under her and sliding off the bar stool. "But I've got to get going. I promised my mom I'd be home in an hour."

She grabs her purse and tries to catch Gunther's eye, but he's at the other end of the bar, talking to a tall blonde in a tight devil outfit. Great.

She's out the door and halfway to her car before she realizes that the pirate guy is following her. "Good night, thanks again for the drink," she calls a little too brightly while hurrying to her Pontiac.

She's just opening the door when the pirate rushes over saying, "Hey, Goldie, don't run off so fast. Wouldn't you like to see my place?"

Is he joking? He didn't even bother to ask her name. She's just about to make a smart remark when she's hit by a searing pain that jolts her off her feet.

It's nearly one o'clock before Gunther manages to shoo the last of the patrons out of the bar. He's been steadily cleaning tables and straightening up since he stopped pouring at midnight, so there's not much left to do other than sweep the floor and take out the trash.

He gathers the jack-o'-lanterns and puts them in a crate in the back. Tomorrow, he'll add the rest of the Halloween decorations. Then Thanksgiving and Christmas and New Year's Eve are right around the corner. Crap, he can hardly believe he's wasted another year here. He's got to find another job. Maybe next spring he'll move to Alaska. Yeah, they say there's good work up there.

It doesn't take long to sweep the floor. No messes tonight. Luckily, nobody puked.

When he's finished, Gunther pours himself one quick shot of Grey Goose—he doesn't get paid enough to go home without some kind of perk—and sips it while counting his tips. Then he shuts off the lights, locks the door, and heads out toward his pickup truck.

The sight of Jenna Dutton's car stops him. He recognizes the Pontiac immediately. He shakes his head, disgusted at the thought that she's gone home with that stupid pirate, and turns toward his vehicle, but then stops and turns back again, considering.

She didn't seem drunk, but more than once, he's found a customer passed out in the front seat. Better than driving drunk, but still, a person can choke on their own vomit.

He crunches across the gravel toward the Pontiac, figuring it's worth checking out.

Peering through the driver's window, he can see that the car is empty.

Okay, fine. Score one for the stupid pirate.

He turns back toward his truck with a grunt, but at the same instant a tune starts up, a cheerful melody carrying through the night.

Gunther freezes, recognizing the ringtone.

He glances around, then drops to his hands and knees, searching beneath the car. It's dark as hell, but the cell phone pulses brightly, shining through the cloth of Jenna Dutton's purse.

FIFTY-FIVE

Seattle, Washington

Shortly past dawn, Reeve hears footsteps in the hallway. She lies still and listens. It's Milo Bender's gait, but his tread is different. He's not wearing slippers. She pictures another sole, running shoes, perhaps.

The footsteps approach her door and she expects a knock, but then there's a pause and a hushed sound. The footsteps creep back down the hallway. A moment later, the front door opens and clicks closed.

She cannot hear his footsteps on the path, but then a car door shuts, an engine turns over, and as Milo Bender drives away, she rises from the bed to fetch the note that he has slipped under her door.

Dear Reeve,

Forgive me for saying good-bye with this brief note. Something has come up that I need to research—perhaps nothing, but it's on my mind and I couldn't live with myself if I failed to check it out.

Forgive me also for not driving you to the airport. If you'd like to call JD, I'm sure he would love the chance to say good-bye.

I can't tell you what a pleasure it has been having you stay with us these past few days, even under these difficult circumstances. Yvonne and I both hope you'll come again during happier times. (She has an early yoga class, by the way, so perhaps you'd like to join her.)

Safe travels, regards to your family, and please come back and visit soon!

MB

She folds the note and presses it between her palms, touched by his words.

After a shower, she gets dressed, makes the bed, and quickly packs her bags, feeling unsettled about leaving. But no amount of argument could persuade her father that she should stay.

"You've accomplished everything and more than anyone could ask," he'd said. "It's time for you to come home."

As she's heading toward the kitchen, she notices a light on in the den and peeks inside. It's empty, but she immediately senses something different about the room. What has changed?

The desktop is just as strewn with files and notes as before. Curious, she circles the room, and her eyes come back to the desk.

The office chair, which is usually angled toward the cluttered desktop, is now facing the computer. She puts a hand on it. Warm.

She sits in the chair and nudges the mouse. The computer blinks to life— *Hello Milo*—and challenges her for a password.

She sits back, crossing her arms. She hasn't a clue what his password might be.

Yvonne is stirring in the kitchen, and she would hate to get caught snooping, so she creeps back to the bedroom to boot up her laptop.

A minute later, Yvonne knocks and whispers, "Good morning, Reeve. Are you up?"

Reeve answers brightly and opens the door.

Yvonne grins at her. She's dressed for exercise, a rolled yoga mat tucked under one arm. "I've got a great yoga teacher if you'd like to come along."

Being simultaneously polite and closemouthed proves difficult. But luckily, Yvonne is in a rush to get to her yoga class. The second she's out the door, Reeve starts scanning headlines.

Bender was investigating something, no doubt. What did he find that compelled him to leave this morning?

She understands the moment she sees the headline: "Seattle Woman Vanishes." The article says a young mother disappeared last night from outside Three Bucks Bar, and Reeve gasps at the photo of Jenna Dutton.

FIFTY-SIX

Reeve tries to explain in a rush, but JD just seems more and more confused. In a low voice, he coaxes her to the kitchen table, hands her a glass of water, and asks if she's had anything to eat.

"I don't need to eat. I need you to drive me to Tacoma. Please? Can you?"

"Tacoma? Why?"

"Because he's doing it again. Didn't you read the news?"

"Yes, about the woman who disappeared last night? Of course, after you called—and woke me up, I might add—I read all about it."

"That's Flint. That's him, there's absolutely no question."

"But isn't he a pedophile? It doesn't make sense."

She needs him to understand, so she starts again. "Listen, Jenna Dutton was my best friend in middle school, and we lived just a few doors apart, so it's my fault that he took her, now do you get it? And she was kidnapped from Three Bucks Bar, so it's all connected."

What is that look he's giving her? Disbelief? Pity?

"Okay. . . ." He takes a breath and says in a placating tone, "So I understand that you're upset, but, listen, why don't we call—"

"The FBI? I did that already. I called Nikki Keswick after I talked to you. They know all about it. They're investigating."

"Okay. Good. So could you please explain why a trip to Tacoma is necessary?"

"Because Flint's mother lives there and she knows! We need to talk to her," she says, thumping the table.

"Flint's mother? What does she know?"

"I don't know, but it's *something*." She sets a piece of paper on the table and nudges it toward him. "Look at this."

He glances at her scribbled notes. "What exactly is this?"

"It's a network, a diagram."

"It doesn't look like—"

"Okay, it's more right brain than left brain, but look, everything makes perfect sense."

He frowns at the confusion of lines, arrows, and interlacing circles, so she taps on the paper, urging him to understand. "Here's Flint, see? Here's Dr. Moody, and here's the accomplice, and here's Mrs. Pratt, Flint's mother. Everything connects *here*, with his escape, and she's the only one who visited him while he was locked up. She *knows*, okay?"

"But I'm still missing something. Why do you want to talk to her?"

"I don't *want* to. It's not that. It's that I *have* to. I know it sounds crazy, but I'm sure she's the key. If I'd talked to her sooner, maybe Flint would be locked up by now." Reeve gnashes her teeth with frustration. This is life or death. Why can't he see that? Trying to sound calm, she says, "I've got her number, so I'll call and set it up. But we need to hurry."

"Um, okay, I can take you," he says, frowning. "But let's look at this logically. Flint's mother has already been questioned, right? And it stands to reason that the bureau has her under investigation."

"Which makes it even more important that I talk to her."

"Why?"

"Because they're getting nowhere."

"But what makes you think she'll even talk to you?"

"Because I'm not a threat to her. I'm not a cop or an agent. Besides, it's a game for her. I'm the reason her son went to prison, which made *her* look bad. And she can't resist pouring salt in my wounds. It's her nature."

The memory is like a knife, still sharp after all these years.

Reeve had steered clear of Flint's mother during the trial until that one afternoon when she'd encountered her in the restroom. She can still picture the sinister way Mrs. Pratt looked at her while lighting her cigarette. She squinted at Reeve as though seeing through her clothes and counting every scar, then smiled at the glowing tip of her cigarette and said, "My boy sure left his mark on you, didn't he?"

Reeve stared at the woman for a long, stunned moment before fleeing the restroom. With those hateful words still ringing in her ears, she'd charged straight into a pack of reporters, where she'd swatted at news cameras, her cheeks aflame, her humiliation recorded for all time.

"Are you all right?" JD asks, peering at her. "Maybe we should call my dad?"

"I tried that. No answer. We need to go." She jumps to her feet, knocking her chair to the wall.

"But won't you miss your flight?"

"I'll get my luggage. Just drive, okay?"

FIFTY-SEVEN

Olympia, Washington

Milo Bender hates lying to his wife, so he has turned off his phone. He knows she'll be calling to ask if he's remembered to take his pills, and the truth is, he was halfway to Olympia before he even thought of them.

Still, it's okay if he misses a day. Hell, he's got so much medication in his system by now, it would probably take a week before he'd drop to normal blood levels.

Of course, Yvonne would not share this opinion, but if he doesn't talk to her, he doesn't have to lie.

He'd slipped out of bed at dawn, telling her to go back to sleep, saying only that he was "curious about something, following up some leads."

True enough.

She didn't need to know that he was getting an early start so he could drive south to Olympia. Or that, just as a precaution, he was carrying the gun that he bought shortly after relinquishing his government-issued weapon upon retirement.

The Glock fits nicely into his old shoulder holster.

Bender has resolved that he will explain everything to her tonight, in person, when he gets home. But not on the phone.

At this point, it seems best to keep his plans to himself. If he's wrong, no big deal.

What he'd learned yesterday had sparked the idea. When Blankenship mentioned that headlight fragments had been traced to a Ford Bronco, he'd almost said, "You know, I staked out Flint's house for a lot of hours, watching vehicles come and go, recording license plates. I could go back through my records."

But then he'd got the message, loud and clear, that Blankenship was working on a hot lead and it wasn't his place to interfere. He would have felt the same way when he was a case agent.

Still, an idea had nagged at him. It woke him up early and wouldn't let him sleep, so he got up and went into his den, where he scoured through notebooks from years ago. When the FBI was having no luck linking their toughest missing persons cases to registered sex offenders, Bender had decided to cast a wider net, looking at minor violations. That's when Daryl Wayne Flint's name had first popped up on his radar.

Flint had Peeping Tom complaints against him, starting when he was a teenager, plus a dropped sexual-assault charge from when he was a student at the University of Washington.

Bender hadn't liked the smell of the guy. Never married. A loner in a big house. And when it turned out that Flint didn't live far from Reggie LeClaire's family, Bender had paid him a visit. He'd gone through his trash. He'd watched the house. He'd noted the vehicles of all Flint's visitors. But he'd never found enough to gain a warrant.

Maybe it was ancient history, but Bender thought he remembered something. So he pored over his old notebooks, and sure enough, he found a license plate number with "brown Ford Bronco" written next to it.

All those years ago, he had traced the registration and came up with a name—Walter Wertz—plus an address in Olympia. The guy's record must have been clean, because Bender can't remember anything about him.

It might be nothing. So, if this trip to Olympia is a waste of time, no one needs to know.

On the other hand, if he finds anything significant, he'll speak to Stuart Cox as soon as he can. In person. Because those damn cell phones only complicate things. They're unreliable. They're always jumbling your words or cutting you off. And Bender hates admitting it to the chatty young people, but his hearing isn't as good as it once was. All that shooting practice takes a toll.

So now his phone is shut off and tucked into the glove compartment, where it can't cause problems while he's out doing something that, yes, could be technically illegal.

But, hell, Milo Bender had dedicated more than twenty years of his life to toeing the line and doing everything by the book, following the bureau's rules to the letter. He never did anything rash, which seemed smart at the time.

But now he's not particularly proud of that fact. Now he's retired, answering only to his conscience. And shouldn't someone named Bender be able to bend the rules once in a while?

Bender finds the address, drives past, and parks just down the street. He puts on his gloves and approaches on foot, noting that "Wertz" is stenciled on the mailbox. With a yard of unraked leaves, the house seems neglected, but he notes that tire tracks lead to and from the garage.

No lights are on and the drapes don't stir as he climbs the front steps. He raps loudly on the door and rings the bell. He waits. He tries the door. No one home and it's locked up tight.

He leaves the front porch and goes around to the back, letting himself through the gate. The house stays quiet—and Reeve isn't the only one who has studied entrance and egress—so he finds a wheelbarrow and rolls it around to the side of the garage, where he's well hidden from any neighbors.

He turns it over beneath a window and climbs atop it, steadying himself against the house. The window screen comes off easily and he sets it down on the damp grass.

Facing the window, he cups his gloved hands around his eyes and holds his breath so as not to fog the glass. The inside of the garage is dimly lit. He can make out clutter, but it's vacant. He sucks his teeth in disappointment at not finding either Dr. Moody's black SUV or a brown Ford Bronco.

He works the thin blade of a modified grapefruit knife between the window's metal frames and lifts the latch. The window slides open. He grips the ledge, hoists himself up and over, and scrambles inside, knocking something to the floor.

He freezes, listening.

Far away, a dog barks. . . . Then the stillness returns. Bender's eyes adjust to the dark interior and he locates the door that leads into the house. As he's turning back to slide the window closed, he kicks something with his toe—the empty plastic container that he knocked to the floor—which he quietly returns to its place on the shelf.

He pulls out his weapon and takes a breath, preparing for trouble as he approaches the door. The doorknob turns easily, and he peeks inside. A laundry room.

Scuff marks on the floor beside the washer and dryer look recent.

He creeps forward and enters the kitchen. A few plates in the sink, an inch of cold coffee in the bottom of a cup. He stands still and listens for a long moment.

The house remains silent.

He moves from the kitchen to the den. Also empty, except for the mounted heads of a dozen animals. Somebody's a hunter, and proud of it.

Bender creeps from room to room, searching expertly, moving with stealth and speed, gun ready for any potential threat. When he's certain the house is empty, he returns the gun to his shoulder holster, ready for a second pass. This time, he looks more closely, checking doors and cupboards and floorboards, looking for locked rooms or a trap door, anyplace where Flint could have stashed young Jenna Dutton.

Once he has searched the house a second time, he returns to the den and, ignoring the staring eyes of the dead animals, scans the room, taking its measure. Something is off. He moves to the adjacent room, which is dominated by a mahogany dining table, and stands in the doorway, studying the wall between the two rooms.

He stiffens, then creeps back to the den. Ignoring his arthritic knees, he lowers into a crouch and examines the carpet. Footsteps seem to disappear into the middle of the floor-to-ceiling bookshelves.

Bender again unholsters his gun. Silently, he approaches the bookshelf, placing his boots inside the indentations. A half-step to the right, on the underside of a shelf at hip level, he finds the button. Holding his gun ready, he pushes it.

The door slides open and lights flicker on. The room is narrow and windowless. Bender scans the table, cabinets, shelves. There are books and several cameras of various types. Long, telephoto lenses. Boxes of high-quality photograph paper and a large printer.

In one corner stands a polished gun case, empty. Are Wertz and Flint out hunting?

Bender peruses the titles on the bookshelves. Yearbooks. High schools, middle schools, elementary schools. Shelves full of them, dating back years.

A cold comprehension falls upon him.

One yearbook lies open on the table, and something catches in his throat as he recognizes a schoolgirl photo of Reggie LeClaire.

Beside the yearbook is a file folder marked with a large "D." Bender scans the papers inside, stops at a property tax document. He studies the information, memorizes it, and closes the file. Leaving everything exactly as it was, he steps out of the room and pushes the button so that the secret door slides closed behind him.

Moments later, he's climbing back out the garage window. He closes it tight, fetches the window screen, and fits it back into place. He turns the wheelbarrow upright and rolls it around the side of the house, returning it to its spot beneath the overhang.

His slick tracks in the damp grass are already disappearing by the time Bender has crossed the street, climbed into his vehicle, and settled behind the wheel. He adjusts his glasses and checks the map, intent on locating the best route to the remote property owned by Walter Wertz.

FIFTY-EIGHT

Cascade Mountains

Last night, he'd been elated by his success. One quick zap and she dropped like a dead cat.

No one saw him wrestle her limp body onto the passenger seat. He quickly got her secure, then got away, clean as you please.

But things started going south once he got her back to the cabin. Even by the kerosene lantern's sputtering flame, he could see the hideous tattoos covering her shoulders and back.

A skin artist needs a clean canvas, but her skin was ruined, useless.

By this morning's light, he sees that it's even worse. She has an ugly C-section scar across her lower abdomen.

"Ugly, ugly, ugly," he grumbles. He couldn't even get hard after seeing her naked.

That's what he gets for grabbing an old one, but the young ones are so goddamn skittish these days, with their cell phones and their meddling mothers. It used to be so much easier.

Now the question is, what the hell is he supposed to do with her? There's no damn way he's going to waste energy keeping this one alive.

"Cover yourself up, I can't stand to look at you," he says, throwing a sheet at her.

She grabs at it awkwardly with handcuffed hands and he slams the closet door.

He stomps back and forth across the floor, pacing like a caged beast. Then he hears Wertz's voice in his ear, telling him he'd better get started. He shoulders on a warm jacket, grabs his gloves, and heads outside.

The temperature has dropped and the air smells like snow. He tips his head back and puffs a breath toward the low ceiling of clouds. The cold feels good on his face.

There's a lot of work to do, but last night's binge has cost him, and a heavy ache fills his skull. He decides to fix himself something to eat first.

He fetches a load of firewood and carries it inside, where he stacks it next to the woodstove. Opening the metal door, he finds that the embers have died. He places kindling and logs inside, wads up a few papers from Dr. Moody's file, and crams them into the crevasses. He lights the paper and watches his secrets burn while pondering the best way to dispose of the girl.

FIFTY-NINE

A single red flowerpot adorns the front steps of Mrs. Pratt's otherwise plain brown home. Reeve sits in JD's pickup, studying the house for a moment, but sees nothing distinctive about Flint's mother's suburban residence. Then she steels herself, climbs out of the vehicle, and joins JD at the curb.

They cross the street together and go through the short gate. The instant their shoes hit the walkway, a dog starts yapping, and the closer they come to the door, the more ferocious the barking becomes.

They mount the porch. The yapping increases in intensity, and the dog bangs against the door, trying to get at them. It's a small dog, given the height and tone of its noise. Reeve pictures its snarling teeth and rings the bell, which chimes while the barking becomes more vehement.

Reeve notes that the large, bright red flowerpot is brimming with cigarette butts.

JD leans close and whispers, "Maybe she's not home."

"Stop that!" cries a woman's voice. "Doodle, you stop right this minute!"

After some minor commotion, the door swings wide and there stands Mrs. Pratt, cradling the angry dog in her arms. Mrs. Pratt is tall and thin and dressed in a pink-and-black leopard print outfit. The dog has yellow fur and black lips that are stretched tight, baring its teeth.

"Here you are," she says to Reeve. She gives JD a flat look. "But I thought you'd come alone."

Reeve introduces JD while the dog yaps.

"Don't mind him. He'll calm down in a minute," Mrs. Pratt says, but this is a lie. The dog has a fit when she steps back to allow them inside.

"I wasn't expecting you quite so soon." She shows them into a living room crammed with dark, heavy furniture. The wood gleams, but the place smells of dog and cigarettes. She tells them to have a seat, and the dog struggles in her grasp, snapping at them as they edge past.

Reeve and JD sit on a swamp-colored sofa while Mrs. Pratt remains standing, holding the dog, watching them. The dog's and its owner's eyes shine, and it occurs to Reeve that Flint's mother enjoys making them squirm.

"Would you care for a drink?" Mrs. Pratt carries the dog over to a huge and ornate sideboard. "Port? Bourbon? Jägermeister?"

JD frowns. "It's awfully early, don't you think?"

Mrs. Pratt makes a dismissive sound. "Suit yourself." She pours herself a glass of something over ice and takes a sip, leaving a pink lipstick mark on the glass, then smacks her lips, all the while cradling the snarling dog in one arm.

"Doodle, you bad little man," she coos into the dog's ear. "Just calm down, will you?"

Flint's mother carries her drink and the dog closer to them and perches on the arm of an overstuffed armchair. She's a carefully groomed woman who might have been beautiful before years of smoking furrowed her complexion. Her eyebrows are drawn on, and she shows an extravagant taste in jewelry. Her rings seem to capture every bit of light, and Reeve wonders if they're as valuable as they look.

Mrs. Pratt sips from her glass, then eyes JD. "Your name is Bender, did you say? So you're related to that peculiar FBI agent with the same last name?"

When he answers that he is indeed Milo Bender's son, the dog snarls.

The woman gives the dog a pat, smiling. "Oh, I am so sorry, but Doodle sure doesn't like you." She sets her glass on an end table beside a stack of paperback books. "Let me just put my little mister in the next room."

Her heels click with purpose across the floor. Just out of sight, a door opens and shuts. The dog continues yapping while the heels click back toward them.

Reeve tips her head toward JD and murmurs, "Maybe this was a bad idea."

He gives her a look. "Ya think?"

Reeve catches herself rubbing the numb spot on her left hand and forces herself to stop.

"Now, I'm so very sorry to tell you," Mrs. Pratt says, settling again on the arm of the overstuffed chair, "but I really have no idea what my son might be up to. I've cooperated fully with the FBI and told them everything I know already." She rolls her eyes. "So I'm afraid your trip is wasted."

"But you were his only visitor at the hospital, weren't you?" JD asks.

She makes a *tsking* sound. "What a dreary place that is. Have you seen it? God, it will be a relief if I never have to go back there." Waving her glass so that the liquid sloshes, she looks around the room as if at an audience and pronounces, "You've no idea how difficult it is having a notorious criminal in the family. No one invites you to the country club, I'll tell you that for sure. It would suit me just fine if my son simply disappeared."

Reeve frowns at her. She'd been more convincing at her son's trial, taking the stand wearing nice clothes and subdued makeup. What makes this woman tick? The manipulative witch.

JD is saying, ". . . because a lot of people are putting a great deal of effort into locating him. He's killed two men and—"

"Why do you care?" Mrs. Pratt squints at him. "Are you a lawman, like your daddy?"

"Um, no ma'am."

"Oh, I see. I suppose you're after that reward is that it?" She coughs a laugh. "Well, no one would blame you. Seventy-five grand, that's a nice take."

Reeve finds her voice, "Mrs. Pratt, do you have any recollection of a place by a lake, maybe a cabin of some kind?"

"A what?" She gulps her drink.

"Someplace in the mountains?"

She purses her lips into a tight smile, looking at Reeve a beat too long before shaking her head.

"Maybe someplace your son went camping when he was young?"

"Camping?" That coughed laugh again. "Daryl was hardly a Boy Scout."

Reeve bites her cheek. She is trying to frame another question when Mrs. Pratt says, "By the way, I'm sorry about what happened to you."

Surprised, Reeve is trying to digest this when Mrs. Pratt continues, "But it wasn't so bad, was it, really? It made you famous, didn't it? I've seen you on TV. You're quite the little celebrity, aren't you?"

The floor seems to tilt.

"Anyway, let's face it, plenty of girls have trouble with men." Still smiling, she seems to be speaking to the ice cubes clinking in her glass. "So what? It happens. You get over it."

Their eyes meet, and something churns in Reeve's stomach.

"After all, just look at you. Young and pretty." Mrs. Pratt's eyes sparkle with malice. "You've recovered all right, haven't you? You seem just fine to me."

Reeve rises to her feet. "We need to go."

JD agrees. Standing, he cups her elbow, and they hurry toward the door.

"Sorry I can't help, but I wish you a heckuva lot of luck," Mrs. Pratt slurs, close on their heels. "I mean, in getting that reward money and all."

The woman laughs oddly, her boozy breath falling on Reeve's cheek with a familiar medicinal stink. The hallway seems cramped and narrow. Is the floor uneven? Reeve stumbles slightly, her shoulder bumping a framed photograph and knocking it askew.

"Watch it," the woman snaps. "Daryl's daddy wouldn't like being disturbed," she says, straightening the photograph.

The picture swims before Reeve's eyes. The man looks exactly like Daryl Wayne Flint.

The other framed photographs draw her like magnets. Here is one of a young Daryl holding a fishing pole in one hand, raising a string of fish with the other. She gasps and brazenly plucks it off the wall, studying it closely.

"Who took this picture?"

Mrs. Pratt snatches it from Reeve's hands. "I've no idea. Probably Walter. He was always taking pictures." She clutches the glass to her chest.

Reeve stares at the golden sticker on the back of the frame: *Walter Wertz Photography*. It fixes in her mind as she escapes out the door and blindly follows JD to his pickup truck.

"Well, damn, was that weird or what?" he says, starting up the engine and pulling away from the curb.

She turns away, huddling low in the seat.

Wertz. The name echoes in her head. *Halloween, Hallo-week, Hallo-Wertz.* She groans aloud.

"What's wrong?" JD asks.

She shushes him, pressing the heels of her hands hard against her closed eyes, hearing that woman's odd cackle, smelling that alcoholic odor. She searches her memory, reaching deeper, descending until she locates a seam, picking at it like a scab until it tears open, and she's in the basement, Flint's hands clasped around her throat while he's shaking her, threatening her, his mouth against her ear, his voice a low rasp. "You know where you're going to end up, don't you, cricket? Dead and in the ground, that's where. Buried! Buried with the others, right next to my daddy." He snickers, his stinking breath hot on her face. "And I'll sit on your grave and laugh while I'm fishing."

She's rigid with fear, gasping—

"Reeve? What's wrong?"

A hand on her shoulder, shaking her. They're in the pickup, stopped at the side of the road.

"Are you okay?" JD's face is close.

She blinks at him, saying nothing.

"What happened? Reeve, tell me what's wrong."

"That photograph . . ."

"What about it?"

"Did you see?"

"See what?"

"In the background . . ." She chokes slightly and tries again. "In the background. I . . . I saw graves."

SIXTY

JD Bender has enough of his father in him to want to puzzle out what the heck is going on, but he has enough of his mother in him to notice that Reeve's color has dropped from pale to ashen. His first thought is to get some nourishment into her, so he stops at the first diner he sees.

He shepherds her inside, insisting she needs to eat. They slide into a booth with red vinyl seats. He opens his menu, but she ignores hers. She's wearing a thousand-yard stare and rubbing her hand as if it has a mean itch.

"They have twenty-four-hour breakfast. How does that sound?"

She doesn't respond.

He watches her a moment, wondering how much to tell her, then says softly, "It's obvious that you're really upset. Can you fill me in?"

Her eyes meet his, unreadable. She gives a quick shake of her head and stares out the window.

When the waitress appears, he suggests two "Bluebird Specials" and Reeve gives a shrug that he takes for consent. He's ordering two coffees when she interjects, "No. Hot chocolate," which he figures is a good sign.

When the waitress brings their drinks, Reeve pulls her cup toward her and holds it with both hands, as if warming them. He watches her until the color starts coming back into her cheeks.

"Please tell me what's going on," he says as calmly as possible. "Come on, you said there were graves."

"You didn't see them?"

"I didn't get a good look."

I was looking at you, he thinks but doesn't say. "Did you have a flashback? Is that what happened?"

She closes her eyes and shudders.

Identical plates of two eggs and a short stack of blueberry pancakes appear before each of them. "Aren't you hungry? Eat," he urges.

She picks up a fork and pushes at some food on her plate while he eats. The waitress stops by to take his empty plate and refill his coffee cup, and when he looks up again, Reeve is watching him.

She pushes her plate aside. "Go ahead and say it."

"Say what?"

"You think I'm crazy."

"I do not."

She puts her elbows on the table, presses her thumbs into her temples, and shuts her eyes.

"Reeve, I do not think that. But you said 'graves,' plural. What did you see?"

"Maybe I imagined it. Maybe I really am crazy."

"Hey, I've seen crazy and you ain't it. But listen," he says, making up his mind, "there's something I need to tell you. Something that was going on behind the scenes during Flint's trial."

She opens her eyes. "What?"

"Well, I was always asking my dad a lot of questions, and he told me something that didn't come out in court."

"What are you getting at?"

"The prosecutor had an interesting theory about Flint's father."

"I don't know anything about his father," she says, looking away. "Please don't tell me about poor Daryl's childhood. If he was abused, I don't want to hear it."

JD leans across the table. "The thing is, his father disappeared when he was thirteen. Disappeared as in vanished without a trace. And eventually Donald Flint was declared legally dead, and then a few years later, Flint's mother married a pharmacist named Pratt."

"So what was the prosecution's big theory?"

"That Flint's mother murdered his dad."

She rocks back in her seat. "Are you serious?"

"It's just a theory."

"Why didn't I hear anything about this before?"

"Because it was just speculation. There was never cause for any warrant and there was never any search." JD reaches across the table and gently touches her wrist. "So tell me, what did you see?"

She gazes past his shoulder for a long moment, then meets his eyes. "By the water . . . in the background, I thought I saw mounds, like graves, and I remembered that Flint warned me"—she blinks rapidly and takes a breath—"that he was going to bury me next to his daddy. He said he'd sit on my grave and fish."

JD swallows hard and waits, saying nothing, holding back questions.

"I thought his father was still alive when Flint said all that. I thought he was going to kill me and then sit on my grave for years and years, until his father died an old man."

"But Flint's father was already dead."

"Murdered. Good lord, maybe he really did sit on his father's grave." The color blanches from her cheeks.

"But you said *graves*. Plural." JD's breakfast turns leaden in his stomach.

"I don't know, I've got so much vile crap inside my brain, but I just . . ." She plunges her hands into her hair. "God, I thought I'd be over this by now. I thought I'd be healed and I could get on with my life like a normal human being."

"I can't imagine what you've had to—"

"Let's call your father," she says abruptly. "We need to fill him in."

JD agrees, places the call, then sets his phone aside with a grimace. "His voice mailbox is full," he says, mocking the electronic voice. "My dad and technology."

Reeve drums her fingers on the table. "I wonder where that picture was taken."

"Yeah, and I wonder when Flint's father died. She said he didn't want to be disturbed. That's an odd thing to say, isn't it?"

"Yeah, I wonder if . . ." She stops drumming the table. "I know just who to call," she says, lifting her cell phone from her purse.

SIXTY-ONE

It doesn't surprise Nikki Keswick in the least when Blankenship tells her to return Mrs. Bender's call. "The old guy's wife wants something," he says. "I'm busy, Nik. You handle it."

His attitude isn't surprising. But Yvonne Bender's very first words make her catch her breath.

"Why on earth did you people give my husband back his gun?"

"Excuse me?"

"When he retired, he promised he was done with firearms, and he handed in his weapon along with his badge. He's no longer an agent, and I think I deserve an explanation."

"Mrs. Bender, excuse me, but the bureau would never do that. That would be one hundred percent against protocol. Isn't it possible that your husband simply bought a new gun?"

"No, it is not. He hung up his holster and started behaving like a normal adult. But now his holster is gone and why on earth would—oh!" Yvonne Bender gasps slightly. "It's that damn Daryl Wayne Flint. That's why Milo is acting so weird."

"Weird in what way?"

"Like he did when he was an agent."

"Like how, exactly?

"Restless. Prowling around the house like a trapped animal. I find him in

246

his office at all hours of the night and morning, mumbling to himself, going through files."

Keswick purses her lips, saying nothing. This exactly describes her own behavior.

"His desk is all covered with maps and papers," Yvonne continues, "just like when he was investigating a case. I swear, Milo has an obsession with that criminal."

"Did you say maps?"

"I've been trying to call him but he won't answer. And when I saw that his holster was gone . . . Oh my god, if Milo has gone out and bought a gun, I'll kill him."

Keswick questions Yvonne Bender briefly, then asks her to go into her husband's office and describe what she sees.

Keswick listens closely, and after hanging up, she cues up one search and then another on her computer. She double checks the timeline, makes a call, and sends several pages to the printer. Then she gathers up her notes, places them neatly in a folder, and tucks it under one arm, eager to carry this news to Blankenship.

She raps smartly on his door and waits.

"Keswick!" says a voice behind her.

She wheels around and sees Special Agent in Charge Stuart Cox leaning out of his office door.

"Have you got something?" he asks.

"Yes, sir."

"Come and tell us about it."

She enters his office to find Blankenship already inside.

"Yvonne Bender just called," she says.

"So did Milo," Cox says. "We've got to check out a guy named Walter Wertz."

SIXTY-TWO

Tacoma, Washington

Reeve insists there's a pattern. When Otis Poe can't follow, she cuts him short, saying, "Can you do this for me or not?"

"Damn right I can do it," the reporter says. "I've checked so many marriage records, death records, and property records, I could moonlight as a county clerk. But listen, Reeve, if this turns out to be something real, then you're giving me an exclusive. Deal?"

"Deal."

It doesn't take long until he calls her back. "Daryl Wayne Flint's father, named Donald P. Flint, disappeared in 1978, declared legally dead in 1985. Then his widow married this guy Pratt, a pharmacist in Tacoma, who has owned the same house since—"

"Forget Pratt," she interrupts. "What about that other guy, Walter Wertz? Where does he live? Anywhere near a lake?"

"Hold on, Reeve. I'm telling you. Wertz has a house in Olympia."

"Olympia? Near a lake?"

"It's Washington, there are lakes everywhere. But no, it's in a regular residential area."

She groans.

"But hold on. The records show that Wertz owns some other acreage, too."

"Where?"

"A couple of places. One parcel is up north by Anacortes, and here's a larger one in the Cascade mountains, beyond Snoqualmie Pass, in the Granite Reach Wilderness Area."

She closes her eyes, recalls the photograph, and hazards a guess. "In the mountains. Is there a cabin by a lake or something?"

"I'm pulling up the satellite image now," Poe says. "I'm enlarging the image . . . No, it's quite a ways north of Cle Elum Lake and looks to me like it's just wilderness."

"But don't you see a lake or a river or something?"

"No, uh, wait . . . here's Shadow Bark Creek, and, oh, here's a body of water. Shadow Bark Lake."

"That's gotta be it. I owe you, Otis. But now I need directions."

SIXTY-THREE

Cascade Mountains

Milo Bender drives slowly, studying the right side of the road. The weather is working to his disadvantage. It has been snowing lightly since he came through the pass, and once he passed Cle Elum, it started to stick.

He eases off the gas and pulls over at Granite Reach Mini-Mart. He unfolds his map and adjusts his bifocals on his nose, but finds nothing distinctive, just narrow roads winding into rugged terrain. He puts the map away and continues driving. No traffic behind him; none up ahead.

He passes a rickety bridge that crosses a creek. The road banks and climbs and then cuts into a rocky hillside. A bullet-riddled sign warns of falling rocks. He drives on, regretting that the tread on his tires isn't the best, given these conditions.

A weathered sign announces the Granite Reach Wilderness Area, and he turns off the asphalt onto what can only be a forest service road. It's snowing steadily now. The light bounces off the flakes, so he turns off his headlights. Soon the landscape will become a pure blankness, obscuring everything, and he'll be out of luck.

He maneuvers his minivan through the remains of a huge tree that must have fallen across the road years ago. A section large enough to drive through has been cut away, and the bisected trunk still brackets the road like rotting bookends.

He peers out the windshield, looking for anything distinctive—for markers, a trail, or some evidence of recent habitation, if that's not too much to wish for, because there's apparently no residence up on this acreage. He rolls down the passenger-side window to get a better look, trying to think like Flint. The cold air rushes in, but he pays no attention.

He spots a moss-covered boulder and a gap in the trees. Could that be a trail? He drives past, craning his neck, trying to judge the opening. It's worth a look. He continues several yards before he finds an opening in the trees where he can park off the road.

He shrugs on his weatherproof jacket, zips it up tight, and climbs out. The moment his boots hit the ground, he smells smoke. He lifts his nose, studying the skyline, but sees only treetops disappearing into a low, gray sky.

He climbs back into the minivan to retrieve the Glock from the glove box. Once it's secure in his shoulder holster, he feels like an agent again.

His boots leave tracks in the freshly fallen snow as he studies the terrain. Now he's sure that the gap between the trees is wide enough for a vehicle. He studies the ground, walking down the middle of what might be a road. It banks to the left, so that trees obscure it from anyone driving past.

Deeper in the trees, where the snow barely filters through the pines, the ground betrays tire tracks, recent and distinct. He hesitates, his breath hanging in the air while he considers whether to go back and place another call to Stuart Cox. Still, what does he have to report? Not much.

He trudges along, the cold stinging his cheeks and numbing his hands. He regrets leaving his gloves in the car, but he'll just take a quick look around, then head back down the mountain out of this damned snow. There's no longer any question that this is a road. It hugs the trees, turning, climbing, and descending in a way that would make it hard to spot from even those high-powered satellite cameras. The snow dusts his hair and shoulders as he crunches along, and his body warms from the effort of climbing.

The smell of smoke intensifies. He's got to be close.

He feels invigorated, alert. The trail becomes slippery and uneven as he hurries on. Something catches his eye in the trees ahead. Freshly broken branches.

He slows, approaching cautiously, and peers through the trees to see a black Toyota Highlander, parked with its nose sticking out from beneath a canopy of pine boughs. Dr. Moody's stolen SUV.

He moves up beside it and places a hand on the hood. Cold.

He knows he needs backup. He needs the bureau to scramble a team and rush up here. But in the meantime it's snowing, and if the roads close . . . what about the girl?

Bender unholsters his gun and his heart begins to race.

SIXTY-FOUR

The ground is so cold and hard that Flint is getting blisters. Even after all this digging, he has only managed about two feet. Not deep enough. Three would be better. Three is always best.

He'd thought about making the girl walk out here and help him dig, but then reconsidered. She'd be whining and crying and trying to get away the whole time. Not worth the trouble.

What's that sound?

He looks up, scans the trees, the lake, the shoreline, the flat water. Nothing.

It's snowing harder now. Big flakes dust his hair, fall under his collar, and melt on the back his neck. He hates this part, but his muscles are strong and warm and he'll be done soon enough if he just keeps at it.

He wields a pickax to break up the hard earth, then uses the shovel. He always hated digging. For grunt labor, it was always better to have two men. Wertz had prided himself on his ruggedness, whereas Daryl was more artistic. By nature, he was much better suited to slipping into the night for rendezvous with his targets, camera in hand. But over the years, Wertz had made a point of toughening him up.

Stepping down inside the grave, Flint takes a wide stance, trying to work the shovel deeper, but flings out only a cupful of dirt. He spits out a curse, jabs the blade in, shifts his grip on the handle for maximum leverage, and heaves. The handle snaps and he cries out as the momentum dumps him on his backside in the freshly turned earth.

He flings the broken shovel aside, his curses carrying though the wintry air.

Milo Bender freezes, locating the sound. He peers all around. Up ahead, a trail of smoke scribbles low across the cloud ceiling. He rushes forward, tripping over rocks, slipping on icy pine needles. He spies a chimney between the trees . . . a rooftop . . . a cabin. He veers between the pines, his heart jumping in his throat.

If Jenna Dutton is still alive, this could be his only chance.

Cautiously, he circles the cabin, staying in the trees, watching for movement. Snow moistens his eyeglasses, blurring his vision. He stops and listens but hears only the whisper of snow. The gun is cold as ice, and he blows warm air on his frozen fingers.

Seeing no one, he creeps out of the trees and crosses the clearing toward the front door, conscious of every footprint he leaves behind.

Flint takes the shortcut back to the shed, straight up from the lake. He's not happy about having to fetch the other shovel, which has a wider, flatter blade. Better for snow, not as good for digging. If he has to, he can switch handles. Or, if need be, he can drive into town, buy a new shovel, plus a six-pack and some beef jerky for his trouble.

Just as he's edging past Moody's SUV, he sees footprints and stops short.

Shit!

He drops into a crouch and looks around. Nobody.

Quietly, he opens the door of the SUV, and for a moment considers climbing in and driving off. He has the vehicle packed and ready to go.

Think, Daryl. Think, think, think!

He studies the direction that the footprints lead through the freshly fallen snow. Just one man? He looks around, listens.

He needs to handle this. The pistol is loaded. He retrieves it from beneath the seat, gently shuts the door, and starts following the tracks toward the cabin.

Bender creeps closer, watchful and alert. The smoke drifting upward remains the only movement.

Maybe the cabin is empty, or maybe the girl is inside. What are the odds? Fifty-fifty. She might be dead, but if there's any chance she's breathing, Bender has no choice but to enter through the front door.

Hard or soft entry?

The man's curses seemed to come from farther off, to the left. If the man is off in the woods, his accomplice might be inside with the girl, perhaps armed. But a hard entry is a loud entry. Has to be soft.

He creeps up to the door, aware of every shudder of sound. Gun ready, he places his hand on the knob, turns, and the door swings wide.

Darkness greets him. He steps inside and sweeps his gun through the shadows.

Nothing but furniture, heat wafting from a woodstove.

He closes the door and moves deeper into the cabin with slow, cautious steps. At the far end, he finds a bed with sheets, a sleeping bag, and a jumble of frilly clothes.

Bender's mouth goes dry.

He looks for blood, for gun shells, then sees the padlocked door. He steps up close and whispers, "Jenna? Jenna are you there?"

A tremulous voice answers, "Who is that?"

"FBI," he says, knowing the lie will calm her. "Stay quiet, okay? I don't know where he is. Let me find a way to get you out of here."

Movement inside. "Oh, thank god. Hurry!"

Knowing Flint is right-handed, Bender searches to the right and finds the key on the windowsill. A moment later, the padlock clicks open and the girl tumbles out. She's small and naked and pale, except for her many tattoos.

"Are you okay?"

Her eyes are frantic. "Get me out of here!"

Bender pulls the sleeping bag from the bed and wraps her in it, noting her bare feet. "Where are your shoes? It's snowing. Can you make it?"

She nods fiercely as she clutches the sleeping bag around her.

"Stay close. I'm parked about a mile away."

Bender holds his gun steady and his chest tightens as they move toward the door.

Flint, crouched low in the trees, watches the cabin door swing open, sees a man and the girl scurry out. The man carries his pistol and scans the trees like he knows what he's doing.

Flint doesn't move. The man's gaze skips past. His face looks familiar.

They dart for the trees. The girl is barefoot and the man shepherds her forward. It would be easy to follow as they stagger along, but Flint concocts a better plan. He eases back and cuts through the trees, heading for a bend farther down the path. He moves quickly through the pines, silent as a fox.

When he's sure he's far enough ahead, he finds a good spot to wait in ambush and steadies himself against a tree trunk. He hears them coming. His pulse quickens. He watches the road, raises his gun, and braces it with both hands.

Steady . . . steady now as they appear . . . first the girl . . . now the man. He sights along the barrel, aiming for the man's chest, tightening his finger, squeezing the trigger.

The blast rips through the air and the girl screams and runs as the man spins, raising his weapon. Flint squeezes the trigger again and another gunshot explodes, punching the man off his feet.

Gun smoke hangs in the silence, then Flint dashes out to kick the man's gun away.

When he gets up close, he sees that he needn't have bothered. The man's face has gone slack. He lies still while blood pools, melting a pattern in the snow. Flint marvels at the oozing redness, then pulls his eyes away.

He studies the man for a moment and recognizes that face. "Agent Bender," he mutters.

He quickly straightens, looking around. The girl has vanished. He could chase her, but if other agents are nearby they'll have heard the shots. He inhales sharply and dashes back through the trees.

Jenna Dutton drops the sleeping bag and runs naked, oblivious of the cold. She runs blindly and fast and scorched with panic.

Where to go? Where?

She races on, her ears ringing, terror thudding in her chest. Her feet fly across rocks and snow. She slips on the icy pine needles and abruptly halts in a patch sheltered by dense conifers. For a crazy instant she imagines climbing a tree, but all the branches are much too high. She spins around, searching for someplace to hide, but sees only trees and more trees. She chooses a direction and rushes on in a panic, gasping. She must hide, but—

There! A rotted stump with a gaping hole in its side catches her eye. She rushes over and drops down on her knees. The hole is a black, toothless maw, just large enough to hold her. She pushes herself into it butt first, the wood scraping and jabbing her skin.

She hears something and struggles to push herself deeper into the cavity, trying to disappear. The sound draws closer. A car engine. She tucks in tight, squeezing her knees to her chest, praying that she'll be spared for the sake of her son. *Dear lord, please!*

A black SUV flashes through the trees, and then it's gone.

She holds still and listens as the engine noise grows fainter, gradually diminishing in the distance until all she can hear is the hush of falling snow.

Aching with cold, she inches forward, unfolds from the tree stump, and crouches there, shivering, wondering what to do.

The man had said his car was parked nearby. She stumbles forward, hunched over and shivering. Her feet have turned numb and clumsy, but she forces herself to keep moving.

She staggers along, and after what seems like miles, at last finds the narrow road. She follows the tire tracks downhill, splashing through icy puddles, expecting to see a car but seeing nothing. A sob catches in her throat. She spins, searching, and glimpses something uphill. A vehicle there in the trees?

She lurches up to the minivan, shaking with fear and cold. Her frozen hands won't obey, but at last her thumb connects and the door opens. She climbs in, pulls the door shut and collapses, so numb that the cold seat barely registers on her backside. Her teeth are chattering and her thoughts are slow, but she rouses herself to search for keys.

No keys.

She continues searching and finds a cell phone in the glove box that she manages to turn on with trembling hands, but her hope disappears when she sees there's no service. She slumps down on the seat and moans a low, pitiful sound, thinking of the man shot in the woods. Dead, surely dead. She moans again, slumps lower and tucks her legs in close, so cold she can't think.

SIXTY-FIVE

The windshield wipers beat aside the wet snow as Flint speeds away from the cabin behind the wheel of Dr. Moody's SUV. The snow-covered roads are slick as he winds down out of the wilderness, but soon after he reaches black-top, the snow turns to sleet and then to rain.

He has the precious metal box on the seat. The gun is ready at his side, but he meets not a single vehicle as he winds past the old bridge. And when he passes the Granite Reach Mini-Mart, he hoots in elation. He has done it again. Too smart, too quick for all of them.

Just outside of Cle Elum, the gas gauge dips low and the warning light comes on. Cursing, Flint veers off the road into a gas station on the left side of the road. He pulls up to the pump, parking nose out, ready to go, then puts on the camouflage hat and the horn-rimmed glasses.

While filling the tank, he keeps his eyes on the road, ready for trouble, but sees nothing special. Five pickup trucks and four beat-up sedans drive by, totaling nine, three threes, which is a good sign.

The gas pump clicks off, and just as he's replacing the nozzle, a massive black SUV flashes past. He freezes.

A second black SUV appears and zooms past, followed by a third. All identical. All with darkly tinted windows and two men up front. All going too fast.

Flint knows what that means. How long until they find their fellow agent in his pool of blood? And what about that girl with the hideous tattoos?

He keeps checking the road, but no more black SUVs come racing past. No flashing lights, no speeding sheriffs.

Lucky, lucky, lucky.

But the cabin is blown. And since the cabin is blown, then the Olympia house is probably blown, too.

Maybe not so lucky. He growls in frustration, holsters the nozzle, and climbs back into the vehicle, his mind spinning like a turbine. He needs to get off the road and start Plan C. He needs to take cover until nightfall. He has Wertz's instructions waiting inside the metal box. And Moody's camping equipment is still loaded in back. That could prove useful, if only for the short term.

He turns the key. The engine sparks to life and he grips the steering wheel with both hands, still watching, in case a fourth vehicle speeds past.

When it doesn't, he shifts into gear and eases down on the accelerator, carefully signaling that he's turning left into traffic.

A pickup truck flashes past and he nearly chokes, because unless he's full-out hallucinating, he would swear up and down and sideways that the pretty red-haired passenger zooming past was none other than his own little cricket.

Flint stares after the green pickup, certain that he's seen it before, certain that Milo Bender's son was at the wheel.

He equivocates for only seconds before turning right and heading back the way he came. He continues north, passes Granite Reach Mini-Mart, and follows the green pickup at a safe distance until he reaches the bridge. Then he turns off, crosses over Shadow Bark Creek, and bumps along slowly until he reaches the far side of Shadow Bark Lake.

SIXTY-SIX

Bright flares sputter with red tongues, marking a wide circle. The cloud cover lifts as if swept away by a merciful hand, and a sudden thrumming overhead grows louder as the helicopter beats down from the sky. Agent Nikki Keswick watches it settle onto a meadow near the crime site.

A heartbeat later, JD Bender appears, hurrying alongside the gurney that carries his father. Another gurney, carrying a pale but wide awake Jenna Dutton follows, with Reeve LeClaire trailing behind.

The medics won't allow Bender's son to board. He steps away and stands hunched beside Reeve as the chopper's blades spin. The noise builds, and in an instant the chopper is in the air, heading to the nearest hospital, leaving behind a whirlwind of conjecture.

The crime scene swarms with FBI investigators. Everyone is asking questions, but the only certainty is that Daryl Wayne Flint has managed to slip away.

"Keswick, can you give me a hand here?"

She looks up and recognizes an investigator named Torres.

"We need to box this stuff up," he says. "We're done processing Bender's vehicle."

"God, I hope he makes it," she says, glancing back at Bender's son. He's walking slowly toward Reeve, who is waving her arms, talking agitatedly with Blankenship.

Keswick would love to know how those two civilians ended up here, but just now, there's too much going on to worry about them. The word is that graves have been discovered. A forensic anthropologist is on the way to oversee the exhumations. Lights are being set up for an all-night shift. Meanwhile, forensic teams are processing evidence in a cabin, a shed, and a Ford Bronco.

It won't be long until a news chopper shows up and all this hits headlines, Keswick thinks, following Torres up the road to Bender's minivan.

Jenna Dutton had been discovered huddled inside, bruised and hypothermic, but once she'd been wrapped in blankets and given a thermos of hot coffee, she'd been eager to talk and surprisingly coherent.

"Okay, look, I've got everything organized," Torres says, handing Keswick a file box. "Just hold this a minute, would you?"

She stands beside the vehicle, gripping the box with both hands while Torres gathers up evidence. The front seats are covered with bagged and tagged items—including maps, binoculars, and a cell phone—which he hurriedly places in the box.

"Let's get these loaded up," Torres says, lifting two identical stacked boxes in his arms.

As they're loading the boxes into an evidence van, Blankenship calls Keswick over to where he's talking with Reeve. "Nikki? I need you double quick."

"What's up?" she asks, hustling toward them.

"Reeve thinks she might have some information. Take her down to the lake and show her the graves."

SIXTY-SEVEN

Daryl Wayne Flint loops the binoculars' strap around his neck, fits the camouflage hat onto his head, and finds the path through the brush. The way is vaguely familiar, though overgrown since he was here last. When he gets close, he ducks under a branch and proceeds forward on his hands and knees until he nears the water's edge. Then he gets down flat on his belly and scoots forward on his elbows until he has a sightline across the lake.

He peers through the binoculars and focuses on the commotion on the opposite shore. They've found the graves.

Or—correction—they've found three of the graves. Flint adjusts the binoculars and watches, rapt.

The FBI has encircled the faint mounds with neat yellow flags. They are measuring, setting up lights, and photographing, scurrying about like the methodical little worker ants they are. It's funny that they walk right past the other graves without even noticing them.

Flint snorts, jiggling the binoculars, and the image vibrates.

Wertz was clever to have found this spot so many years ago.

Once they had covered that first grave with pine needles, Wertz said, "We need an observation post in case somebody comes looking for your daddy."

Then he'd taken Daryl all the way around to this side of the lake, where they hid his car and then hiked to this place on the opposite shore. They'd had to scrunch low through the brush, and Flint recalls crawling on his elbows, terrified and thrilled by what they had done.

"No one can ever know," Wertz said. "But you and your momma owe me big time."

And so their pact had begun. Shortly after that, Daryl went to live with him. He'd expected that his mother would object, but it seemed like she thought it was her idea. Like she thought he was payment, almost, for helping to get rid of that mean son of a bitch.

But he and Wertz knew the truth.

Daryl had worked hard to prove himself to Wertz from the very start. He'd paid attention and soon recognized that, despite the age difference, they had shared interests. He seized his first opportunity to make an impression one afternoon when he caught Wertz hiding in the bushes, snapping photographs of nude sunbathers.

Wertz had given him a hard look, like he thought a thirteen-year-old kid might raise a fuss.

Instead, Daryl signaled that he could climb a tree for a better shot. He shimmied up the trunk, and Wertz grinned as he handed up the camera.

Wertz treated him differently after that, like he was testing him or something, giving him tasks. But Daryl didn't mind. He knew he'd have to jump through a few hoops if he wanted to team up with someone like Walter Wertz. Getting rid of his brute of a father was a bonus.

As Daryl matured, Wertz gave him more responsibility, and they honed their complementary talents. Daryl was good at improvising, while Wertz was always methodical, always thinking ahead. For instance, Wertz had explored all around Shadow Bark Lake long before their first encounter. He knew all the best spots.

Flint smiles at this thought, refocuses the binoculars, and stares intently, because there she is, his own little cricket. Her skin is lovely, even at this distance.

He likes the red hair.

Next to her is another woman, taller, with long black hair, wearing a vest with "FBI" in bold print. Reggie grabs the woman's elbow and points. And Flint can practically hear her say, "Look there," as she points at where another girl is buried.

SIXTY-EIGHT

Harborview Hospital

The whole time Reeve is with Jenna Dutton—holding her hand, offering words of comfort—she has the oddest feeling of déjà vu. It makes no sense, because she hasn't seen Jenna since middle school. Now they're adults, and Jenna even has a son, but while holding her friend's slim fingers, she feels like she's a kid again. It's comforting and familiar, even in this bizarre circumstance, and she wants to hear everything about her old friend's life, but this is not the time or place. When Jenna's family arrives, Reeve listens to their tearful reassurances to one another that everything will be all right. Then, promising to stay in touch, she says good-bye and slips out into the hospital corridor.

She hurries upstairs to the ICU. When she enters the waiting room, she finds a half-empty coffee cup on the table next to the chair where JD had been sitting. She shoots a fearful look at the heavy, locked door, and pictures JD hovering at his father's bedside. The horrible details of the past hours kaleidoscope through her mind, and she swallows a hard lump.

Her head hurts and her body aches. She heads toward the restroom to use the toilet, wash her hands, and splash water on her face.

"You look like hell," she says to her reflection.

When she returns to the waiting room, she finds JD sitting hunched over his phone. As she perches beside him, he glances up. His face has aged a decade.

"How's your father?"

264

A heavy pause. "The same."

She places a hand on his. "I wish there was something I could do," she says, but the expression seems weightless. What can anyone do while monitors tick and screens flicker? She casts about for something better to say, but any further comment seems pointless, and any question seems cruel. They sit in silence for several minutes, hoping for the best, fearing the worst. Her chest aches as if she were the one who got shot.

JD gives her a bleak look and says, "My aunt and uncle are flying down from Calgary in the morning."

The next instant, there's a distinct metallic click and the door yawns open. Yvonne emerges from the ICU, pale but erect and alert as a soldier.

A nurse, Reeve remembers.

She stands before them, palms clasped together, as JD questions her about his father's condition, his collapsed lung, his blood loss, his heart. Yvonne answers in medical terminology which seems paradoxically vague and specific, like naming stars in some remote galaxy.

Touching her son's shoulder, Yvonne adds a few soft words that Reeve doesn't catch, and they all fall silent, each studying the floor, each wanting to know the one thing that cannot be answered: Will he survive?

The question hangs over them like a shadow, and Reeve suffers a hard pang of guilt. If only she'd stayed in California, if only she hadn't dragged Milo Bender back into this case . . . She feels responsible for every awful thing that has happened.

After a moment, Yvonne suggests that they all head down to the cafeteria for coffee, and they move toward the elevator. Reeve stays silent, listening while the mother and son gravely discuss the pending arrivals of various relatives.

The elevator dings, the door opens, and out steps Agent Nikki Keswick, looking fresher and more alert than any of them.

After a rush of questions about Bender's condition, she turns to Reeve and proposes: "Why don't you come home with me? You have your luggage with you, right? I've got a comfortable guest room, and I'd be happy to take you to the airport in the morning."

"That's probably best, dear," Yvonne says, patting her shoulder. "Go get some rest. We'll call you when there's any news."

SIXTY-NINE

Mercer Island, Washington

Keswick talks fast and drives faster, saying, "God, I'm wound up. I'm running on adrenaline and coffee." She grips the steering wheel, accelerating around a truck. "This case has blown wide open. We've brought in teams from all over."

Reeve listens in amazement while Keswick talks about how a jumble of events fit together. A dozen scenes flash through Reeve's mind, and then she asks, "Do you know how Bender ended up at that cabin?"

"We've been piecing it together. Did you hear about the yearbooks?"

"What yearbooks?"

"Walter Wertz, the guy who owned that property in the mountains, worked as a school photographer. He had a huge collection of yearbooks. And it looks like he and Flint worked as partners."

"Partners?" She frowns. "As photographers?"

"Yeah, they had a legitimate school photography business that provided the perfect cover. And he and Wertz ran a kiddie-porn business on the side. At least, that's the theory."

"School photographers." Reeve swallows dryly. "They took kids' pictures."

"And that's how they found their victims. Some of our missing girls were high school students in those yearbooks. You were the youngest, as far as we know. The only middle school student."

"So . . . schools were their stalking grounds." Reeve stares glumly out the window, where trees tremble in the moonlight.

"Anyway, we'll know more tomorrow," Keswick says. After a moment, she adds, "I hate to think about what would have happened if we'd arrived at that cabin even a few minutes later."

Reeve's heart skips. "You don't think Bender would have made it?"

"He would have bled out for sure. We figure Flint had just left."

"What?"

"We must've just missed him. Flint must've headed east, otherwise we would have seen him. He would have driven right by us."

They ride in silence while Reeve grapples with this.

Keswick makes two quick turns and winds through a residential area. In a few minutes, she steers up a long driveway and parks in front of a one-story home with contemporary lines.

Reeve climbs out of the car feeling stiff and lightheaded. "Nice place," she says absently, as she carries her luggage inside.

"Isn't it? My aunt is letting me house-sit while she's in Hawaii with her grandkids. I can't even imagine what I'll do when she decides it's time to come home. I'm drawing a total blank."

They move through a living room decorated with cheerful colors and quality furniture. Keswick shows her to the guest room, where Reeve stashes her luggage.

"I know it's late, but I'm starved. How about you? Are you hungry?"

Reeve nods mutely. She can scarcely recall her last meal.

A minute later, Keswick is peering into the refrigerator. "I've got nothing to eat but rice and eggs. Oh, wait, how about fried rice?"

"Anything is fine. Can I help?"

"Nope, I've got it. Let's see . . . soy sauce, ginger, celery . . . You're going to love my mother's recipe. Quick and healthy."

Reeve leans against the counter behind her and watches while Keswick dices vegetables, her fingers a blur of chopping.

"Does the bureau have any idea where Flint is hiding?" Reeve asks, rubbing the scar on the back of her neck.

Keswick sets down the knife. "No clue."

SEVENTY

A fist of moonlight punches through the clouds, throwing beams and tossing shadows while Daryl Wayne Flint moves closer. He crouches deep in the darkness, feeling comfortable as he settles into old patterns. It had been simple to follow Reggie from the lake to the hospital and then here. And from this vantage point, he can watch the whole house, front to back.

There are no curtains on the kitchen windows. Peering through the high-powered binoculars, he feels as though he's part of the domestic scene inside.

He recognizes the one with the glossy, black hair. She has shed the bulky FBI garb that she wore at the lake, and looks so much better now in her blood-red sweater.

He watches her cooking, noting where she reaches for the knife, which she leaves atop the cutting board. When she steps away from the window, he can see all the way inside the kitchen, to where his girl stands, fine as ever.

Most girls have only a short period of beauty before the acne and awkwardness of adolescence, but his cricket was always blooming. Her skin still glows. Her gestures have the grace of a dancer. When she stops to think, the tip of her tongue reaches briefly for her upper lip. He hungers for that tongue.

The dark-haired agent plates the food, and when the two of them move deeper into the house, away from the window, he steps from his hiding place. He crosses the lawn, moving farther from the street. The wind stirs the clouds and whips the trees.

There is no hurry as he approaches the house. He imagines them eating their food, talking about him. They will speculate about the graves, and he enjoys thinking about those who await exhumation.

He moves in closer, slow and stealthy, keeping to the shadows as the moon waltzes in and out of the clouds. The dark-haired agent's house stands unobserved by any neighbors. He approaches the back, wondering where the agent will have stashed her gun. By the front door? Perhaps a second weapon in the bedroom?

It doesn't matter. She won't have time to reach for a gun.

SEVENTY-ONE

You don't like the fried rice?" Keswick asks, eyeing Reeve's plate.

"No, actually, it's really good. Better than anything I could make." Reeve takes another bite and swallows. She scarcely tastes the food. Now and then her phone pings, and she apologizes to Keswick about responding to a text.

"No need to apologize. I'll bet your family is worried sick."

She nods, texting. "And my roommates are insomniacs."

"Oh, I almost forgot to tell you," Keswick says, putting a strand of hair behind her ear. "You know that woman you asked about, Cybil Abbott? The one who used to work as Dr. Moody's assistant?"

"Yes?" Reeve sets her phone aside.

"We took a closer look, found some interesting credit card activity. She bought gas in South Turvey, not far from Church Street Storage, a couple months ago."

"So, is she under arrest?"

"I wish."

"What happened?"

"She's dead. Looks like a drug overdose. Suicide."

Reeve puts down her fork. "It's not suicide."

"What makes you say that?"

"Flint's mother killed her. I'd bet you anything."

Keswick gives her an uncomfortable look, starts to say something, then changes the subject, saying, "I'm going to make some tea. Would you like some?"

Reeve nods. While the teakettle boils, she silently resolves to say nothing more about Flint or his sick, twisted family.

But Keswick's mind is still back at the crime scene. "These types of predators, they dedicate themselves to their crimes. And they perfect their skills over time," she says, setting two mugs of tea, spoons, and a jar of honey on the table. "But Flint was off the charts. I mean, we found a whole damn graveyard, six so far. And who knows how long he'd been doing this? You're lucky you weren't killed."

This last comment stings, but Reeve tries to keep it from showing on her face. "I don't know why he didn't kill me," she says softly.

Keswick raises her eyebrows. "I've got a theory about that."

She seems to be waiting for permission to continue, so Reeve meets her eye and nods once.

"It was your skin."

"You think Flint was creating designs on my skin." She looks away. "Yeah, he was."

"But it was more than that. I think you became his obsession."

Reeve gives a twitch of her shoulders.

"No, listen. When I was growing up, we had a neighbor who grew bonsai trees. It's a Japanese art form that requires a lot of dedication."

"I know what bonsai is. But what does—"

"It takes years of careful pruning to perfect bonsai. The roots are cut and bound. Each branch, each bud is cultivated. It's a kind of artful torture of the plant."

Reeve scowls into her mug of tea.

"So my neighbor had lots of bonsai," Keswick is saying. "It was his business. But there was one tree that he refused to sell. It wasn't the most beautiful or the most impressive, but he was fixated on that little tree. He eventually fell ill and sold all his bonsai, everything, all his family treasures, but he kept that one special tree. And they say it was at his bedside when he died."

Something crackles inside her. "That's a sickening theory. You think Flint was so obsessed with me, he would have kept me forever, like a plant in a pot?"

"It's just that Flint doesn't fit any profile. I mean, he's insane, for sure, and he must have been abused because—"

"Oh, please. I'm so sick of hearing about how poor Daryl Wayne was abused." Reeve feels the heat rising in her cheeks. "Because then it's his father who was abused, and then it's his grandmother, and on and on until it's just an endless string of blame. And I don't care who abused who first, because I'm the one who was abused last, and it has to *stop*."

She gets up from the table and pours her tea down the sink.

"Oh, god, I'm so sorry," Keswick says, following Reeve and placing a hand on her shoulder. "I can't believe I said that to you. That was thoughtless of me."

Reeve takes a breath. "I didn't mean to snap at you. It's just, well, this is not my favorite topic."

"Of course. And I really, really apologize. The words just flew out of my mouth before I realized what I was saying. Honestly, you seem so self-possessed that I just forgot that . . ."

"Okay, so could we please not talk about Flint anymore?"

"Cross my heart," Keswick says, drawing an index finger across her chest. She glances at the clock. "God, it's later than I thought. We'll have to get an early start tomorrow. Will 6:30 work for you?"

"I hardly sleep anyway. I'll be up."

Reeve offers to help with the dishes, but Keswick waves her away, saying, "Go on to bed. I'm just going to get the coffee machine ready and take out the trash."

"Okay, I'll see you bright and early."

As Reeve retrieves her bag of toiletries and carries them into the bathroom, she hears Nikki Keswick's light tread in the kitchen, cabinet doors opening and closing, the rustling sound of a plastic bag. She turns on the faucet and brushes her teeth, rinses, spits, and shuts off the faucet. The house is quiet. She's using a washcloth on her face when she hears movement in the kitchen again.

The hair stands up on the back of her neck.

She goes still, listening hard, hoping she's wrong. But no, the footsteps are different. Heavier. And horribly familiar. For four years, she listened to that same tread going back and forth across the floor above her head.

Her chest constricts as she looks around, wanting scissors, something sharp, but seeing nothing but soft, pretty things. She shuts off the light, afraid that it might shine beneath the door, and holds her breath in the darkness, desperate to hear something from Nikki Keswick.

She hears only his footsteps coming closer.

Her mind is frozen with fear. She listens to the sound of the footsteps change as they leave the tiled kitchen floor and come into the hallway.

Moonlight spills through a window too small for escape.

Where is Keswick's gun? Reeve tries to picture where it might be stashed, but she has no idea.

She looks around, seeking a weapon. Even a can of hairspray and a match might work. Her eyes stop at the toilet. Quickly, she removes a box of tissues from atop the tank, grips the ceramic lid firmly with both hands, and lifts it off. Keeping her eyes on the door, she shifts her grip on the lid and raises it above her head.

Her heart thuds in her throat. The footsteps come closer, closer . . . and move past, creeping toward the front of the house.

Should she bolt out the door and try to escape? Or does she have a better chance if . . . There's no time to equivocate, because now the footsteps return and the sound has changed, as if he's on tiptoe.

A floorboard squeaks.

A shadow falls across the threshold.

Her eyes water with fear as she widens her stance, watching as the door-knob slowly turns. Gripping the heavy lid, she raises it higher, arms trembling.

Flint bursts in, and she smashes the lid down with all her might—but it glances off his shoulder and flies from her grasp, crashing to the floor. She cries out and tries to dash past him, but his fist smashes into her face. She stumbles and he grabs her by the waist, lifting her off her feet with astonishing strength. She screams and thrashes. Her feet touch the floor and she bucks hard, throwing a knee at his groin, but not connecting. She struggles wildly, but he throws her to the floor so hard that her head bounces on the tile. And then he strikes like a viper with a searing hot jolt.

SEVENTY-TWO

She chirps sweetly and drops, just as she did the first time. He bends close and breathes in her scent.

His little cricket. His again.

He stares at her limp body, marveling at how superb she is, with her clear complexion and trim physique. He tilts his head from side to side, admiring the artful way her red-bronze hair spills across her cheek. Then he spies the scar at the nape of her neck, peels off her sweater, and gazes at her back for a long, thrilling moment, recalling how he created each detail.

The photographs don't do her justice.

Tremendously excited, he imagines what he could do right this minute—now!—but he cannot trust this house, these neighbors all around. He needs to get somewhere safe.

Time for Plan C.

He secures the zip ties to her wrists and ankles and drags her down the hallway, leaving her there while he hurries outside to move his vehicle closer to the house.

He's back a moment later, sealing duct tape across her lips. He covers her with a blanket and carries her outside. Once he has her secure in the back, he wraps a heavy black cargo net over her and fastens it tight as an added precaution.

When he climbs into the driver's seat, he notices the wonderful aroma that permeates the interior. He fills his lungs.

He shifts into gear, leaving his headlights off until he reaches the next intersection. Then he speeds onto the freeway. He's unconcerned about when or how the female agent's body will be found. He's thinking instead about the distance from Mercer Island to Anacortes, estimating how long the drive will take. Two hours, maybe three.

He remembers the place clearly, a two-story structure of concrete block. Not a place to stay permanently, just long enough to arrange for a pick-up time. He glances at the thick envelope beside him on the passenger's seat, the one Wertz marked "Plan C." The final escape plan.

Burn the bridges, leave it all behind, and head north, north, north. By this time tomorrow, they'll be starting a new life in Canada.

SEVENTY-THREE

Her head is swimming and she hears herself moan. Each breath requires effort. Duct tape seals her mouth. Her arms are pinned, her back twisted, her face pressed to the floor. She hears the vehicle's tires spinning and fear coils in her gut.

She tries to roll but cannot. Plastic ties bite into her wrists and ankles, and she's covered by a musty blanket, wrapped tight. Cocooned.

Her sweater is gone. She feels no other body heat. She's alone.

She thinks of Nikki Keswick and a lump swells in her throat. She swallows painfully and tries to picture what will happen tomorrow. How long will it take the FBI to wonder where they are? How long until they begin to search and then discover mayhem at Nikki Keswick's house? What will happen when her plane ticket goes unused, when her father's phone rings with such terrible news?

His heart will stop. This will kill him, and it will cripple her sister.

Reeve yanks against the ties. She tries to shriek but manages only a strangled cry. Her face is wet, and she's choking on tears that make it hard to breathe.

Stop it!

She must not to panic.

She must not hyperventilate.

She inhales through her nostrils, taking deep, shaking breaths, telling herself to calm down, forcing herself to concentrate.

She can tell that the vehicle is moving fast through minimal traffic. A freeway late at night? Flint has a destination in mind, she's sure of that. She tries to calculate direction and figure distance. But north or south, it doesn't matter. Because once he has her locked up, escape becomes impossible.

Lurid memories of being held captive flash through her mind.

No, don't think about that.

The vehicle rolls on into the night for what seems like hours. She can't help but pray for someone to come and save her, but knows it's futile. She spent four brutal years hoping for rescue, but was saved only by accident. No one will come. Her picture will be pinned up on a crowded wall with countless others who are missing and presumed dead. Her photo will fade and she will wither and perish.

She suffers an image of a plant with bound roots.

Stop it! Figure it out.

She's still wearing her bra, her jeans, her boots. At least she hasn't been stripped.

She hears him talking. From the cadence, it sounds like a phone conversation, but she can't make out the words.

There's silence for awhile, and then he seems to be muttering to himself—something unintelligible—over and over, in sets of threes.

If only she could speak with him, concoct some sort of lie, create a diversion.

There's a sudden change in road noise and her weight shifts sharply as the vehicle turns. A freeway exit? She jostles for comfort, struggling against the ties that cut into her wrists, wishing bitterly that she had some kind of weapon.

Yes, a weapon must be her first priority. Somehow, she must find an opportunity, act fast, and gain the upper hand. But how? If only she had more skills, more strength . . .

She pictures that wicked stun gun, probably tucked into the pocket of his cargo pants. He's right-handed, so right side.

And the gun that he used to shoot Milo Bender?

She squeezes her eyes shut and suffers a wave of emotion before she can force herself to think about the gun. She's certain it is somewhere in this vehicle, likely up front, perhaps under the seat, somewhere handy. And Flint will have knives or scalpels. He always loved sharp blades.

Flint's elaborate designs flash across her vision. She feels him cutting into her skin, slicing a pattern here, an embellishment there. . . .

Quit!

The vehicle makes a sharp turn, forcing her face hard against the interior. It starts to climb, crests a hill, and begins to descend with slow, sweeping turns, again and again, a disorienting distance. She hears no other traffic and wonders if they're getting close.

Where is he taking her?

He will have to unload her once they arrive.

Will he use the stun gun again? Only if she resists. He'll threaten to, of course, but he won't want to haul her limp body. It will be easier for him if she walks. So, with luck, he'll free her ankles . . . but her hands? Not likely, but at least they are bound in front of her instead of behind. Maybe she can grab something.

Their speed abruptly slows as the vehicle maneuvers over rough terrain. One hard turn and they jolt to a stop.

SEVENTY-FOUR

An old pickup truck is waiting just where it's supposed to be, just inside the gate. Flint puts on his jacket and his camouflage hat, grabs a thick envelope, and climbs out.

A heavyset man in a down jacket and a red knit cap gets out of the pickup and walks toward him, saying, "I was beginning to wonder if you were gonna show."

"It was a long drive."

The heavyset man peers over Flint's shoulder toward the SUV. "Where's Mr. Wertz?"

"It's just me."

"But is Mr. Wertz coming?"

"You have trouble hearing? Wertz isn't here. I'm the one you're dealing with."

The man makes a face as though he's tasted something sour.

"Listen," Flint says, "it's all set up, right? The boat's ready?"

"I was expecting Mr. Wertz, though."

"Where's the boat?"

The man shakes his head, saying, "I don't like this."

"Look, Wertz told me to come here. And I called you with the code words, didn't I? And now I'm here, with cash in hand," Flint says, waving the envelope in the man's face.

He squints up at Flint. "Did you do something to Mr. Wertz?"

"What kind of question is that? I'm like a son to him, okay? And I've been here before. Not recently, but lots of times."

"Is that right?" The man kicks the gravel with the toe of his boot. "Well, okay, I guess. But I'll need some cash up front. Pay me half now."

Flint scoffs. "Not half."

"Look, I need to gas her up. Both tanks. That ain't cheap. Call it good-faith money."

"Money, money, money."

"Damn right."

Flint opens the envelope and counts out ten hundred-dollar bills. "That should be more than enough good faith. I'll pay you the rest as soon as we're underway."

"What? No, I'm not going with you," the man says, pocketing the cash.

"Are you kidding?"

"No, man, you're on your own. I ain't goin'."

"Well, shit."

"What? You can't handle a boat? Forget it, then."

"That ol' Grady-White Marlin? I'll manage."

"You sure you know how?"

"Like I said, I know the boat, and I know these waters."

The heavyset man crosses his arms across his chest. "Okay, the most important thing, listen, you gotta get clear of here as fast as you can. Be gone before daylight, got that? Because if anything goes wrong, it's on you. You screw up, I'll report the boat stolen. Never seen you before, understand?"

"You think I'm an idiot? I'm just out fishing, is all." Flint casts a glance up the long driveway. He can barely make out the building's roofline. "Is there coffee up there?"

The man gives a shrug. "I don't like that place."

"If I'm going solo, I need some coffee."

The man grumbles something, shaking his head, then fetches a backpack from his truck and holds it out to Flint, saying, "Here's everything you'll need. There are pills inside. Take one now and two later, that ought to keep you awake till you make Dale's place."

"Who's Dale?"

The man squints at him. "I thought you said Mr. Wertz had you up to speed."

"Oh, his cousin, right? His cousin in Canada. Plan C. Okay, so how does this work?"

"I'll get the boat and bring it around. Meet me down at the dock. It won't take long, an hour, maybe." The heavyset man cranes his neck to look again at the SUV. "That yours?"

Flint glances over his shoulder. "Why?"

"You can't leave it here."

It takes a minute for the men to work out the details. The man in the wool cap will meet him at the dock with the boat and they'll exchange keys.

Flint nods at the SUV. "You should paint it."

"You don't need to tell me how to do my job." The man holds Flint's eye for a moment, then looks down the path toward the boat dock. "You'll need to carry your gear down. There's a flashlight in the backpack. It's a little tricky in the dark."

"Like I said, I've been here before."

"Okay, I'll meet you down there. Those pills will keep you awake, just pay attention and keep well clear of the islands. And remember, you gotta be gone by sunrise. And I mean plenty gone. Out to sea."

"So hurry up then, why don't you?"

The man gives Flint that sour look again. "Just don't screw up," he says, before climbing into his pickup and driving out the gate.

SEVENTY-FIVE

She listens to the other vehicle drive away, wondering what conversation was swallowed by the howling wind. Then the SUV door opens, and there's a weight shift as Flint climbs back inside and slams the door.

He drives forward, gravel crunching beneath the tires. It's not long until the vehicle turns and comes to a halt.

She takes deep breaths, feeling cramped and hot and feverish.

He gets out and comes around to the back. The tailgate opens and cold air rushes in. The tightness loosens, the blanket comes off, and fresh air meets her nostrils.

She squints into the glare of the dome light. He looks different without his beard; the stubble on his cheeks seems almost obscene.

"Hello, my little cricket. Did you miss me?"

His comes so close she smells the stink of his breath.

"Sit up," he says, and when she does, he grasps her ankles and pulls her roughly toward him. "Are you going to behave?"

She nods, making a noise in her throat.

"You're not going to scream, are you?"

She shakes her head, thinking she must do as he says and try to lull him into a false sense of security.

"Okay, then." He grips the back of her head in one hand. "No one can hear you, anyway. But no screaming. You know I don't like that."

He rips the duct tape from her mouth in one fast move that makes her eyes water and sets her face burning. Then he looks at her closely, saying, "Mine again. How sweet is that?" and presses his lips hard against hers.

Revulsion rises like bile in her throat.

He quickly shifts his grip to the back of her neck and folds her forward so that he can stroke the scars on her back.

Her gut twists but she tries not to respond.

The next instant, he jerks her toward him and cuts the ties from her ankles, telling her to stand up and walk. Her boots find the ground, and an icy wind turns her skin to gooseflesh.

"You cold?"

She shivers and tries her voice. "Yes, c-cold."

"Hurry up then."

He grips her arm tightly, yanking her forward, and she stumbles along the walkway, scanning the moonlit surroundings, desperate to get her bearings. They're heading toward a concrete building, a two-story box with a metal roof, hard edges, and narrow windows. Ugly as a bunker.

"Where are we?" Her voice sounds small and weak.

"Don't worry about it. We're safe and sound."

Grasping at an idea, she repeats it back to him, "Safe and sound, safe and sound, safe and sound."

He looks at her sharply, and she smiles in a way that she hopes is disarming. When he looks away, she stretches her fingers, wrenching against the ties toward his pocket, angling for the stun gun, but it stays out of reach.

The building rises before them like a prison, gray and ominous. He ignores the metal front door and steers her around to the back, where the concrete is covered with dark moss.

Her eyes dart left and right, searching for some means of escape, seeing only a ragged field rimmed with forest. "Where is this place?"

"It doesn't matter. We're only staying here until the boat's ready."

"B-boat?"

"A boat for Plan C. Canada. Cricket. Three Cs." He coughs a dry laugh and grips her arm tighter.

A boat to Canada? The idea seems chillingly plausible. Puget Sound offers the perfect escape route to the sea. Her knees weaken as she pictures the FBI searching Nikki Keswick's house for clues while Flint is loading her up and smuggling her out like small cargo.

He forces her toward a metal staircase that zigzags upward. The cold wind whips around them. Clouds scud across the sky and the moonlight falters as they start to climb, their boots ringing on each metal step. She needs to stall, needs to distract him, but her teeth are chattering and she can't form a single sentence.

Panic rises in her chest as they climb higher into the blackness. They reach the landing, turn, and continue climbing. His grip on her arm is tight as a tourniquet.

Another few steps and they've reached the top landing, which seems narrow and perilous as a diving platform. She looks down, suffering a rush of vertigo.

Flint retrieves a ring of keys from his pocket.

Hearing that fateful *clink* of keys, she's again a child chained in the dark, and the horror of those years howls around her like the wind.

He faces the door, releases her arm, and bends close to the lock, straining to find the keyhole in the dark.

Her heart pounds, and in one fast desperate move she shifts her weight and swings her knee up, smashing it hard against his face.

He grabs his nose and she turns to run but he seizes her hair and she falls, landing hard. He looms over her, but before he can strike, she kicks out, cracking the sole of her boot against his shin. He yelps, bending to grab his leg in pain, and she kicks again, catching his chin with the toe of her boot. He staggers backward as she jumps to her feet and leaps toward the stairs.

Her boot soles beat out a staccato as they carry her down. She reaches the landing, hears Flint behind her, panics, and misses a step. She's in the air, tumbling, and lands hard, but Flint is coming fast and there's no time for pain.

She scrambles awkwardly to her feet and runs across the open field, heading for the trees. She races blindly into the night, her hands still bound and her knees pumping. The ground is slick as ice, and her pale skin is like a beacon in the moonlight.

She sets her sights on the dark perimeter, hears him gaining ground behind her, and runs faster. Her feet fly across the ground. The wind snaps and howls, the moon casts shadows that dance with menace.

As she nears the trees, she glances back and nearly runs headlong into a fence.

She stops, gasping, and looks back to see Flint charging on fast. A wail escapes her throat as she clumsily leaps onto the fence, using her bound hands together to shimmy up and over. She falls to the ground on the other side, where she jumps to her feet and runs on.

The terrain turns rocky. She hears Flint scale the fence, thud to the ground, and come charging after her.

She sprints through a clearing without looking back, then dodges through brush and trees, keeping to the shadows. Her heart hammers in her chest. Her lungs are on fire.

The ground suddenly slopes and she's hurtling downhill, slipping and sliding on wet leaves, trees flashing past. She hears Flint curse behind her, but doesn't dare look back. She pushes herself to keep running, sucking air, desperate for somewhere to hide.

She catches a toe and stumbles, but stays upright and keeps running.

"Give it up," he calls in a raspy voice. "You won't make it far."

Gasping for breath, she escapes into the brush. Limbs snatch at her hair and scratch her skin. She hurries forward, crouching low until she finds a path.

The moon disappears and the night deepens. She rushes forward, and then the ground abruptly stops and she nearly falls. She latches onto a sapling and teeters on the edge, her heart thudding as moonlight glitters on the water below.

His voice rises from the darkness behind her. "You might as well give up. There's no way across those rapids."

She inches away from the steep drop and hurries alongside, searching for a bridge, a log, any means of escape. The noise of the wind and the rushing water cover the sounds of her footfalls.

She glances back to see Flint lurch out of the brush. He stands in the open, eyes shining, as she hunkers down beside a fallen tree, trying to catch her breath.

"There's no bridge, I'm telling you. There's no way across. You might as well come out. I know this place, you don't."

She hunches lower beside the dead tree, unseen but trapped, with nowhere to go.

Flint steps closer, looking in all directions. "Come on out now. You know I'll find you. You know it's hopeless."

She backs closer to the edge and looks down at the fast water below. Dampness rises to her face, carrying the water's fresh, metallic scent. The rapids have cut a deep gorge. How far is the drop? She peers down, calculating a jump, but sees only disaster. She cranes her neck, trying to see a way down the cliff face, but knows she couldn't manage even with her hands free.

Her mind reels as he looms closer. Wind gusts around them. The clouds part, moonlight cuts through the night, and a slice of brightness falls across her pale skin.

He spots her instantly and smiles, showing his foul teeth. "There you are." He closes the distance. "I knew you'd come back to me. I knew you couldn't resist. I knew, I knew, I knew."

Panic knots in her throat.

"We'll start all over again in Canada," he says. "There's a place up there, all set up, all part of the plan, you'll see."

She backs away from him, trembling as he lifts the stun gun from his pocket and holds it high.

"Don't make me use this," he warns.

"Y-you don't want to do that."

"No? Because you're going to behave?"

She watches his hands. "You won't want to carry me. It's a long way back."

He glances over his shoulder. "Yeah, well, I wouldn't have to carry you, because once this thing wears off"—he says, waving the stun gun—"you can walk, can't you? I'll just wait. I'm awful good at waiting." He smiles and takes a step closer. "I waited a long time to get you. You don't know how long."

"W-what do you mean?" she asks, desperate to keep him talking while she casts around for a stick, a rock, any kind of weapon.

"The first time I saw you, you were with your sister."

She freezes. "With Rachel?"

"Yeah, we were after her at first."

"What do you mean?"

"Wertz liked her. And we almost got her, too, one night."

She fixes her eyes on his and a white-hot hate combusts inside her.

"But once I saw you, I knew you were the one I had to have," he says, coming closer. "So then it was just a question of waiting until I had my chance. I told you, I'm good at waiting."

Her focus narrows until nothing exists beyond the darkness between them.

He lunges at her but she sidesteps, seizing his wrist with her bound hands, wrestling with him, hooking a heel behind his ankle and frantically trying to swipe him off his feet.

He laughs, his breath hot on her face, and suddenly she's thrown flat on her back beside the tree.

"You shouldn't have done that," he says, raising the stun gun. It crackles and sparks as he jabs it at her, but she rolls onto her stomach, seizes a tree root, and swings away.

She dangles over the edge for a split second before the root slips through her hands and she falls, landing on the rocky shore with a bone-splitting jolt that sends stars bursting behind her eyes.

Flint stomps and swears on the outcropping above. She tastes blood, but stays immobile. He shouts at her to get up, but she concentrates on keeping still. He rants that she has ruined everything, cursing and fuming while the frigid water soaks her clothes. The rocks are like ice beneath her, but she doesn't move.

At last his voice falls silent. She waits a long while, playing dead until she's certain that he's gone. Then she painfully gets to her feet and staggers upright. It hurts to breathe. She fingers a painful knot below her left breast, fearing a broken rib.

Clouds churn overhead as she stands ankle-deep in fast water, shuddering with cold and fear and looking all around. Flint seems to lurk in every shadow, but she shakes herself and heads downstream.

She stumbles and falls, stumbles and falls, cracking a knee this time, bruising an arm the next. She moves along the shore until it becomes impassible, then pushes herself to wade in and out of the freezing stream, slipping on the rocky bottom.

The elements—water, wind, stones—are her only company, save for a fat slice of moon that winks through the trees overhead. The water speaks ceaselessly, now murmuring comfort, now urging her forward, now daring her to chance a stretch of rapids. She wades through them with a dogged mindlessness.

The wind is brisk and sucks all remaining warmth from her body. Her sodden boots make every step an effort, and she scarcely realizes that she's limping.

She trips over a branch, pitching forward, landing heavily on hands and knees. Tears flood her eyes as she rests there, panting like an animal on all fours.

As she starts to rise, a searing pain shoots down her side. A jagged rib can puncture a lung, tear flesh, cause internal bleeding, but these thoughts merely flit through her mind. She gets to her feet and trudges on, dazed and unthinking. She keeps looking behind her, but Flint does not reappear.

How long has she been walking? It feels like hours.

The trees gradually thin and the landscape opens before her. The creek bed widens and the water grows shallow, burbling over the rocks. The moon reappears, and the rushing stream glitters like tumbling diamonds. Up ahead, the stream spills into a large expanse of water. Puget Sound.

She's approaching the shoreline when a dog barks in the distance.

Reeve snaps to attention. She searches for lights, a roofline, but sees nothing beyond trees and darkness. She's listening, waiting, hoping the dog will bark again so that she can get a fix on its location, when a sound behind her makes her heart jump.

She whirls around to see a figure with a flashlight.

She stares hard, recognizing Flint's gait. He is coming downhill, yards away. Reeve is exposed. She goes rigid with fear, comprehending that her long hike downstream has done nothing but circle around, returning her to danger.

SEVENTY-SIX

Daryl Wayne Flint aims his flashlight down the path and shoulders the backpack, which reminds him of college and makes him feel young. He's buzzing with the pills, having taken two already, and feels a pleasant surge of confidence. Everything can begin again in Canada. And everything is going as planned, except for the major aggravation of losing the girl. A damn waste. All that work he put into her . . .

He'll have to start over with a new one once he gets set up. Young skin, a blank slate.

He steps onto the wooden boat dock, and his boots make a loud, pleasant sound with every step. He stops beside the boat and taps his toe three times before stepping aboard.

Setting the backpack on the captain's seat, he takes a look around, getting reacquainted with the boat. It's a good-sized fishing boat, thirty feet, not too old. He sets down his flashlight and switches on a light.

Down below, a cabin runs all the way forward. A musty odor rises off the old mattress. There's a sink filled with dirty dishes, a cushioned bench, a head. The basics.

He climbs three steps back to the helm, puts the key in the ignition, and scans the familiar controls. Turning around, he notices that Wertz has replaced the old outboards with new 225 horsepower Yamahas. Sweet. To clear the fumes before switching on the engines, he switches on the blower and decides to leave it running while he heads back uphill to get the rest of his gear.

Reeve sees Flint's flashlight aiming back toward shore and drops into a crouch.

The dog barks again, somewhere behind her, and she holds her breath, afraid that Flint will turn toward it and see her. But he doesn't seem to hear the dog and continues uphill. She doesn't move as the flickering glow of his flashlight disappears through the trees, where she can just make out the roofline of the house.

Her eyes return to the boat. Flint has left a light on, which glows a dim yellow. Which means he'll be back. Soon. And then he'll launch his escape to Canada.

Behind her, the dog barks again.

She turns toward the sound, filled with longing. She pictures a warm house, a phone. She searches the dark hillsides, but there's no welcoming porch light, no happy pooch bounding toward her.

She turns back toward the boat's yellow glow, and suddenly hears her own voice: *"If I can stop him, I have to try."*

The words fill her with despair.

Milo Bender.

Nikki Keswick.

The dog barks again, as if calling to her. She looks in its direction for a long moment before turning her back.

The anguishing truth is that she has no choice. Because she's certain that Flint will never stop. He will catch another girl and etch himself into her skin. And she's certain that her nightmares will never cease, that her life will never be her own, as long as Daryl Wayne Flint runs free.

It takes all her resolve to put one foot in front of the other and walk toward the boat. Her legs are rubber and her feet are leaden. Driftwood litters the shore. She stumbles forward, intent on getting aboard the boat before Flint sees her, praying that she can find some means to stop him.

She has no plan as she steps onto the wooden dock. She moves with little stealth, limping along, repeatedly looking over her shoulder to check for the flicker of his flashlight.

Every nerve burns with cold. She's exhausted, and the closer she gets to the boat, the weaker she feels. But now there's no going back.

She climbs aboard the vessel and looks around, hoping for a sharp-tipped weapon, imagining a speargun or harpoon, but seeing nothing but fishing tackle.

When she spies the backpack she lifts it, hoping to feel the weight of a gun, but then drops it back on the seat.

In the dim light, she notices that her wrists are bleeding. It's obvious that she needs to free herself. She descends into the cabin and searches, rummaging through a cutlery drawer until she finds a sharp knife.

She thumbs the blade, and a terrifying memory swims behind her eyes: Flint holding a similar knife to her throat, saying, "Stop whimpering or I'll cut out your voice box and use it for bait."

Hearing a noise, she turns toward the window and peeks out the curtains. Flint's boots resound on the wooden dock, his flashlight swinging before him.

Quickly, she sets the knife on the counter, blade up, and tries to saw the plastic tie. But the angle is wrong, and the knife jiggles back and forth, then flips onto its side.

She moans. The footsteps draw closer. She fumbles with the knife, then sits on the bed and grips it firmly between her knees.

Flint's heavy tread draws steadily nearer as she saws at the plastic tie. The pressure dislodges the knife and it falls to the floor as Flint steps aboard.

She freezes, watching his legs move past the opening. She hears him flicking switches, muttering, "On, on, on."

The motors roar to life, then settle into a heavy growl as her nostrils fill with the stink of fuel.

She snatches up the knife and sits on the floor to try a new approach. As he moves back and forth, she grips the knife handle between the soles of her boots.

There's a shift in weight as he steps off the boat. She has a split second of hope that he'll walk away, but hears him moving around on the dock.

He's untying the boat. Her pulse races. Sawing desperately, she's all too aware of Flint moving from stern to bow. The knife slips and as she bends forward to reposition it, the boat comes unmoored with a lurch.

He climbs back aboard and she goes dead still, realizing with dismay that fumbling with the knife has cost her precious minutes.

The boat begins moving forward with Flint at the helm, out of her line of sight. But directly in front of her is the gun. It sits atop a duffle bag on the passenger seat. Flint could reach out and snatch it up in half a second. Her only chance is to climb the steps, exit the cabin, and grab the gun before he can react.

Gripping the knife, she swallows dryly and gets unsteadily to her feet. She takes a step, thinking she needs to act fast, grab the gun, and shoot. She can't afford to miss.

The boat gains speed, surging through the choppy water. Is there a safety on the gun? She hesitates just as the boat bucks, and she staggers slightly, her boot knocking hollowly against a cupboard.

His shins appear before her, blocking the exit. He bends down to have a look as she straightens, quickly turning the knife blade to lie flat along her wrist, pointed toward her. She holds it hidden between her clasped hands, meets his eye and says, "I came back."

His face lights with surprise. "Well I'll be damned."

"You were right," she continues, taking half a step toward him. "We should be together."

"I can't believe you're alive. But you shouldn't have run away like that. I'll have to punish you, you know that."

"Yes, but it's better than having you leave me all alone." She tightens her grip on the knife and thinks about the gun. There's no way she can reach it. She has to buy time and get close enough to stab him.

"I was thinking about those designs you were working on at the hospital. Your artwork."

"You saw those?" His eyes seem wild and strange, like he's high.

She nods. "They're . . . they're very impressive. Especially the ones of the cricket."

"That's my favorite." His eyebrows lift. "So then you understand what I want, don't you?"

She feels ill. "Of course. You want to embellish the design on the back of my neck." She takes another step toward him, but he's still too far away. "And I think you'll like my idea."

He rolls his tongue over his teeth. "What idea?"

Her knees are shaking. "It would be best to have three designs, three grouped together. Don't you think so?"

Eagerness shows on his face. "Come up here into the light, where I can get a good look." He steps back, watching as she ascends the steps out of the cabin to join him.

She glimpses the gun—so close—but is it even loaded? Clutching the knife with both hands, she dips a shoulder and lowers her head, saying, "Look, you could put three designs in a group. There's room for two more, isn't there?"

She watches him out of the corner of her eye as he sweeps her hair aside. Her heart gallops. The knife's handle feels wet in her hands.

He says, "Maybe so, maybe there's room enough."

She widens her stance, tightening her core as he touches her skin, saying, "I'll put one here, and here, and—"

She wheels at him with the knifepoint aimed at his throat, but the blade only nicks him. He jerks back, grabbing his ear. "You bitch! I should have killed you years ago!"

They both grab for the gun, knocking it to the floor, where it slides away. He's faster and snatches it up, but she reacts instantly, driving a shoulder into his diaphragm. He staggers while cracking the butt of the gun hard against her skull. The blow sends her sprawling with an explosion of pain.

The boat slams through the waves, sending up spray as he fires the gun, sending a bullet through her hair and into the gunnel. She scuttles blindly on the slippery deck. The boat bucks underfoot and Flint loses his footing, skidding sideways. She sees her chance and grabs the wheel with both hands. She cranks it hard and the boat spins like a demon, hurling him overboard.

There's a splash and a sudden *thump*. She gasps, staring back at the boiling wake, guessing he's been hit. Scrambling to her feet, she searches the water's surface, but sees nothing but inky blackness.

With effort, she gets the boat under control, slows its speed, and then finds the flashlight. Grasping it in her bound hands, she begins scanning the water's surface in all directions. She sweeps the beam across the choppy water until—*there!*—something catches her eye. She loses it, then finds it again, but has to set down the flashlight in order to steer the boat toward the spot.

It's hard to judge distance. When the boat seems near where she last spotted him, Reeve leaves the helm and again grabs the flashlight. Its beam barely cuts the darkness. She sweeps the beam left and right, seeing nothing but whitecaps, until . . . She catches another glimpse, sure that it's him. It must be him. She struggles to keep the beam fixed on that spot, but it wobbles and sways as the boat rolls underfoot.

She has to set the flashlight down to steer closer. Gripping the steering wheel, she closes the distance, but he seems to have disappeared. She grasps the flashlight, playing the beam across the surface.

The black water suddenly lifts him, and the flashlight's beam seems to intensify until it's bright as a spotlight, illuminating him. As the boat approaches, she expects him to shout and curse, but abruptly sees that he's floating face down.

She peers over the side at his floating body but cannot trust her eyes. An incomprehensible pattern of slashes runs across his back. With a hard shudder, she realizes these must be propeller wounds.

As the boat glides past, a flap of scalp floats beside his head, still attached and tipping like a cap. Tipping, tipping . . . and then his body is claimed by the waves.

Her mind is reeling. The flashlight slips from her grasp, and she's overcome with a strange sensation, as if she has left her body and is rising up and up into the night air. She feels untethered, weightless. For one sublime moment, she is free of gravity, free of time and cold and pain.

But then her stomach clenches and she's snatched back to the boat, where she's bent over the side, vomiting.

When her stomach empties and the spasms cease, she straightens, wipes her mouth, and approaches the helm feeling shaky. The display panel swims before her eyes. She knows she cannot think about Flint. She must force all else from her mind and focus instead on the switches, dials, and gauges. She tries to get her bearings using the electronic map, but it's unfathomable. The throttle and the wheel are the only things that make sense.

When she looks ahead, the shoreline is approaching fast. She grabs for the throttle and quickly shifts to neutral. The boat wallows in its own wake, decelerating so sharply that she nearly falls. She fumbles with the controls, shifts back into gear, and spins the wheel, swerving and overcorrecting as she executes a U-turn.

She has no idea how to get her bearings, but steers toward what seems as good a direction as any, searching the horizon for signs of life. The only lights seem to waver many miles away.

Is that mist? Is she seeing clearly?

It occurs to her that it might be smart to go below and look for something to keep her warm, but somehow she cannot pry her hands from the wheel.

After what seems a long while, a small light twinkles ahead. She steers toward it, and gradually the light draws nearer, brightening until she can make out a boat dock. The light tops a post. A single boat is tied beside it. She searches the shore and hillsides for signs of a house, but sees only trees and darkness.

Moonlight shines on the approaching shoreline. Steering parallel to the dock, she eases back on the boat's speed. She knows from riding ferryboats that you have to reverse engines to stop a boat, so several yards from shore, she shifts the throttle into reverse, but she's too late. The boat grinds on the bottom and slams to a halt, knocking her off her feet.

SEVENTY-SEVEN

Annie Swann's dog occasionally barks at bears or raccoons or other nocturnal creatures, but he has never sounded like this, with such urgent baying. And he has never behaved like this, up on his hind legs, pawing at the back door.

"Moose! You stop that!" Annie Swann commands, but the big hound just looks over his shoulder and barks sharply, as if throwing her words back at her, and continues scratching at the door.

She peers out the window. The sky is barely beginning to brighten, and her night-adapted eyes see nothing but the familiar blue-black shapes of the patio furniture. She snaps on the light. The back deck glares empty.

"There's nothing out there," she says to the dog, but her words only encourage him to drop to all fours and bark louder. She has never seen him this insistent.

She takes a breath. She had always feared it would come to this—a woman alone in this remote old house—but has prepared for danger since her husband died last year. She puts her shoulders back and quickly pulls on some warm clothes, steps into her galoshes, and fetches the rifle. She makes sure it's loaded. Then she grabs the big flashlight and debates whether or not to step into the glare outside the door.

No. She switches off the light.

Moose whines at her, dancing anxiously.

She puts her hand on the knob, steels herself, and says, "Go get 'em," opening the door.

Moose charges out to gallop across the deck, down the steps and away. Annie cautiously follows, scanning the lawn, the garden, the surrounding woods. The beam of the flashlight pierces the darkness, but Moose has already run well beyond its reach. She sees nothing unusual as she moves away from the house and down the path.

Following his noise into the dark, she is surprised that the dog is racing downhill to the boat dock. She hurries across the dewy grass and down the slope, wondering what kind of creature could have excited him like this.

Please god, not a bear. Annie Swann hurries forward, ready for some kind of fight with an animal, fearing rabies, wounds, and veterinary bills.

SEVENTY-EIGHT

The boat lists on its side, pitched at an angle. Reeve rests where she fell, eyes closed. The pain in her side only flares when she tries to rise. But that doesn't matter, because now she can think of nothing other than sleep. All urgency has drained away, replaced by a numb indifference. Her thoughts drift.

Somewhere far away, she hears—what? A dog? Not the same dog as before, she reasons dimly. This is a baying dog, with a deep-throated voice.

The dog falls silent, and the night folds over her. Waves slap against the hull. Wind churns the sky.

The dog's baying resumes, louder, closer, rising half a tone.

A woman's voice calls, "Hello! Who's there?"

Reeve's eyes flutter.

"Is someone aboard? Are you all right?"

A bright light pierces the darkness, waving back and forth.

Reeve opens her mouth and tries to speak, but the sound she makes isn't quite human. The dog *woofs* in response.

She rises painfully onto her elbows and stares into the blinding light.

"Oh, dear god!" she hears, followed by running, splashing, a scrambling noise. In half a minute, the woman is kneeling beside her, whispering, "Oh god, oh god, oh god."

The woman's face hovers. She wears a halo of white hair. Pressing warm fingertips to Reeve's cheeks, to her neck, she asks, "Can you speak? What's your name?"

Reeve mumbles and manages to sit up.

The woman gasps. "Your wrists! We need to get you to a doctor. We'll do this together, okay? Can you stand? Can you? Let me help you up."

Her legs wobble, and the woman helps her to her feet, saying, "We're just going a short way, just to my boat. That'll be easier that getting you up to the house. That's it, that's good, come along now."

The woman keeps talking as they make their way ashore. She steers Reeve along the dock, the dog dancing at their heels. A minute later, they are stepping over the gunnel and boarding her boat. She settles Reeve on a cushioned bench, and then finds some scissors to cut the tie, freeing Reeve's wrists.

The relief is exquisite.

While the woman cleans and bandages her wrists, Reeve tries saying, "Thank you," but her tongue feels thick and foreign.

The woman peers into Reeve's eyes, saying, "You must rest, understand? My name is Annie. We're going to the hospital. It's faster by boat, anyway."

Annie grabs some blankets and tucks them around Reeve. "Moose, up!" she says to the dog, patting the cushions. He jumps up, and she tells him, "Settle down right here. That's a good boy."

The dog's breath is hot on Reeve's face.

"He smells, I know, but he's a furnace. And you can't beat a dog for warmth." Annie climbs out onto the dock to quickly untie the lines, then hurries back aboard. She takes the helm, starts the engines, and throttles forward. The boat's hull cuts through the black water, trailing a fat wake.

Reeve swallows, coughs, and settles back on the cushions. The stink of dog wafts around her as the engines roar and the boat gains speed. She looks up, hoping to see the moon, but it has slipped out of sight. Dawn begins to blush, and the big dog stays warm at her side as she surrenders to exhaustion.

SEVENTY-NINE

Reeve can't help feeling sorry for Case Agent Pete Blankenship. He wears a stricken expression as he sits at her bedside, appearing much paler and older than the first time they met, just days ago.

After he has dutifully taken her official statement, he sets down his pen and says to her, "Okay, now it's your turn. Any questions?"

She goes rigid. "Did you find Flint's body?"

"A local fisherman found him. No need to wait for the official autopsy. Propeller wounds are pretty distinct."

She closes her eyes, clamps her palms together, and searches her feelings, expecting something heavy and profound. What rises instead is a relief so powerful she can scarcely catch her breath.

Opening her eyes, she asks, "How's Milo Bender doing?"

"Uh, still in the hospital, recovering, last I heard."

Before she can ask for more details, Blankenship says, "He sure opened up a can of worms. Did you hear about Walter Wertz?"

"No, not much."

"That fishing cabin wasn't his only property. Wertz's family owned acreage all over the Pacific Northwest, plus a house in Olympia that Bender tracked down about ten years ago."

"Ten years ago? You mean, Milo Bender was investigating Wertz while I was locked in Flint's basement?"

"Right. Bender checked his old records and acted on a hunch, then went to Olympia to search the house. Looks like Bender did a little B and E, and—"

"What's B and E?"

"Breaking and entering. Pretty illegal, but I doubt that anyone's going to press charges."

"Why? What happened?"

"Well, everyone seems to believe that Walter Wertz is dead."

"Dead? Flint killed him?"

"Everyone thinks he died of renal disease. Kidney failure. Because according to medical records, the man was on dialysis and in serious need of a transplant. And here's the interesting part: Wertz stopped getting treatment and disappeared a few months ago, but his neighbors saw him return to the house a few days after Flint escaped."

"Meaning what, exactly?"

"Seems that Flint was in disguise."

"What? So Flint was pretending to be Wertz, a man who is actually dead?"

"That's what everyone seems to believe."

"You keep saying that. You don't believe it?"

"Let's just say our investigation remains open, and I'm reserving judgment. This guy Wertz was pretty smart. Plus, he's wealthy, and he has connections. Seems to me, a man like that could arrange a kidney transplant if he wanted one."

"Oh, man. This is making my head hurt."

"I know, it's crazy. But what's unequivocal is that Flint's fingerprints were all over Wertz's place, plus we found wigs, IDs."

"And yearbooks, right?" She suffers a sharp memory of her conversation with Nikki Keswick.

"Yeah, Flint and Wertz had a photography business. We always wondered how Flint made his living. But he mostly mooched off Wertz, who had a whale of an inheritance."

"Psychopaths tend to be parasitic."

He gives her a half smile. "Yes, they do."

"And speaking of psychopaths, what about Flint's mother?"

"What about her?"

"Is she under arrest?"

"No. Why?"

Blankenship takes notes, mouth crimped shut, while Reeve explains her theory that Dr. Moody's former assistant, the blond woman named Cybil, didn't commit suicide. Reeve says she's sure that Mrs. Pratt killed her.

Blankenship scarcely responds, and when she runs out of words, he gives her a quick nod, glances at his watch, and closes his notebook. "Your father ordered me to keep it short. As did Dr. Lerner. He says you've got a lot of people waiting for you down in California. Pretty nice that he brought his private plane to take you home."

"Yeah, I never expected that." She takes a breath. "Before you go, I wanted to tell you that I'm really sorry I won't be here for Nikki Keswick's funeral."

She watches his Adam's apple slide up and down, his eyes water.

"Are you okay?"

"Not really." He sighs heavily. "I feel like . . . I don't know . . . like somebody took a sledgehammer to my chest."

"You liked her a lot."

"I loved her. Everybody loved her. Nikki was so . . . filled with promise, so . . ." He looks down at his knuckles, shakes his head, then opens his empty palms.

"I know how terrible it is to lose someone you love," Reeve says, thinking of her mother.

He clears his throat and changes the subject. "So, anyway, I hear that your prognosis is not too bad."

She gives a small twitch of the shoulder. "Hypothermia, lacerations, some spectacular bruises."

He frowns at her. "Yeah, plus a couple of broken ribs."

"Could be worse."

He gets to his feet, saying, "Well, it hasn't exactly been a pleasure, has it? But you sure surprised the heck out of everybody."

"I guess that's one way of putting it."

"So, what are your plans after college?"

"Who knows?"

He gives her a level look. "You have a talent for this, you know."

"A talent for what?"

"Criminal investigation, forensics."

Her eyebrows lift, but before she can respond, the agent has turned his back.

"You take care," he says, raising a hand as he disappears out the door.

An hour later, Reeve is swinging her legs over the side of the hospital bed, anxious for the nurse to bring the discharge papers. She's dressed in jeans and a sweater, clothes that her roommates sent up with her father. She sends a quick text message thanking Lana, while her father and her psychiatrist linger at her bedside, waiting with her.

Years younger and several inches shorter than her father, Dr. Ezra Lerner is such an energetic, fit, compact man that he almost appears primed for a gymnastic competition. Her father, on the other hand, looks in need of rest, with dark circles under red-rimmed eyes.

Reeve has been trying hard to seem perky, hoping to ease the worry lines etched deep into her father's face. But he responds to her every comment with the patient nods and wan smiles always granted the sick.

"You didn't need to fly up here, but thanks," she says. "If the news people are watching Sea-Tac airport, they're going to be disappointed."

Dr. Lerner grins. "You don't get airsick, do you?"

She shakes her head. She has seen photographs of Dr. Lerner's Cessna, but has never flown in anything other than a commercial airliner. "I'm actually kind of excited about flying in your plane. But you're just back from Brazil. Don't you have jet lag?"

"I'm back on Pacific time already. And it's perfect flying weather."

At last the nurse arrives with a wheelchair and discharge papers. After a few signatures, Reeve is free to go. She gets to her feet, trying not to wince. Her muscles feel as though they're stitched together with barbed wire.

Her father is watching her closely.

She meets his eye and smiles, saying, "Just a little stiff, Dad."

He pats her shoulder. There are a thousand unanswered questions between them, but there will be plenty of time to sort everything out.

"I feel fine, really. Just a little bruised. I don't need a wheelchair to take me out."

The nurse insists on hospital protocol, but allows Mr. LeClaire to steer his daughter's wheelchair along the corridor toward the exit. Dr. Lerner hurries ahead to bring the car.

Soon the front doors whoosh open and Reeve emerges into a crisp, fall day. She inhales the fresh air. As she stands, she briefly closes her eyes to savor the warmth of the sun on her eyelids.

During the ride to the Anacortes airstrip, her phone rings. The man identifies himself as Dr. Moody's attorney, calling to notify her that the Moody family is sending her a check for seventy-five thousand dollars.

She nearly chokes. She'd forgotten all about the reward money. When she starts to protest that she doesn't want it, her father raises a finger, saying, "Might I suggest something?"

Reeve asks the attorney to hold on for a moment.

"If you don't want the money for yourself," her father says, "perhaps there are others with whom you'd like to share it? Just a thought."

"Dad, that's brilliant."

She quickly asks the attorney if the reward can be divided equally among the families of Daryl Wayne Flint's victims. He sounds surprised, but agrees that can be arranged.

"Please make sure that Jenna Dutton gets a share. And Nikki Keswick's family must be included, too, of course."

The attorney points out that seventy-five thousand dollars split nine ways won't be a large sum. But Reeve does a quick calculation in her head and says, "I think eight thousand-plus will buy a lot of baby clothes. Jenna Dutton. You wrote that down, right?"

They arrive at the small airport while she and the attorney are making arrangements. Dr. Lerner has just parked the car when she disconnects.

As she gets out, she sees JD Bender leaning against his green pickup truck, waiting for her. He looks so tall and handsome and healthy that she can't help but say, "Wow."

"How are you feeling?" he says, walking toward her.

"I'm just a little bruised, is all."

"A little bruised? I heard you thought you could fly."

She starts to laugh, but winces. "It only hurts when I laugh."

"I'll try to be more serious, then." He pauses. "We've all been so worried about you."

She gives him a searching look. "How's your dad?"

"He wants to talk to you."

"What?"

"Yeah, one minute and I'll get him on the phone."

She cups JD's phone to her ear. A rush of relief flows through her the instant she hears Milo Bender's voice.

"Good morning young lady," he says. "Was the food as bad in your hospital as it is in mine?"

She starts to chuckle but stops, pressing her fingertips to her taped ribs. While they make small talk, she tries to match his light tone.

After a minute, his voice seems to weaken. "These doctors are keeping me sedated. But I just wanted to say . . . I'm proud of you. You did good, kid."

Tears stand in her eyes. "Hey, that goes double for me, right back at you."

She hands the phone to JD, blinking rapidly. After he says good-bye and pockets the phone, she asks, "So your dad's really going to be okay?"

"He'll be in the hospital a couple more days, but it'll take more than a bullet to stop him. That heart of his is turbocharged." He grins, his face glowing in the sunlight.

Together, they notice that Dr. Lerner and her father are standing beside a shiny aircraft, waiting.

"I know you need to go," JD says, "but before we say good-bye, I wanted to personally share a bit of good news."

"I like hearing good news."

"We're going to be neighbors, kind of."

"What?"

"I got a teaching gig at Cal State Monterey."

"That's fantastic."

"I start in January, but I'll be heading down a little early. So I was wondering if you'd like to go sailing. I mean, maybe I could stop by for visit. What do you think?"

She recalls the stink of diesel and the roar of engines. "I've never been on a sailboat, but I always wanted to. It seems so quiet and clean."

"Great. It's a date then. I can't wait to show you my boat," he says as they walk across the tarmac toward Dr. Lerner's plane. "She's a beauty. Her name is Eleuthera."

"I've never heard that before, but it's pretty. Is Eleuthera a woman's name?"

"It sounds feminine, doesn't it? But it's actually a word with two meanings. For one, it's the name of an island in the Bahamas."

"Nice. And the other meaning?"

"Eleuthera is the Greek word for freedom."

She stops and looks into his eyes. Feeling emboldened, she rises up on her toes to lightly kiss him on the lips, then quickly turns and climbs into the plane.

The next instant, the engines are roaring and she's waving good-bye. An unfamiliar sweetness fills her chest as the plane accelerates down the runway and lifts into a sky of flawless blue.

TWELVE YEARS AGO

Rachel Lynn LeClaire
Seattle, Washington

For the first time in her young life, seventeen-year-old Rachel LeClaire believed she might actually have a future as an actress. She had played the lead in *Grease* at the high school auditorium for three nights, and she hadn't flubbed her lines or hit a wrong note or missed her mark even once.

She'd heard nothing but compliments shouted across the theater and whispered in her ear after each performance. And she was starting to believe that people weren't simply being nice. They seemed to be looking at her differently. Complete strangers approached her, eyes shining, to say things she'd never heard before. They touched her elbow and claimed that she was by far the best one in the entire play.

"You have an extraordinary stage presence, my dear, absolutely extraordinary," one woman gushed.

"You were dazzling! I was completely swept up in your performance," said another.

Even Chad Hart, the class president, had made a point of approaching her backstage to tell her that she was "totally, amazingly talented."

The last three nights had been a dream come true. Standing ovations! And after tonight's performance, she'd been handed a huge bouquet of gorgeous long-stemmed red roses.

"We'll take these home and put them in a vase for you," her mother had promised. "You stay and have fun with your friends."

The next instant, Rachel had been swept up in the cast party. Everyone was buzzing with excitement about how well the play had come together, despite wardrobe malfunctions, stage fright, and tears.

Rachel declined a second slice of pizza and allowed herself only two bites of cake. She would have to watch her weight if she seriously hoped for an acting career. This was her dream. She liked her other classes well enough, but performance was her passion. She couldn't imagine anything better than dedicating herself to music, dance, and theater.

The only bad thing about tonight was that her cat was having kittens—if that was even a bad thing—so she would have to say good night and head home early. She didn't want to miss her cat's first litter.

With final hugs all around, Rachel put on her coat and stepped out of the overheated room, thinking that, if even part of what all these people said was true, she might actually major in theater arts when she got to college. And if she worked really, really hard, maybe she could even make it to Hollywood or New York.

The idea made her shiver with pleasure as she descended the well-lit steps and moved out into the night. The rain was coming down in earnest, and she clutched her purse tightly against her while fishing in her coat pocket for the car keys.

"I've got an umbrella," a man said, stepping toward her, opening his umbrella with a flourish. "Let me help you. Where are you parked?"

"Oh!" Startled by his sudden appearance, she blinked at his uneven yellow teeth, but then smiled brightly, assuming he must be another fan who had seen the play.

At that instant, a familiar voice called from behind, "Rachel!"

She turned to see her kid sister come barreling toward her through the rain. "Rachel, wait up!"

She groaned. "What are you doing here?"

Reggie splashed to a stop in front of her. "I was checking out the theater lights and stuff."

"I thought you went home with Mom and Dad."

"No, I'm riding home with you."

"Well, hurry up then," she said. And as she hustled Reggie toward the car, she forgot all about the man with the umbrella, scarcely noticing as he slid away, silent as a ghost.

ACKNOWLEDGMENTS

Many kind souls deserve thanks for helping with some aspect of this novel, but the single most important person in the publishing process is you. Whether you're holding an e-reader, a first edition, or a tattered copy, whether you chose this title on a recommendation or on a whim, you bring meaning to the arduous and privileged endeavor of putting ideas on the page. Without you, there would be no book.

My thanks also to the many patient, insightful, and talented individuals who allowed me to impose on their goodwill. Deepest thanks to my critique group, Authors All: Karen Engelmann, Rachel Goldberg, Lynn Grant, and Marissa Silver. A thousand thanks also to Lois Gordon, Dr. Brian Grant, Dr. Robert Jones, and William A. Powers. And a special bow of gratitude goes to Sue Grafton.

I pestered various authorities while researching this book, and I'm grateful to all who shared their time and expertise. In particular, I must thank Ayn Sandalo Dietrich, FBI Seattle public affairs officer; George Fong, former FBI special agent and current director of security for ESPN; Dr. Bruce Gage, chief of psychiatry for the Washington Department of Corrections and clinical associate professor at the University of Washington; Roy Hazelwood, former FBI supervisory special agent and cofounder of the Academy Group, Inc.; and Ben Reed, Jr., chief of police, Elko, Nevada. (These kind people deserve a ton of gratitude but not an ounce of blame. All errors are my own; please grant poetic license where you can. In particular, I ask the citizens of

Washington State to forgive mischaracterized or fictitious institutions and topography.)

Luckily, this book had the backing of a brilliant team, starting with my agent, Liza Dawson, and the excellent staff at her agency. Next, I owe endless thanks to my extraordinary editor, Hope Dellon, who worked tirelessly at getting my unruly manuscript into shape. I'm also grateful for the dedication and energy of everyone at Minotaur Books, particularly Andrew Martin, Jennifer Enderlin, Paul Hochman, Sarah Melnyk, David Rotstein, Meryl Gross, Silissa Kenney, and the many others who helped prepare these pages for publication.

On a personal note, my love and gratitude goes out to my wonderfully supportive family.

And finally, my most heartfelt thanks to Allen, who makes all things possible.

DO YOU NEED HELP?

If you or someone you know needs help, please act as quickly as possible. For an immediate response, call 911. Some additional resources are listed below.

- National Center for Missing & Exploited Children, 1-800-THE-LOST (1-800-843-5678) http://www.missingkids.com/ or http://www.ncmec.org/
- National Domestic Violence Hotline: 1-800-799-SAFE (1-800-799-7233) http://www.thehotline.org/
- National Human Trafficking Resource Center / Polaris Project: 1-888-373-7888 http://www.polarisproject.org/
- National Missing and Unidentified Persons System: http://www.namus.gov
- Office for Victims of Crime: http://www.ovc.gov/help/index.html
- The Elizabeth Smart Foundation: http://elizabethsmartfoundation.org

If you need help, please don't wait. Be safe and act today!